THE SECOND STONE

THE TRIEMPERY REVELATIONS
- BOOK III -

L. L. STEPHENS

Copyright Information
THE SECOND STONE
Published by

FOREST PATH BOOKS

THE SECOND STONE Copyright © 2023 by L. L. Stephens. All rights reserved.

This is a work of fiction. All characters in the publication are fictitious, or are historical figures whose words and actions are fictitious. Any other resemblance to names, incidents, or real persons, living or dead, is purely coincidental.

Forest Path Books supports writers and copyright. This book is licensed for your personal enjoyment only. Thank you for helping us to defend our authors' rights and livelihood by acquiring an authorized edition of this book, and by complying with copyright laws by not using, reproducing, transmitting, or distributing any part of this book without permission.
Forest Path Books publications may be purchased for educational, business, or sales/promotional use. For information, please address the publishers at:
info@forestpathbooks.com
or
Forest Path Books, LLC
P. O. Box 847, Stanwood, WA 98292 USA

Stay informed on our releases and news!
Join the reading group/newsletter at:
https://forestpathbooks.com/into-the-forest

Front cover art © 2023 by Larry Rostant
Map © 2023 Christina Wooden
PR Compass Rose font © Peter Rempel (licensed for use)
Cover and interior design by Mahli *https://bookdesignbymahli.com*
Cover content is for illustrative purposes only, and any person depicted on the cover is a model.

Library of Congress Control Number: 2022923555
ISBNs:
978-1-951293-67-3 (hardcover)
978-1-951293-65-9 (trade paper)
978-1-951293-68-0 (e-book)

Reviews for
The Triempery Revelations

"Two elements elevate this work above standard fare. First, it's a character study at its heart, driven by the growth and evolving relationships of complex people, vibrant and varied, without any reduced to stereotypes of good or bad. Second, the mysteries of the Rill and the Wall are compelling and drive readers to explore this world more deeply. Stephens serves up a terrific first entry to a fascinating new series."
—*Booklist*

"An incredible introduction to a new fantasy series… layered, flawed characters within a fascinating world with a rich history and intriguing magic system that you can't wait to learn more about."
—*Smyco*

"*The Kheld King* takes all the elements that made *Sordaneon* great and expands them. A character-driven story with high stakes, with politics as the main focus of this fantasy."
—*Jamreads*

"If *Dune*, *Lord of the Rings* and *Game of Thrones* all got together and made a book baby, it would be rather like *Sordaneon*, which is to say that it's brilliantly done. … It was easy to sink into the world along with Dorilian and the others. I'm absolutely in awe of how many layers Stephens brought to the strange world of the Rill and all those fighting for power."
—*Rebecca Crunden*

BIBLIOGRAPHY

The Triempery Revelations

Sordaneon
The Kheld King
The Second Stone

The God Spear
(forthcoming)

Moon Blood and Salt Flowers

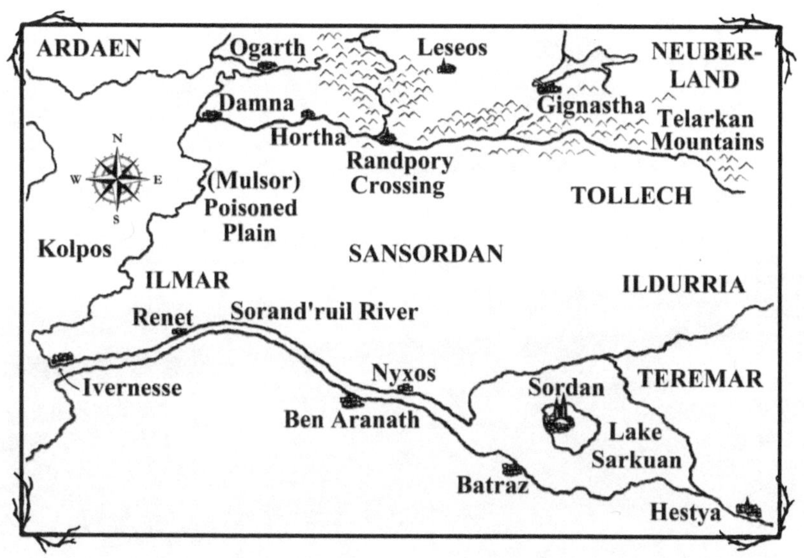

ARDAEN
Ogarth
Leseos
NEUBER-
LAND
Damna
Gignastha
Telarkan
Mountains
Hortha
Randpory
Crossing
TOLLECH
(Mulsor)
Poisoned
Plain
N
W E
S
SANSORDAN
Kolpos
ILMAR
ILDURRIA
Renet
Sorand'ruil River
Nyxos
Sordan
TEREMAR
Ivernesse
Ben Aranath
Lake
Sarkuan
Batraz
Hestya

To Mary,

who I hope will be happy to read the result of all
those hours spent listening to teenage me telling her
this story—and that Endelarin made the cut.

THE
SECOND
STONE

1

Cut off the head of government and it will grow
another. Sometimes it will grow several and they
will gnash at each other until one dominates.
Occasionally they will agree to cooperate. But in
all of human society, there is no such thing as a
political vacuum.
—Marc Frederick Stauberg-Randolph,
Discourse on Politics

Sunlight filled the open space between the twin spires of Permephedon's High Citadel. A decade ago, the mighty third tower had shattered, and forty-seven godborn Princes had met their Demise. Now Emyli Stauberg-Randolph faced Essera's Prince Regent, Erenor Tholeros, across a floor upon which death had written its poetry in undying blood.

"If you are trying to avoid me, Princess," Erenor snapped, "you must work harder. I know you come here every day at this hour to commune with your ghosts."

Not all of them. Not the ones you killed. Emyli gazed at her confronter with a steady defiance. It dared him to continue, which of course, he did.

"If you do not present your son to the Archhalia before the month is out, I will order your arrest."

"On whose authority?"

"Your son's." Erenor eyed the blood-scrawled paving between them but declined to cross it. Instead, he paced the perimeter with the taut rage of a caged and thwarted lion. Had he a tail, it would have twitched. "I am Handurin's regent. And you, not I, are obstructing his ascension to Essera's throne."

Emyli laughed. "Me? Hardly. I want him on that throne far more than you do."

"Then produce him!"

"Could I but wave my hand and make Handurin appear before us, I would have done so already."

She stood at the edge of a fractured medallion of gold veined with crimson. At the medallion's center hovered a blue bowl within which burned tongues of cold white flame. Like so many of Permephedon's mysterious structures, the Arcana Memorial occupied a space more akin to dreams than reality's tangible elements. Towering white pediments upheld by ghostly pillars—all that remained of the Arcana's former architecture—crowned the lush banks of a river of silver water laced with blood-red lilies. The gentle waterfall from which the watercourse originated simply appeared in midair. The ethereal water meandered through the ruins until its stream spilled over the distant edge of the building. Spectral arches, rib-vaulted and crowned by starbursts, soared overhead, reaching the clouds etched against a vivid blue sky. Bracketed by the corridor of those arches was a view of impossible mountains and an even more impossible half-finished moon.

Emyli doubted Erenor knew what he looked upon. Permephedon's reality was unfathomable, and knowledge of the Creation's current composition had died along with its guardians.

"At least make Handurin appear *somewhere!* You have one month, or he will forfeit his right to the throne." Erenor extended his right hand to Emyli, the documents he held rustling sharply. With his left hand, he held out a stylus. "Sign these, as the Archhalia ordered. The Manor at Gustan is Crown property, not yours, and must be inventoried."

He was changing the subject. The threat to depose Hans had no teeth. These documents, for one thing, bestowed the estate of Gustan Manor on Hans. Emyli honored the legitimacy of that assignation and signed both pages, surrendering her right to dwell at the Manor or on its grounds until such time as her son became king. As for inventorying the place… Erenor was welcome to try. She watched him tuck the papers and writing implement into a packet he carried on his hip.

Behind the scowling Prince Regent, another person emerged from the shimmer of the Memorial's angled, gilded portal. Ionais of Merrydn, wearing a close-fitted jacket of gold-stamped midnight leather atop wide velvet skirts the somber color of dark wine, stiffened when she saw them. Erenor's frown deepened.

He walked to the portal, bowing to Ionais when she stepped aside and turned back to give Emyli one last warning. "Handurin. Here before the Archhalia. One month." He held up his forefinger. "One! Until then, you are not to leave Permephedon."

As if Emyli would attempt it while this man waited to seize her. She watched him leave before allowing her shoulders to drop and her head to fall back.

Ionais's annoyance, always high, now focused on Emyli. "Much as I loathe that man, he's right. Handurin's continued absence is causing conjecture. Are you *sure* he's not dead?"

"Yes. Of course, my son is alive." Emyli clung to that hope. No one had seen Hans in nine years, not even her. She had only Marenthro's assurances. Her son lived… somewhere. Some*when*. Hidden away in one of the First Creation's archived pasts. She had not heard from Marenthro in weeks, however—not since the day the Archhalia had named Hans to be Stefan's successor. They had talked then, for perhaps a full minute.

Ionais looked doubtful. "I hope so. If he can find his way home, there's still a chance this kingdom might avoid war."

"You gave away that chance when you voted Erenor to be his regent."

"For the love of Leur, don't tell me you still resent that some of us voted against you—"

"I will resent it to my dying day."

Ionais walked slowly onto the Memorial pavilion, careful not to tread upon the bloodmarks on the patterned floor. "Then resent while you still breathe. You are handing your enemies too many chances to move against you."

"Better me than my son."

Emyli had never been warm with Ionais; the ties that bound them were woven of the men who had given them life, taught them and shaped them, and died. Their fathers, both murdered in this very place. Jonthan, brother and beloved husband. Stefan, son and king, also stirred between them as a haunted and tormented presence.

"They will move against Handurin too, you know, as soon as he is in reach." Ionais stopped walking when she came to a place on the floor marked by a serpentine scrawl of red. She knelt and removed a slip of ivory paper from inside her jacket, which she kissed and then touched to the crimson mark on the floor.

Emyli watched in silence.

Father. Ionais's lips shaped the word. Regelon had died at that very place. Marenthro had identified the dead Highborn Princes, and a chart of the bloodmarks had been filed with the Prime of Permephedon's Sages. Tears stung Emyli's eyes. Though her father had died here, no bloodmark noted Marc Frederick's passing. Human blood, merely mortal, did not bond with the Leur matrix. Nor had Marc Frederick died *here.* His body had been found in the rubble. Emyli remained silent as Ionais rose and walked to the white flame at the medallion's center, where she set the tiny slip to burn. Fragile, the paper flared blue and dissolved into a curl of smoke and ash, to be carried upward on the rising air.

Smoke becomes air... ash becomes earth... and memory becomes forever part of the World.

"We have our memories of them, at least," Ionais said.

"For now."

"Do you think it true? That we face a peril greater than *lr* weapons or war from that throne-grabbing Mormantaloran?"

Regelon would have warned Ionais about Nammuor, armed his daughter with truth. The Malyrdeons were good at holding secrets—and even better at building foundations.

"Yes. Marenthro—" Emyli stopped, the name frozen on her lips.

As if summoned, he had appeared in front of them. Tall and gracefully made, Marenthro's physical perfection jarred even more than usual. His skin seemed to glow faintly in the same way as the arches around them; his hair shone with the bright molten tones of the gold medallion at Emyli's feet. Everything about Marenthro's appearance matched the grandeur of their surroundings. Even his garments repeated the colors of the ethereal place within which they stood: white and red and blue. The Leur's Ring, moon-bright, glowed upon his left hand. Ionais gasped before dropping into a deep curtsey. Emyli followed suit, for Permephedon's wizard merited nothing less. Though her heart hammered with surprise, she forced herself not to besiege Marenthro on the spot. All these weeks and all these questions!

To demand answers now, in front of Ionais, would be unseemly. Emyli did not doubt why Marenthro had appeared at *this* moment and not one more private. He had, however, miscalculated if he thought Ionais cared about the propriety of bespeaking wizards.

"Eminence. *You* certainly must know where Handurin is being kept. I think it is high time you, or someone, bring him back!"

"He never left." Marenthro's slight smile widened as he caught Emyli's astonished stare. Raising his left hand with its shining ring, he pointed along the corridor of ghostly arches to the distant mist-blue line of mountains. "The Second Creation is connected, always, to its manifold pasts."

Ionais slid her gaze to Emyli, eyes narrowed with under-standing. "Clever girl, you sent him to the realm from which Endurin plucked your father."

"No." Marenthro's smile faded. "The enemy might think to look there. Nammuor has Vllyr's Crown and holds captive the life forces of Wall Lords. He could, conceivably, find a way to locate *that* realm and destroy it, but he does not have the ability to search or destroy every past. Not yet." Marenthro gazed upon distant peaks, and as he did so, vistas shifted and flowed. Mountains became sand… became grass… cities rose in towers of stone, then of glass… to be followed by landscapes of ice and snow beneath a full, fat moon. Many hundreds of thousands of worlds and moons had preceded the Second Creation.

"Of course!" How had she missed it? Emyli ran to the edge of the medallion, toward the vistas and their promises, then looked back at Marenthro. At Ionais. "Permephedon connects to *all* worlds!"

"That's convenient," said Ionais. She tugged at lace cuffs. "If that is the case, we can get him back. You can present him to the Archhalia within the hour."

Emyli faced Marenthro and, for the first time, feared how little she truly knew this man. More than anyone, she understood what he had done, the terrible fates from which he had saved her son. Stefan's troubled reign. Sordan's invasion of Gignastha and the bloody Rannul War. The slaughter of the Wall princes. Marenthro had removed Hans from Essera so Hans would not be caught up by

Stefan's ruin or Dorilian's violent hatred. Had found a place where none of them, including Nammuor, could distort or harm Hans.

But Emyli and Marenthro had known from the beginning that Hans must someday return.

"Now is the time," Emyli agreed. A light touch landed on her arm, and she looked down to see Ionais's hand. Surprised, she placed her own atop it and clutched at the offered support. It should not be necessary to beg. Marenthro had approached Emyli *first*, had included her in the decision to shield Hans by spiriting him away from the World. Marenthro would—he must—heed her plea to return him to it. "Hans is my son. Stefan's Heir. If Essera falls to Nammuor, so falls the Wall. So falls the World. We need him."

To Emyli's relief, Marenthro nodded.

2

What have we taken from the World? How are we
going to give it back?
—Endurin Malyrdeon,
Address to the Wall Initiates

The black eyes in the handsome face studied Hans, and he studied them back. He could do nothing else, not even breathe. Hair of silver gilt slashed like brushstrokes across the man's forehead beneath a crown ringed by tall blood-red spikes. A knife glinted in the man's right hand and something else—a long black shard—menaced in his left. *Run!* The word sang along Hans's nerves, but his arms and legs refused to obey. The man smirked and plunged the blade into Hans's neck. A scream without sound gargled in his throat, followed by a red spray he knew was blood. His blood. The black shard in his attacker's hand bloomed crimson.

Vision scattered. Glass shattered upon a floor splashed with gore. Bodies—so many bodies—bloodied, heads askew.

A crash louder than any thunder; a roar of wind filled his ears as the world broke apart. After that, there was nothing. Nothing but black fire and oblivion and a name.

Dorilian!

The name clawed from Hans's throat, seeking to become a scream—then he was awake, breathing hard in his bunk, sheets tangled about his legs.

The dream would fade. It always faded; already it had thinned into nothing. Yet each time he managed to hold onto a piece of it.

That piece.

"Dorilian," he whispered.

Groping his way to the trailer's small bathroom, Hans turned on the light, looked at his face in the mirror on the back of the door. The dream always left him wondering whose face he would see. Again, as always, he saw his own: wide-eyed and scared. He went to the window and moved aside the brightly striped curtain to peer into the cold night.

The lonely, moonlit plain was flat but for distant lights of houses and the serene glow of an all-night rig resting beside the highway. High, white-crowned mountains defined by starlight marched to the east, dwarfing the new civilization built atop the ruins of several that had come before. It was the same world in which, just a few hours ago, he had gone to sleep, but which always, after the dream, felt like the wrong one.

"Damn it." Even his voice seemed off, the language discordant. Every. Time.

In the morning, he had to go to Chuquiago to meet the project coordinator from the Yachaywasi, the Inka university, about his internship. Spending another sleepless night revisiting his demons was the last thing he needed. After kicking his feet into slippers, Hans left the light on so he could navigate the jumble of desks and storage that took up most of the trailer. Stepping outside, he quietly closed the door before he sat on the wooden step. How long until dawn? He hadn't looked at the time. An hour? Two?

Moonlight bathed the archeological site. Shaped by darkness and shadows, Tiwanaku's ancient stone walls and mysterious monoliths commanded the velvety night. Something sparkled, bright and glittering, within the ruins, near the excavation. There was nothing there that should have glittered. Intrigued, Hans got up and walked across the road. He saw no sign of movement or other people. The guard post looked dark, even though it was supposed to have been manned. The government was an unreliable one, its civil servants even more so. The gate creaked under his hand when he pushed it.

Beneath looming stone walls, Hans walked toward the top of the Apakana, where a shining point burned as brightly as though one of the stars themselves had fallen to earth. It was winter on the high plain of the Qullasuyu, and the air was crisp and thin, the silence deep, drawn from a lingering past. Lured on, Hans mounted the great stone steps, each a massive shin-high slab. At the landing, the remaining door into the temple loomed, brooding. That was where he found it: a bright bit of clear fire. He approached the anomaly and knelt upon stones worn smooth by millennia of weather and use.

A ring. A wide band of misty metal encircled a single oval stone that was at once translucent and filled with color, glowing even more brightly than the moon. Intrigued, Hans reached out his right hand.

The sky had paled to a deep pearly midnight. The moon had fled. Hans sat up. Cold pervaded his limbs, and he had a splitting headache. All around him, Tiwanaku was losing its magic. The ghostly stone pillars marched inexorably toward a daylight that would bring tourists and gum wrappers and words spoken in foreign tongues. He looked for the ring, but it was gone. The massive doorway rose overhead, simple and unrevealing.

Hans staggered to his feet and placed a hand against the doorway's stone frame when lightheadedness seized him. Had he seen a ring or not? Maybe he had dreamed that too. He scanned the half-restored temple and froze, arrested by the surreal vision of an audience of monoliths that stood there, had stood there for ages—and the man who stood beside the low wall under their gaze.

"Hello, Handurin."

The name locked around Hans with a naturalness he could no more explain than the man who had spoken it. Shimmering in bright gray shadow, the man wore garments that belonged to another world. Even his face was one the Romans of antiquity would have immortalized in marble, perfectly beautiful. Time seemed to stand still. Hans simply stood there and stared, struck by the realization that he *knew* this man.

Marenthro.

This didn't fit. *Marenthro* didn't fit. Not here.

Images slammed into place, newly remembered. A bedroom... his? But not the poster-hung one Hans had known as a child in Portland, across a hallway from Irmgard and Geraldine, his adoptive mothers. In this memory, he clasped a toy horse carved of wood, painted with gold, and stared up at—

"Y—you." Though he stood rooted, Hans could neither enter

the temple nor turn and run the other way. For some reason, he wanted to do both.

"Why so surprised? You always knew I would come for you."

"Mother said—" Hans stopped. No... neither of his mothers. He had just referred to a person who, until now, had been accounted for as a legal note jotted on his adoption papers. "Mother: Unknown." Right next to "Father: Unknown" and a line down from "Birthplace: Unknown." Yet his mind now held images and memories of a brown-haired, pretty woman named Emyli—yes, that was her name—and a father he had never known. And a dark-haired older boy, a brother named Stefan.

Stefan had been coming to see him. Hans was eight... no, he had just turned nine. It was his *birthday*. And he had been in bed sick, had dreamed the world was burning—had seen Stefan burning.

Had that been what had happened? Somehow Hans had woken up after that with no memories at all. His childhood before his moms was a blank slate.

Until now.

Another house... a different house. Different people. A woman speaking in a language he had not heard since *that* day.

"Marenthro wants to send Hans away."

And Stefan's voice. *"No!"*

Hans backed away a step. "You came to me because I was sick. I remember that now. But I don't understand. Why was I told I was an orphan, given to Irmgard and Geraldine? Did my family *die*? What did you do?"

"I helped you. Only that. You're not an orphan. Your mother is alive."

That was probably a good thing. Still, Hans frowned at Marenthro. "You helped me? How?"

"You were having too many bad dreams. Nightmares, but waking ones. Unrelenting and crippling. The only way to stop them was to keep you drugged and in bed. That was no way for a child to live—or develop. So I brought you here. A place free of trouble, where you could learn and grow."

"I still have those dreams."

"But you didn't, not for many years."

That much was true. The dreams had returned again only in the last year.

"Where… am I?" Hans asked. This wasn't the same place he had left behind. Not even close.

"One of the First Creation's many pasts."

Not just a different place, then, with different people. A different *world*. Another memory intruded, of an illustration of overlapping circles. An older man's finger traced one of the drawings. *"This is the Second Creation, where we live. And this the First Creation, its pasts forever preserved."*

Hans remembered the rest of that conversation, and with whom he had shared it. "This is a *past*? Of the world I belong to… like… grandfather's was?"

"Not the same one. But similar."

"So everything here—this world, its people and the things they do or will do—has already happened?"

"Yes."

As unbelievable as that explanation should be, as impossible as it should have been, Hans knew it must be true. It *felt* true—and it fit his new memories too well.

"But was that really necessary? Was it even fair?" Hans walked toward Marenthro across the temple yard. He stopped before completely closing the distance between them. "You never told *me* what you were going to do. No one asked me. What you did… you *stole* my childhood! You took away my *life*. Everything that I knew and was. Even my memories, of my *home*, my family—"

"Your confusion and terror and exposure to harm. You were more vulnerable than you can imagine. The World… changed very quickly after your grandfather's death, and not for the better."

"And this one is better?"

"It was for you."

"But I knew. I've… *sensed* it. It happens all the time. I wake up and I feel like things around me are… off, like I'm not where I'm supposed to be! And now—" Hans looked around, but the stone-faced monoliths among which he stood seemed to glare at him in hollow-eyed, silent agreement. "Now I know why. It explains so much. Even why I sometimes feel like I'm… not *who* I'm supposed to be."

"You will never be other than who you are supposed to be."

Which at that moment meant Hans Gerard Stoll-Becker. He had always called himself Hans, even before placement, even at the time of his adoption, when he was nine. The Dominion official had asked him what name he wanted to be called—Gerard, perhaps, to combine the names of his two moms?—and he had insisted, "No. I am Hans."

"Does anyone know what you did? My… mother—" Again a memory rose to the surface of the woman, probably his mother, saying Marenthro wanted to send Hans away.

"Your mother agreed it was for the best. Your world knows you exist. When you return, you will regain everything that was set aside."

Hans barely remembered what that might be. His toys? His pets? He didn't remember any pets. "I… none of this feels right. For years and years, I—" He shook his head. "Children may not know all there is to know about the world, but they understand when they are out of place. I never fit in, not completely. Other kids knew I was different. I made a few friends, but they never stuck. Even my moms… they tried so hard to figure out what kind of kid I was, what I needed to make it work. They really wanted to. And then they died—"

Last year. He had just settled the estate, a small one, back home in the Dominion. The land was worth something and he had given the proceeds to Irmgard and Geraldine's favorite charity. He was living off his own accounts now. He stared hard at Marenthro as a new realization hit him in the gut.

"You knew all along. You knew my moms would die." *And when. And how.* "The accident. The explosion."

"I knew. And you were a good son to them."

"As you knew I would be."

Not quite a smile. "I hoped. Their lives were fixed in ways yours is not."

"Fixed?"

"It's complicated." Marenthro approached, a man strangely at home among the monoliths. Perhaps, Hans thought, he fit in everywhere. "They were a quiet couple, bookish and open-minded, desirous of leaving a legacy. I knew they would provide you with opportunities to learn and travel."

"They did."

It was thanks to Irmgard and Geraldine that Hans had traveled and learned languages, fallen in love with other cultures and believed those cultures to be living, growing and changing—a kind of ecosystem. He'd pursued his interest into the study of history, which had led him here, standing in a temple complex that had preceded the Inka Empire.

Finding out it was all for nothing.

"I have been here with you all along, in small ways." Marenthro squinted outward at ruins gilded by the rising sun.

"I feel that it's true. You *are* a wizard, just like Stefan always said you were—like… like Grandfather told me." Hans tested his memory for his grandfather's name and found it: Marc Frederick. His heart swelled and he wondered why. Love? Pride?

"Did they? I suppose children require such explanations." A timeless quality, quiet and impending, resided in Marenthro's smile. It was not unlike the sunrise he watched. And yet Marenthro was young, so young that Hans wondered how he had ever thought him old. Or did all adults seem old to a child?

Together they ascended the platform and walked through the high stone portal beneath frowning gods. From a stone landing they overlooked the ruins while sunlight from behind the mountains turned to rose fire.

"How did you do it?" Hans asked. "My childhood—I forgot it all, until tonight. I'm still not sure I remember everything." And yet he remembered so much. The thunder of ivory-white horses upon the road, himself seated in front of his grandfather on the saddle. His laughing, dark-haired brother. Oak trees blazing red across hills of wilderness. A vast city of canals, reflected in water, crowned by light. Hans closed his eyes against the flood of images. "This thing that's happening to me right now—being here, seeing you, remembering… all of it—it feels like a dream. Or a summer vacation when you get home. It's simply… gone. Nothing feels real anymore."

Even the moment in which they stood, together upon Tiwanaku's stone ruins, wavered between realities, placing him solidly in neither.

"Give yourself time," Marenthro counselled. "You were just a child when you left, and your memories are that of a child. I have noticed that when children look at a certain tapestry I know, they first see the unicorns—and often that is all they see. Later, when asked to describe what they have seen, the unicorns are all they remember, but they remember it vividly."

As Hans did now. He saw that tapestry, hanging on the wall of a landing atop a great stair in the manor where he had lived. Surprised, he laughed out loud. He wished he could have sworn otherwise, but it was true: the unicorn was the only thing he remembered.

"I used to study that tapestry for hours when I was a boy," he confided. "And now all I can think of is that one silly unicorn tossing its head. So much for having regained my memory!"

"Children have excellent memories, just highly selective ones. If you would see that tapestry again, you would recognize it in an instant, in all its forgotten detail. So it will be with your own country when you return."

Marenthro was right, and not just because Marenthro could not be wrong. If Hans did this—if he went back to whatever world he had been born in, to that world he remembered—it would be as though he had never left. His grandfather had once said the same about his own birth world, that if he could go back he would feel right at home.

Hans was not enjoying this whole integration process. His warring memories were giving him a headache.

"Why did you do it? Block my memories?"

Marenthro sat upon one of the steps and patted the stone. Hans took a seat beside him, and only realized after that he had done it without question.

"I did it so you could more easily adapt," Marenthro said. "Your memories as they are now—as you have regained them—are untouched, untarnished by exposure to this world, a culture and way of life that conflicts wildly with that into which you were born. Children are so very vulnerable. What was to be gained by having you feel more different and more isolated than you already were? You navigated this unalterable world better without them."

Such reasoning made more sense than Hans would have liked. Knowing nothing, or close to nothing, about himself, he had taken whatever had come his way. He had been told he was the only survivor of a terrible accident, that no one knew who his parents were. He had not spoken to anyone for two months. But then one day he did speak, and he went on to advance rapidly in school, become the adopted son of Irmgard and Geraldine, learn new languages, and enter college by age sixteen. He had been uncommonly fortunate. His childhood had been ordinary, rich with experience, and trouble-free. But before that...

He had left behind a very different world: a world without cars, electricity, or airships. Now that he thought of it, his birth world was considerably *less* advanced than this one. Except—

He pondered Marenthro.

Marenthro had always been a friend of the family. That much Hans remembered very clearly. Whether Marenthro was in fact related, Hans wasn't sure, although he doubted it. He recalled his brother Stefan saying that Marenthro was probably Staubaun, and Hans knew—probably from Stefan also—that their family was Kheld. But it hadn't seemed to matter. Hans's mother had always welcomed Marenthro warmly on his frequent visits, and Marc Frederick—the other towering presence in Hans's early memory— had set great store by the wizard and had often sought his counsel. Even more amazing, though...

He frowned at Marenthro. "You're leaving something out. A lot, actually. Like about my family being royal."

With a nod that indicated he had expected this issue to arise, Marenthro turned his hand. Between his thumb and forefinger, he held the ring, bright as a star in the pre-dawn gloom, that had drawn Hans to the ruins just an hour or so before. Hans had not recognized it then, but now he did.

It was his grandfather's ring.

"I keyed your memories to this."

Marenthro set the ring upon the stone surface between them. Hans reached, thinking to pick it up, only to have Marenthro's hand clamp upon his wrist.

"Don't," Marenthro warned, guessing his intention. "If you were to put it on, you would not be able to take it off. And that means for as long as you live."

Snatching back his hand, Hans left the mysterious ring on the step, where it continued to wink at him like a mischievous bit of captive light.

"Is it magic, then?"

"Yes, as humans would define it."

"What kind of magic does it possess?"

"Whatever kind the wearer can summon." Marenthro tapped the ring so that it wobbled and flashed. "This is the ring of the

Highborn Kings of Essera, worn by every king since Ergeiron Malyrdeon, who received it from the hand of his father, called Amynas, who got it from the Hand of Leur."

"The Leur's Ring!" Hans peered at it more closely. As a child, he had been fascinated by his grandfather's ring, which never left the royal hand. "It doesn't look the same. On Grandfather it looked alive, kind of. It had colors."

"That's because it was alive—and is. It lives with the wearer, bonding to the flesh for as long as that flesh lives, thereby providing that the true king shall always be known by its presence. It is a true symbiont, rare and powerful. They take many forms." Marenthro plucked the ring from the step and held it on his outstretched palm. The ring, merely bright and clear before, burned now with fires of blue and gold and green, its silver brilliance stirring deep within those undulating fields. A thing of impossible power and beauty. "This is the Ring of Leur, linked to the life force of the Creation itself, which only someone also bound to the Creation may safely wear. It cannot be removed in life. But in death, from wherever the vacant body lies, the ring always returns—to *me*."

Hans knew then, beyond all question: every one of Stefan's crazy allegations were true. A blond enchanter with strange and wonderful eyes offered Hans a living gift. Unthinking, he put out a trembling hand and laid it palm down over Marenthro's. He felt with eerie clarity the warmth of the wizard's living skin, the heat of the Leur's Ring pressed between their palms. Felt, rather than saw, those resplendent copper eyes bridging the distance between them, taking hold of him, an alien awareness sliding over the skin of his mind, not hostile but not Handurin.

Hans jerked his hand away, tore his gaze from that hypnotic other, and squeezed his eyes shut against the unwelcome intrusion.

"Good God, what was that?" he said. "Were you trying to hypnotize me?"

"No. I was assessing your ability to eventually wear the ring."

"*Wear* it?" This was getting preposterous. "I don't want to wear it, not if I can't ever take it off again. I've read enough stories to know that magic things always carry a price."

"They are a weighty responsibility, to be sure. You do not have to wear this ring to become king, of course. Stefan never did, but—"

"Stefan became king?" Hans vaguely remembered that, too, though the knowledge felt unreal. Because he had been sick at the time, he had not attended the coronation. Their grandfather had died. Horribly. Hans had seen it somehow or imagined it. Death and more death, himself but a flicker among so much carnage, struggling to break free—the swirling confusion of his mother's grief and his brother's accusations and feelings and pain—

"Yes. Stefan succeeded your grandfather. He reigned for nine years." Marenthro's face clouded as he looked across the soft gray shadows of the awakening land. "He died a few months ago. You have been declared his Heir."

Hans felt as though the steps had dropped out from under him. Tiwanaku's ruins loomed to either side but felt far away somehow, like the mountains so far in the distance. Two worlds that must never, ever meet, met in him. "My brother's *dead?*"

He'd only just remembered him again.

"You are the last of the Stauberg-Randolphs." Marenthro's chill expression informed Hans what that meant. "Stefan's Heir, by declaration of the Triemperal Archhalia, Prince-Apparent of Dazunor and rightful king of Essera."

"Stefan's dead." It was like the dream, death piled upon death. Hans closed his eyes but could not keep from crossing thresholds of memory. He remembered Stefan alive, storming against Marenthro and his mother. *What are we waiting for? For Dorilian to kill me next? Then Hans? The way he killed our grandfather...*

There was that name again. Dorilian.

"Your brother was murdered." Marenthro continued to fill in missing information. "The men who did it were executed because the law demanded it, but they were not truly the ones to blame. Their deaths compounded the tragedy. After that, it took several weeks to convene the Archhalia to secure the vote."

Hans drew a breath. "I wish you hadn't. I wish someone had asked me first. I don't want this."

"Handurin, I—"

"Do you need an answer right this moment?" Hans swallowed to buy time for his thoughts to settle. "I hope not, because I don't have one. I need to think about this. About my future and what I want it to be. Irmgard and Geraldine had a dream for me too and, well... I don't think being a prince or king, of anywhere, was part of the plan. Certainly not *my* plan! And I just signed a contract to serve a year-long internship. Don't you think I should honor that?"

"If that is what you wish."

"I feel like I need to think about this."

"Then you should. You have some time."

Newly hopeful, Hans lifted his head. "I do? How much?"

"A few days at most. Your enemy is not unaware of this effort to bring you back."

Enemy? Hans shook his head. It was bad enough finding out he did not belong in this world and had a host of expectations waiting for him in the one he *did* belong to—he also had an enemy to contend with?

"You could hide here for a while, of course," Marenthro granted. "This is a large and currently stable past, with billions of people and many ways to create a good life among them. But that would not save you. You would just die along with them." He rose to stand beside Hans. He was taller, in the way Staubauns were tall, with the same golden assurance, his garments brilliant against a world painted in tones of earth and stone remembered. "Come, I will show you."

They descended the steps of the ruined courtyard, silent as the stones among which they wandered beneath the cold first light of day. Marenthro did not act like a stranger to this place; he walked like a man who had trodden here before, beneath a younger sun than this one. They passed wall upon unfallen wall, courtyards smooth and pale with dawn. Ahead, a sky brushed with blue showed through the portal of the Door of the Sun.

"Scholars will tell you they do not know the origin of this gateway." Marenthro watched his face. "I will tell you that the other ruins were built by men who came later. This gateway was built before they ever arrived here. It was built by the Aryati, who used it to cross between temporal planes."

"This?" Hans saw only an artifact he had studied: a giant doorway of stone, its cracked headpiece carved with unrecognizable gods. Its open door might seem alive, but only from heat and the sheen of an earthly, familiar sky.

"It is dormant now. The gods themselves disabled it." Marenthro stepped to the arch and put his hand upon it, palm pressed flat against the pitted surface. As though Time itself fell away, Hans saw the Gate as it must have been in its pristine state—smooth-clean and shimmering, its uncracked lintel covered with gold blazing like the sun, atop a base and walls like quicksilver. Bright against the dawn, it revealed, suddenly, a clear blue sky vivid within.

"The Aryati built it in the days of their glory. They had studied with Leur and mastered infinite Time itself and for them this age in which we stand now was but one of the Creation's variations. Through this Gate and others like it, they came to this place, exploited it, and enslaved its people." Marenthro removed his hand. The image wavered, and the Door of the Sun faded to but a ruin again. "That was many thousands of years ago. Tens of thousands of years. In their star-conquering pride, the many-crowned Aryati destroyed the One World, the First Creation. Only the sacrifice of Leur, who separated the World in Time, creating three Worlds out of the One, spared the Creation. Billions died, but before the barriers fully formed, some of the Aryati fled to this past, this one and a few others. They brought their knowledge and their technology. They were gods, Handurin."

"Viracocha." Hans softly spoke the name of the god most associated with the gate.

"Viracocha had another name, an Aryati name. It has been forgotten." Marenthro ran his hand over the stone again, then sighed. "They are gone now, of course. Amynas Malyrdys and the Three cast them out and hurled their Gates into the Rift. Only a few, like this one, remain—and barriers can be breached."

Hans himself was proof of that. "But what does this have to do with me?"

Marenthro told him gravely, "Only this: your enemy is not unaware of the existence of these many pasts. In time, given his nature and that of the thing that compels him, he will seek to gain dominion over the Second Creation and all its pasts—to rule or destroy. He was weakened for a time, but grows stronger. You may not get another chance to fight him as effectively as you can now. And if you wait until he finds *you*, you will fight him alone."

"*Fight* him?" Hans did not like the direction of this conversation. "I don't want to fight anyone. I don't even know who my enemy is. Besides, I am nothing; anyone can see that. If this enemy is so strong, he's probably Aryati or something, right? Well, I'm not Aryati—and I'm not one of the Highborn princes Stefan used to rant about, the ones with unnatural powers. The Stauberg-Randolphs are just ordinary."

"That is not entirely true. Your grandfather was endowed by the Malyrdeons with Highborn gifts. That was quite extraordinary."

"Yes, well, that was Marc Frederick. And if you're suggesting you or someone else is going to give me Highborn gifts, I don't want them. I wouldn't even know where to begin with that."

They walked back toward the Apakana and the steps descending to the plaza. With morning full upon it, the plain spread from the ruins like a brown sea, desolate and remote. Already workers had begun to arrive near the fence line, while in the distance the sun glinted on approaching rigs.

"I need time to think, Marenthro. This is too much too fast. And I'm meeting the person in charge of my project at the university today. I can't miss that. It's important."

Maybe the meeting was important. And maybe it wasn't. But in the scheme of things, Hans wanted it to be. He needed to hold onto something that still felt real.

Marenthro sighed but nodded. "Your brain is piecing together two very separate lives. They may not always fit together peacefully. If you need me, there is a house in Chuquiago." He pressed a card into Hans's hand. Hans looked at it and recognized the address as one in the *missionario* section of the city. "That is where I will be."

3

The great irony of the Epoptes is that they understood their Entity's nature least of anyone.
—FAHME D'SORDANEON, *ANAMNESIS*

The moment his perspective locked into place, Dorilian recognized the bone-white architecture, even as sunset dipped beneath the clouds and poured red light into the solitary pavilion overlooking the Prism. Twelve circular columns ringed a mosaic floor and lifted high a dome painted with a fresco of the Rillbirth. Rain recently fallen from the clouds now hanging over the lake slicked the nearby ravine and the smooth paving stones of the pavilion's skirt.

Moments ago Dorilian had been standing on a carpet among books in the library at Rhondda, his estate on the south side of the island.

Levyathan sat on one of the two marble benches at the pavilion's perimeter, feet up and arms about his knees. As they had agreed, he had waited here for Dorilian's return. "What are you testing now? Your limits… or *that*?" Levyathan's gaze landed unhappily on the Sordan Coronal, the gem-tipped points of which smoldered green above Dorilian's brow.

He removed the device, which he placed into a heavy pouch of leather and quilted velvet at his hip. "I am practicing. Skills are of no use if not kept sharp."

"No one has sharper skills. You practice all the time."

It was only the truth. In pursuit of perfecting every gift at his command, Dorilian had handed over the greater part of his administrative duties to others and had also stinted time with his family. Hours spent cultivating the discipline needed to manipulate his arcane blood-born gifts—the sources of it, the applications— could not be regained. It was only right to acknowledge the wellspring of Levyathan's resentment.

"I practice while I can; our time may be running out." Dorilian joined Levyathan on the bench. The pavilion was part of the Sordaneon Serat's extensive grounds, private and secluded. They would not be interrupted or overheard. Most importantly, only Levyathan had witnessed Dorilian's translocation. It was imperative to keep such talents secret. "I will spend more time with you and Fahme now that the Illumination draws near. I will also start teaching you."

"Me?" Levyathan's eyes widened.

"You are getting older and more able. You can send to me now and that is something no one else can do." Levyathan had just turned ten and they had tested his nascent ability by playing "catch", sending cylinders throughout the confines of the Serat and, just this past week, to Rhondda.

Levyathan grinned. "Even the Rill cannot obscure you from me."

Dorilian grinned also. "Never. You know me too well. I encourage you to practice other skills also. *Orbi* are useful. Separation of densities. Matching of resonances. Differentiation is the key to everything in this thrice-cursed world. It took me too many years to figure that out, so allow me to hand my hard-learned lessons to you on a platter."

"I can differentiate things other than just you from the Rill," Levyathan said. He winked as he recited dichotomies. "Sanity from insanity. Good from bad."

Human from... not human at all. Dorilian regretted where his thoughts were taking him. "We should go to dinner. I am hungry and you should be too."

Using the powers of the Sordan Coronal drained him still. The device was one of the greater enhancers and drew heavily on his merely mortal energy. Though Dorilian carried a flask of restorative, he much preferred eating and drinking food fit for humans. When Levyathan stood, Dorilian hugged the boy and together they left the pavilion, following the wet path to the first rampart of the sprawling eighteen-hundred-year-old wonder they called home. Scented evening roses blossomed on thornless stalks beneath the warm glow that spilled from the Serat's many loggias and windows. Waterglobes discreetly lit the terraces.

Levyathan, at least, had more to say. "I beg you to tell me you are being careful. I cannot help but worry over these dangerous powers you seek."

How not, after all he had seen? Dorilian hastened to reassure him. "Making these abilities familiar means less chance for harm, not more. None of these powers you fear are as dangerous as the Rill."

"Except you are not seeking the Rill."

Not yet. That day would come, though at least for now Dorilian could avoid his bloodline's ancestral calling.

"What has Nammuor done now to make you think our time grows short?" Levyathan asked. They had reached the outer terrace and walked along its vine-draped overlook.

"He is no longer only in Aral—he has stationed troops in Trulo. It's only a matter of time until he moves into Stauberg. He has taken control of the port already."

"I thought the Wall would not abide his Diadem."

"I think it would not—if our knowledge is true. The Rill does not tolerate the thing. I witnessed that for myself." Sordan, too, enjoyed the protection of an Entity. "I don't believe Nammuor has entered Stauberg while wearing it. However, the Entities do abide dangerous things... and people: the Wall will tolerate enemy troops. It allowed Kheld troops before, even knowing what they might do." Dorilian stopped walking and paused at the terrace edge. From this height he looked out over his City and hoped to convince himself that he and Levyathan enjoyed some safety from their enemy.

The world had become uncomfortable, less and less a realm into which Dorilian fit. He was too cognizant that he and Levyathan were the last of their race. Loyal courtiers and administrators surrounded Dorilian but he wanted more. Respite, perhaps, such as he had found for a time with Palimia, whose lovely body and generous spirit had relieved his yearning to feel more... human. She and Marc Frederick had put that longing in him, the weakness to his strength. He wanted… no he *needed* to act, to move—against Nammuor, against lies, against beliefs that reduced the Rill, and him, to useful prisoners.

"Dor?" Levyathan had noted the darkening of his thoughts.

"Nothing can harm us here," Dorilian said.

They resumed walking toward the residence. Below them, Sordan's streets etched the island with trails of light, while above them the City's Leur might cradled the Rill's massive architecture and glowed with the beauty of its eternal dance.

The god-machine, forever in motion.

The detailed map and colored markers on the conference table revealed the extent of Dorilian's fear. He had guessed before now that the Epoptes were colluding with his adversaries in Essera. It was bad enough that Erenor, as Prince Regent, controlled Essera's Crown Rill slots; that the villain was using those slots to supply Nammuor's increasingly large army in Tahlwent struck Dorilian as the worst kind of treachery. And the scoundrel was doing it in plain sight.

Sordan to Dazunor-Rannuli. Randpory to Dazunor-Rannuli. Hestya to Dazunor-Rannuli.

Sordan to thrice-cursed *Permephedon* and then to… Dazunor-Rannuli.

What irked Dorilian most was that he could do nothing to stop any of it, short of abandoning the Rill as his Hierarchate's primary means of getting goods from one place to another. Just as irksome was the way Sinon Kouranos watched him like a pot he expected to boil over.

"You know what these reports suggest, don't you?" Dorilian was aware the question sounded like an accusation. "The Epoptes are conniving with my enemies! They are facilitating the diversion of shipments I have been sending to Lacenedon."

Military supplies for that domain's eventual defense. Horses. Arms.

"Yes, Thrice Royal." Sinon, Sordan's Ambassador to the Triemperal Archhalia, had owned Dorilian's full trust for nearly a year and had earned the privilege of being seated in his Hierarch's presence. He occupied the facing chair. "I have compiled the reports as you requested. This degree of sabotage could not have occurred without the knowledge of the Brotherhood."

In violation of their Charter, and the Rill Covenant too. The Brotherhood of Epoptes was supposed to remain outside of political jockeying, though they had certainly flouted that part of their mission on the day Marc Frederick had gained his throne. They had only grown more power hungry since. It wasn't a big step from power brokering to power grabbing.

Sinon leaned forward to press a point. "If you will not talk with the Seven Houses—"

"I will not. Anything they wish to say, they can say to you or my trade minister."

"Which they do. I believe it is notable that *their* shipments are not being diverted. Not from any of these ports. Only yours are, and those of other slot holders who sometimes act as your surrogates."

Which meant that *some* provisions—slotted through other holders or the Seven Houses—*were* getting through to Hebron and his allies in the Royal North. That vital supplies must be routed through the cartel going forward irked Dorilian even more. Everything about this situation could not have been better designed to force his hand.

"They want me to know what they are doing. Erenor. The Seven Houses. The thrice-cursed Epoptes. They are showing me that they, not I, direct the Entity."

"What do you plan to do, Thrice Royal?"

After a long moment, Dorilian pushed away from the table. "Nothing. I will stop sending through vendors I know to be compromised and Hebron will have to stockpile what we are able to get through to him. But I will not let this continue into another winter."

"Before you go, there is another bit of news." Sinon produced a note.

Curious, Dorilian took it. He recognized the handwriting. "Ionais?" Dorilian and his cousin, the Princess of Merrydn, spoke as seldom as possible. His last communication had been a blistering excoriation of Ionais's refusal to grant the Esseran regency to Emyli. He had yet to forgive that offense.

Sinon distilled the note to its essence. "She wishes you to know that Prince Handurin will soon be in play."

That… was interesting. Emyli had been promising—or threat-ening—to bring back the missing prince for months. Essera's instability had only gotten worse as a result. Clearly Dorilian's frown conveyed his thoughts, because Sinon sought to reassure him.

"According to the Princess, she herself witnessed Emyli make the arrangement."

"Good." At least now the question of who would succeed to Essera's throne might be settled. Dorilian held no illusions about the ambitions in play.

"Does this not interfere with your own plans?"

Dorilian shrugged. "I don't see how. Handurin's return to Essera won't change anything, except perhaps to delay the inevitable."

4

Amynas knelt beside his friend and clutched his
wound, but there was no stemming the life from
leaving him. "Did you think it would last
forever?" the Leur whispered. To which Amynas
answered, "Why should it not?"
—Cibulitus, *Annals of the Return*

The meeting with the project coordinator went smoothly enough, but still left Hans feeling off course. Once he had left the administration offices, he sat on a low retaining wall and stared at the eroding features of the Yachaywasi's monolith. Hollow-eyed, the stone god stared back. The more Hans tried to embrace the world surrounding him, the sharper its alienness became. Could it be true that his presence in this world—this sliver of an archived past—might be all that was needed to destroy it?

Maybe, if he had an enemy who might track him here.

Troubled, he picked up his knapsack and walked back to the Plaza Inti. Even the gold-sheathed Inka temple dedicated to the Sun no longer evoked a sense of wonder. As he moved through crowds of tourists, listening to the polyglot of languages, some of which he understood, he felt overcome by banality. *These people aren't here, not really, not any more than I am. They're taking in just enough of the sights to say they have been here, but they will leave no trace behind when they return to their own countries.*

And now he knew their lives were doomed to leave no trace at all.

Behind the church of San Francisco, with its foundation of Inka blocks and interior that had known the boots of the conquistadors before the Reconquest, thrived the teeming Witches' Market. Although the street suffered its share of gawkers laughing uncomfortably over offerings of dried llama fetuses or bins of tiny trinkets, most of the patrons of this crowded alleyway were indigenous. Before the Inkas had established their empire, other people had populated the Qullasuyu and they lived here still. In the Witches' Market, as much as anywhere, Hans embraced the lingering traces of their ways.

There was a woman whose knowledge of native herb lore and witchcraft often informed Hans's studies and who still was his primary teacher of the local non-Quechua language. He found Felicia in her usual place, presiding solemnly over her wares in a makeshift stall, her black hair streaked with gray and crowned by the high-topped conical hat favored by indigenous women when marketing to tourists. Her black eyes peered at Hans from beneath heavy eyelids.

"This time, *joven*, you seek something," Felicia said in Spanish. Because Hans had fair skin and light brown hair, she liked to tease that he was from New Spain.

Hans smiled, but knew it to be less light-hearted than usual. "Just some green tea with coca. To relax me. I have a lot on my mind." He laid two square coins on the cloth draping the counter.

Felicia waved her left hand. "Young people should not look too much at what is in front of them. Those things are already known."

Taking the coins, she tucked them into the bulging sash under her shawl. Her fingers moved across the many mounds on her table, gathering seeds, leaves, roots and powders. She picked a little from this pile, then a little from another, adding each pinch to a cheesecloth bag. Hans enjoyed watching her work. Felicia would peer at him with her pitch-dark eyes, her face drooping with years and secrets, while assembling a bag of herbs which she then handed to him with a pronouncement of what ailed him. Many times Felicia's preparations had provided ease where alcohol and conventional medicines had failed. He was curious to know what she would make of his current melancholy.

"Now, tell me what you seek," Felicia said.

Hans shrugged. "Answers to my questions."

Felicia snorted. "You are looking in the wrong place." Hans

watched her grind something red in her pestle and add it to the bag. "You will not find answers in a lie."

"Lie? What lie?"

She grunted something noncommittal. Her gnarled but nimble fingers tucked and stitched, sealing the bag with needle and thread. That done, she put the pillow of coca and herbs in Hans's hand. Bending stiffly, Felicia reached under the table and brought forth something brown, flat, and stiff. It was a dried llama fetus, but different from the many piled in the basket at the end of her table. This one had three eyes and six tiny, shriveled legs and a tiny pouch tied around its desiccated neck. She put it in a paper bag and handed it across the table. "Put this under your bed after you drink the remedy."

Hans decided it was probably bad luck to decline a shaman's prescription, even if it was grotesque. He accepted the paper bag and tucked it under his arm, then rummaged in his pocket for the extra money to pay her. "How much—"

"Next visit," Felicia made a dismissive gesture with her hands, "you pay me what it was worth to you."

He looked at the tiny woman skeptically. "Marmi Felicia," Hans used a cordiality marker and emphasis, "I don't think this will answer my questions."

Felicia turned from him and eased herself back onto her chair, hands folded. "It will do better than that. It will show you the lie."

The local professor overseeing the students at the dig owned a formerly grand but currently run-down house in central Chuquiago. Two retainers lived there, keeping up the place. Marta and her son had been told that Hans was to have use of the house whenever he was in town. He went there now, carrying his paper bag with its odd contents. After letting him in and locking the door securely behind him, the son left Hans alone. Hans made his way to the courtyard where in the spring blood-red geraniums would bloom like roses against stone walls and among the golden bells of prized cantuta flowers. He sat at a rusting iron table and simply stared at the walls. He didn't have the energy to pick up his coursework. Now he wondered if he would ever finish it.

After asking Marta for a cup of boiling water, he made Felicia's tea. He watched colors unfurl as the contents settled into the shell-pink cup: green first, from the leaves, then traces of red and purple that quickly blended into a rich brown. The brew smelled heavy and strong, different from straight coca tea. It tasted different too, vaguely unpleasant, almost like chicory. After drinking the remedy, Hans carried his bags upstairs, dumping his knapsack on the chair in his room and emptying the paper bag onto the bed. The dried llama fetus, the tiny red pouch around its neck brilliant against the white coverlet, seemed to eye him balefully.

This is ridiculous, he thought. Then again, his day had long since passed the point of absurdity. *Oh, what the hell.*

He took up the dead thing gingerly and put it on the floor under the bed, then realized that wasn't right. The usual treatment of llama fetuses was to bury them, traditionally right next to the foundation of a new house, covered with earth. Last night he had watched on viewer as the Sapa Inka himself did so for the construction of a new government building. Hans picked the dead thing up again and lifted the mattress, inserting the stiff bit of arcana between that and the box spring. Better.

Hans wondered if he would feel it when he lay on the bed, but the mattress buoyed his body as it always had. Outside the thick walls, traffic dulled to a drone. His breathing deepened and slowed and then the world itself gently slipped away…

A vast white dreamland opened before him, only mountains against a gray sky, marching in a line unbroken, while in the distance, hounds bayed.

A young man older than himself, dark-haired and proud, stood beside him. Hans recognized his brother. "I didn't get him," Stefan said, but his blue eyes were focused elsewhere.

"Who?" Hans asked. He could not hear his own voice, but his breath created mist as he spoke.

Stefan's did not. "Dorilian. But I killed the rest of his demon breed."

Hans wanted to know more, ask more, but the mist had risen again and no matter which way he turned, he saw nothing, only heard the horrible baying sounds. He ran past fallen trees silvered with dew. The land around him was wet and dark, shadows and twilight.

…the hounds baying…

And there was Stefan again, sprawled on the ground, leaning back on his elbows… and standing before him was another man with hair of silver, wearing a tall crown of red crystals. A man Hans had seen before, in a different dream.

…laughing…

Run, fool, run! You have done your part! Sordan stands alone!

Starting, fear in his eyes, Stefan scrambled to his feet, then ran.

…and then it was not Stefan running, but Hans, into a field where grasses released clouds of mist. Hunters were coming, shadows cresting the rise, and he knew they were after him. Arrows, released, whistled through the air… pierced his side. Pain, then blood, filled his lungs. And the dogs, the dogs were baying, and he could not run anymore. Then the hounds were on him, teeth tearing into his flesh, rending him… bringing him down.

The silver-haired man looked down on him. The gems on his crown looked like fresh blood. You thought to cheat me, but I need him more than I need you.

And there was blood, blood everywhere. Fingers closed over his hand, a hand that looked like a hoof… then an ax came down and severed his hand above the wrist…

… and he woke up screaming.

Only this time he remembered the dream.

The next day was Saturday, and even in the early morning the Witches' Market was busy. Hans found a younger woman in Felicia's booth, black hair shining and big gold earrings bright in the sun. The lack of afternoon shadows gave the market a festive, less sinister air.

"Where is Marmi Felicia?" he asked. The young woman turned and pointed to the brown rear wall of the church of San Francisco.

Though the nation's Inka elites worshipped the Sun, the Roman church of the defeated conquistadors flourished among the lower classes. Hans dashed around to the front of the church, weaving through crowds thick with tourists and merchants from nearby villages. At the door to the church, he paused to catch his breath and bought two candles from a woman who had set up her folding table just outside the entry. He found Felicia inside, kneeling at the wooden gate before a wall of blazing candles at the foot of the Virgin. Lighting his, he added them to the conflagration of prayers.

After several minutes, Felicia rose, and Hans followed her to a bench beside the reliquary. "What did I see?" he asked.

Felicia lifted a crucifix that hung from a chain about her neck and kissed it, then made the sign of the cross. "I am not a taker of souls. I do not know what the magic revealed to you. I do not know why I cannot read your truths or your lies. But I will pray for you." She wrapped her fingers around the small cross. With a sigh, she looked about the church. "Last night, there was thunder without rain. Lightning without thunder. Even the sky was disturbed. I do not know if it was because of you."

"I cannot disturb the skies, Marmi Felicia. I don't think bad dreams do, either."

She shook her head but still would not meet his eyes. "In a village I know, high in the mountains, a child was born who would throw fits and stare at the sun. One day the animals in the village started to sicken. The hens laid green eggs, the cows grew thin and gave no milk, the llamas died for no reason. Until the day the villagers killed the boy. After that, the animals thrived. The boy did not know he was evil, but evil does not always know itself."

Hans blinked. *Evil?* This was getting surreal.

Felicia pushed aside her shawl to pull something from her sash. She pressed a small flat disk into Hans's hand. He looked at it—a piece of carved ivory painted and touched with gold leaf.

"I asked the Virgin to protect you from evil. I found this where I put my candle. She means for you to have it."

A medal of Saint James, a gold-haired man astride a white horse, fiery sword raised high. "To protect me?"

Felicia shrugged to indicate she did not know how the sign should be interpreted. She pushed upon the seat and rose, preparing to go. "Yesterday, *joven*, I saw that a black shadow had fallen across your path. You owe me nothing for the spell that showed you its face."

5

Time is not a linear dimension. It is a mistake to
think of Time as a constant, that a year in one
World is a year in another. We have but to
consider the existence of Gsch, which is forever a
single moment. A moment can be an eternity. A
year can be ten thousand. And ten thousand years
can be a World reborn.
—CIBULITUS, *ANNALS OF THE RETURN,*
DISSERTATION ON IMMORTALITY

"I need to know more about the dream."

Hans stood before the windows of a house in the oldest part of the city, though not the wealthiest. He had found it only after much searching, at the end of an alley lined with shops, boarded-up doors, and iron-barred windows. The rustic wood-panel entry had displayed the number he sought. However, the afternoon-shaded courtyard behind it was completely at odds with the shabby environs of the run-down neighborhood. Paved with tiles and surrounded by walls covered in vines and dainty white flowers, the courtyard suggested an unassuming permanence.

Hans found the sight of Marenthro seated on an antique chair to be both odd and disturbingly familiar. His memories had integrated enough that Marenthro no longer seemed strange, or maybe it was just that so many odd things were happening to Hans, this was simply another occurrence.

The cabinet beside which Hans stood was certainly antique. Its carved dark wood gleamed with an intricate design of flamingoes and llamas and proud men in Inka headdress mounted on horseback. Something about it struck Hans as very *this* world and he appreciated the contrast with the man he faced.

Relief showed plainly on Marenthro's face.

"I'm glad you came to me. I would not have forced your return."

Hans resented the assumption. "I'm not here because I want to return. I'm here to tell you I haven't decided. I can't explain at all why part of me thinks I could do this. I'm not even sure I *should*. I cannot get past the dreams and… other things. Every hair on my body tells me going back might be dangerous."

"It will be."

"You're not exactly helping your cause." Hans paced toward the table. "The only thing I've decided is that I need more information. As things stand, you're the only one I know who might have it."

Though clearly disappointed, Marenthro nodded and settled back in his chair. "You have questions, of course. If I can answer them, I will."

"Mine are simple enough. My family is dead. My grandfather, my brother. Other people too. I remember that. It wasn't just dreams. I remember being at Gustan and people talking and the things they said. Somebody killed a lot of people. Who did it?" Hans would never forget the hideous visions haunting his mind. "Was it Sordan?"

"Whatever gave you that idea?"

"'Sordan stands alone.'" Hans said it dully as he turned away and paced back. "I had… a dream, last night. A new one, about Stefan and how he died. And that's what the voice of whoever killed him said: 'Sordan stands alone.'"

"I see." A kind of grim understanding fell across Marenthro's perfect features.

Hans wished he possessed the same comprehension. He leaned his forehead against the polished edge of the cabinet and closed his eyes. "For years I have woken up from horrible dreams about my grandfather. I mean, I know now that it's my grandfather. And it's always the same. He's dying, burning, and he cries out a name: Dorilian. And in last night's dream, Stefan's dream, I heard that name again, and I saw the same man. That is when he said 'Sordan stands alone.'" Seeing that Marenthro watched him intently, Hans sought to explain. "I've heard that name before, a lot, and now I remember where. I used to hear people talk about Dorilian when I was a boy. Stefan said Dorilian belonged to some kind of demon breed, that he wasn't even human. He said it last night again in the dream. And Dorilian is from Sordan, I remember that too, and that his family is sworn against mine—blood sworn, bitter enemies. My mother and Stefan called him a killer."

"Stefan hated the very sound of Dorilian's name. And your mother should have known better." Marenthro sighed, then looked away. An ineffable sadness lurked in the hardness of his features and the dead tone of his words, as if some hope had already died within him. "Your family's enemies led many astray after Marc Frederick's death. It was easily done. Dorilian is not an easy man to like, and the enmity on both sides is genuine. You will hear much of it should you return. Yet things are not always as they appear on the surface."

"Are you saying Dorilian is a friend?" Everything about that idea went against what Hans knew.

"No. He may well prove the greater enemy. If so, he will be a terrible one. He is not the enemy you seek, however, nor will he be the one that seeks you."

"But he killed Marc Frederick."

"A great many think that. I tell you he did not."

"Then who did? All I ever see is a man wearing a blood-spiked crown. If that's not Dorilian, then who is *he*? And does he want to kill *me* now? Why? I can't make sense of shadows and dreams!"

Marenthro set down his wine glass. Whatever substance filled it looked velvety and rich, red as blood. "Marc Frederick died because he shared in the deaths of hunted princes—and Stefan died because he insisted on slaying the Highborn."

"The Highborn." It was a word that as a child Hans had overheard often but never really understood.

"You call them 'not even human'."

"Then Dorilian—"

"Dorilian is Sordaneon, and the Sordaneons are Highborn, very high and very proud. Their lineage goes back to the days of the first kings and the gods who defeated the Aryati. His bloodline is bound to that of the Rill, one of the Entities upon which the Triempery is founded." Marenthro stood and placed his hand upon the naked table between them. The wood surface shimmered, became smooth and pale and fluid, and then an image appeared there. Hans drew closer and saw that it had become a map with every mountain, every river, in perfect relief. Marenthro indicated the singular land mass of ivory, gold, and green framed within blue. "The Highborn Triempery was a confederation of nations: the Kingdom of Essera, which Marc Frederick came to rule"—he pointed to what was probably the north, then moved his hand to the middle, which was dominated by a large inland sea—"the Hierarchate of Sordan"—then lower still—"and the Nuarchate of Mormantalorus."

"That's practically the whole continent."

Marenthro nodded. "World ruling. It was intended to be. The Second Creation was new and needed builders." He pulled back his hand. "Until eighty years ago, all three parts of the Triempery were Highborn ruled. But the bonds between them had begun to decline. And then Marc Frederick ascended to Essera's throne."

My grandfather. Hans glanced up. "That mattered?"

"Greatly. Mormantalorus refused to align with a ruler who was not Highborn, who moreover was half-Mentan with Kheld blood in his veins. The Sordaneons," Marenthro redirected attention to the belly of the land, "would have joined with Mormantalorus had Marc Frederick not prevented them from it. But the bond of Highborn brotherhood was broken—and people have been trying to rearrange the Triempery's pieces ever since."

"Rearrange them? Into what?"

"Empires take as many shapes as those who would rule them."

Hans touched the map, traced the bright silver line that bisected the continent from north to south. More childhood memories pushed to the fore: of a river thick with barges and ships, and also a city of canals and palaces above which rose a hill crowned by something immense and shining.

The Rill.

The memory startled him because he had never seen anything like it anywhere else, neither before nor since.

"Stefan rode the Rill once," Hans remembered. "He called it unnatural."

"It is as natural as a Creation's eternity sundered into three parts. Or a structure that exists through the whole of Time." Marenthro allowed a hint of a smile. "Leur's Creation includes many wondrous elements. You are heir to all of them."

Which was part of the problem. Hans's inheritance was incomprehensible, but the dangers that awaited him were crystal clear.

"You still haven't told me who killed Marc Frederick. Or who killed Stefan. Don't you think that's something I ought to know going in?"

"Very well. For the good it will do you. It was Nammuor Varehos."

Nammuor. The answer settled between them like a lump of stone: shapeless, dull, and undefined.

"All right, then. Who, or what, is Nammuor?"

"The ruler of Mormantalorus."

Though that explained a little, it wasn't much. Nammuor was a person, then—maybe even the man with the crown—but Mormantalorus was a land so distant that Hans had only heard rumor of it and whispers of rebellion, nothing that he had understood as a child. Now he saw it on the map, a shape of green and blue and red. He still knew nothing about it.

"But Sordan has just as much reason—"

"Maybe more," Marenthro agreed. He sat again in the chair, the grandness of which lent him a professorial solemnity. "As I said before: that enmity runs deep. I did not say enough. It runs far deeper than your brother Stefan's hatred or its repercussions. It goes all the way to the last years of a Wall Lord's rule and the first of Marc Frederick's reign. With your family gone, the Sordaneons hold clear claim to Essera. There are ancient reasons why they should, and ancient promises to bind them to it. If you do not return, Dorilian Sordaneon will have no choice but to pursue that claim."

"And you want me to believe he had nothing to do with my family's murders?"

"The only thing I *want* you to believe is the truth."

Hans brushed his hand on the edge of the table, testing the grain of its dark ancient wood. "I wish I knew what that was."

"I can only tell you what I know. It is for you to believe—if you can."

"I have a hard time believing things just because someone says so." Hans took a seat across from Marenthro, a chair also of dark wood. "Can I see my grandfather's ring again?"

Hesitant but curious, Marenthro brought forth the Leur's Ring and laid it on the wooden table between them. The map vanished as abruptly as it had appeared. Now the table held only the ring, enfolded in gray silk, a threat and a promise of all that existed between the two people—one mortal and one very likely not—who studied each other warily across that tabletop domain. Hans reached out, with a steady hand this time, and unwrapped it, retrieving the ring and holding it carefully between thumb and forefinger just as Marenthro had done. Above that ring, his gaze met that of the wizard.

"Marenthro," Hans spoke slowly. He took care to phrase his next words as a request. "If I ask but one thing of you, one thing and never again—"

"Handurin—"

"Just hear me out. This is my grandfather's ring. Marc Frederick was wearing it when he died, right? He had to have been, because you said it yourself: it never left his hand while he lived. You... can take me back to the day he died."

Marenthro inhaled sharply and turned his face away.

Undeterred, Hans pressed on. "I know you have the power, Marenthro. I overheard Marc Frederick say you have command over Time itself. You brought him from another world, a world like this one! A *past*. So why not use your power to help me understand what happened—what really happened? Send me back to the day Marc Frederick died and make me the ring upon his finger. This ring. It was there. That is all I ask, that you *show* me the truth. I want to see who killed my grandfather and all those others—see it for myself. Show me the face of my enemy. Then I will know."

"Magic does not work the way you are asking—neither does Time."

"Then do it a way that does work."

Marenthro's calm, questing gaze melted first into perplexity, then retreated further yet into a mask of regal detachment. His handsome face became ominously stern, as though he were a schoolmaster staring down a schoolboy who had suggested an obscenity. His copper-bright gaze narrowed.

"Do you realize what you are asking?"

"Nothing that does not lie within your ability." Hans was suddenly sure of it.

Marenthro remained silent and would not answer, though indecision weighed in his unwavering stare. That look etched a path into Hans's very mind. How not, when what was asked was so much? So intense was that gaze, so unrelenting, that Hans fought down a rising fear of this man who but moments before had smiled upon him so warmly. He held up the ring and watched Marenthro's gaze follow it.

"This is the ring you would have me claim as heir to my brother and grandfather, a ring and a throne with a history of bloody death. You want me to go back to a home I barely remember to pick up a birthright I never asked for and face an enemy I don't even know. All I ask, before I make that decision, is a chance to know who that enemy is. To really *know*. Is it Sordan? Mormantalorus? Someone else? Whatever or whoever it is, I need to be sure. Otherwise I will distrust every person I see, question every ally I find to help my cause. You say you cannot give me a future, but you took away my past—and I think I deserve to be given back a piece of it."

"It is not your past you ask for, but another's."

Marenthro rose and walked to the windows overlooking the night. Beyond the glass, a network of lights spread itself, a city clinging precariously to a mountainside. Watching Marenthro in such deep contemplation, Hans grasped the enormity of what he asked—and that it was not impossible. Had it been, Marenthro would have denied him at once. That there could be a choice in such a thing at all put an unbridgeable distance between the wizard and other men.

"Marenthro?" Hans pleaded. "If I return, I will be surrounded by lies. Lies about what happened and who did it. At least arm me with the truth."

It might have been minutes, or hours, but Marenthro withdrew from the windows, pulling the velvet draperies shut to darken them. Then he walked to each fixture, turning out the lights. Briefly light from the courtyard flooded the room, then that was also shut out. Darkness closed over them but Marenthro's presence seemed even more acute. Hans's heart leaped, pounding, into his dry throat. *For you, Grandfather*, he thought. *Because you died... and Stefan too. Because I don't know who killed you, or why. I have just asked Marenthro to prove he's a wizard—and it looks as though he's going to do it!*

Hans jumped when Marenthro's hand closed warm and solid over his own and the ring he still clutched in his fist.

"Give me the Leur's Ring, Handurin."

Hans complied, glad to be rid of it.

In the soft glow of the ring itself, Hans watched Marenthro slip it over his left forefinger. Light bathed the wizard's hand as the Leur's Ring took on its characteristic opalescence and Hans saw again that silver gleam, starlike within an ever-changing firmament, glittering deep within the stone. Marenthro extended that hand to Hans.

"Give me your hand."

Acutely aware of how tight his breaths had become, Hans laid his left hand over Marenthro's. The ring's light did not die but glowed living red through his skin, lighting only their two figures in the darkness. All else was pitch black and nothingness save themselves and the ruddy light between them. Hans thought he detected the shimmer of hidden things: Marenthro's life, a discernable thread of Creation, of Here, of Now and Then and the weighty barriers that divided three Worlds out of One. He let that energy flow into him, through him, fill him somehow. Their joined hands lowered to rest upon the table. Looking up, Marenthro's copper-colored eyes met his, red reflections lending an otherworldly heat to the gaze that pierced to his very core.

"Handurin Marc Frederick Stauberg-Randolph, Prince of Dazunor, heir to a line unbroken since the Beginning, you are about to witness Leur art, the delving of Time. This is no game or pleasure ride. A change of this nature is difficult to work and rarely invoked. Never have I done so with an unschooled mind. As you have requested, you shall be sent to view firsthand the events of your grandfather's demise in the Citadel of Permephedon ten years ago. Since you were not present at that event, and the fabric of Time will not permit your bodily attendance, you will witness the Demise through the eyes of another. Do you understand?"

"Yes," Hans whispered.

"You are about to acquire intimate knowledge which you could not possibly have witnessed on your own. To reveal this knowledge could be perilous, to you and others. You must keep secret what you have done. Will you do this?"

"Yes."

"Will you trust me completely?"

"Yes."

"I will be with you, though you shall not sense it. If you wish to return, I shall know."

Marenthro lifted his right hand and traced a sign in the air between them. It remained there, fixed, transparent, dark against the dark. "*Kronos*," he muttered. "*Aeios Ergeiron.*" He grasped Hans's right hand and placed it so that the Leur's Ring was clasped between them. "*Ys alnyr'rynysyr*," he intoned in a language musical and unknown. "*Permephedon beorynos.*"

Hans exhaled. His sight blurred and the room spun. He felt, unerringly, when his mind separated from his body, a thousand filaments pulling away. Even before he could think to fight it, it was over and all he could do was remember to trust.

The wildly swirling colors of the Leur's Ring spun a web around his disembodied identity, tightening, enclosing some essential part of him for a moment before he was torn, ripped, away from all light and flung into a vast darkness. For a moment, there was nothing. No sound, light, smell or taste or touch—not even the movement and weight of his body—nothing to connect him to the world in any way. But then light burst upon him and it was too bright, too brilliant, more painful than the dark. As the light acquired shadows, it coalesced into reality, expanded into a Time, shifted into a place... a person.

He was within another mind, another body.

6

I don't know what to tell you about the Highborn.
Don't really know the kind. But among
Staubauns, it is said that the Highborn can open
the gates of men's souls and command mountains
to bleed stone.
—Tobold Forbasson,
North Country Narrative

A vault of ceiling cradled the blue cup of the sky. That sky, so blue against the brilliant white of the ornate architecture surrounding it... it was beautiful, but Hans had hoped to see more. Where was he? Permephedon? What he was seeing could be anywhere. The voices surrounding him spoke clear and fluent Stauba, the language of the proud race he knew to rule the Triempery. It was the language of his dreams. Hans understood every word, which was good because he *heard* every word—everything, every cough and footstep and scrape of a chair—without discrimination.

The person whose senses he inhabited might be able to block out the confusion; Hans could not. Like now, forced to stare lazily at the sky while voices swirled around him, without any ability to redirect. Perhaps it was a good thing Hans couldn't detect other senses like smell, taste, and touch.

A voice intruded to his right, louder than the rest.

"Look at them. Barbarians! Self-satisfied and smug, all of them. They think they have our Rill upon their platter. Do they realize, I wonder, that you are simply playing a game?"

Hans heard a sigh. He knew it had come from the body he inhabited when his vantage changed. He was seated at a table with two other people, his viewpoint focused on an older man with gilt-bright hair and gold-brown eyes that regarded him with barely veiled distaste. Hans's host spoke then, a male, controlled voice much different from his own.

"When the treaty is before you, sign it—or, by the Leur, you will have no throne come nightfall."

His gaze shifted along the length of the table to land upon a group of three men. Finally, Hans looked upon people he knew. Two men he had seen often, whose names he remembered—Redd and Reggie—and...

Grandfather! Marc Frederick—alive and wearing Esseran blue and gold, the glittering state crown of his kingship seated on silvering dark hair—looked relaxed and happy. And very much a King. Marc Frederick lifted his eyes for a moment so that Hans felt as though their gazes met—but no, it was Hans's host for whom the royal smile deepened.

Did his host smile back? Hans couldn't tell.

His vision shifted again, this time to where several dark-haired, bearded men, their clothing less fine than that worn by the bright-haired majority, laughed uproariously at some private matter. It made a discordant note in so decorous a chamber. Only when they saw that he watched them did their laughter cease, as abruptly as though he had thrown water on their small flicker of a fire. Their blue stares turned steely and cold. Hans found it alarming. Khelds had never looked at him with hostility. Not once in his whole life.

The man seated at his side—Hans thought of him as Gilt Hair—refused to stop grumbling. "You would do it too. Rob me of legacy and birthright, and for what? That *he* might fawn and smile upon you? I should have smothered you at birth."

"Sign it."

The treaty—surely the piece of paper being passed around—currently lay under the pen of a handsome older man wearing an impressive circlet. Marc Frederick rose to speak. On his left hand glowed the white ring Hans had just minutes ago seen Marenthro wearing. A pair of men had brought out a huge golden bowl and set it on the table in front of the King.

My grandfather looks happy. He is proud of this day—this treaty.

When he had fallen sick as a boy, in all that upheaval, Hans had overheard people say Marc Frederick had died on the brink of accomplishing something great. Hans also remembered that Stefan had been angry about being told to stay home.

"You will notice the wine being poured into the bowl," Marc Frederick said. "I wish this to be a celebration, a marriage, as all true covenants should be." Again the King looked in the direction of Hans's host.

Whoever this body belonged to was someone important.

Movement. Hans recognized the motion of standing, then of walking to the ceremonial bowl, from which he drew three cups. These he carried back to his table and handed to its occupants. The man to his left, who gave him a meager smile, looked incredibly old and slightly dotty. Gilt Hair, however, on the right, wrinkled his nose at the wine and continued his litany of complaints.

"You won't drink wine with me, but you'll drink with him!" Gilt Hair reached a jeweled hand to a nearby silver platter, plucking a grape which he then placed between thin lips. Making a show, he sucked out the pulp and juice, then flicked the empty skin into, not his own goblet, but the goblet in front of Hans. *What the—!?*

Hans knew his host had seen the disgusting act because he heard a barely restrained hiss of anger.

"Let us drink to a Triempery renewed and reborn!" Marc Frederick raised his cup. From every table, the guests did the same.

Hans watched his host's sun-browned hand—youthful, it looked—grasp the goblet and raise the gold-rimmed thing high with the others. But though the rest of the gathering downed their drinks with victorious flourish, Hans's host did not. Instead, he stared into the cup at the grape skin bobbing like a pustule on the surface. Without comment, he lowered the goblet. The metal base settled with a bright note upon the table of blue glass as he set it aside.

Gilt Hair sniggered. "How unfair. 'Tis your favorite vintage." That man took a second, even deeper drink. On his left hand flashed a large ring with an emerald stone bracketed by green gems and silver talons.

With an inhalation clearly that of someone striving for patience, Hans's aggrieved host looked away again to where Marc Frederick, the sculpted stylus filling his hand, affixed his signature and seal to the document in front of him. That document was then carried to the glowering Gilt Hair, who snatched up the signed paper. The room itself fell silent. Then, with a growl and a venomous glance at Hans's host, the man took up the stylus.

"So be it!" he spat.

Somewhere to the left, someone moved or twitched. One of the Khelds clutched at his chest and slumped forward. The man's wine cup tumbled, red liquid splashing onto his neighbor's papers. Then Gilt Hair, stylus in hand, fell forward also, onto the table, where he lay with eyes open and staring. But not moving.

"Father?" Hans's host touched the main's throat with sun-browned fingers. "Father!"

Gilt Hair was his host's *father*?

Hans struggled to feel something, anything other than horror at what he knew was beginning. On every side now, other men, Kheld and Staubaun alike, fell to table or floor, gasping and gagging, eyes open. Marc Frederick also swayed, groping at a chair as his advisers fell around him. *Do something!* Hans urged, but already his host was on his feet, running toward the King.

"Guard!" Arms that seemed to be Hans's own caught Marc Frederick, holding him upright. *I didn't ask for enough*, Hans thought. *I can't feel him. Hold him.* A glance toward the chamber's great doors. Toward safety. Pounding and shouts from the other side filled his hearing.

Get out! Hans wanted to scream. He knew what was to happen. Had seen it in visions and dreams. But he was trapped behind another man's mind, removed from acting by an irrevocable assignment of matter. Helpless, merely a passenger, he could only watch.

"You are not harmed?" Marc Frederick gasped.

"No, thank Leur! Come with me—"

They moved toward the doors but didn't make it. Just as in his nightmares—which he was seeing play out right before him through another man's eyes—Hans saw six men materialize in front of the closed doors. Tall, wearing black cloaks lined with dark-red satin over crimson robes cinched at the waist with belts of gold and buckles like open-mouthed serpents. Two of the men bore swords. From within the black hoods of their cloaks, dark eyes glittered beneath bright hair bound by circlets of glowing crystals. One man, white-haired, wore a crown of glittering blood-red spikes.

I know that face! Felicia's magic had shown it to Hans.

"Go." Marc Frederick's blue eyes seemed to lock onto Han's… only it wasn't Hans he urged. "Now!"

There was no time for escape. The two men with swords caught Hans—no, Hans's host—by the arms, wrestled him away. Marc Frederick fell to the floor.

No. Hans couldn't watch now. He knew too much of what would come. But neither could he turn away. Damn! *I asked for this… I wanted to see….*

"Nammuor!" The angry voice vibrated through air and bone— and through Hans's own chest. "You are thrice-damned to any hell I can reach!"

Nammuor. The face of Hans's nightmares bore the name Marenthro had given.

"Do you like my work?" The voice sickened Hans. He *knew* it. Silken. Deadly. "It's but the first stroke of a masterpiece. Nay, the second, as it appears my dear sister did her part well."

"Rhypos take you! May you drown in Mulsor's hell! And that whore with you!"

Nammuor's black gaze hardened beneath its crown of red spikes. "Silence him!"

The floor rose in Hans's host's sight, followed by walls, then a fist. Hard breathing and scuffling ensued. Hans could only guess his host was fighting back. But it was futile. Soon his head was wrenched back and he stared into the smirking face of a man with a scar marring his lower lip. Hans glimpsed a leather strap and by the sounds that followed he knew his host was being gagged.

Too many voices. An avalanche of sound. Too much noise— scrapes and clatters. Crashing. Laughter. Nammuor's hideous voice. The others. The room. His sight blurred, bending and blinking. Maybe his host could sort out the chaos, but Hans could not. Not through this. Not until Nammuor's words took shape again, and Hans found focus: Marc Frederick, seated on a chair.

"…you… surprise me. How are you still standing?"

"What foul—"

"The Leur's Ring, perhaps? Its powers are rumored to be life-binding. Killing you, then, will be a pleasant bonus." Nammuor turned to face the rest of the room. "But that must wait. Just watch this."

Pulling a blade from within his robe, Nammuor strode to the man wearing an impressive circlet, the one Hans had watched sign the document earlier, and plunged the knife into the man's exposed throat. Blood erupted in a great gout across the table, then spilled in a stream onto the floor.

Nammuor studied the spreading pool of red. "Such a waste, isn't it? Immortal blood. Fortunately, I don't need much."

Again, the nightmare living. Nammuor pulled from his clothing a shard of black crystal and touched it to the spilled blood. Almost instantly it filled and glowed red, and Hans saw the bleeding man's eyes glaze, the life light in them quenched. The world went dark and he heard more struggle. *Stop it! Stop fighting!* Hans futilely berated his host. *I need to see!*

Vision returned in time to see Nammuor approach another victim. *Redd*, Hans remembered. *Grandfather's friend*. The man had carried toddler Hans on his shoulders. Nammuor sliced Redd's throat so brutally, the head flopped back and hung like a sack.

"No!" Marc Frederick cried and Hans heard agony in that protest. A second black crystal drank blood. Glowed red. Nammuor yanked something from around the man's neck. The head, severed, fell to the floor.

By the way his vision shifted and from the ragged exhalations he heard, Hans knew his host was feeling… something. Pain. Terror. Perhaps both.

Nammuor turned to his mages. "I want them all."

They circled the room, Nammuor and his mages singling out the Highborn princes, slicing flesh and collecting blood. Filling crystals. His host did not watch every killing. His gaze often darkened, filled with tears. Gulps. Muffled curses. Just as in the dream, the floor flowed crimson.

Nammuor came to where Gilt Hair lay sprawled upon the table, hand still upon the document he had been signing. "Alas, Deben. There's a fitting end. As usual, you have left the thing unfinished."

Hans's vision went dark. Why? The name? Hans didn't recognize it. He knew only that he was seeing nothing now.

What are you doing? I need you to look! And then something hit hard, something Hans had heard his host say: *Oh fuck, no—it's his father!*

"You should watch." By the way Nammuor said it, Hans knew

the words were meant for the man he inhabited. "You'll want to see this."

Vision returned again. Nammuor twisted the massive emerald ring from his victim's finger. The treaty lay abandoned and blood-soaked under the man's naked hand. Nammuor held up the ring like a trophy. "My Heir will need this."

The ring joined the crystals in the pouch. Nammuor then walked closer, boots treading blood. "So what is *your* story, Brother? How are you still here? The Rill, perhaps? Is it trying to *save* you? Or did you simply fail to drink your own sweet wine?"

Closer, and closer still, gaze locked on gaze, Nammuor approached. "My opinion of you differs from my sister's. She's blind to your appeal, but I'm not." One blood-stained thumb traced his host's face, the cheekbone under the eye, and Hans was thankful he could not feel the touch. "You have some value. The Seven Houses would pay a lot, so very much, to get their hands on *you*." Avarice stole over that elegant face, corrupting the beautiful Staubaun features to a leer. "And then there is another reason."

Again blackness. Had someone struck him? Stabbed him? Hans heard gasps for breath and Marc Frederick crying out.

"Damn you! Don't hurt him!"

When Hans's host's eyes opened again, the world swam with tears.

Nammuor's horrible voice spoke. "But I am going to hurt him, my usurping martyr. I am going to hurt him in ways no other man has ever dreamed. You see, I know how you are able to wear the Leur's Ring."

"No! What was done to me cannot be done again! That was Endurin's work!"

Nammuor signaled. "Do it."

Disruption. Movement. Following Nammuor's cue, Scar Lip and another man forced Hans's host over to a table. Roughly, they slammed his hand hard against the edge, fingers splayed.

Scar Lip drew his sword, raised it. The blow descended. Metal cleaved flesh. Darkness. Hans heard his host's raw scream, muffled by the leather strap. Then he saw the hand: the left forefinger and most of the second finger had been chopped off, not neatly at the knuckle, but deep past the joint into the hand. Gasping loudly, through eyes blinking with pain, his host watched Nammuor pick up the severed fingers and, taking only the forefinger, discard the other.

"This should live for a good long while." The black eyes seemed more reptilian than human, gauging prey. "Seeing as you did not die, I'm going to take your body apart, again and again, until I get it right."

Nammuor turned to Marc Frederick. "Now for you."

Marty. The name Hans had used as a child a world ago came to him now. *Marty, no....* Hans had asked Marenthro for this, demanded it, yes, but... he'd seen enough, hadn't he? Did he need to see more? Did he really want this much truth written into his mind through another man's pain?

Marc Frederick looked grim, more determined than frightened. Hans saw why when Marc Frederick lunged from the chair, a greenish blade in his hand. But the King crumpled and the blow went wide. Nammuor raised his hand and unleashed a bolt of blue fire. Trapped behind a captive's eyes, Hans screamed as he had in his dreams, silently, without even a throat to express his horror. His host's vision went dark again and Marc Frederick cried out in anguish.

No... no.... Hans needed to see!

The darkness lasted but a moment. Vision returned but Hans couldn't tell what was happening. A grunt... a black-robed thug slumped to the floor. A loosened sword clanged and then the floor rose like a wave, bringing the sword with it. Yet another sweep of confusion as the weapon flashed briefly, contested. It emerged, gripped in a young, now-familiar hand. His host's right hand—unmaimed, strong. Free. In almost the same movement, Hans saw that sword plunge through one captor's ribcage, jerk back, and then slash across Scar Lip's red-robed abdomen. Both men crumpled to the floor.

It left only Nammuor within reach.

A leap, and this time the blade knocked the bloody dagger from Nammuor's grasp, nearly taking his hand with it. The dagger clattered across the floor and into a wall. The blade flashed again. Nammuor dodged, but the blade glanced across his face, biting deep to lay open the left cheek down to bone. As Nammuor stumbled back, blood flowing between the fingers held to his face, a third blow hit a metal ring on his belt.

The pouch fell to the floor.

Again the room spun. Hans rode along as his host's body rolled to the floor and then to his side, half sitting near a table. Hans realized why when he saw the pouch now clutched to his chest with a maimed, bloodied hand, the blood-covered sword in his other. Heavy breathing filled Hans's hearing. Panting. Wet. His host's gag was still in place.

Nammuor hissed a word. Hans's host's right hand fell open and the sword clattered to the floor.

Then Hans heard something more. Marc Frederick's voice, soft, confident… and singing a language Hans did not know.

"Nas ancyarie!"

Hans stared as Marc Frederick's left hand, held out toward Nammuor, blazed whiter than the Leur's Ring.

An eruption of colors burst through the room. A scramble backward, away from Nammuor, toward Marc Frederick. Red energy met white. Power crackled from ceiling to floor and both shattered. A scarlet-robed man running toward them burst into flame.

The floor shifted violently. A tumble, with glimpses of furniture and corpses swirling to every side… and then he saw only ceiling. His vision leaped around until he spied Marc Frederick. The King had pulled himself upright and stood near the window, clutching a handful of drapery.

Between them yawned a gulf of broken floor and ruin. A wall of white energy shimmered across the remainder of the great chamber. The gag was ripped away, then tossed aside.

Hans stared down at a hand with missing fingers, covered with blood, then the stare moved to Marc Frederick.

Go to him! Hans willed. But just as it appeared his host was moving in that direction, he was thrown to his knees again. The floor heaved and several bodies slid, then tumbled over the edge, becoming tiny as they fell to the ground so far below. What had been a crack was now a chasm. Another bolt of energy struck the white shield emanating outward from Marc Frederick's hand.

"He's got my crystals!" Nammuor shouted. "Get them!"

Nammuor's two remaining mages strode toward the barrier but could do nothing while the energy held.

Go to the King! Hans begged again.

Why was his host scanning the floor? Hans knew why when he

saw the pouch. With his unmaimed hand, his host grabbed up the sack and emptied its contents onto the floor. Seven long crystals, blood red, pulsing with either evil or power. His gaze shot to Nammuor. Hatred and greed glared back—but the once-red spikes of Nammuor's crown had dimmed. All but two were dark and lifeless. More floor. More looking and groping, seeking something... ah! The milky green blade Marc Frederick had sought to use against Nammuor, fallen to the floor nearby.

Hans watched his host's right hand close over the hilt, raise the blade, then quickly stab point-first at the nearest red crystal.

The thing exploded with a spray of splinters and blood.

What is he doing? Unmaking them?

"No!" Nammuor's shriek pierced the roar of wind through the gaping wounds in the tower.

The blade destroyed a second crystal, then a third. Nammuor hurled another bolt of red against Marc Frederick's shield.

"You are their murderer!" Nammuor screamed.

Another glance at Marc Frederick. Though wounded, the King nodded. Hans wondered what it was Marc Frederick approved, what he was urging this man to do.

It did not matter. Sobbing, vision blurred by tears, one by one Hans witnessed his host shatter every crystal. Nammuor kept screaming. After, there were only two items remaining, placed with swift care into the pouch: the glowing green ring and the white stone on a chain.

More booms sounded at the door. But Hans knew there would be no rescue.

"Leave!" Nammuor shouted to his mages. "Take what you have! I'll finish here."

Another impact shook the door. The mages had gone. Only Nammuor remained against a fading power. With a mighty crack, the floor in front of Hans dropped and tilted, furniture sliding. More bodies fell. The slab where he sat was still sound. Though he crawled toward Marc Frederick again, he could go no farther than the broken edge.

Almighty Sun! There's no way! We're too high! Hans had stood within the belly of an airship and been closer to the ground. And Marc Frederick's piece of the building... was floating, not attached to the main structure at all.

"Sire!" Hans's host shouted. "You must get to this side!" His strong and unhurt right hand extended over the chasm.

Marc Frederick shook his head. "No. I can still hold him a little longer. Run! Nothing you do here will save anything! Not me, not Sordan, not the Rill, and not the Creation."

"Grab my hand!"

"When the Ring's power is spent, I am dead anyway. I drank the poison. I have only this to give you. Promise me—"

"Anything!" It was as if Hans's own arm stretched until bones cracked. "Just take… my… hand!"

Marc Frederick's fierce gaze locked hard onto his. "Look after my family."

"I will, I promise—my most solemn vow. Just take it." The tears were blinding.

"You are the only thing here worth saving. Finish what we tried to do here this day."

"I promise! Now try—" A section of the outer wall cracked and fell away. "I can't reach you!"

Take his hand! Hans begged Marc Frederick, though he could see for himself how dangerous that would be to both. *Take it, please take it.* The shimmer holding Nammuor was fading along with the force of the Leur's Ring.

"Leave me! Run!"

"I can't!"

Red energy exploded.

"Run, damn you!"

No! Don't leave him! But for Hans the world dissolved. Darkness enveloped him, even as Marc Frederick screamed a name. *That* name.

Magic closed again around Hans, a maelstrom of colors, then the lightless, timeless place where he had no mortal being. He sought relief from the darkness engulfing him, deeper and darker than death.

7

Amynas achieved fame first among his own people
for his exploits in defeating and acquiring the
technology of Vllyr, the god Amynas and Leur
slew. The Aryati stripped the slain god of its
things of power and brought these to their home
world. That was their great undoing.
—Cibulitus, *Annals of the Return*

Dorilian enjoyed early morning views of the Dekkora. Open and filled with light, Sordan's central plaza with its star-shaped footprint and smooth white paving looked like a proper place of reverence. Sunlight kissed the floating orbs of the Three Sisters as they hung above the three broad landings leading to the Rill station and set aglow the blue-green roof tiles of the Temple of the Inception.

The City of Amynas, whose statue commanded the Dekkora below. Peaceful. Secure. About to be invaded by believers.

Pilgrims would soon descend upon the City for the annual celebration of the Illumination, or Coming. The next few weeks would see the Dekkora's approaches and walkways become swamped with vendor stalls and makeshift living spaces. Dorilian trusted that the City Guard would keep the plaza itself clear.

"I tell you the danger is too great. Someone else can deliver the Proclamation."

Vexed by the interruption, Dorilian looked to the speaker. Scarred and war-hardened, Tutto Rhunnard saw peril in any act a Sordaneon undertook. The two swords of that morning's weapons practice hung from his sturdy belt. Dorilian had wanted to hold practice here and Tutto had accommodated his request. Sparring at dawn fit well into a day constrained by demands. It also meant that, like now, he could cool down his tested muscles while enjoying views of his City. Dorilian didn't think Nammuor would pop up in Sordan to attack him with a sword—but other people might. Despite Dorilian's busy schedule, it was important to maintain his weapons training.

"I will not abandon this tradition," Dorilian said in response to Tutto's warning. "The entire point of the Proclamation is that the people of Sordan see their Hierarch and hear him proclaim."

"You do not have to appear in person," said Legon Rebiran from his stance at Tutto's side. Legon was the Commander of the Sorda-neon Eagle Guard, charged solely with the protection of the Hierarch and his family. The eagle emblems clasping Legon's cloak to his shoulders matched those embellishing the helm he carried tucked against his side.

"People who make this pilgrimage want to witness a god, not a surrogate. Do I need to remind you how important it is for them to see *me* crowned by *that*." Dorilian turned his back to the City view and pointed to the soaring structures behind Tutto and Legon, both of whom turned their gazes to follow the gesture. Sordan's splendor— its Leur Citadel and Serat and Temple—and the rings and arches of the Rill itself, pierced the pink-blue shell of dawn. Dorilian knew a statement piece when he saw one and the Proclamation welcoming pilgrims to Sordan had been a statement of grand proportions for two thousand years. "Displays of power and stability matter. I have delivered the Proclamation every year of my reign as Hierarch. I will not take the path of my father and appoint a surrogate."

Tutto rubbed a hand over his thinning, close-cut hair. "I expected this stubbornness. Let me remind *you* that our ears in Essera have detected chirps of a possible plot against you originating—"

"And you told me," Dorilian interrupted, "you had nothing concrete."

Plots against Dorilian's life were common events, nigh monthly. Reason enough for these men to be concerned. It would serve no purpose to belittle their efforts. They were his friends as well as his protectors and he valued their bonds to him.

"You know me too well," Dorilian continued, "to think I will act upon rumors. And you know too why I must not. My enemies use such devices to maneuver me, and you, and others into creating situations that could advantage them. It advantages them if I am fearful, and silent, and bound by lies."

Legon scoffed. "No lie can bind you."

"No, they use lies to make me bind myself. And with this one they would make me invisible."

The Eagle Guards stationed at the entry to the terrace let out a "Hai!" to alert the Hierarch and his companions that they were being joined by one of the few people Dorilian had instructed them to let pass. The tall figure of Tiflan Morevyen, Bas of Teremar and Dorilian's cousin, ambled past the border of clipped cypress and flame flowered shrubs. Tiflan's long tunic, woven of cerise wool and belted with costly stamped leather, flaunted gold-stitched hems and other noble adornments. Dorilian knew Tiflan had just come from Permephedon, where he had gone to cast Teremar's vote for an inconveniently early Archhalia session.

Dorilian gestured for the news. Tiflan grinned.

"Your veto of the proposal to transfer the Aesa Eranos into Essera's Crown estates was successful. Sinon's argument about the palace's provenance and record of habitation placed your interest in it remaining a Highborn property above dispute."

"The Aidion beneath the Aesa Eranos provides access to the Wall," Dorilian pointed out. Though he had never personally visited the Wall Entity by way of that access, he knew it existed. And he would be damned before he would let a traitorous worm like Erenor Tholeros lay claim to the Malyrdeon palace. It was a sore point already that Erenor squatted there illegally.

Tiflan paused before proceeding to another matter. "A point was raised needing clarification. Sinon will be contacting you about it." To Dorilian's look of interest, he spelled it out. "Handurin Stauberg-Randolph will soon return. It's likely he will make Stauberg his capitol and take up residence in the Aesa Eranos. The Archhalia is concerned about... what stance you might take."

And so, as predictably as the sun rose every morning, the Sordaneon family history with the Stauberg-Randolphs had reared its ugly head.

Marc Frederick had lived in and ruled from the Aesa Eranos. Dorilian had accepted the legitimacy of that occupation.

Stefan too had made the Aesa Eranos the seat of his capitol and even dwelled there for short periods. Though Dorilian had despised the Kheld King, he had not challenged Stefan's right to inhabit the palace from which his family had ruled.

How like the Archhalia to have not noticed the pattern.

Not that it mattered.

"They concern themselves needlessly," Dorilian said. "If either the boy or his protectors have a thumbnail's worth of sense, Handurin will not return to Stauberg."

"He might use the Stauberg Rift," Legon suggested. "People have done that before. He could return by ship."

"Why not to Permephedon?" Tutto offered. "If the wizard is involved—"

"Witness Princess Emyli's fate," Tiflan explained solemnly. "She's all but a prisoner there. The prince would be trapped into the Prince Regent's custody and then the Archhalia would almost certainly hand him over."

"Which is why a ship makes sense," Legon seized again upon that means. "He need not go to Stauberg. If he follows Stefan's habit, he would seek out the Khelds. Amallar can be reached by the sea, though the cliffs are forbidding."

"Perfect," Dorilian said, and took his first steps toward the pavilion where he knew a table would be set. Weapons training had left him hungry. "Then Handurin can be trapped in Amallar instead."

Hans awoke between clean linen sheets, covered by a blanket of thick vicuña wool. It was night and low light from a jaguar-faced lamp pot pooled on the table beside him. A strange lethargy pulled at him, but he fought it and pushed one foot out from under the blanket. A leg followed, then the rest of him. Except for not wearing shoes, he was still fully clothed. The narrow bed in which he had slept—with its four posts of dark carved wood, velvet draperies, and stark white linens—was unfamiliar and Hans wondered if, during the dream that had not been a dream at all, he had somehow left one world for the other. But when he brushed aside the lace that covered the window, streetlights told him he was still in Chuquiago. Night had begun to pale behind the triple peak of snow-crowned Illimani.

Hans padded from the room into the empty hallway, wood floors gleaming with lamp light. A stronger glow drew him to the dining room where dark furnishings vied with silver plates and goblets and a candelabra bearing stately pillars of flame. As he had suspected he would, he found Marenthro there, reading a book at the head of the table.

"Marenthro?"

Hans pulled out a chair and sat. Marenthro closed the book and pushed it to one side. The leatherbound tome was ancient, a copy of the chronicles of Fernando Tupac Inka. Hans was still mulling why a wizard might want to read about an archived world's half-Spanish Inka reformer-king when Marenthro set a cup before him. It rattled reassuringly.

Hans sipped the tea. It had been prepared to his taste, light and sweet. "How long have I been out?" He reached for a roll of bread from the plate on the table.

"Almost six hours. It's nearly morning."

"I saw." After devouring one roll, he decided he needed another. The bread's honeyed taste at least fueled his wakefulness. "What I experienced tonight—was it for real?"

"Do you think I would concoct that sort of slaughter for sport?"

Hans considered himself properly chastised and set down his cup. "I'm sorry. It was horrible. I had no idea. My dreams... my dreams left out the worst parts." He looked up again, to see if what he had guessed was true. "They were killed by sorcery, a sorcerer of some kind. Even though I saw, it's still hard to believe that sort of ability is real."

Marenthro pondered Hans solemnly before answering. "The Second Creation works within laws most humans can neither grasp nor manipulate. Some few can. Of those few, most, like that man, use devices."

"So now I know who he is and what he did—but not *why* he did it."

"Nammuor had many reasons. Doing so removed the Triempery's leadership, of course, and threw its remaining realms into chaos, making a strong foe into a weaker one. He also wanted to complete his device. The Diadem of the Devaryati covets things of power, even living things."

"The Diadem? That ruby crown I saw?"

Marenthro frowned. "One of the artifacts of the Aryati Hegemons. Indeed, it was the ruler's crown." He spoke slowly, as though explaining was difficult and he wanted to be sure to do so correctly. "The Diadem is a symbiotic device. It has a sort of life and even intelligence, though not a proper mind. It has another name, an older name: the Undying Crown. It belonged to—or rather it was created from—a being, a very powerful being whom the Aryati slew so they might obtain its power. They did not know the device they salvaged retained a piece of the god, or that it would engineer their world's destruction."

"The Devastation," Hans said.

"Yes. The Undying Crown played a part in that. It was thought lost, destroyed during the Return, frozen on the moon or drowned beneath the sea, but Nammuor found it in the ruins of the World, and it is again aware of its purpose." With a sigh, Marenthro continued. "There are other crowns, lesser ones, but few mortals are suited to wield such devices. At best, using one drains them terribly, so much so that they cannot sustain the effort for more than a few minutes. The strain on mortal minds is such that they risk insanity to try. But Nammuor, who you saw, is very close to pure Aryati—and he has learned to use the Diadem."

"Is he insane?"

"At this point, he very likely is."

"Did Grandfather ever have a chance?"

Marenthro's regard was uncompromising. "No. But he did make a difference. He forced Nammuor to pit the Diadem against the Leur's Ring, something Nammuor never expected. Nammuor's power—and that of the Diadem—was broken for a time. Marc Frederick died and Nammuor fled, albeit wounded, taking the Diadem with him."

"But why—how come you let it happen? You dwell in Permephedon. Mother told me once that you know everything that happens there. Why didn't you protect them?"

"Protect them from what? The Time paths that brought them there? Paths they themselves created? The consequences of their choices?" Though his face betrayed no sign of age, Marenthro spoke as though he looked back upon uncounted centuries of watching mortals live and die, all beyond his ability to aid them.

"Handurin, some things *cannot* be prevented, and there are others that *must* not be. I cannot decide people's fates for them. Neither can the Creation. It must obey its own Laws. When a stone is thrown, what can be done to keep it from striking down those things in its path?"

"You could catch it."

Marenthro acknowledged that answer. "It was I who threw the stone. I could not intercede in their battle without creating ripples in Time that would have led to greater harm."

"The Wall told you not to." The Wall Entity was mysterious but had something to do with Time.

"No. The Wall tells no one what to do."

So it… what? It allowed people to look, but not touch? Not knowing what to believe or feel, about that or anything, Hans ran his hand over his face. He was still bone-tired, and rubbing his eyes helped to banish the blur. "Well, at least now I know who really killed my grandfather. And Stefan too. Is it the Diadem that makes Nammuor so vicious, or was he just born that way?"

"People bring their own malice with them. The Diadem is infected by Vllyr, the god from whom it was created. Because Vllyr was not completely unmade, the god's residual malices persist in the Diadem. And Nammuor is a cruel and calculating man even without it."

Hans shuddered. "I felt so helpless. It was the way he touched me, made me look into his eyes. Like he wanted something. But what? Only my fing—fingers?" Hans broke off, startled, and sank back into his chair, staring at his left hand. It was whole, his own again. He curled his fingers into a fist. "Not me," he whispered. "It wasn't me. He didn't know I was there."

"Nammuor did not know," Marenthro affirmed. "Neither did Marc Frederick, nor even the man whose senses you inhabited."

Hans swallowed. "Who was he?"

"Your grandfather cried out his name, at the last."

"Dorilian." The revelation crashed against everything Hans had ever heard. Dorilian to him had always been the monster, the man his mother and Stefan had denounced.

Marenthro bowed his neck and sighed. "You witnessed the events of that hour as he saw and heard them. But do not think your experiences to be the same. Dorilian experienced that day in ways you did not, and these events through the lens of a life you never lived. The things he knew, you did not know. The things he felt, you did not feel. His thoughts were not your thoughts and may never be known to you—if the Universe is kind."

Hans's experience had been terrible but how much worse must it have been to live through it? Dorilian had lost his fingers, his father. "He was either very brave or very foolish, attacking Nammuor the way he did!"

"He was a little of both, and desperate as well. But that is Dorilian's nature, to attack problems head-on."

Hans caught the conflicting emotions that briefly crossed Marenthro's face, mingled approval and uncertainty, a vague unease, as though Dorilian were himself a thing not wholly known and therefore to be feared. But of one thing Hans was sure and would always be sure: Marc Frederick had trusted and perhaps even loved the young man whose safety had been his last thought in the world. And Dorilian had tried to save Marc Frederick with all that was in him.

"He ran, then."

"At the very last when all hope of help was past, yes, Dorilian ran. Had he not done so, he too would have died."

"Did anyone else survive it?"

"No. He was the only one. Many people still believe it was he who killed them—*because* he survived. I daresay at first, he would rather have died with them. But he continued his life. He is Hierarch now in Sordan."

A few things, at least, now began to make sense. All his childhood life, Hans had heard that Sordan was an enemy. It must have seemed natural for Stefan and others to continue to paint things that way.

"I might meet up with him, then, one day." What might that be like?

The candles had burned lower while they spoke and now were pillars of glowing wax. After a minute, Marenthro said one thing more. "The Triemperal Archhalia and Prince Regent Erenor have ordered your mother to return you to Essera, or face arrest on charges of high treason."

"High *treason*? They're going after my mother?" Emyli. Hans had been recalling more about her and how she had always protected him fiercely. He had been a runt of a child among his roughhouse cousins.

"For now, she has sought sanctuary at Permephedon and I have granted it to her, so do not fear for her safety. However, the Archhalia can be expected to force the issue. Nammuor cannot like having an heir out there to be sprung on him in the future. Furthermore, Essera's domains are in disarray—they need a ruler."

"*Ruler?* Wait just a minute." Hans couldn't believe they were back on this king notion. "You said I have a regent, right? Even if Essera wants a change from him, I'm sure there are better people they could turn to."

"They don't have that option. You and Dorilian are the only legitimate heirs under their law. Anyone else would have to take the throne by conquest."

That hardly sounded like a bloodless solution.

"I'm not a monarchist, though. I mean, I think the Sapa Inka and his family are fun to read about, and the whole Euro thing, but... I think people should have rulers they pick for themselves."

Marenthro grinned. "That's exactly what happened. The Archhalia met. Essera's ruling body picked *you*."

Had they? Hans doubted that process had involved elections or any other way of regular people having a say. No. He'd been selected by those already in power, probably as a way of keeping theirs. Hans tried to imagine ruling his grandfather's kingdom. Sure, he managed things here pretty well, but the life he managed consisted of sleeping on other people's couches and living off the proceeds of a grant he had procured with the help of his advisor. Not to mention he was hardly anybody's idea of a leader. Because people never felt quite real to him, he seldom worked closely with others. Hans had helped out at his moms' bookstore on Moulton Street—but he had never been anyone's boss. That Essera's nobles would choose someone like him to run things was laughable. But *this*...

Could he even attempt to rule... anything? Set policy, give orders? Or battle someone like Nammuor? Marenthro said Marc Frederick had broken Nammuor's power—for a time. How long a time?

Marenthro continued to speak, though Hans had yet to agree to, well, any of it.

"While she can pave the way for your return, your mother agrees with me that you must not return to Permephedon or the Archhalia. If you did, you would be taken immediately into protective custody by men who have anything but your protection at heart. Even if you petition for sanctuary yourself, chances are you would be dead within weeks."

So Essera was out. And he had almost talked himself into going back there.

It was strange how the more Hans thought about going back, the more he thought maybe he should do it. His childhood memories of his home world were so strong now, so clear, so close. For all the nine years he had spent in this world, it had never felt completely whole or real. Even Felicia had sensed that he didn't belong here. Maybe he had somehow discerned all along that he was simply a visitor, a tourist inside a history already written, a world in which he would never make a single bit of difference.

But could he make a difference, maybe even a lasting one, in his home world? Not if he ended up dead. Now that he knew for a fact who had killed Marc Frederick, Hans also knew that hiding his head in the sand was not going to make him less of a target. Nammuor hadn't stopped with Marc Frederick—he had gone after Stefan next.

"So I can't go to Essera because my regent is in Nammuor's pocket," Hans agreed. The longer he put off meeting Nammuor, the better, as far as he was concerned. He remembered enough of his home world to know there were other places in the Triempery he might go. "What about going to Amallar? The Khelds are my kin. My people, right? I spent some summers and a winter or two at Rhodhur, and they practically worshipped Stefan. They would rather follow me than some Staubaun noble they don't know much about. They would harbor me and help me fight any who wants to kill me."

"Yes, they would, with all their hearts." Marenthro traced a knot in the wood plank of the table. "The Khelds are loyal and tough—and increasingly numerous—but they are no match for Staubaun might. Not yet. They do not have the power politically or militarily to sway matters beyond their own borders. Though they might mount an insurrection, the result would be the same: you would alienate any Staubaun domains that might have stood with you. You would find yourself contained in Amallar, without allies or any hope of success. The kingship would be stripped from you and given either to Erenor or to some faction Nammuor deems malleable. At that point Dorilian would be forced to press his own claim. And you and your Khelds would fight for your lives to the ends of your days."

"Well, that's llama spit!" Hans protested. "I'm dead if I go one way and dead if I go the other. If I can't go to my family or friends—"

Marenthro lifted an eyebrow. "You are thinking too small, even in terms of what family and friends might be, or where you might find them. You must start thinking like a prince."

"No one taught me how to think like a prince. Certainly not Irmgard and Geraldine. They were true Mainers, they joined committees and brewed their own beer. Thanks to them, I buy my clothes at resale shops and think like a Dominioner. And all my coursework ever taught me was how to think like a historian."

"Thrift and history are useful tools for a prince. Dominioners have nearly three hundred years of stable and successful government, and historians look for facts and collect evidence. Those are lessons and skills you can put to good use. Your affiliations are going to be complex, not simple."

"Yes, because I have been away for *nine years*. I have no affiliations. I'm starting from nothing."

"Nothing except who you are and what you stand for. You have yourself. For most men, that is all that they have. Learn what you are. It is enough."

Hans shook his head. "I don't know about that. In case you haven't noticed, I'm not much of anything except a reasonably good student. I can drive a rig and sail a boat, but I have never handled a weapon that wasn't tagged in an exhibit. I'm certainly no match for a sorcerer. And I haven't exactly been hanging out with royalty, or even politicians. I avoid them! I don't know the first thing about being a king."

"A king?" Marenthro granted a wry smile. "You are not going back to *be* a king, Handurin—you are going back to be a prince and possibly win the chance to *become* their leader, their king, if you wish to be one. Even if you win back the leadership that Stefan lost, there is no kingdom left intact for you to inherit. There is, however, a great one to be forged out of the remnants of the one that was shattered. You may well be the only person who could do it."

"Yeah, right."

Hans couldn't believe he was even thinking about doing this. Not a thing Marenthro was talking about attracted him, other than a desire to put things right. And *that* felt more like obligation. A sense of family history and duty. His grandfather had talked with him and Stefan about how important it was for the Stauberg-Randolphs to serve as a model for their people. To lead by example and serve the greater good, though exactly what that might be had been a little vague. Still, Hans had idolized his grandfather and had wanted to be just like him. Like Marc Frederick. It still felt like a worthwhile goal, especially given what he had just witnessed. If Hans could help the people of his home world, really help them… perhaps he should. Doing so might also get his mother—the only relative he still had—off the hook. And while he was at it, he could introduce new ideas, maybe change things for the better. A less deadly form of government, for starters.

It occurred to him that Irmgard and Geraldine would approve.

"If I do this, you will help me—won't you, Marenthro? You'll be with me?"

Marenthro pulled back from the table. "I will help you as I can. But no, Handurin, I will not accompany you. That would not be wise, even if I thought it best. You will not see me again after tonight, not in this world, not even if you change your mind and choose to stay. What you do now, you must do of your own mind and will—make your own path, find your own allies—else my choices would find their way into yours. Once before I threw a stone. Now at long last I throw another."

"Me?" Hans looked up in surprise.

Marenthro nodded, his expression solemn. From behind the copper gleam of his ageless eyes, something of that other world looked back at Hans. Hope, perhaps, of seeing him again.

"I will find you," Hans promised.

"When you know where to look. I will be aware of all you do. But first," Marenthro held out his left arm, then encircled that wrist with the fingers of his right hand. With a swift pull outwards, he seemed to skim light itself from his skin and, when done, held a glowing ring of diffuse energy. That circle of light shone blue as he extended it to Hans. "I do have some influence over the firmament of Creation, of which Time is an element. Touch this ring to the headstone of the Door of the Sun, and it will return the Gateway to its original working state in *this time*. But only for a few minutes. After that, it will close again—forever. Just remember that Gateways, of all kinds, are well guarded, and the faint of heart never cross the threshold."

Hans took the circlet, finding it cool and completely without substance. If he squeezed his fingers together, they passed right through the thing. What held it together?

"And where will the Gateway take me?"

"To one named Thaa, who will know you are coming."

Hans found that the circlet fit into the oversized pocket of his camp shirt. He put it there but then had to look again, to see if he still had it. It was so weightless that he could not feel it on him. Though it continued to glow, the ring's light did not show through the cotton fabric. "And then?" he asked, once satisfied that he had the key to the Gateway secured. "Once I am through the Gateway? Where do I go?"

"You must find your own way. Nammuor knows you must return, but he will not know where you are until rumor of you informs him of a location. Use that time wisely. Others will be awaiting your return as well, but there is one destination none will be watching because no one would think a Kheldish prince, Emyli's son and Stefan's brother, would ever go there." As the room brightened and morning sun touched them both with brilliant fingers, Marenthro waved his hand again over the table between them. Once more the map appeared. Marenthro laid his finger in the middle of the map, on the blue shimmer of an inland sea surrounded by golden lands and a blaze of pure light at its center.

"You must go to Sordan."

8

The Rift is a transdimensional artifact. Human
senses cannot detect the full extent of its
disruption. The anomaly exists throughout the
entire Creation.
—Cibulitus, *Annals of the Return:
The Aryati Problem*

"Really? You're giving away all this stuff?"

"Yeah, I am. Take what you want."

Hans was leaving it behind anyway. The trailer belonged to the Yachaywasi, but there were books, clothes, music—hundreds of possessions—he could not fit into his backpack.

His undergrad student, Qhapaq, eyed him suspiciously. "You're not killing yourself, are you?"

Hans laughed. "No. I'm going home. I just can't take all my stuff with me."

Qhapaq held aloft a jacket with a jaguar leaping over the left shoulder. "This is a killer piece of outerwear."

"Yours. If you want it."

"I want it. I want all your things and so will the rest of the class. But this doesn't feel right. These textbooks, they cost a damn fortune."

A small one, maybe. Not that Qhapaq needed the money. His family in Cuzco was old Inka aristocracy and rich. As Hans watched his bespectacled friend assess the clothing and books, it struck him that by leaving this world he might be saving Qhapaq's life. A life already lived, determined from beginning to end, but one that Qhapaq appeared to be enjoying. Even as he stood here now, Hans knew himself an outsider. A voyeur. Although he was currently alive in this world—this past—he could not change it, neither by being in it...

...nor by leaving it.

Nothing he did here could alter this world's outcome. It would be a coward's move to stay, knowing every day what he had refused to do. He preferred the course he had chosen, that of knowing he could alter things—for the better, with honor—where he was going. His decision had come down to fighting to not be a dead prince on a living world or being a live grad student on a dead one.

Hans turned so he could look out the trailer's dusty front window. The massive Door of the Sun stood in a barren field apart from the other ruins. Now he knew why it stood so alone. In his pocket, he carried a key that would turn back Time itself.

People in Essera were putting their lives on the line for him. His mother, Emyli, who faced charges of high treason if Hans did not return. The Khelds, whose fierce devotion to his family meant they would welcome and follow him, but who stood to lose the most if he failed. The loyal remnants of his grandfather's friends in Essera, dwindling by the day if what Marenthro had told Hans was true. And Dorilian Sordaneon, who might help him or might not, but who Hans now knew had tried to save Marc Frederick. Had made a promise.

Look after my family.

Well, Hans was Marc Frederick's family. And Dorilian was Highborn, which meant he might have powers or something. In a world that had once defeated a god, maybe there still existed the kind of power that could defeat it again.

Hans left the trailer before dawn, quietly closing the door behind him. Just two days ago he had made a similar trek across the road. This night the site stood silent, darker because clouds obscured what little moonlight remained. Even so, the ruins were crowned by distant mountains. Ten thousand years ago, the Aryati had chosen this place to build a piece of their transit system. That thought caused his heart to beat faster.

The Door of the Sun loomed in blocks of shadow and broken light beneath a sickle moon brushed by high, thin clouds. Hans fished in his pocket for the circle Marenthro had given him. He held it up, a ring of light glowing softly in the velvety dark surrounding him. Once he touched it to the headstone, he would have just a few minutes. He had brought nothing with him but a change of clothes and some photos, the Saint James medal Felicia had given him, and a few antique gold coins. He didn't know what he would find on the other side, though Marenthro had promised there would be someone to assist him on his way.

"Well, here goes," he muttered.

He stood at the front of the Gateway and reminded himself of all the reasons he had decided to leave. Even though he believed he was doing the right thing, to actually take that step seemed monumental. Tentatively reaching up, Hans touched the glowing ring to the headstone.

At once the circle vanished and light flowed from his fingers into the stone, across its surfaces. He stepped back, mouth falling open, as the doorway sharpened and brightened. The Doorway's God blazed on a headstone now golden, atop silver pillars, light bracketed inside the facing sides. Within the Gate itself, suspended in some unknown matrix, hung a quicksilver orb reflecting all the World. Drawing a breath, Hans stepped forward as a tonal hum emitted from the portal.

Forbidden!

Stunned, he stepped back for a moment, then pressed forward again.

Don't… Don't… Don't!

Driven back by a portal suddenly rife with madness and death, Hans felt nothing but stark, uncontrollable terror. The urge to run away caused him to stumble backward. He tripped over one of the stone blocks scattered throughout the site and went sprawling. Within the Gate, the silver orb spun.

Gateways of all kinds are well guarded, and the faint of heart never enter there.

Marenthro had been referring to this. Such a Gate, if it were to serve its creators, must have had some means of keeping out the uninvited. A warning, especially one that induced paralyzing fear, served to ward off birds and animals that otherwise might stray into the passage. Unwary and primitive humans, likewise, would flee from such supernatural terror. Only someone who knew the Gate's purpose might gather enough will to face it.

Hans sprang to his feet and approached a second time, prepared for the terror as the orb pulsed its vibrations into his brain. Resisting his own impulse to flee, his sense of panic began to fade. Only the glinting otherworldliness of the sphere remained within, hung on a veil of blue sky.

There are only three Worlds, he reminded himself, *and to one no Gate goes.*

Through the Gate, from somewhere or when, a red glow of fading sunlight streaked the clear blue sky.

He stepped into the stone opening. As he did so, he heard an ominous grinding as the headstone, cracked, slid down. Without thinking, Hans threw himself the rest of the way through the portal as—its bounds broken—it began to shift, Time's barriers resealing the man-made breach...

...and found himself falling backwards, the Qullasuyu already gone. He landed on his back, slamming unceremoniously into whatever World awaited.

9

Hans drew a deep breath and sat up under the red glare of a setting sun. The land revealed by that swollen, sinking orb rolled and puckered all the way to the horizon, a wasteland devoid of any feature worthy of hope. Even the wind stroked like claws across his cheek and stirred sand into his eyes and mouth. He groped about, then looked around for his backpack. Gone. He must have lost it when the Gateway had crashed in.

So much for having packed stuff he wanted to keep.

Bleeding and stiff from the Gateway's wreckage, Hans pushed to his feet and clambered to the crest of a nearby dune. No signs of habitation. Or mountains. The Andes were gone and so were the ruins of Tiwanaku. To every side lay a twisted, tormented land.

Other than the air being breathable, nothing about this place resembled the world of his childhood.

He stood dismayed, his lightweight trousers flapping against his legs, as wind gusted past rocks. Hearing a small noise behind him, Hans turned around. A short distance away stood a figure, someone slender and tall, clothed in filmy black robes. What looked like smoke-black hair or a veil floated across an unseen face. The best Hans could say for the apparition was that it looked vaguely human.

Marenthro had provided a name, so he used it.

"Are you Thaa?" he called.

The shadowy form lifted a limb and gestured for Hans to follow.

Hans picked his way to the base of the hill and a winding, sandy gully. The figure led him through this until they reached a trail, which led to a cave halfway up the steep side. Striations in the rock beckoned and Hans touched the fine-grained bands, thinking they had been carved by some long-vanished river. Seeing a warm glow within the cave, he entered.

The steady fire showed his host no more clearly. Low light rendered even the simplest movement dreamlike. Thaa's smooth hands, cupped as though the fingers would not be parted, moved in strange and fluid ways. Those hands directed Hans to a table set with a plate of bread and some strange fruit, with an ewer of water standing beside a bowl. He was bidden to partake, not with words but with a kind of expectancy. A bed followed the meal, a rock shelf heaped with blankets, spare yet comfortable enough. Exhausted and without knowing why he trusted, Hans slept.

He woke again. Time must have passed because his cuts and bruises had faded. Time... which might not be the same here. Looking around, Hans saw that he had not dreamed the cave and that its rock walls were bathed in the flickering light of a strange clear fire. Thaa sat before that fire, unmoving, hood flung back and face bared. Small, almost tiny, features—too small to be purely human—looked insignificant in a pale face dominated by huge black eyes without any white at all. Overwhelming and demanding of attention, those eyes gave the impression that they saw nothing... and everything.

Hans spoke first. Hopeful of being in the right place, he used the language he had spoken as a child. "Thank you, Thaa, for taking care of me."

"I attend all who arrive here." Tones as deep as the dark place in which they huddled called to mind the wind outside. "Most never wake."

"Are you some kind of guardian?"

"I watch."

For many heartbeats, they watched each other. Human or not, Thaa reminded Hans, vaguely, of someone's sister. He couldn't tell for certain if Thaa was female or male, or neither or both, and that he could not do so put Hans off balance. He did not want to offend.

"Marenthro sent me," he said when the silence became too much. "But I have no supplies. It all got left behind, everything—"

"Nothing lost but what Was. When the light of day permits you to travel, take what I provide and go out into the World That Is."

"But I don't know where to go. Or rather, I don't know how to get there."

"All knowledge you need, this World will provide."

Hans was convinced, if he had not been before, that his host wanted as little to do with him as possible. Thaa lived alone and obviously preferred it so. Still, there were questions Hans found imperative to ask.

"Might you tell me… where am I? Is this Sordan?" That was the question foremost in his mind. What if, in the Gate's destruction, he had missed?

"You entered the Rift between Worlds," Thaa said. "You are where the Wall determined you belong." Those strange hands cupped the white incandescence at Thaa's feet. When drawn back, fused fingers glowed with a brilliant white light that blazed across Thaa's eyebrowless face, so small of feature and so smooth of complexion that it seemed a mask. Black within black, those eyes fastened on his. "I know the old ways, the ways of the World That Was before. The Creation is old—old, yes. Old and vast. Leur gave their Creation many gifts. Mortals were not the first, nor the last, born of the World That Was. Mortals are not all that remain. Hidden power dwells in these hills where the Three Worlds meet."

As a child Hans had heard that there were places where the boundaries between the Worlds had never healed, into which people might wander never to return. Some such rifts were famous—one in the mysterious Bogs had permitted Khelds to cross into the World, and another lay offshore of Stauberg.

"Few come here. Fewer leave. I know a way that is safe." Thaa rose in a swirl of black veils. "Come. Daylight grows, and you must go. It is dangerous to tarry here—the land is too strong."

Thaa presented garments Hans supposed were of the kind worn by males in this world—woven trousers and a tunic of plain cotton, a jerkin of leather dyed with diamond shapes of muted blue and red, a sturdy belt and shoes of soft leather laced with what looked like hemp. Before leaving his garments behind, Hans checked the pockets and found the two gold Inka coins and, to his surprise, the Saint James medal he had been given by Felicia. He rolled it in his fingers, feeling the embossed shape of the horse and rider.

When Hans had dressed, Thaa led him from the cave.

Outside the underground shelter, dawn brushed a cloudless sky with pink, the sun not yet risen above a line of hills to the east. Though Hans had seen no sign of horses the night before, one awaited him now, dun like the land that had bred it, grazing on a patch of meager grasses at the entrance. It was saddled with a low wooden frame covered by leather and a few worn blankets, water skins slung from the front saddle rings, packets of food and other items tied to the back ones. Thaa pressed the reins into Hans's hand.

"This is yours, and all it carries. And these for you also, to see you on your journey." Thaa held out a purse. "This to purchase help along your way." The pouch weighed heavy when he took it in hand. Thaa offered a dagger. "This to use when all else fails." Hans took that too and tucked it into his belt. "And this, from the one who sent you here."

A medallion, gray and lusterless, lay in Thaa's cupped palm. Hans knew better than to judge the thing by its appearance. He took the medallion in hand and watched as colors blossomed from its matrix. Not just color, but brilliant color. Bold and bright. Background of blue. Gold crown and sword imposed over the silver image of a winged horse. There was more, banding and symbols Hans did not understand.

"It is your *deiknya*," Thaa said when he looked up with the question. "A bit of your life is in it. And this word to you from the giver: You will find what you seek at the headwaters of the River of Blood."

"But I'm going to Sordan."

"Even so."

Thaa did not speak again. Perhaps, as Thaa led Hans away from the cave and whatever sorcery it provided, speech was impossible. Perhaps Thaa was not truly there, walking ahead of Hans, showing a path through the poisoned land. Not once did the shadowy guardian turn to see if he followed.

Their surroundings passed as if in a dream until the sun sank low to cast long shadows and they stood atop the last scorched ridges of the hills. There, black against the growing darkness, Thaa pointed. In the distance, barely visible past a wide green land, shimmered a faint dark line, a suggestion of a great river.

The River of Blood, Hans guessed.

"You have my thanks," Hans said to Thaa as the lighter breeze of evening drove off the desert heat. "I want to tell you now because I do not think that I shall pass this way again."

But the dark-clothed figure did not turn or give any sign of having heard before starting off down the hill. Looking back but moments later, Hans saw that Thaa had already gone and he was alone.

10

Khelds looked to the north and saw a mighty
country, a monolithic fortress of Staubaun
affluence and privilege. We did not see the cracks
in its foundations. With its Highborn rulers dead
and no king to unify them, Essera's many factions
lacked the resources and will to successfully
defend themselves from the Sorcerer's predations.
—Robdan Aelfricson,
The Stauberg-Randolph Succession

"What are we waiting for?"

The sailor stood on the amber planking of the deck, the cerulean and white banners of Stauberg unfurling overhead in the sluggish breeze. The air itself was heavy, the sky mottled with impending weather. Zepheron, Lord Admiral of Royal Essera, gazed unhappily at the copper sky. Overhead, the Rift shifted its energies in flickering sheets of purple and curling edges of black.

"We will know when we see it," he told his crewman. He marked how the sea had flattened under the oppressive atmosphere that barely swelled his ship's sails.

After eighty long years at sea, he still disliked being near the Rift. The thing sucked ships into its maelstrom energies and created whirlpools that pulled them beneath its waters. Ships also appeared in the Rift, strange vessels, though never large ones. Gone were the ages when armadas sailed between Worlds to wage war across Time itself.

What he did not tell his crewman was that he had brought his flagship, the *Ariande*, to these forbidden waters without the Regent's knowledge, and that he had done so for reasons which Essera's Halia would not approve. His crew did not know that they rode the Rift because Zepheron Elmarachos had been called upon to do one more service for an old master.

Marc Frederick was my King. And I honored Stefan as his heir, kept my command. The Stauberg-Randolphs were and are our proper rulers.

Zepheron frowned at the way Erenor Tholeros had stolen the regency. And he frowned at how black-hulled Mormantaloran ships now commanded Aral's harbor. How even now they roved the northern seas, policing the shipping corridors, conveying the Sorcerer's power and troops. Nammuor himself, it was said, had taken up residence at Aral, sitting upon the High Seat of the Halasseons.

Zepheron saw his country being conquered from within.

And now Emyli Stauberg-Randolph wanted to bring home her son, the Triempery's rightful Heir, to put a stop to it. She had asked Zepheron, her father's old friend and comrade in arms, to keep watch on the Rift.

Today the barriers looked disturbed. Always a bruise on the skin of the sky, today the Rift looked fresh, its colors unusually vivid. In the coppery light of sunset, the shifting energy fields purpled already dark and angry clouds. From time to time, deep, hidden lightnings flashed white, then black.

Leur help us—it is active tonight! Zepheron made the sign of the Sword. Emyli had written that Marenthro would bring the boy home as once he had brought Marc Frederick.

He heard the lookouts holler before the first crewman ran up to him. "Mormantalorus," the man said, pointing. Zepheron brought the spyglass to his eye. A black crow of a ship rode the waves of a sea already in the first throes of storm.

The way was watched, just as Emyli had feared it would be.

"Turn about." Zepheron put away the glass. "We head to port. There's a Rift storm blowing up."

"It is the Sorcerer's ship," his officer pointed out.

"Yes. Yet more reason. Make for the Eye!" Zepheron had set the course for Stauberg ahead of time but wanted them to know they must not wait. If the winds were kind, the *Ariande* would have enough speed to outrun Nammuor's pursuit.

Ariande pulled into the wind and with a surge gained speed. The Rift was not far off Stauberg's shore, where it could be seen from the tall towers that the Malyrdeons had built for the purpose of watching it. Even as far out to sea as they now were, they could see the white wings and spires of Stauberg's Wall.

"Why do we run?" the officer demanded. Fear slashed the man's face. The Mormantaloran vessel, though still but a black blot on the storm-dark sea, had clearly engaged in pursuit. "We are not enemies."

"Ask, then, why the Sorcerer gives chase," Zepheron countered grimly.

The man took him by the arm. "Have it that way, then—why does he follow?"

Zepheron gave a feral grin, an urge for battle unfolding within him. "He thinks we have the Prince on board. That we picked the lad up at sea. And that is exactly what we want him to think."

Soon every man aboard the *Ariande* could see the great yawning beak at the prow of the Mormantaloran ship. To them it seemed the red eyes of the thing were fixed on them like those of a demon's beast. The nearer it got, the more it drank of the *Ariande's* wind. Ahead of them, Stauberg's Wall tipped the horizon, the city yet unseen.

Ergeiron, Protector of Men—come to us! Zepheron prayed. But only Highborn voices had ever moved the Wall.

Looking back, Zepheron saw the Sorcerer himself, red-cloaked and terrible on the deck of the sinister vessel, framed by its taut sails and clouds of storm. Against Nammuor, he and his crew had no weapons. Speed had been their only hope, and that dependent on the wind. *Ariande* was still lengths in front of the black-sailed ship. Still had hope of the Wall...

Sorcery, even the most benign of its ilk, smelled of volatile vapors. What drenched the *Ariande* stank of sulfur and the fire at the World's end. The golden-hulled vessel at the last moment appeared to fill her brilliantly emblazoned sails with wind, to leap forward through the brightening water. Then the whole vessel, every glowing board and gilded mast, the shimmering sails upon her and the men screaming on her incandescent decks, took on the look and texture of flame. *Ariande* wavered, a ship of fire. And then that vision dissipated into the wind that tore into her. There was not even smoke but simply ash, blowing across the water to fall there like snow.

11

Sorand'ruil! Was ever a river more blessed with
riches? The Dazun does not flow into the sea and
so does not bear upon its bright waters the ships of
many nations. The Randpor is ugly and brown and
the lands through which it passes are poisoned.
The Geroe is wild; the Stariel plunges over cliffs;
the Kav ruled by hull-breaking beasts; and the
Epporos is shallow. But the Sorand'ruil! The City
of the Sordaneons stands as a haven to great ships
sailing upon a road of silver, and towns along the
way dot the emeraldine shores like jewels.
—Patroculos, *Journeys to Many Lands*

The river was farther away than it looked. Hans spent that first night in the desert, without a fire to warm him—there was nothing to burn, and even if there had been, he was not inclined to announce his presence. Instead, after tending to his horse, he settled back against the saddle and its pad in a clearing ringed by sun-warmed boulders, and watched clouds scutter across the dying curve of the moon. That, at least, was the same—the same moon—as it was, as it would be, forever floating above the Creation's earthly plain.

Well, Marenthro, Hans thought, *I'm home. I'm not sure where I am. I don't know anyone. I don't even know where I am going, not really. But I'm home.*

For as far as he could hear, nothing but the whisper of the wind across grass and stones came his way. Only now did it hit him, what he had done in leaving one world for another. He'd lost his photos of Irmgard and Geraldine yet they remained in his mind, happy and excited that he had embarked on an adventure. None of this would have frightened them. Knowing that reassured him. Maybe they would not mind so much that he had traded everything, even the life they had given him, for a vast unknown.

A host of unknowns, not the least of which was himself. Who was he, after all? Hans Stoll-Becker, student of a world long vanished? Or Handurin Stauberg-Randolph, a prince without lands, significant only in that his name and blood bore a claim that might inconvenience or benefit just about everyone else he might meet? At least Nammuor would find it hard going to locate him; even Hans didn't know where he was. The only map Hans had was the one in his mind, memory of an image Marenthro had magicked onto a table. Somewhere there was a lake and a river and the sea.

Ahead, not that far away, was a river.

The river would take him to Sordan. Marenthro had explained the need to go there.

"Of all the lands remaining of the Triempery, Sordan stands the tallest. It is the last Highborn throne and Sordan has the resources to oppose Nammuor. It may also have the will. You are the rightful heir to Essera—even Dorilian did not put his claim against yours. Dorilian did not approve of the regency put over you and has refused to recognize it. Whatever may come, he would not remand you to Erenor."

Reasonable as that sounded, however, there had been more.

"Unfortunately, Dorilian's history with your family is an uneasy one. You will find yourself on a road populated by the ghosts of those who went before you."

To just walk into a lion's den didn't sound like much of a plan—and Marenthro's warning of ghosts felt all too real. For now, though, it was the only plan Hans had.

He started out again before dawn, glad to have a sound horse and for having learned to ride and care for horses in his youth. By evening he had reached the river, and the smell of water urged his tired beast to continue. A broad, beaten swath of reddish-copper reflections beneath a swollen, setting sun, the river passed in a stream so mighty that the opposite bank was but a heavy, dark suggestion. Hans rode until he found a place where the higher bank gave way to trees and a sandy shore. There he dismounted and lowered himself to refill his canteen, just upstream of his mount.

He was not prepared for the rough voice that spoke up behind him.

"*Chi'ya kara!*"

The voice was hale, not threatening. Only the language was unfamiliar—a bastardized dialect of Stauba. *River friend*, Hans translated, thinking it must be a kind of greeting. He turned to see a short, ruddy man dressed in skins that had been softened and tanned to clothlike lightness and hemmed with fabric, wearing broad sandals and leaning on a heavy staff he held clutched in one sturdy hand. The man pointed to the horse.

"You travel?" This time the man spoke in broken Stauba.

"Yes." Hans dragged on the reins, leading the horse from the water.

"Where?"

"Sordan."

With a low, guttural sound that could have meant anything, the fellow lowered his staff and approached the water. He knelt and splashed his arms and hands, then dunked his head up to his neck in the river. Rising to his feet, he shook himself like a great shaggy dog and confronted Hans once more.

"Overland, she is bitch, no?"

Hans looked out at the wide arid land and nodded.

The man bared his teeth in a big, friendly smile and put a hand on his chest. "I am Cef. You?"

"Hans." He wanted to kick himself as soon as he had said it. He should have lied. But it was beyond unlikely that this man was an enemy who had followed him through the gate or traced his footsteps upon leaving the poisoned land. Cef was just another traveler sharing river water and a few words while he was at it. Hans didn't need a historical perspective to know that a river of this size had served as a major artery of transportation and culture for thousands of years. Meeting with strangers would be commonplace.

"Is this the River of Blood?" he asked.

"Sorand'ruil." The word as literally translated meant "god-ruled river." Cef considered, then added, "The blood Sordaneon gives it life." He pointed upstream.

"So this river will take me to Sordan?"

"The river comes from Sordan. Follow it to beginning, find Sordan. Even child knows that."

"I wanted to be sure it was the right river."

"There is no other river." Cef looked Hans over. "You Trongorian? Trader?"

Hans had no idea what he might resemble in this strange land or by way of the strange clothes he was wearing, so he said simply, "Maybe."

"Can tell. Blue-eye." Cef pointed to his own dark eyes. His gaze narrowed, probably also noting Hans's lighter hair. "Maybe Staubaun goat a Kheldish maid, eh? Happens. But you dress Trongor."

It was better than being branded as a Kheld in this land where Khelds were hated. "Then Trongor it is," Hans said easily. He checked the harness of his horse.

Cef gathered up some waterskins he had apparently filled earlier. "Come my camp. Folk is herders. You welcome to share our fire." He pointed upstream, to a line of trees. Against the twilight, Hans saw curls of campfire smoke. "Come, *adon'i.* Do us honor."

Relying on instinct, Hans accepted. He took his horse by the reins and led it, not wanting to display arrogance by riding while the other man walked. And what had the fellow called him? *Adon'i* meant "lord" in the formal Stauba mode and was probably a term of respect. A man on horseback in these lands might indeed seem a lord to those who walked. Or possibly, all guests were called so.

The herdsfolk to whom Cef led Hans were brusque and coarse of manner but accommodating. Caps of twisted, colorfully dyed cotton sat atop heads of short dark hair, men and women alike, and gray-haired elders wore breast ornaments of carved and painted bone. The only questions they asked concerned possible markets for their animals or skins. When Hans claimed to have had no contact with nearby villages or traders—and showed no interest in their goods himself—they had little more to say to him. Still their fire was warm and bright, and the food that the loosely garbed women set before him was wholesome. Fat-fried patties of ground corn and meat and deep cups of warm beer soon put him in a mood for slumber.

"Is Sordan far?" Hans inquired of Cef, who was more articulate than most of his fellows and who, acting as host, stayed with him. Hans knew his questions displayed an appalling ignorance of the land he traveled but he saw no other means of improving his knowledge.

Cef, however, did not seem to care about his guest's failings. "Very far." He slowly chewed the dried, stringy meat the herds-people favored. "To ride there would be hard, take long. Easier to ride the water."

Ride the water. Of course. Hans had already seen several ships. "How?"

"Big boats, trade many goods, they no stop. Want the City, only the City. Some traders, they take goods for passage. Not all. Some do not. But there are many, many boats that trade with the City of the Sordaneons." Cef told Hans to try his luck upriver, where another day's ride would bring him to the trading village of Renet.

Hans took his leave the next morning. The sun spilled gold upon the grasses and reeds that bordered the river and soon the rough path he followed brought him to a clearly marked road. Though merely hardened dirt, the road bore evidence of horse traffic and the ruts left by loaded wagons. The land was greener near water, and for as far as Hans could see, windblown grasses rippled away from him like the crests of a pale green sea. He kept the river to his right hand, and all day long in procession he watched boats passing in either direction, a river of goods flowing along an artery of commerce. Most of the vessels were low-slung barges or barques, but he saw several massive, seagoing ships with tall masts and wide sails. He had been fascinated by books about the sea during his boyhood and had memorized the sails of the many nations. Now those memories reasserted. Red sails could only be Ardaen, the mighty seafaring nation famed for its ships. White- and blue-striped sails announced Merced. Sails crossed with blue and red signaled Trongor. The many black-barred sails belonged to Lahgael. Green and gold meant Teremar. And the white sails broadly bordered in green belonged to Sordani ships.

He had not, so far, seen any ships from Essera.

The ships and the sails reminded Hans that soon he would be coming to inhabited places, and with them the perils of human contact. The herdsfolk had been an isolated group and ignorant, so there had been little to trip him up. River people would be worldlier. Hans recalled that Cef had taken him to be an Estol—a person of mixed blood—a horseman and a trader, albeit a young one. That was a role he could play.

For one thing, he *was* of mixed blood. As a child, he had learned that his blue eyes would not let him pass as Staubaun, but he was also not quite dark-haired enough to be taken for a Kheld at first glance. Hans decided to be glad of the latter. Though the herdsmen cared little about such things, he would soon be among folk who might hold stronger views. Fortunately, his looks and the clothes Thaa had given him, the Stauba tongue that he spoke so fluently and so surprisingly, even his horse and its trappings—all played to the role of a Trongorian.

No one will know that I am Handurin Stauberg-Randolph unless I tell them. And Marenthro is right—no one would think to look for a Kheld on the road to Sordan.

Renet was not much of a port. Poor land surrounded it and the town lured only occasional business from the big trading vessels that sailed past it on the way to more prosperous destinations. Most of the boats docked at the ramshackle piers looked to be small fishing boats, bearing only jugs or textiles to barter among other river villages. Little Sordani traffic—and none of any importance—stopped at Renet.

It was already dark when Hans tied his tired, dust-covered horse to one of the posts outside a riverfront tavern. While the patrons of such a place might turn out to be rough characters, they would be no worse than anything he might meet wandering the wharf at night, and one of them might know of a boat that would be willing to take him upriver. He lifted the leather flap over the doorway and walked into a dusty, smoke-filled room that smelled of grease fires. Someday, probably, the place would go up in flames, but tonight it merely stank. A sparse sprinkling of listless customers gathered about the tables, barely glancing up at him. Ill at ease, Hans stood there until a surly, gray-haired man approached and greeted him indifferently.

"Eats or room?"

"I'll take a room," Hans said, hoping for the best. At worst, he would at least spend the night indoors. "And I am looking for a boat to Sordan."

The man studied him for a few seconds, then shrugged. "Sure, why not? Yey, Yanpo!" he bellowed across the room. "What got goin' big time?"

General laughter broke out from the smoky corner across the way, and someone barked in a loud, deep voice, "Who say?"

"Trader here. Talk to him sharp yourself!" With that the man retreated again to the back room.

Out of the haze appeared a wiry, broad-shouldered man reddened by a life under the river's broiling sun. Yanpo kicked a couple of chairs out from under a nearby table and Hans sat down as Yanpo made himself at home. "Sordan, yo' say, heh?"

"That's right." Hans began to question what he was doing. Going by river would mean trusting in men he did not know, the kind of men who might think nothing of killing for a few coins. The only weapon he had was the dagger in his belt—and he had never used a dagger in his life. All he had was his instinct, which told him that the tavern keeper seemed honest, if harried, and Yanpo looked hard-worked but not much like a pirate.

Although Yanpo was working toward drunkenness, he still had his wits about him. "What yo' willing to pay?"

"I have a horse outside, but not much else."

"Horse for Sordan? That won'd go. Too far. And anyway, our boats, they don'd go that far." Yanpo rubbed at his nose. "Then again," he said, seeing that he had a paying customer, "Can'd promise yo'll get there for First Day, but… tell yo' whad—yo' come up with ten krugs and I can get yo' to Ben Aranath."

"Ten silver?" Hans mentally tallied the coins in the purse Thaa had given him.

"And the horse," Yanpo emphasized. "I wasn'd planning to go that far, but I could use that horse."

"Where is that place, Ben—"

"Ben Aranath. Trader port, Lahgaelan side. Big port. Big ships. New about it, aren'd yo'? Ten on one yo' turn up big boat there will work yo' for passage, if yo' don'd have the coin, that is. So many pilgrims, be hard chance. Best I can do."

Grimly decided, if only because it would save him the long overland journey, Hans bartered using tactics he had learned from the women in the Witches' Market. "Three silver," he offered. "I ordered a room, and I have to eat."

"Let me see the horse," said Yanpo.

In the end Yanpo settled for the horse, its gear, and four of the small silver coins, two of which he spent that evening fortifying himself for the trip upriver, proudly stating that he never drank while on the water. Hans kept him company, listening to a loosened tongue spin tales of life as a small-time trader along Sordan's most traveled highway.

About Sordan, Yanpo could tell him little. For one thing, the man had never been there. "Big" was all the riverman could say for certain. Home of the Rill and source of riches. Tales ran rampant about its beauty and might, blending with belief in the godhood of its rulers. About Dorilian, Yanpo knew even less. "He drove out the looters, fought the northers" was about the gist of it. That and an unfailing certainty that the Sordaneon ruler was divine. "Derlon's own blood, Rill blood. May he live forever and his blood, that is the life of the World!"

The most useful bit of information had to do with the upcoming Malyrdean New Year. It seemed Amynas Malyrdys, ancestor-god of the Highborn rulers, had arrived in Sordan in spring when he had first Returned from a period known as the Exile. Amynas and his Leur companion, the last of that magical race, had at first found only desolation. But when they crossed the lake, they had seen that Sordan had survived, so they celebrated. Now, every year, the god Returned.

The Coming, a three-day cycle of religious observances, was celebrated around that event, drawing hundreds of thousands, perhaps millions—Yanpo had little grasp of such large numbers— of pilgrims annually to the island City. Under other circumstances, Hans wouldn't have welcomed that kind of crowd but, in his current situation, he saw his chance to blend in, to be one of many, just another visitor from a far land come to worship in the presence of the Highborn god. Already, Yanpo told him, river ports teemed with travelers heading for the Coming. In fact, Yanpo had from the start taken Hans for a pilgrim and continued to address him as one, asking him to offer up a prayer at the sacred grove which grew at the foot of Tur'Ahraean, where the god Amynas had walked.

"Amynas Malyrdys had sons, and his sons had sons. Derlon sired the Sordaneons in that grove, he did. Laid his woman down among the lilies. People pray for sons there—straight, strong boys like the Highborn themselves—an' it works, hear say. Wife gave me three girls and I'd like to get a son on her this time."

Ben Aranath was a much larger port than Renet. A pillared blue palace inhabited by the Lahgaelan governor dominated the city, which boasted many impressive buildings and markets. The busy docks, and the district of storehouses and taverns, covered an area many times that of the entire village Hans had seen downstream. The three-day journey upriver had been uneventful and pleasant. Yanpo had been a serviceable companion, good with his small trader's skiff, true to his word about not drinking. From him, Hans picked up a working knowledge of the region and its peoples.

All during the trip he had taken note of the many larger vessels that traveled the river with them, surging ahead with the greater power of vast sails or banked rows of strongly muscled men and women straining at the oars. Distant Sordan began to take on shape, beating with the pulse of those many ships. Those vessels were the ones Hans knew he must seek out, ships that would take him to a city that would not welcome him and a man he still felt uncomfortable about needing to find.

He left Yanpo at the docks with a handful of pleasantries and the last two coins he owed him. The riverman weighed them in his hand and wished Hans well, then walked away to seek a tavern in which to squander his gains. Hans, in turn, walked the docks in search of a ship that would carry him to Sordan. He soon found there were plenty of ships to choose from—and plenty of cargoes. Many barges bore loads of such local staples as goatskins and caged poultry, oils and fruits; other barges carried more exotic goods, cargoes of value such as wool, timber, or spices. The docks fairly reeked with this prosperity. Livestock lent its strong odor to the rest: sour sweat and unwashed humanity; the sweetness of ripening fish and blood from slaughter; musty bales of cotton; and a stifling aroma of rotting wood from the docks themselves. The heat of the day, the sounds, the thick smells of the waterfront—all left Hans groping for something, anything, familiar to him. But nothing was. He stopped for a moment to get his bearings, surrounded by bales of cotton and huge stacks of tanned leather. A trio of clattering carts passed him by.

A disturbance begun on a nearby barge cascaded his way, followed by loud swearing and the crack of blows landing across bare human skin. Someone careered around stacked barrels of sweet *kormos* oil before tripping on a length of rope that sent him sprawling at Hans's feet. The unlucky runner's pursuer, burned and burly like most dock workers under this sun and dressed only in a loincloth but with a quirt and a dagger strapped to his thigh, followed. With a cry, the young man being chased attempted to scramble back onto his feet, trying to get away, but slammed into Hans and fell back to the planks, staring up at the person he had run into. Hans looked down, startled, into frightened eyes as blue as his own. Traces of scant beard shadowed the youth's jawline.

What was a Kheld doing so far from Amallar, deep in lands close to Sordan?

With a muttered curse, the burly man shouldered Hans aside and reached down to grasp his quarry. Thick fingers curled brutally into the Kheld's sunburned, scabbed skin. All fight left the Kheld as he was hauled to his feet only to be thrown across the dock, hard, against some boards. There he cowered, hands covering his ears, as the man brought the quirt down on his back. Blood welled in stripes under a shirt already torn and stained with brown streaks from previous beatings.

"Stop!" Hans interceded when he saw the man raise his quirt to strike again. "You're hurting him!"

"Damn right! Get out of the way!" The man tucked the quirt into his thigh strap, then drew his dagger and knelt. With his other hand, he grabbed the Kheld by the hair and slammed his head down on the dock. "And I'm going to notch his flea-bitten ears, too!"

"No!" Hans protested. When he looked around, he saw that he was the only one. Most people simply walked by without looking and of those who watched, none seemed to care.

"Have you a stake in it?" The burly man took a good look at him and scowled. "Another blue-eye! Go pick your own toenails, pilgrim. This stinking Kheld's a thief, and his miserable ass is in thrall to my ship. He's a lazy hedgepig too! It's none of yours how he gets paid for it."

"You don't have to maim him. You've got him back, isn't that enough?" Hans saw that the Kheld breathed raggedly as he cowered, no longer resisting, neck extended cruelly by the man's heavy grip.

The riverman gaped for a moment in disbelief, then erupted. "What's this? Grief about how a damned Kheldish thrall gets his goods put to him?" Though he continued to hold his captive to the planks, he focused now on Hans. "He's gods-damned property, that's what he is—and he'll get his beatings 'til he learns it. Now move on before I give you a good taste of what those blue eyes will get you if you keep with that talk!"

Wisely or wrongly, Hans stood his ground. "What do you mean, he's property?"

"You don't think I birthed him, do you? This ship bought his hide in Damna. We get 'em from the wars, down from the mines. They're worse than animals but, what the curse, I needed the hands and his came cheap."

"But that's—" Hans caught himself. Slavery was about as common to human cultures as warfare itself. There was no reason not to find it here. He changed his approach to one that better suited the waterfront. "How much did he cost you?" At the question, the Kheld looked up at him with something like hope in his eyes.

The man drew back. He was a trader, with a trader's sensibilities. "He's young... strong too." He fingered his chin, as if he would consider any reasonable offer.

"Yes, but he's been hard used. You said he came cheap."

"Didn't say he'd come cheap to you. I could sell him to the galleys for fifty—more if I notch his ears and he survives it."

"Fifty silver?"

"Hell, no! Fifty gold."

"Fifty gold!" Hans's indignation was unfeigned. He was hazy on the exchange rates, but fifty gold sounded exorbitant. By the laughter some of the onlookers gave him, he knew he was right. "I wouldn't pay ten for his brothers—all thirteen of them!"

More laughter from the small crowd swelled the air of bartering as they were reminded of Kheldish fecundity, which was famous. The Kheld probably did have thirteen brothers and as many sisters.

"What the hell." The man laughed. "So he's a louse-bitten Kheld. Offer me forty and I might take it."

"I can get a horse for forty."

"A lame broke-backed nag, maybe. We're talking different animals here. He may be a shittin' Kheld, but he's human. He'll do what you tell him—if you beat him enough."

"Ten gold—*krugs*, not *malyr*," said Hans.

"Hell, he ate more than that!" The man pondered. He had probably gotten the Kheld for less and would be rid of a troublemaker besides. "Tell you what," he offered, "Thirty-five and I'll throw in his shoes."

"Twelve is my limit," Hans said. It was only the truth. He had twelve gold coins in his purse and several pieces of silver. He remembered the two Inka coins in his pocket and pulled them out. "And these."

"Let me see those." The man gave each coin a bite and a once over. "Good enough," he decided, seeing he would get nothing more. "But I keep his blanket and his shoes."

The transaction complete, the man stomped back to his ship and Hans found himself walking the docks of Ben Aranath with another mouth to feed and no money. He alternated between pride at having redeemed a man from an obviously cruel existence and consternation at knowing he was now nearly penniless. He could no longer afford passage to Sordan. If getting there had been difficult before, it would now be impossible. What had he been thinking?

Turning to the Kheld, who was more perplexed than he at what had transpired, Hans said, "You have a name, right?"

The Kheld nodded. Though he looked like he could use a few meals, he was sturdily built with brown shaggy locks and enough body and facial hair to make his race inescapable. One of the major differences separating Khelds from Staubauns, beards particularly offended the ruling race. Probably due to his own Staubaun blood, Hans had yet to be able to grow one.

"Arne Anseldson." The young man cast a wary sidelong look.

Hans drew him into the shadow of some nearby bales. "My name is Hans," he said. Now they were safely out of earshot he used the Kheld tongue he remembered from his youth. "I'm Kheld, like you… a little anyway."

"I thought maybe you were." Wonder colored young Arne's voice. And skepticism as well.

"I come from Gustan, on the Dazun river," Hans said. "You know where that is?"

"Who doesn't? Everyone in the *kelds* knows the high king's town. But if that's the case, what're you doing here?"

"It's a long story." Hans glanced quickly about. "Look, let's start speaking Stauba or Esta or something. People around here might not like us speaking Kheldish. You speak Stauba, don't you?" He steered them around the bales and back into the swirl of people moving along the dock.

"A little," Arne managed. "Esta is better."

"Then suppose you tell me where you're from—and how you got *here* of all places."

Arne began his story haltingly at first, then with increasing confidence. Although born in Amallar proper, Arne had gone off to the Neuberland wars full of righteous zeal—the same kind of righteous zeal that had brought Sordan's soldiers there. He didn't know how the conflict had originated and said it didn't matter. "It's Sordan we're fighting now." A badly planned and led raid on a town outside Gignastha had resulted in his capture. Kheldish prisoners were commonly killed or ransomed, but on that day there was a man among the locals who looked to make a profit by choosing the younger, healthier prisoners to sell to quarries in Anit-Rebir.

Arne never made it to the quarries; he was traded for supplies to a merchant who fancied youth. After several weeks of hard use, that merchant in turn had traded him to the overseer of a trading barque taking cargo on consignment down the Randpor River enroute to Lahgael. Ben Aranath had been the barque's last stop. Agonizing over what was to be done with him and what other masters might be awaiting him along the road, Arne had stolen some food and the ship master's dueling knife and had sneaked off the deck, hoping to lose himself among the many races and nationalities swelling the waterfront of Lahgael's largest river port. It was the overseer's pursuit that had brought him to Hans.

"You bought my life, and it's yours to do with what you want."

"I'm not a slave owner, Arne. I don't believe in that."

"No, you don't understand. You saved me from the Staubauns. It doesn't matter to me what made you do it. I'd be a dead man if you hadn't bought me off. And that makes me your man."

Hans felt a sinking in his stomach. "My man?"

"Sure," Arne said. "I stick with you, watch your hide. Just like you was a lord or something."

"But I'm not—" Hans cut himself off when he realized that he was a lord, or rather a prince. Only there wasn't a need for Arne to know that just yet. "Look, Arne, I wanted to free you, not the other way around. No man has any claim on you now."

"You do," Arne told him bluntly. He shrugged and something stubborn took hold around his mouth. "You saved my life, and I'll stay with you 'til I can return the favor. I owe you that, and it's what I want to do. It's not like I have a whole lot of ways to go about it. I'm farther from home than I ever wanted to be—than I ever thought I *could* be—among people who think I'm lower than the dogs in the street. I know they'd kill me for less than the dogs get away with, first chance they get. Where would I go? I don't even *know* the way back to Amallar. And yours is the first friendly face I've seen in six months."

Hans could hardly ignore Arne's desperation. Sordan was at war with Amallar, if not formally then at least in fact, and while Ben Aranath was not Sordani territory, it stood on the border. Hans could hardly leave Arne alone and without means among enemies. They might well be *his* enemies too. So far, he had not heard Essera or any country known to him even mentioned. Chances were good most people along the way weren't going to be happy when they found out who Hans actually was. It might not be so bad to have someone else to fall back on, even if that someone was a Kheld who might attract more trouble than he ever got Hans out of.

"All right, you can come with me, if you want to," Hans said to the hopeful Arne. "But I really did spend all but my last few coins to buy you. That was supposed to be my passage money. Now it looks as though we will have to work our passage to Sordan."

Dismay flooded Arne's features. "Sordan! No Kheld living's ever been to Sordan! At least, none that's ever come back to tell about it. I just ran the hell away so I wouldn't have to go there!"

But Hans was in no mood for argument. "That's where I'm going, Arne. I already told you, you don't have to go with me."

For a long minute Hans thought that Arne might, after all, refuse to go with him. But at last the young man threw up his hands. "That's it, then, if that's where you're going," he consented unhappily. "I don't have no place telling you what to do or where to go. But Sordan ain't no place for Kheldsmen."

"Neither is Ben Aranath," Hans reminded him. "Sometimes we go where we have to."

"But why Sordan? Or ain't I supposed to ask?"

Hans sighed. "You can ask. But I'm not sure I can explain it. Maybe you should just trust me for now."

"I reckon I got no choice."

A party of loud-mouthed sailors strolled past, moving Hans and Arne both to silence.

It was well into evening before Hans turned up a barge that

would let them work their passage, signing them up for loading in the morning. It was dirty work, transporting valuable salt, hard labor because the salt permeated everything. Ezhno the shipmaster, an Estol out of Sordan, had merely looked them over and lamented the quality of that year's pilgrims. As he was in a hurry to be home in time for the Coming himself, he had taken them on.

Spending the few silver coins left in his purse, Hans bought two meals at a cheap tavern that Ezhno had recommended. The place was hardly more than a few planks and a firepot, but the food was clean and plentiful, and the owner gave them soap and water to wash with in return for sweeping up after. They chose the table farthest from the door, in a corner removed from the worst of the traffic. Arne hauled a small packet from under his oversized tunic.

"It's food," he offered, looking chagrined. "I took it before I ran off. Wouldn't you know I never was a thief in my life before this?" Wrapped in the cloth was a hunk of hard cheese and a short knife with a nicked blade. Arne picked up the latter and looked at Hans asking if it would be all right to keep it.

Not willing to sort out the morality of it all, Hans gave Arne his blessing. "You might need it, I suppose." Everyone else Hans had met on the road or along the river carried a blade of some sort, as much for slicing fruit or meat, or cutting rope or leather, as for use as a weapon.

The food was warm and filling, and Hans kept the conversation away from Sordan. Much as he already liked Arne, and glad as he was for the companionship, he felt uncomfortable with laying out his real reasons for going to the island City. It was safer and easier to travel in secret, protected from questions by a layer of imposed ignorance. So they talked at length about Amallar and Essera, carefully avoiding any place names that might enable a listener to pinpoint what they were discussing. They disguised their conversation to sound as if they talked about Essera alone. Hans was not surprised to hear that the Khelds were restless.

"I've been gone a year in all," Arne sighed. "It's probably worse now. I heard that the king died, that they got Stefan. Always knew the Sordaneon would try it." He looked up beneath his shaggy hair to see what Hans thought. But Hans was not about to voice an opinion of any kind on that subject, which sat too close to home. He could see in the Kheld's bright gaze that devotion to Stefan ran deep, however, and so too the grief of losing him. "There ain't much chance of a Kheld king now, I don't reckon. The Staubauns will see to that." Arne's light voice was soft with anger. "Stefan had a brother, though, and he's the true king. We won't support no other—and the Sordaneon can rot on his island."

As he sat in a smoke-filled, noisy tavern on a waterfront crowded with pilgrims heading to Sordan, Hans was finding it more and more difficult to convince himself of the necessity of going there. The picture of Amallar that Arne painted was endlessly more appealing. He would be closer to Essera. If Arne was any indication, Hans could gather support there, set up some kind of grassroots movement, get things going.

But Marenthro had warned against such thinking. *You and your Khelds would fight for your lives to the ends of your days.* For a moment Hans sensed that fate, of being trapped in Amallar, struggling and never succeeding at getting any Staubaun land to believe in him. *If the world is to change, it needs something new that was not here before. My going to Amallar now would just be the same old thing, no different from Stefan.* During his journey so far, Hans had learned enough about Sordan to know some people, at least, regarded it as the last bastion of something great in the world. As for Dorilian.... Arne hated him, the Khelds despised him—their conversation so far made it abundantly clear that both blamed "The Sordaneon" for Stefan's death and the war in Neuberland. Yet Marenthro had called Dorilian the ally Hans must have above all others.

The last of the Highborn princes, the holy blood of the Triempery. Is that what matters? Or is it that he tried to save Marc Frederick? Hans felt a pang as he remembered his grandfather's scorched visage, his blazing blue eyes, the plea in his gaze.

Marc Frederick had trusted Dorilian, made him promise to finish... what? Something important. The Rill maybe, though Hans barely knew what that was.

What is the Rill? he wanted to ask people. *Tell me about the Rill....*

Seeing the uncertainty in Hans's face, Arne ventured hopefully, "You know, we could still—"

"Cut it out, will you?"

After eating, they wandered back to the salt barge, where the master gave them a tarp and a mat and pointed to a corner between some bales where they might sleep.

12

With his omnificence, Derlon bestowed upon the
Rill his own abilities to regenerate and heal. After
completing his body's transformation of the Aryati
mekhos that ordered the machine and learning how
to utilize core energy from the Permephedon and
Sordan arrays, Derlon's priority was
reconstruction of the primary corridor.
—Deben III Sordaneon, *Life of Derlon*

There was no need to row. A strong spring wind had swelled
and the master ordered sails hoisted on the barge's two
sturdy masts. By the grace of Leur, a god known to favor
Sordan, winds commonly rose from the west. It also favored them
that the Sorand'ruil was a sluggish river with very little drop in
elevation between Sarkuan and the sea—indeed, salt water often
flowed upstream as far inland as Renet—so that the river gave way
easily, allowing them to glide inland to Sordan's heart.

But if travel was easy, the work was hard. The salt had no mercy.
By afternoon Hans and Arne's eyes were red and tearing, and even
the cotton kerchiefs they wore over their faces did not prevent
them from breathing in enough salt dust to set them to coughing
their lungs raw. Dern and Terk, the two regular barge hands, jibed
at them for their weakness—though they did give Arne an old pair
of too-big sandals so he would not be barefoot.

"Wear yer masks double next time if yer smart," Terk said only
after all was done. "An' don't salt yer damn food for two weeks or
yer'll be sicker'n an Ardaenan cat."

When not manning oars, Hans and Arne joined the crew in stitching sacks, scraping rot or rust, replacing nails, and scrubbing down the bargemaster's small cabin at the rear. There was never much idle talk, but an easy camaraderie with the crew developed, and Arne quickly picked up more words in Stauba. Of course the dialect spoken on the barge was Sordani, heavily flavored with Lahgaelan and Trongorian idioms, and Arne soon sported a colorful vocabulary. He sounded like a deckhand, but he was communicating in a language he had never thought to learn.

The best times were when daylight died and evening set both sky and river aflame with red-streaked clouds, the winds rising again with the coming of night. Before sleeping, the crew would gather on deck around a brass brazier, its pyramid of hot coals glowing, to eat their evening meal. Poor as it was—hard flat bread and skewers of olives and meat, with warm Sordani beer to wash it down—the food was a feast to hard-worked men.

This night was no different. The food was no better, the work no less hard. But there was anticipation in the air, a sense of something drawing near. They were four days out of Ben Aranath and drawing near their destination. Arne and Hans, exhausted, rested against the heavy, tarp-covered salt sacks and listened to the rivermen talk of reaching port with the hope of being on time for the festivities of Coming.

"Lights the World like the sun, she does, and at night Leur's Citadel is brighter than the moon," said Terk, speaking of Sordan. The faces of Ezhno and the barge crew shone with the reflected light of men proud of the land from which they hailed. Natives or not of the island City, they stood taller because of her.

Dern owned a gitar, a homely instrument with a cracked neck that would not stay tuned, but he counted it as his most prized possession. While Terk talked, Dern strummed chords and some snatches of tune, searching for one that would bring forth a song. Terk laughed and pounded his feet upon the hollow planking, his hand slapping the lid of the fresh water keg every time the gitar slid into a melody. The songs of the plains were sharply melodious, defiant, and soaring. The words moved. River songs flowed like the waters that had shaped them.

"What are they singing now?" Arne asked about a song that had the men laughing.

"It's… a bawdy song," Hans explained, knowing no better way to say it and using a Kheldish word he hoped conveyed the proper meaning.

Arne lifted his head to pay closer attention. "It is? What about?"

"You know, it's… well, bawdy." To his own delight, Hans found that he could understand the words and he laughed along with the others, while Arne tried gamely to follow.

That song ended and the laughter died. For a long while there was silence. Then Dern slapped his instrument and broke out in a new song that brought immediate approval from Terk, who picked up the rhythm and added his voice to that of the bargemaster.

…Go on then, live in your cold mountains!
One day you will long for the warm winds of Teremar…

It was a lovely melody, Hans thought, with a breadth like that of the lands it evoked. What about it, then, made him uneasy? He paid closer attention to the lyrics, knowing the song to be not of Essera's north, but of the south, of Sordan.

…Fools, you think we have forgotten,
We who you have begotten will someday claim our own.

He realized, then, what it was. It was a song of defiance against Esseran rulers. Hans felt a chill go down his spine at something he had never stopped to consider: Sordan might have reasons of its own for hating Essera and Amallar—and him. That Dorilian might not welcome him was worry enough, but he had never sought to understand why.

Abruptly, Hans recalled where he was—he walked, however concealed and anonymous, among potential enemies. No, he reminded himself sharply, these men were not his enemies, although they might think him theirs if ever they learned his name. One look at Arne's blank face, distorted by the brazier's ruddy light, let Hans know how close that fear was to truth. The bargemen were like Arne; their hatreds simple and close to the skin, enmities learned at the knees of bitter parents. They had never met a Kheldman that they knew of, yet they shied from Hans's and Arne's blue eyes, seeing in their azure gazes some taint of a threat they barely understood.

Essera had lost its hold over this land long ago. It was Sordan that moved them: their songs and their hearts, their tales and their laughter, their blood and their sinew born upon this great desert river beneath this southern sun.

Hans leaned back against the side of the barge. The music wove its chorded spell amongst reedy tunes played by the marsh grasses lining the Sorand'ruil. Tonight maybe, or tomorrow, they would enter the vast inland sea of fresh water that was Sarkuan, and still they would be a day's journey from Sordan. How vast was Sarkuan, Hans wondered, that it could be the source of a river as great and wide as the Sorand'ruil, great enough to keep Sordan free from attack by all but a seafaring nation? No enemy fleet would ever make its way up the Sorand'ruil without incurring heavy losses, and Sordan surely had some way to block the river in such an event. A fortress—in every sense of the word.

What would he find when he reached the City of the Sordaneons? The haunting tunes teased him with verses he, as a stranger to this world, could not fully grasp.

> *…Tall lady, Highborn sister,*
> *Arya's daughter of old,*
> *Upon your stones there linger yet*
> *a thousand tales untold!*
> *Kneeling in Forever's waters,*
> *your mystery to behold…*

"There now's the holiest spot in the Creation," Ezhno intoned when the song died away. It was the last they would sing that night. He proceeded to tell how he would celebrate First Day, and Second Day as well. First Day was for feasting, from what Hans could gather, and Second Day was for revels—and a darn good excuse for the rite of drunkenness. Third Day, the first day of the new year, was a day of grace.

"Those who believe in magic climb to the mountaintop." Dern smirked. "The rest of us mere mortals sleep it off!"

"Those what climb to the mountaintop get to see the High Folk," grumbled Terk. He was a full believer in the Malyrdean mythos. "The rest of yer, the unbelievers, belong in the gutter where yer lie."

"'Tis true," said Ezhno. "It is a holy rite and not to be made little of."

"Highborn glitter," said Dern. Beer, in him, prompted mild blasphemies. "Right up there with talking fishes."

Terk had his own take on that. "What can open mountains, glitter or no glitter, ought to be worshipped."

"And next tell me the Rill once walked the World as a man."

"Mind of the god—"

"Enough now!" Ezhno admonished the two men. He drew a deep draught on his pipe. When he exhaled, a long trail of bluish smoke drifted downstream. "I traveled on ship with a Highborn prince once," he said. "The Bas of Teremar that was, the Thrice Royal Sebbord. Was his own flagship and I one of the crew. He stayed top deck all night while a storm raged across the Kolpos over the City of the Dead. You know the like, one of those storms a sailor fears in his very bones, caught between wind and wave and the rocks the sea throws up to snatch the wicked. All our lanterns blew out in the rain and the wind, so he made light for us in his hand. And when all was done, he lit the fires again with but a touch. We lost not a plank that night, nary a spar cracked or cringle torn, and the masts were as tall and straight as you please. They say he held the ship together, that Highborn prince."

Terk nodded as if a point had been made. Dern leaned back over the rail and tossed the remnants of his drink overboard. "That may be, and stranger things have happened," he conceded. "I'd be the last man to deny that the Highborn are of godsblood."

"Our own Hierarch is such," Ezhno agreed. "If he would will it, the Rill itself would answer his whim."

"That he might clothe himself in glory, as his forefathers before him!" Terk pronounced.

Dern grunted. "I'll be happy if he just keeps as he's been doing. He needs neither Rill nor glory to toss Essera on its ear and Mormantalorus back into the sea."

"The northers don't bother us these days, true." By the look on Ezhno's face, there had been a time he would have said differently. "Not since the Hierarch took the throne. We can consider ourselves blessed. Leur has favored us with rulers above those of other lands."

Dern nodded. "Look what happened north. Turned from Leur, they did, from Permephedon and the Wall, and saw their Highborn princes all dead or killed off, and the kingdom falling to Khelds and pieces." There were general nods and grunts of agreement.

Hans kept his eyes and ears trained on the men, attending every word. Beside him, Arne's body had grown tense.

"That damn lot can go the way Stefan did, that Highborn killer—all twelve curses be on him!" Terk spat.

Highborn killer? Stefan? Hans knew nearly nothing about his brother's troubled reign. A glance at Arne's closed face showed only that it had darkened. The Kheld cared enough for his life—both their lives—not to speak up. But if he did, what would Arne have said?

Another barge drifted past on its leisurely way downstream, silent because its rowers slumbered, unneeded, bright fireflies of lanterns lining the rails in warning. Several men huddled around that vessel's brazier, bathed in a warm orange glow, looking much, Hans knew, as he and his companions must look themselves, a ghostly ship bearing a low point of light on an empty, night-dark river.

"That's all underwater. Stefan is dead and the Khelds might as well be." Dern lifted his blond head to stare after Terk, who loomed sullenly nearby. "Sordan is still far away, Terk-boy," he jibed. "You won't see your Shining Lady tonight."

Terk scowled, his rough features chiseled by the lantern light. "I know. Just a horizon glow would lighten my soul though, it would be so like the sunrise. I want to see Sordan standing bold as yer please, looking like she'll stand forever. Ruled as is right by a prince of sacred blood."

"It's the Hierarch, Dorilian, you're talking about, right?" Hans seized the opening and a chance to glean something useful. Though Arne's face tightened, he wisely said nothing.

"It must be so," Ezhno granted. "That's all the Highborn blood left in this world, Sordan's own. And there's no denying *he's* Highborn, bred and true. Look into his eyes, folk say, and you see the Mind of Leur looking back. The World Itself. The Highborn cannot go mad, cannot forget, cannot believe a lie. If they did, so would the World."

"Leur save him," said Terk as a refrain.

Hans looked over the side, at the sleek, black river with its shadowlands that passed by in the night, knowing where it took him but not what it took him toward. "I was wondering what he's like, as a person, that's all."

Ezhno sighed. "That's beyond me, lad, or any man to tell you. Only the highest ever get to see him face to face. The days are long past when the Highborn walked abroad in the world like other men, sure they would come to no harm. From what I hear, he goes forth not at all unless accompanied by a guard of hundreds and with the streets emptied ahead of him. It's not likely any of us would ever so much as brush his shadow with the likes of ours."

"He's unapproachable?" Hans felt his hope fade. How would he ever meet with Dorilian if the man was always surrounded by guards?

"Might as well be, for the likes of us." Dern laughed. His teeth flashed in the dark. "Just as well, from what I hear. Stefan put ice in his heart. The Thrice Royal kills men soon as look at them. A thousand in one night, he did, the day he gained his throne. Folk take their own lives rather than face his wrath. But Sordan hasn't suffered by it. The Rill gives him wealth without end, and the City through him. He's kept Sordan strong. If the rest of the Triempery falls apart, then to Gsch with it."

Gsch, the World of Fire. The End of the World, always and forever burning just on the other side of this fragile plane.

"And the Highborn will keep you from Gsch?" Hans asked.

"From ruin?" Ezhno asked. "Maybe not. But the godborn alone can keep the World from Fire."

13

One of the most pervasive and least understood of Highborn gifts is the stabilization of reality. The Highborn perceive the World through others nearly as powerfully as through themselves. During the first millennium following the Return, societies that were Highborn-ruled exhibited a strong sense of identity and a deep habit of consensus with their rulers. This consensus fragmented when the Highborn became increasingly isolated by the aristocracy they had themselves created—the world the rulers perceived less and less resembled the one beyond their palaces.

—ZAMENES,
CIBULITUS AND THE FIRST TRIEMPERATE

He stood upon a high place surrounded by water, the world to one side of him and to the other, spires and rings of light. Night jasmine laced the air he breathed, potently fragrant. He reached his hand into the fading night and plucked a leaf from one of the branches that etched its shape against a troubled sky. Casually, he broke off a piece of the world. Someone addressed him from behind, a young voice breaking the silence.

"What in this darkness keeps you from sleep?"

And he heard his own voice answer across a great distance, "There's something coming."

Something coming.

Hans struggled awake. He thought he smelled night jasmine still, but there was no tree. And he was not standing but lying on a pile of old sacks. Becoming aware of his surroundings, he pushed his way out of the dream and looked up at the flapping of a tarp over his head. Rain poured down in sheets of gray just beyond the edge of his shelter and cascaded in waterfalls. Wind whipped across the deck and waves loudly slapped against the sides of the barge. The floral scent had vanished, replaced by the smell of unwashed bodies. Taking care not to awaken Arne, Hans eased himself from the makeshift bed.

Something coming.

Reaching the side of the barge, Hans stood staring into the maelstrom blackness of night, rain pelting his skin, his eyes, running from his flattened hair. Something coming. He sensed it, bearing down on him, just on the other side of the slashing curtain of rain and night.

Something... but what?

His ears picked up the first and only warning, a change in the tone of the rainfall, waves breaking against wood, wind cracking sail. Sail... a ship. A damn galley. Before his eyes, the dark shape of it emerged from blackness, wind driving it hard toward them, sails clinging like tormented wraiths to towering masts. Lanterns swung from its rail, making wild orange circles against the night. Lanterns! What had happened to their lanterns? Hans scrambled forward to the prow of the barge, only to find it dark, its warning lights doused by drenching rain. Terk lay slumped in the cramped shelter of some nearby bales.

"Terk!" Hans shouted, shaking the man, dragging him out upon the deck. "Terk, wake up! Our lights are out—they can't see us!"

But the man simply rolled over, a drinking flask falling from his hand.

"Get up!" Hans shouted and kicked him. Looking over his shoulder, he saw the great ship still bearing down on them. He leaped towards the rail.

"Ahoy!" he shouted, waving his arms. "Stop! Turn! Turn!"

Voices, thin and high, answered above the sounds of storm and crashing waves, telling him that the barge had been spotted. Still, even knowing the barge was there, the galley's crew could not control the storm-tossed ship. They were just as much at the mercy of the wind and waves as was the barge. The great bow rose, caught by a mighty swell, and plunged down again into the trough, sending a spray of water across the barge, driving Hans to his knees upon the deck.

As if from very far away, Hans heard the cries of his shipmates. Ezhno had awakened. Somewhere, Arne was screaming Hans's name into the wind. Hans could see only the galley, feel only the galley—waves and wind, a war between heaven and water. The larger vessel's heavy shape towered above the tiny barge and those upon it, blotting out even the tempest with blackness. If they collided the barge would break apart.

No. Not like this!

This wasn't Nammuor, not intelligent, not the enemy. It was a sudden, capricious storm.

"Stop!" He shouted at the black thing bearing down upon them. "Turn, you bastard! Turn!"

From out of the roiling heart of the storm, the winds shifted, sudden and cold. The barge swung violently against the hull of the galley. The impact threw Hans across the deck, against the side, as the barge, carried by galley and wave alike, swamped with water. Arms clasped his shoulders, and he found himself in Arne's desperate grasp. Ezhno and Dern were manning stout poles, driving these against the other ship's ribbed side, pushing with all their might. Men on the galley were doing the same.

Hans leaped to join Dern, putting all his strength into the pole. Arne did the same with Ezhno, giving his all. The gap between the vessels grew, then grew again. The larger vessel slid past them into the night.

Hans released the pole and dropped to the deck. His limbs trembled, suddenly weak. Black water still swamped the deck and wind still drove rain into their faces.

"We turned, or she did," Ezhno said.

"The poles." Hans pointed to the stout lengths of wood resting against the racks.

"We barely scraped past." Water ran down Ezhno's face as he stared at Hans. "If you had not awakened us in time, or we hadn't come up along her side… I don't know the Devastation how, but we made our way clear."

"I was praying for that."

Ezhno's tight smile hardened. "I would like to meet your god."

Wind snatched at the tarp, and the barge groaned beneath a sudden wave that washed the decks, drenching Hans as he struggled to his feet. The rain came again in sheets, stronger than before.

"God or no god, this storm heeds no master," Ezhno shouted. "Get you to cover, lad, you've done your night's work. The lads will bail and I'll stand watch over the beacon. It'll be over by morning. With luck on the morrow we may yet reach Sordan before the Coming."

Later, after bailing and in the damp confines of the make-do shelter they shared, Arne wrapped a blanket around Hans's shoulders. Now that it was over, they were both bone-tired and shivering in wet clothes.

"Nothing to change into, neither," Arne complained. "Just these rags and not much else."

Hans didn't care. He stretched out on a pile of old sacks that served as a mattress, his wet hair sopping the coarse fabric. Overhead, rain drummed on the tarp. It was very easy to fall asleep.

The waves woke him, rapping the sides of the barge with gentle rebuke. Gulls screamed overhead. Hans shook himself awake and cleared from his mind the remnants of a night spent in fitful dreams. The storm had passed and given way to another dawn. Pulling on the tunic Arne had been so insistent he remove the night before and that had dried only a little, Hans made his way to the front of the barge and stared in dismay at the flat, wavering horizon. No sign of land, not so much as a smudge. Somehow, through the night and the dreams, he had been sure he would see Sordan in the morning.

"We're in for it now, you know." Arne flopped down on the neighboring bale. "There sure ain't nowhere to go."

Hans looked around at the vast lake. All about them was a wide expanse of water as unending as the Sansordan plain. "Not unless you want to swim for it," he conceded.

"Can't swim. Don't have to, where I come from. And don't have to now, I reckon."

"No. We'll be in Sordan soon, before the day is out. I can feel it."

"So can I, like death at the door, you know."

Dern, testing the tarps for storm damage, eyed them scornfully. "You got out of bed a half day too early for seeing the sight. Won't spy the island until the sun sends our shadows on ahead to greet it. Take all day, and maybe then some. This is the biggest lake in the world, not some lord-fancy lily pond—good thing that storm dumped us a good half day east of where we would have been."

East... closer to their destination.

The breakfast was spare but their mood buoyant as Dern and the normally taciturn Terk, humbled by his lapse of the night before but glad to see the voyage end, openly anticipated reaching Sordan. Bowls of coarse tasty porridge chased the morning chill, and they downed cups of warm beer before setting to the day's work. The storm's violence had left behind torn tarps and broken boards. Even so, cool lake winds out of the west filled the sail and flapped lines strung with an assortment of finery being aired in anticipation of going ashore. Feeling that they might as well do the same, Hans and Arne also strung up their washed garments—plain dark tunics and mended trousers, as homely as they were functional. These evoked snorts from Dern and Terk, whose brightly colored hose and quilted tunics gleamed of silk and brass buttons and danced a far merrier jig on the wind-tossed lines.

"The port master might not let yer in, boys," Terk ribbed. He sat cross-legged on the deck, stitching tarp. "Look damn poverty-ridden yer will, dressed in those rags."

"Probably best that way." Hans was resigned to his meager possessions. His lost backpack had included a nice belt with a sun buckle, at least. He hammered a hinge that had bent, forcing it flat again. "Who knows—maybe they'll feel sorry for us."

"Not sorry enough to let you in wearing those! Look like yer going to a wake," Terk snorted. "What kind'er pilgrims are yer, anyway, to go like that into the Presence?"

"Aw, the damn Hierarch ain't going to see them—not himself, anyway—so what's to worry about?" Dern grumbled. "Ain't likely the Thrice Royal's going to see you, either, and you'll be dressed to humble a lord."

"But look at 'em, filthy as goats! That ain't respectful. Pilgrims ought at least to be clean for the holy days." Terk looped another stitch onto the edge of his tarp. Then he brightened and turned to

Hans and Arne, saying, "There's a bathhouse I know. Yer can do it proper there. Water's from a spring, out of the island. Damn near holy, that water, not like those what use the common beach. Lake water comes from Suddekar and Pessach and Leur knows what awful places or bodies soaked in it. Do it right, though it costs a shaved silver."

Hans shook his head. "No money."

"Too bad. Yer won't get as clean at the beach. Yer'll stink of fish."

"He's a pilgrim, ain't he?" Dern laughed. "Most pilgrims smell like fish—or worse."

"He looks a cut better, that's all. Why, he even got him a servant, looks like." Terk pointed to Arne. "Follows him like a dog, that one does."

"Just want to make sure he don't get hurt," Arne spoke up, glaring. He bent again over the broken hatch edge he was sanding down with a pumice stone.

"You're more like to get him hurt than not," said Dern. "'Less you keep your eyes down and your mouth shut. Look like a thrice-cursed Kheld, you do. You dirt-footed Trongorians breed with most anything these days, seems like."

"You can cut that out." Ezhno had come out of his cabin. "We're born what we are, that's a fact. And there's no changing it."

Terk snorted. "World's getting stirred up so yer don't know what's where no more. Even Staubauns don't keep to their own the way they did. Not like Mormantalorus, where I hear tell they keep the blood true. Make sure their pure women get a Staubaun man to seed them."

"Sounds like a fine bit of cock-lore to me," said Dern.

"Cock-lore or not, they're starting it in the northlands too, up Aral way. Man at Ben Aranath said it was so. He came off a trader from Merced. Said the Mormantalorans boasted they only sleep with gold-haired women, keep the blood up. Not like we do. Hell, even our Hierarch has foreign blood."

"'Cuz of the Wall Lords and what they did to his line." Dern scowled to display his disgust. "Those damn norther lords think the world is a brothel stocked for their pleasure, leaving bastards like there weren't nothin' to it. Them and the Trongorians, breeding like barn cats. Hell, even the stinking Khelds stick tighter than they do."

"Trongorians ain't so bad," said Terk. He glanced doubtfully at Hans and Arne, looking for signs that they were taking offense.

"That's decent country," said Ezhno. He turned to Hans. "Have you a place to go in Sordan? If not, I could recommend a woman who might give you a room on hearing my name."

"Thank you," said Hans. "But I have… people there, who I hope will take me in. We'll manage all right."

Terk nodded his approval. "Hope yer right. They're sleeping on doorsteps, the pilgrims are, this time of year. Go out at night, yer got to walk around them and their messes."

To which Dern added, "Unless, of course, you don't care to bother. Then you work up a chorus all up and down the street." Terk guffawed loudly, and even Ezhno chuckled his understanding of the annual nuisance.

With Arne squatting at his side, Hans watched fretfully as the sun climbed to noon. They had made the needed repairs and there was enough of a wind to fill the sails. Far away, but often, they saw the shapes of other ships or barges that traveled as they did toward a point none of them could yet see on the horizon. The sun glinted on the water, white as diamonds. Hans squinted and rubbed at his eyes.

"Go blind, you will," a voice spoke beside his ear.

Hans jumped. He had not heard the bargemaster's approach. "I was just looking."

Ezhno merely nodded. He understood, of course, having ferried a few pilgrims in his day. "Well, I can't let you go on staring at this vacant lake and sky, the sun so bright and all this water. Sordan, now, is worth a look, but she shouldn't cost your eyes. Come into my quarters—yes, and your friend too—and we'll share a jug of wine."

The bargemaster's cabin was toward the stern, just fore of the rudder deck. Two deep plank steps led down from the main deck into a spare but uncluttered space with good light and air. Three windows provided good views of Ezhno's domain, and the master himself took the single chair. Since there was no other furniture than a table and rack of charts to be had, Hans sat on the unmade cot and Arne on the floor. Relieved of the overwhelming urge to watch the horizon, they watched instead as Ezhno took up an earthen crock and poured cups of clear red liquid.

"Drink it slow now," he directed. He handed each a crude

pewter goblet half-filled with ruby nectar. "This is real Teremar wine, not that poison other people drink when they don't know any better." He lifted his cup. "To Leur," he said, "and to the Three, and to Sordan that renews the World."

They drank. Then, holding out the jug, Ezhno turned to Hans. "Will you honor your god? It seems last night he was quick to grant you favors."

Hans gave a gentle shake of his head. "That was simply blind luck, bargemaster, and little enough to do with gods."

"That's no way to honor the wine. Come, lad, salute—and let it be to something worthy."

Hans hesitated, then said, "To Permephedon, then—where the sleeping god lies."

Satisfied, Ezhno nodded, though he wore a stunned stare. "Now that's deep, it truly is. And northern talk if ever I heard it. But no harm to the wine." He drank to Hans's declaration as solemnly as to his own.

Hand shaking, Hans set his cup down. That last bit, about the sleeping god, had leaped to his tongue without warning, a forgotten fragment of some childhood memory. *Five Cities did the Leur folk raise, One of Sun and One of Moon...*

"I'm not much for the legend, myself," Ezhno said. He set his own cup to one side. "I prefer living gods to sleeping ones; find them easier to believe in. The godborn, you know—there's no telling what form Leur will take with them." He leaned back in his chair. "But you can't evoke that god and be false, that I know. Tell me the truth now, why a pair of Kheld folk would travel to the City of the Sordaneons."

Hans froze, staring. Arne, sitting on the floor beside him, barely breathed.

"You're mistaken, bargemaster," Hans said. "My companion and I—"

"Now lad, hear me out. I've been north in my day—north and more! I know Kheldish blood when I see it, and the both of you got the taint. You can't fool an old seaman like me the way you can these river folks what never got north of the Telarkans. It's not just the eyes, lad, that give you away, or the beard on his jaw. It's the shape of the face and, for him especially, all that curl in his hair."

"But I had my face, and he had his hair, when you took us on in Ben Aranath."

"Aye, you did, and I fooled myself into thinking you must be Trongorian, the way most blue-eyes are in these parts, until I got to noticing things. But then I said to myself, Ezhno, they're honest with their work, and there's no Kheld in the world would go to Sordan unless there were good reason for it." The bargemaster drained his cup of wine, then frowned into it. "Last night you proved your mettle, lad, and saved this crew, and my barge and cargo too. I won't forget it. I owe your god a service. But I wonder what your purposes be. And I wonder if I'm doing you a favor to bring you to Sordan. That is not a City to welcome your kind. The Hierarch himself is set against you." Ezhno looked Hans in the eye. "And the Kheld folk are set against him."

"Not this time," Hans said. "Not me." His hand strayed to the pocket he had sewn into his tunic. "I must go to Sordan, captain. You don't know how important it is."

"That would be true. So tell me."

"I have this." Hans drew out the medallion Thaa had given him. The oval glowed warm and brilliant in his hand, then the colors faded when he placed it onto the wooden tabletop in front of him. "Will this serve as an answer?"

Ezhno stared at it, his face and his eyes as still as stone. He did not move to touch the thing.

"It's a *deiknya*," Hans explained.

"The Sword is Permephedon's sign—I have seen the mark. Holy, it is, and rare. But never have I seen one of these, though I have heard of such. They are said to be tokens of the High Citadel. Pick it up, lad," he ordered, not taking his eyes from the *deiknya*. "Pick it up again!"

Hans did so, the colors warming again to his touch.

"So it *is* yours," Ezhno acknowledged and raised his face in wonder. "Though I know not what it tells, I can see it bears Essera's seal and Permephedon's mark. Did you get it, as the high lords do, from the hand of the Unchanging One who dwells there?"

"It was Marenthro himself who told me to go to Sordan," Hans admitted. At his side, Arne gaped and let the cup tip in his hand, though he recovered before spilling his wine upon the floor.

Ezhno, too, looked amazed. "Has the Unchanging taken side with the Kheld folk, then?"

Sensing the fear behind the question, Hans moved to dispel it.

"No, nothing like that. I don't represent anyone—no purpose but my own."

"And yet here you go to Sordan on a mission blessed by the Unchanging? That's holy work." The bargemaster clearly pondered what that might mean.

Afraid that he might still say something amiss, Hans couldn't look at Arne, though he could feel the young Kheld's stare of stark disbelief. Marenthro was something of a legend among Khelds and Staubauns alike.

"But why the river?" Ezhno persisted. "If you have Permephedon's favor and blessing, why not take the Rill? Or is that because of your Kheldish blood?"

The Rill. Everywhere Hans turned, he seemed destined to dance around it. "I started west of here. The Rill was too far away." That, at least, he knew would be true.

"But you had to come to Sordan, eh? No place else would do. Who are you, that the Unchanging would give you a thing like that? Or send you with your Kheldish eyes to the stronghold of their mortal enemy?"

Who was Hans indeed; a forgotten prince more afraid than sure of what he would find, who had come to Sordan only because he had nowhere else to go? What might this stalwart bargeman—or Arne, for that matter—think of him if he told them that?

"Does it matter who I am?" Hans asked the question softly. "It seems to me the less I say, the better. But Marenthro sent me to find the Sordaneon prince, Dorilian. To speak with him, to—"

"The Hierarch?" Ezhno's amazement, already high, rose further. "His is the last blood on earth that would welcome yours!"

"That may be true. However, he is the man I must find, if he will see me, with my Kheldish eyes and blood. If he will listen to what I have to say." Hans unfolded his hand and wondered at the *deiknya's* vivid colors and design. He was vaguely aware of Arne sitting on the floor, stunned into silence. "I have to talk to him. About so much."

Across the table Ezhno studied Hans like a man transfixed. He too seemed unable to look away from the medallion that blossomed like a flower cupped in Hans's hand. The mark of Permephedon, the High Citadel of the World, the last bastion of Leur, save one.

"Here," offered Hans, extending the *deiknya.* "You can hold it, if you'd like, to see that it's real."

Ezhno waved it back, alarmed. "I'll have no traffic with the Unchanging One's work," he said, "but I know its worth. And I know one thing more: what happened last night was your fate at work, or maybe the Unchanging works through you. You are meant to go to Sordan—and to the Hierarch himself, if that's where you're bound. I'll not stand in your way, or his, or that of the Unchanging. This is too great for me."

Nervously reaching into his coat, Ezhno brought out his pipe and rapped it on the table to clear out the residue of a previous smoke. "But what you're trying to do—if it's what I think you're trying to do—well, I'm an old man, and I've lived long enough now to see the worth of it. I have been to Essera, which is more than most in these lands can say. I remember the days of the Wall Lords, when the world moved with more mystery. That doesn't change the fact that Kheld blood isn't welcome in these parts—not in Sordan, where that breed are held as Highborn killers."

Hans returned the *deiknya* to his pocket. "That's a chance I'll have to take, because Sordan is where I must go."

Ezhno nodded and turned to Arne. "And you, lad, what have you to say?"

"I'm with him," Arne said doggedly, though he looked scared to death.

Hans and Arne emerged from Ezhno's quarters into afternoon's cool shadow, onto the deck and a world where water no longer reigned supreme. An island of silver rock rose from the blue lake ahead of them like some ancient stairway to the clouds, vast terraces of greenery and stone, cradling a great natural harbor between mighty arms. And upon that island was a City.

Sordan.

A city built not by men, but gods. The great sky towers of a white citadel vied with the mountain for dominance, a lofty diadem of battlement upon splendid battlement, fortifications high and far-seeing. Even from far away, across the water, those towers looked formidable. They also looked new and unworn, monuments to another time when men had set their mortal sights on the stars and set forth to conquer them. In that moment, Hans understood what his shipmates had been saying, how this unassailable citadel uplifted the hearts and souls of those who lived there and drove despair as a bitter spike into the wills of those who would oppose them.

Even as Hans and Arne watched, an array of fantastic arches and spurs near the citadel's base *moved*, rings and arches rotating and extending to create a corridor. A flash of silver briefly sparkled in Sordan's heart and shot forth through that corridor at unbelievable speed, vanishing north across the dying void of afternoon.

Almost instantly upon the heels of that passage, another group of rings rearranged to capture a flash that appeared south of the city. The flash slowed, assuming a shape—long, sleek, and immense— that glided through the arches to vanish into the City's heart.

Arne gaped. "What *is* that?"

"The Rill." Hans had seen it before, in Essera, in a city he now knew had to have been Dazunor-Rannuli.

Hans had expected Sordan would be a great city, but great only against what he had seen along the river. Marenthro had warned him rightly against thinking too small. The shining towers of the world Hans had left behind were like mud huts next to this.

"They call Sordan proud, but Leur knows she has a right to it." Ezhno had joined them on the deck. No doubt he saw on their faces the awe of two thousand years of pilgrims. "Can you look upon her and tell me that the gods did not set first step upon this World at Sordan, or that Sordan stands other than at the center of this Creation?"

The barge slid past the towering lighthouses of the harbor entrance, joining other vessels large and small. Great metal-clad Sordani warships, tall and bare masted but ready, rode at anchor just inside the harbor entrance, reminders of a war against an enemy that had not yet penetrated this sea. But beyond the harbor's fortifications, within the vast harbor itself, congregated a flotilla of color and movement, the trading ships of the world come to this city, their brightly painted sides reflecting off the water. An Ardaenan ship, its masts even at half sail effortlessly pulling its massive hull, glided past, its bronze-tipped spars glinting like spears against the dying sun. The crew, intent only on getting the great ship to harbor, paid scant attention to the barge that wobbled ponderously in their wake.

The sun had sunk into the western waters of Sarkuan and the harbor had already gone to shadow when the salt barge drew into a slip in the maze of piers and wharves hemming the port's southern end. Huge warehouses loomed, indifferent observers as Dern and Terk scrambled onto the wooden wharf and lashed the cumbersome vessel to two huge pilings that supported the platform solidly above the harbor waters. Heavy machinery, great constructions of steel and wood, sat idle in the open spaces, some seemingly arrested in the motions of their trade. Although the port still teemed with activity and life, it was slowing down for the night. A tall man wearing a meticulously pleated mantle over his tunic met the barge as its crew prepared to disembark.

"You're late," he admonished Ezhno crisply.

"Short-crewed. Two of my men made shore at Ben Aranath," Ezhno said. He gestured offhandedly at Hans and his companion, who had caught the man's eye. "Brought on these pilgrims, though."

"Ben Aranath, you say?" the other remarked. "They don't look Lahgaelan to me."

"Don't suppose they are. But then, pilgrims come from all over. These said they came down Trongor way."

The man strained to see them through the gloom. "These don't look like the worst kind of pilgrims we have had crawl out of the lake this year. Seems every vessel that docks brings in another handful of wretches." The port man sighed, then went on heavily, reciting the rules of the City. "There will be no talk against the Hierarch or his kin. Should you find yourself in the Thrice Royal's presence, you are not to approach or speak to him in any familiar way—the penalty for such is flogging. The penalty for touching the Highborn without permission is death. There will be no doing what the body orders in public places. No fighting, no stealing, no killing, and no selling your bodies without license—do any of those things and the City Guard will slap you in chains for the trouble, if they do not take your heads off first. Understand? Good." He nodded to Ezhno. "I will consider you checked in—but sign your port papers before turning in that load."

As the official walked away, thoughtfully ruffling the barge's permits, Ezhno slapped Hans on the shoulder. "There you go, lad. It seems your god is still with you. He didn't quite catch you in the light. All set and get on with you. The dark hides many things but it won't make your way any easier to find. I've got to stay with the load, else I could guide you."

Hans watched as Arne climbed off the barge. He stayed back a moment longer. "I would like to thank you, bargemaster, for your help and your discretion."

"It's in the hands of Leur. I've done my part. But if ever you want to get off the island, or have to, you can find me. I have a house just uphill of the south wharf road. You'll know it by the green capstan."

"I wish I had some money, or something, to give you." Hans felt in his clothes, but all he had was his dagger and his empty purse—and the medal for Saint James. Gold over enamel, with dots of brilliant color, it was at least pretty. He cradled it in his fingers before extending it to Ezhno. Would Felicia mind? He didn't think so. "Take this," he said. "It is a token of protection."

Ezhno examined the piece, then shook his head. "You will need protection more than I. This is a symbol I dare not offend."

"It is?"

"A Highborn prince with a flaming sword? No symbol is more powerful than *that*."

Hans could hardly argue the difference between Highborn princes and a patron saint from one of the Creation's severed pasts. Not with this man. Dissatisfied by having nothing else to offer, he tucked the medal back into the pocket.

Ezhno chuckled and the aroma of pipe-scented breath filled the air. "You earned your passage, lad, and I'm not one to cheat an honest man. Go now, it's getting dark—and may Leur light the path before you."

14

The City of Sordan has never been invaded. No
fleet has been built that could storm such a
fortress. The only way to conquer Sordan was to
seize control of the Rill.
—Robdan Aelfricson,
The Stauberg-Randolph Succession

Hans and Arne left the barge under a growing veil of darkness. They aroused no attention as they walked past barges and other vessels and skirted numerous large warehouses. Many nations and peoples showed among the folk who crowded the busy docks: black-haired, gray-eyed Ardaenans in rich shore garb; brightly dressed Lahgaelans riding past on desert chargers they would sell after the Illumination; mixed-blood Trongorians, less splendid but more numerous, looking to reaffirm their faith. But overwhelming all of these in number were the native Staubaun-Estol race, tall men and women with fair hair and suntanned features and dark, haughty eyes who bent to each other to speak the clear, bright Stauba of the southern lands. Arne combed his hair down over his eyes and kept his head low as they left the harbor area and set out into the city.

"Marenthro!" Arne muttered as they followed a road that wound steadily uphill. "Nobody's seen him since the day the Wall princes died. So where'd he turn up with you?"

"Best he could get on short notice, I guess."

"You're not just some out-Kheld, are you?"

"No."

Arne gave Hans a sharp, sideways glance but didn't say anything more. They were surrounded by a thick and noisy crowd of travelers and pack animals as they made the tiresome trudge uphill, and it wasn't a fit time to talk. It was all they could do to stay out of the path of passing horses and the elegant conveyances of those who could afford such. Hans recognized at once the level of skillful engineering that had gone into making this road. There was artistry in its pavement and considerable skill in laying the evenly jointed blocks of stone, complete with grooves that offered traction for cart wheels and the metal shod hoofs of horses. Stately pillars bearing inscriptions and reliefs lined the way, topped by orbs that burned with clean, white light—chemical salts, not oil-soaked rags. Hans had reached a strikingly advanced level of civilization; maybe not quite the level he was accustomed to in the past he had recently left behind, but higher than he had imagined.

The harbor road led to a narrow plaza fronted by pillared buildings, from which streets diverged to other parts of the city. Hans stopped and pulled Arne with him into the shadow of an establishment roofed with beams and vines, just out of sight of seated patrons who quaffed wine at stone tables. The torches here were pitch and rag, and even the light was oily.

"I'm not quite sure where to go from here." Brighter lights lay ahead of them—and so did the luminescent spires of Sordan's soaring center. "I think we have to go there." Even without their otherworldly glow, the skytowers looked daunting.

"Why now?" Arne kept his voice low. "We can wait out the night, keep our ears open, get the goods on what's going on."

"Come on, let's go." Hans could not explain why he felt it was so important to see the Hierarch right away. Maybe it was the swirling confusion around him, the mad jumble of sights and sounds.

For the moment, it seemed best to follow the flow of pilgrims. The crowd poured onto a broad avenue lined by towering obelisks commemorating the noble founders of the city. The buildings on either side of the way became larger, more ornate, and more imposing. By the way people gathered on what looked like balconies or terraces, Hans guessed they were residences.

Before they had gone much farther, they heard shouts up ahead and the rumble of disruption. Night had finally fallen over the city, but beyond the dark silhouettes of the surrounding buildings spread a dull orange glow that could not be sunset. Above everything shone the amber-pearl arching structures of the Rill that loomed over the city like the bones of some exotic life-form.

The reddish glow flared, then spread. Sordan did not rest easy.

"The Dekkora!" someone shouted, and soon other voices shouted the same. "The Dekkora!"

Jumping down from the wall they had climbed to get a look, Hans and Arne joined the crush of bodies that pushed up the boulevard. Although he knew nothing of the city, Hans surmised that he had reached the Dekkora when the crowd abruptly let up and he and Arne found themselves in a vast, open plaza fronted by taller, grander buildings than any they had so far seen. A handful of fires burned in a maze of makeshift shops and booths that sprouted along the walls and the surging crowd seemed undecided as to whether it should flee or fight the flames. On the far side of the Dekkora, broad flights of steps ascended in a series of three landings, each lit by a floating orb of pure light. Splendid and perfect, the orbs looked for all the world like three moons.

Soldiers, some mounted, all uniformed and bearing steel, barred access to the landings.

As people dashed around him and Arne, Hans tried to gain some bearing. He was somewhere important, maybe the center of the City. Every building he looked up at was monumental and, behind what might be a temple at the top of the stairs, rose the Rill. It moved like something out of a dream, its majestic thrums heard even above the roar of the crowd. Taking Arne by the arm, Hans pointed to a reflecting pool bordered by a low wall.

"Over there."

Fire had spread among the stalls and tents near one of the grand pillared buildings and high flames licked at the edifice. In an effort to fight the fire, a line of people had formed to convey water from the pool. Other people screamed at them to stop.

"Holy!" they cried. "Sacred! Don't empty the Promise!"

What promise?

Bumped and buffeted, Hans kept his grip on Arne and soon they stood at the pool's edge, facing the towering statue at its center: a majestic human giant with sword in hand, saluting the City. They'd both heard Terk talk about this statue and its fountain, the three arcs of which splashed back into the pool. Amynas Malyrdys, the deified Father of the Three, whose City this was and who had founded the Triempery.

"It don't look real," said Arne. The statue, though perfectly representative of a human in every other way, had no face.

"I guess his face is a mystery because it belongs to his descendants," Hans said. At least one of whom ruled Sordan. New sounds of violence erupted from somewhere near the steps and they both turned to look in that direction.

Brazen horns trumpeted an alarm. From somewhere, hidden by the crowd and confusion, a phalanx of mounted men entered the Dekkora. Wielding long clubs and blunted swords, the heavily armed riders charged headlong into the crowd. They cut a wide swath across the Dekkora, then turned to double back upon the shrieking and disorganized mob.

Flee! Hans thought. But there was nowhere to go. The horsemen had cut off hope of retreating into surrounding streets. Arne stumbled and almost fell under the clattering hoofs, but Hans pulled him to his feet. Hemmed in by frightened people who also hoped to escape, it was all Hans and Arne could do to keep their footing as well and their holds on each other. Hans backed up and felt his right leg scrape something hard, solid. Putting out his hand, he found his fingers splayed against a smooth wet surface.

The wall of the reflecting pool. He grasped at its angled edge. In his ears, the fountain's dull roar vied with that of the crowd.

"I'm going to step up!" he shouted to Arne.

Using Arne as a support, Hans clambered up onto the wide ledge and used the bodies nearest him for balance, little caring that they cursed him soundly. He looked over the heads of the crowd and saw the reason for the determined charge in that direction. The Dekkora in front of the steps had been cleared of the crush of humanity and was now ringed by horsemen. Soldiers still commanded the landings beneath those three perfect orbs of smooth, serene light.

Though the Rill and whatever else stood above the stairs was now barricaded from the crowd by battalions of armed men—some groups wearing green and silver armor, others wearing yellow and white, all with blades of naked steel drawn against any who pressed too near—a part of the crowd continued to surge forward. Angry, distraught men and women shouted and demanded attention from the several men that looked down at them from atop their ivory horses on the highest landing.

Hans indulged a renewed hope. Here, surely, were the leaders. Only nobles born into the most royal of Staubaun bloodlines ranked the privilege of riding that breed of blue-hoofed shining horses. His grandfather had talked about the importance of their family having been granted that honor. Hans was about ready to climb down again when his feet were knocked from under him and he slipped into the cold water of the fountain.

"Did you see anything?" Arne grabbed Hans by the arm and dragged him out again.

Hans shouted in Arne's ear. "We're going over there!"

Together they pushed and shoved a path away from the fountain, clawing their way in the general direction of the Rill against the swell of bodies. After considerable struggle and not a few bruises later, Hans pulled Arne into a protected corner against the high wall beside the steps and huddled there with him to ponder his next move.

He had no clear idea of how to approach the nobles on the top landing. They were surrounded by armed men and an unruly mob. Even if Hans did, somehow, make it far enough to speak with them, what would he say? Sordani noblemen had not exactly frequented Marc Frederick's court. Not even one Sordani noble name came to mind save that of the man he had come to this city to find: Dorilian Sordaneon.

Was Dorilian even among them? And if he was, could Hans pick him out from the others? Dorilian to him consisted only of fragments. A name. A voice. A maimed and bloodied hand. *Two fingers*, he remembered, *two fingers off the left hand*.

"You don't think *he's* up there, do you?" Arne looked terrified. "Those Staubaun big togs?"

"I don't know," Hans admitted. He was about to say more when a great light, a blinding brightness that stabbed eyes and brain with pain, burst upon the packed Dekkora without warning. For a moment, no one moved. Then a rearing horse's hoofs clattered harshly to break the silence, and a roar issued from the stunned crowd as they looked for the source of that light.

Within seconds they had found it.

"*Sigislanj Amallar!*" A voice cried triumphantly above the screams of the stricken people crowding the Dekkora. "*Unsibjis Sordan lethei!*"

Arne's fingers dug into Hans's arm, but he didn't need the warning. Those words had been spoken in the Kheldish tongue—but not by a Kheld. From the steps above came an answering retort of Stauba commands, barking authority, demanding order. And all the while, misspoken Kheldish words rang out in obscene challenges.

"That's no Kheld!" Someone on the steps above shouted angrily. "Remove that man!"

Hoofs and feet pounded into action; metal sang as weapons were drawn. Armed men surged into the crowd and every third man of the green-clothed mounted guard rode into the fray. Hans pressed Arne into the corner, deep into the wall's protective shadow, and stood in front. The last thing Hans wanted was for either or both of them to be taken for the taunting dissenter being sought by the soldiers. If it had been up to Arne they would never have come. *Me,* Hans thought. *Arne is here because of me, and I am here because of… what? A dream, a wizard's words, and a hope I don't understand.*

"They're coming mad." Arne's voice clotted with fear.

Hans braved an arm's length of exposure to get a better look. The soldiers had cornered their quarry at the fountain, where the man claimed the dubious refuge of the statue by entwining himself about its legs. Although they had nocked their arrows across ready bows, the archers were reluctant to loose them. Pilgrims and citizens thronged the fountain. Several of the horsemen dismounted, swords drawn, and prepared to go after the dark-clothed dissident.

"Sanctuary!" the pursued man screamed. "As Aldymion was granted in Dares' time, as Amynas asked of Leur, I claim sanctuary! Would you desecrate the god?"

The man's Stauba was bad, crudely accented and slurred, but even so it was better than his rudimentary Kheldish. Hans grimaced, knowing that few in Sordan would be capable of detecting the latter. He certainly could not expect a mob of frightened, angry people—many of them from the provinces and other lands—to recognize that the stranger's accent, while guttural and foreign, was that of neither Amallar nor Essera.

The man chortled and made obscene gestures to the powerful ones who watched from the Rill landing. "Where are your mighty rulers? Look how they lord above you, safe on fine horses, guarding the Abomination!"

The crowd roared and would have torn him to pieces, but they revered the statue. Still, several people plunged forward, only to be restrained, while others shouted at the landing, demanding action. From the horsemen on the second landing, one of the nobles detached himself from the others, his ivory horse picking a careful way down the steps. Hans caught murmurs of recognition, nods and gestures from the crowd. Behind him, Arne stirred, looking around his shoulder. The mounted man glittered. Gilded talons poised upon his shoulders, holding fast a cloak woven and lined in a way that proclaimed his lofty birth, gems blazed upon his crested eagle-winged helmet. His saddle cloth flashed with importance. Even his sword hilt was crusted with rubies.

"Madrock! Would you look at that!" Arne whispered. "It's him!"

Hans shook his head. "I don't think so."

The man raised his hand, then his voice. "You have nothing to gain here. Come quietly and we will spare your life."

"No! No!" The taunter climbed higher onto the statue. Firelight reddened his bony features to a disturbing malevolence against veils of smoke pervading the Dekkora. "I've come to warn you—yes, to warn you all!" He laughed. "Sordan the Tall, Sordan the Mighty!" he mocked. "Sordan, whose gods are helpless! Where is your Hierarch now, afraid to make the Proclamation? He sends your sons to bloody deaths in far lands, then places lackeys among you to answer for him. I piss upon his statue."

He then proceeded to do just that.

The crowd screamed hate at the troublemaker and pressed forward, but again the ring of soldiers held them back. The mounted nobleman shouted to them that the man was not Kheld, that he was a disruptor, but the crowd roared too loudly for his words to make much impact. Hans, looking on, saw what the pretender was doing. But why? The stranger laughed again as the mob's displeasure spread and shook his arm at the crowd, hurling at them a string of Kheldish invectives.

As disorder increased on every side of Hans, the frustrated

Staubaun nobleman gave up his attempt to deal with the insurgent. He wheeled his beast about and spurred a path back up the steps. The crowd, inspired by the troublemaker, began to call out in one voice.

Sordaneon! they chanted. *Sordaneon! Sordaneon!*

Hearing the call of tens of thousands, Hans blanched. Like rolling thunder, the chanting gathered force and took on a disturbing, threatening note.

"This isn't good." Arne tugged at Hans's shirt and urged him to listen. "We're in a seat of trouble already. And more if that one shows up! He's more like to kill us all than put things right. Murder is what he does! Let's get out of here. There's some here look just about mad enough to take a shot at *him*."

Thinking Arne might be right, Hans resolved to leave. A loud clatter on the steps above him and a sudden deep hush—unexpected and commanding—made him stop. And look. And freeze.

Ruddy firelight bathed the Rill steps and also the ivory horse that pranced precisely down the stairs. Blue hoofs overlaid with silver filigree tapped sharply on each step so that each report resounded across the dead quiet of the Dekkora, where now only the fires raged. The horse's polished harness shone like silver, and yet it was plain and functional, purpose without pageantry—but the dark green cloth beneath the saddle blazed with silver thread and white gems in a pattern of sweeping ellipses, sword and eagle too majestic to be anything but royal.

The crowd's silence became deeper still. Hundreds—no, thousands… *tens* of thousands—dropped to their knees. Many bent to the ground.

A breastplate of silver wings spread across the man's chest and a circlet of cold metal and icy gems rested upon his brow—but Hans did not need to attend to the crowd to know that he looked upon the Hierarch Dorilian.

15

It was a foreseen consequence of the Demise that
Highborn power would be compromised and a
way opened into the Mind. What was not
foreseen was that Dorilian Sordaneon would
survive the slaughter. Instead of being left
weakened and easily ruled, Sordan emerged with a
Highborn ruler dedicated to freeing his nation of
every tie but to him and the Rill.
—Preface to a Sordaneon history in Kheldish

Time had passed—twelve years—but its passage had not
dimmed Hans's memory of that day. The Sordaneon Heir
had been the same age Hans was now, and Hans had been
but six, yet the single glance that had passed between them during
a brief and unforgettably hostile introduction effected by Marc
Frederick had impressed Hans to fear the youth who would one
day rule Sordan. It was a meeting he had blotted from his mind.

Until now.

As Dorilian rode his magnificent ivory horse into a naked circle
of fire glow and silence, Hans saw him again with the eyes of a
frightened Kheld child. Except that now his mind held two
conflicting visions—the one remembered, in which he knew Dorilian as Stefan's enemy and his own—and the reality of the moment,
wherein that same man reined his horse to a halt, alone before a
multitude, cloaked in a baptism of fire. Hans looked through veils
of smoke and wonderment at the man he had traveled so far,
through so much doubt and hardship, to enlist.

As did all Highborn princes Hans had ever known, Dorilian bore the stamp of Staubaun aristocracy. He had strong, clear features, the same arrogant posture, and his hair, reddened by the glow of the Dekkora's fires, was certainly a dark shade of blond. But Dorilian's eyes, when he lifted them to look upon the statue of his ancestor, reflected firelight over irises that were clear and silver-pale, evidence of other bloodlines to which he was heir. This was the man, Hans knew without a doubt, who had been at Permephedon that fatal day.

A few in the crowd, still on their feet, now pressed forward and Dorilian, to stay them, raised high his left hand, the smaragdine signet there flashing a brilliant light of its own. As though commanded, those approaching drew away like the tide retreating into the sea.

Hans, seeing that same gesture, started forward, consumed by disbelief. He felt a pressure on his arm, Arne holding him back.

"Hans, no!" Arne pleaded. "Don't—"

"But, his hand—he's got five fingers! He's supposed to have only three on that hand. The finger that has the ring on it—he lost it at Permephedon!"

"Look, maybe not. It's all rumors about him."

"No, you don't understand, Arne, I saw it." Hans stopped, knowing he had already said more than was wise, and let Arne draw him back into the shadows. They crouched, looking out at the one man in control of this crowd of thousands.

It was Dorilian's voice that broke the spell of silence he had cast. "If you listen to this creature, you heed only lies!"

It really is him. That voice, it's the same! Hans closed his eyes for a moment, reliving when he had last heard it.

The man hugging the statue glared at the Hierarch and grinned not unlike a malicious cat. "And why they listen to you? Why not they listen to me, to Mallogh of Amallar? Why should they not hear the truth, that their great prince stood by, impotent, while Khelds slaughtered his demon kind in Essera!"

"Because you are false. You are not Kheld!" Dorilian sharply challenged the man, interrupting the response from the crowd. "You neither speak like one nor look like one. Indeed, you more resemble a hireling of the Seven Houses, or that creature who squats in Aral."

"Mock me, Sordaneon, if that's what you are," Mallogh taunted. "You are half-blood only! Weak blood! A goat ruling over sheep. Sordan is an abscess on the ass of the world—lance it and the pus will run out, and the stench of corruption will rule the land! Already it swells with viciousness and stink." He stretched his hand out over the crowd and chortled gleefully, slinking under the statue's leg and up again behind it. "Amallar knows what will bring you low, you and all these fine, fine towers. Your enemies have promised us royal blood from which to brew our mead! Soon you will have war, war in plenty, from the north and from the south! All lands! And it is we who will open your treasure chambers and enjoy fucking your women! Your wives! Your daugh—!"

A groundswell of noise drowned Mallogh out, the crowd screaming back at the mocking figure in outrage and anger and fear, moved by hatreds as strong and violent as those sent against them. Many had gotten to their feet again. The multitude grew bolder and, stirred by emotion, encroached little by little upon the open space that still divided them from their Hierarch and the statue. Dorilian was frowning, but less with concern than simple vexation.

Arne caught the mob's volatile mood and turned to Hans with anger and dismay written across his face. "That man's lying, Hans—as if he weren't causing trouble enough! I never heard no talk like that, not like he's talking—Khelds don't rape women. Our Mothers wouldn't have it. Even if we did, no Kheld would boast about it or come down here to throw it at *him*!"

Dorilian apparently agreed with Arne on that point. "Enough!" That one word sufficed to silence the crowd. "Amallar does not presume we need reminders of their feelings against us. This creature but casts seeds of hate. He wishes to grow, then reap, a crop of violence! You are playing into his hands." The Hierarch gave the Dekkora a glance that left no person there undisdained. "Believe me when I say I can see what this man intends—only fear piled on ignorance could allow you to believe for even a moment that this mannequin is anything but a fraud!"

The crowd vacillated, uncomfortable, half—if not mostly—convinced they were being led astray. Their Hierarch's words held more power over them, that much was clear. None wished to be recipients of their Hierarch's scorn.

"How far does this creature wish you to descend? Does he wish you to riot? To kill?" The note of shaded violence in the Hierarch's voice sliced knifelike across the moods of all who listened. Dorilian renewed his attention on Mallogh. "Whatever you may be, you are not a Kheld—or you would at this moment be using this podium to address your grievances before us. Khelds like nothing more than to declare themselves grievously wronged. You, quite the opposite, are intent on urging this assembly to do harm to themselves and this City. You are placing a cancer into their blood, and we will know why."

From their niche tucked deep in the darkest shadows under the Rill landing, Hans and Arne lost the thread of the confrontation as it drowned again in confusion and disorder. Dorilian was speaking, Mallogh dancing and shouting, but there was no way to hear what was being said. Hans stepped away from the wall, thinking to push his way through the crowd, but turned back when Arne refused either to move or to release the back of Hans's jerkin.

"Hans, are you crazy?" Arne's voice was ragged with fear. "You can't go out there!"

"I have to!"

Those blue Kheld eyes widened incredulously. "But what if someone spots you? What if *he* does? He hates Khelds! What then?"

Hans shook his head and sought urgently to explain. "Arne! Don't you see? I will be more worried if he *doesn't*. You don't think they are just going to leave everybody here and go home after this, do you? Everybody in the square will be rounded up—everybody— and they will be checked out before being released. What do you think they will do when they find *us*?"

Arne groaned as he grasped the unpleasant consequences. But he could hardly say he favored the alternative either. He grinned weakly at Hans, trying to brave it but unable to muster more than resolute resignation. "I said I'd stick with you, and I guess this is it," he said. "I just don't understand it, why you think he'd give you a hair off his ear."

"I'm not sure myself. But if I can get close to him, maybe I can still pull a rabbit out of this hat."

"What?"

"Just a fancy way of saying I hope to pull off a miracle. Come on, let's go."

Hans forced and squeezed his way through the press of bodies until finally, damp clothes sticking to his skin and his breath coming hard from the effort, he and Arne emerged into the foreground of the dense crowd nearest the Hierarch.

Though much of the crowd, particularly that nearer the fountain, remained on their knees, many had resumed standing.

The human press made the Hierarch's great horse restive. It tossed its wedge-shaped head to and fro, eyes swiveling, white mane flying as it stamped under the iron hand upon its rein. Arne eyed the beast warily and increased his already tight hold on Hans's arm.

Hans, however, felt the most heartened that he had since arriving in Sordan. Whatever the consequences, he and Arne were probably safer near the Hierarch of Sordan than they would have been away from him. Now that he was within armlengths, Hans could see and hear that Dorilian retained at least some control of the crowd.

He's real. And he is right in front of me. Hans looked upon the face and body within which he had been clothed at Permephedon— only to realize he knew nothing. Dorilian remained a cypher. A total stranger.

Hans had traveled all this way, and now he was at a loss as to what to do.

How do I get him to notice me, one among thousands? And not just notice me, but know who I am?

At the moment the Hierarch was preoccupied with the dangerous temper of his subjects. The Sordaneon bodyguards, their winged eagle helmets and emblems as bright as their swords, had moved into a half circle separating the crowd from their prince, who appeared unconcerned about being surrounded by a potentially violent mob. Dorilian was angry and he looked it. As Hans began to sense a developing tension touched off by the presence of the guards, he found himself caught suddenly by a surge in the crowd. Knocked off balance, he stumbled, only to feel a heavy hand grasp his upper arm to hold him upright. Fearful and half-grateful, he looked up into the glinting dark eyes of a man dressed in the robes of a desert trader. His hair, however, was bright Staubaun blond. The man's smile widened.

"Kheld," the man spoke under his breath so that none overheard him.

The man could hardly have missed the blue in his eyes, but Hans knew it was more than just that. After his fall into the water, his soaked hair looked darker too, heightening his Kheldish appearance. He froze mutely, too blank to think. From the corner of his eye, he noted that Arne was more engrossed with the shrieking man at the fountain. The stranger's grip tightened.

"So," the man said, slowly, still using that low voice. "I've caught myself a country mouse, or it may be a rat. Taking in the scenery, eh? *Knenawlleyu Brennan?*"

Hans gaped in surprise. The man had just spoken to him in Khelda. He had thought himself merely found out, but the question, which anyone unfamiliar with Khelds would take to be a simple inquiry, was part of an Amallaran folk riddle and had a response. Hans swallowed to clear his throat.

"*Faedu narlfoen, sonne rithonder, fyndye ne sae anye thaelyther,*" he recited in the high clan Khelda of his childhood. *Do you know Brennan? Father of forests, right-handed son, finds the one that leads to the Sea.*

The Staubaun nodded, satisfied. He jutted his chin in the direction of the Hierarch, who was gesturing at his reluctant bodyguard to pull back to appease the crowd. "There sits a true prince." The stranger smirked. "Holds Sordan with all the power of the Rill Lords of old. These people worship him."

Hans braved a doubtful glance at the belligerent crowd, a large number of whom had gotten to their feet and were becoming more vocal by the minute.

The dark-eyed stranger laughed, then continued. "You Khelds are all the same—you see only the surface. I know it looks right now as though they would tear his heart out, given the chance, but the truth of their madness is they would forgive him in a minute for all wrongs, real or imagined. He has only to say the word and they will follow. These fools look for victory if ever he should go to war."

"Not against the Khelds," Hans countered. He started to say that he didn't think the Hierarch was in any hurry to war with Amallar, but the stranger had taken the first meaning. Strong fingers dug again, holding Hans fast.

"Against anyone. Haven't you heard? His people say he is Derlon Reborn, Rill Lord, perhaps immortal—the next Highborn King. But today we prove them wrong."

Despite being relieved that his accoster had not turned to the crowd and shouted out about having discovered a Kheld, Hans grappled with a growing unease. For one thing, the man continued to hold him. For another, Hans spied a glinting, topaz-adorned, glassy dagger tucked into the bulk of the man's trader's sash. As the stranger gazed upon the mounted Hierarch, his fingers touched the dagger's hilt. Hans felt his blood turn to ice as those hardened eyes attended him again, and the man laughed at his expression.

"You remember what to do this night, don't you, Kheld?"

Hans nodded but could not bring himself to reply. Now everything, even the fires in the Dekkora and Mallogh's insane tauntings, made terrible sense.

"Like Teyek arranged, right?" the sneering voice reminded. "You got your end—kegs of foul water to poison the wells at Gignastha. In return, a few fires, a little disorder, all well and good. Tonight, like Stefan promised, we free your people from the Highborn curse at last."

Hans forced himself to stay silent. Even ignorance could betray him. If he tried to back out, the assassin would not hesitate to kill him.

"Do your part now—and make it look good," the man sneered. "Approach his Thrice Royal Grace, distract him. Think you can do that?"

Hans nodded. Would Dorilian remember him? Maybe he looked like Stefan. If so, one sight of him and Dorilian would probably be more than merely distracted. "Yes. That's easy."

"Good!" With a grunt, the man released Hans. "I thought you were up for it. Khelds usually are. Your people have the cunning for such low jobs as this." That dark gaze strayed once more to the villain's target, still occupied by the verbose Mallogh. "That cur Mallogh has done well enough, but I think you'll do much better. Grab what attention the Sordaneon will give you—assault him if you must—but keep him focused on *you*! The headstrong fool has withheld his bodyguard. Just do your part, and I will finish the job." He smiled thinly. "Who knows? Maybe you'll be lucky enough to make good your escape when Sordan descends into chaos."

Not much chance of that. The assassin did not expect either himself or his accomplices to come out alive.

Hans gave the man a look he hoped would be construed as sullen acceptance. "I'll do my part. I'll do what's best for Amallar."

With a mocking half smile, the dark-robed figure melted into the crowd. Smoke and darkness soon concealed him. Hans stood where he was for a long moment, unable to bring himself to move. Background movement and sound—Mallogh shouting, horses and soldiers moving into the crowd, which resisted the incursion, hurling abuse—surrounded him. Arne must not get involved in this. Hans turned around and saw that Arne was near, puzzled and frightened to have seen him talking to a stranger. He made a gesture to reassure Arne but wondered if it would be enough. The only chance for them both was to somehow warn the Hierarch. But how, when approaching Dorilian was in itself a distraction that could prove fatal? Considering Hans's Kheldish looks, it would be folly to attempt to alert the guards.

Hans dropped his hand to the hilt of the dagger he wore. He must try to warn Dorilian himself. He alone could do it. There might be a way to turn distraction to his advantage...

Only a short distance and a few soldiers separated him from the royal steed and its unsuspecting rider. Few people dared to approach the Hierarch. His person remained sacred—by their own laws. To touch Dorilian meant death, something the guards could enforce on the spot.

Another outburst from Mallogh incited the crowd to roar. Two mounted men rode toward the fountain. The guards ringing the Hierarch tensed and looked. Hans slipped between two of them. Wary of heavy hoofs and a sharp temper, Hans placed himself at the sleek, well-muscled shoulder of the Hierarch's horse. There he mustered every grain of courage to do what no other person in all of Sordan would have dared. He reached up and grasped the bridle, firmly mastering the leather straps.

He held on tightly as the high-strung stallion danced to the side. Staying with the horse, before anyone could descend upon him, he put his hand upon the saddle, within an inch of contacting the royal thigh.

Such insolence rewarded him immediately.

Dorilian eyed him with the uttermost annoyance, a freezing silver-gray stare that instantly renewed all the old terror Marc Frederick's young grandson had experienced twelve years earlier. Hans felt himself become a shell, his insides turned to water, his knees traitor, as he forced himself to meet and hold the challenge in the Sordaneon's gaze. A touch like fire shot through his mind, consuming thought, then withdrew, and Dorilian responded with an incredulous fury that also mirrored recognition.

"Is this *your* doing?" he snarled.

Hans opened his mouth to answer. At that same moment he saw a dark, shadowy shape leap forward from the fringes of the crowd, its hand holding an unsheathed arc of bejeweled metal. No time. Seeing the knife drawn—separated from him only by a nervous horse and a thoroughly distracted Hierarch—Hans darted under the horse's neck and jabbed the stallion's shoulder on the other side with the point of his dagger. He then lifted up his arms and waved and shouted, hoping to spook the beast. Blood already welling against its ivory coat, the horse reared without warning, at the same time pivoting away from both Hans and the assailant before unseating its rider. A less alert horseman might have fallen beneath the animal's hoofs but, as the crowd screamed, Dorilian jumped free and tumbled to the ground some feet away from his horse. He was promptly surrounded by soldiers and scores of his alarmed subjects, who had forgotten their anger of moments before just as certainly as the assassin had told Hans they would.

A hundred hands, it seemed, grabbed hold of Hans, throwing him down where fists and feet could rain upon him. Blood exploded into his mouth. Armed men descended on him, showing swords and pulling his attackers away, suffering blows and punches themselves for the effort. A few of those men kicked and hit at him as well, but at least there were fewer of them and their goal was to get him away. The knife-wielding stranger too had been caught by the crowd. They also laid hold of Mallogh—who had attempted to flee—and the soldiers added Arne when he ran to Hans's side. Neither they nor the crowd had missed the Kheldish look of him.

Hans fought to look behind him as he was being dragged away and saw Dorilian's ivory charger standing between two men in uniform, but he caught no glimpse of the Hierarch. Then a burly guard cuffed him solidly into line. He did not get another opportunity to look back.

16

All *lr* technology is antithetical to Leur. Every
Aryati attempt to meld their creations with Leur
failed. Omnificence cannot inhabit nonliving
systems. When Derlon integrated his immortal
life into the damaged but extant Leur elements of
the Rill, it was not that he inhabited the Rill—he
invited the Rill to inhabit him.
—Epoptean text on the Life of the Entities

"Handurin."

Dorilian spoke the name to spare himself having to listen to the other men in the room speculate about the identity of his attacker. The *deiknya* sat as a gray lump beneath a waterglobe, its colors obscured and design all but invisible against the table. Tutto, standing cross-armed beside a second, smaller table nearby, frowned at the thing. Legon scowled as Tiflan bent over the device, jaw clenched as he looked for clues.

All three heads turned to their Hierarch upon hearing him speak.

"Handurin *Stauberg-Randolph*?" Legon practically gnawed on the surname before he spoke it. "*Stefan's* brother?"

"That would… make no sense at all," Tiflan said, though he abandoned the *deiknya*. He picked up a small round object embellished with a white horse and rider. "This is interesting."

"I saw Handurin once. A long time ago. I got a good look at him then, and now. Look into it. You will find I am right." Now that he had settled the matter, Dorilian pointed to the table where Tutto stood. It held something else he wanted—no, *needed*—to be answered. "But Handurin was not holding *that*."

Three weapons lay upon the red cloth atop the rough-hewn table. One was but a knife such as common folk used for eating. Beside it lay a well-forged but otherwise unremarkable dagger. The third weapon, however... golden *lr* gems of various sizes gleamed within a length of reddened metal warped and fashioned into a deadly blade. A larger *lr* gem glowed orange in the hilt. A mage weapon. Or something worse.

Legon indicated the knife. "This one was taken off the Kheld. It was still in his belt. He never sought to use it even for defense. And the dagger appears to be the blade your attacker used on Caillessar." He named Dorilian's horse, the wound to whom had been minor. "He deliberately startled the horse. Perhaps to place you in the path of..." He too pointed to the third weapon.

"A translocation device." Tutto named the thing.

Although called a sword master, Tutto had made the study of weapons his life work. *Lr* weapons, while rare, were among the deadliest. Especially so in this case.

"Plant that in you, maybe your leg, maybe your neck—" Tutto made a jabbing move with his right hand, then twisted. "Make it hard to remove, then—" He clenched his fist. "Activate. The victim either vanishes or the device malfunctions and he dies a gruesome death along with every living soul in the Dekkora."

Dorilian's bet was that Nammuor wanted him alive. For a while. Being Nammuor's captive, anywhere, would be a living hell—and it wouldn't end there. It would end with Dorilian as an immortal life force welded onto the Undying Crown.

"One way or another," said Legon, "it appears Handurin was not trying to kill you. But he may have been enlisted."

Perhaps. Dorilian was dealing still with how near he had come to disaster. Again and again he relived the vibrant energy of the Dekkora, the crowd, his command of them. Save for the years his father had declined to do so, Sordan's Hierarch always appeared before the Rill and beneath the Three Sisters, showing himself to his subjects and delivering the Proclamation on the eve of First Day. Doing so last night he had felt nothing out of the ordinary, until... the unexpected violence, the now-obvious diversion with the statue, Caillessar's movement that had caused Dorilian to look down at a hand so near his leg. A move designed to distract?

"...the one named Mallogh swears"—Tutto was speaking now,

reading from a paper in his hand— "that both Khelds are accomplices, recruited in Amallar—"

That last gave Dorilian pause. *Amallar* made no sense. Handurin's interrogation and that of the Kheld had contained talk only of boats. And Handurin was supposed to have been hidden somewhere in the First Creation. How could the boy have possibly been in Amallar to begin with? Or have reached Sordan from there in so short a time? Unless Marenthro...

Dorilian had finally reached a point about which he was certain: Marenthro didn't want him dead, nor would the Stauberg-Randolph's pet immortal thrust Handurin into such a plot as this. Shifting his weight, Dorilian winced as his ankle throbbed. It was not quite true that he had escaped the attack uninjured. Attention renewed, he listened to the rest of Tutto's report.

"—the man who bore the *lr* device claims that the one who distracted you, Handurin, responded correctly when given a code phrase."

"In Kheldic?" Dorilian knew the answer already but wanted to hear it.

"Yes."

There again. Evidence that meant nothing. Handurin had spent enough of his childhood with Khelds that he almost certainly spoke the language. So many things about how this night had happened felt wrong, out of alignment, as if they belonged to... separate events. Still, Dorilian's history with Khelds was murderous enough that Kheldish participation was not impossible.

After speaking to someone at the door, Legon trotted over to Dorilian and drew him aside. "You heard the report of what Mallogh and the other said under torture? The one Tutto just read?" Concern sharpened Legon's already sharp features. "Well, they said it again and again that they and the Kheld prisoners came here solely to attack and kill you. My men are bent on serving up punishment. Now. All of them. I have had to remove two men already for proposing summary execution."

Damn. The last thing Dorilian wanted was for the Eagle Guard to take things into their own hands, especially with passions this high. The City was already on high alert.

"I am not yet satisfied. Handurin looked terrified. And I don't think just of me."

"Maybe he was terrified of having not succeeded, Thrice Royal. The men may have the right of it. These Stauberg-Randolphs have always had it in—"

"Stop."

Legon didn't. "We have to consider every possibility, including that one. Many think you Stefan's murderer. It might be your enemies in Essera have joined Nammuor against you. Do not discount how likely that is to have happened—or do you believe all this is a coincidence?"

Dorilian did not discount a Wall design. "Probably not."

Resolve hardened the set of Legon's jaw and a knowing glint entered his eyes. "We know you were close to the grandfather, and so do your enemies. We know you promised him something, and so do they. Perhaps they are counting on that. Maybe you cannot kill this Handurin, Thrice Royal, but there are others who will do it for you."

17

Staubaun society has founded itself on powerful
pillars of belief—most importantly, that it is
divinely ordered. Not a Staubaun Lord gazes in
the mirror but he believes his god gazes back at
him with special favor.
—MARC FREDERICK STAUBERG-RANDOLPH,
WORLDS APART

Metal clanged harshly against metal. Long wands of brass rattled and scraped at the door before one was found to key the lock. Hans winced as he struggled to a sitting position. The beating he had taken in the Dekkora last night had left him a mass of bruises. He hoped he didn't look as bad as he felt. Or maybe, it occurred to him as the door opened, it would be better for him if he did. He fumbled for his clothes, hoping that the guard would at least let him talk this time. But his clothes were gone, taken from him when the guards had questioned him and thrown him into this cell. He barely remembered it happening.

The guard, tall with tanned skin and flat eyes, came in and tossed a wad of fabric at his face. "Put it on."

"My things, where are they?" Hans asked him. "I had a *deiknya*, a small round thing, this big."

Had they given it to the Hierarch? Hans had asked them to. He had given them everything they wanted except his Esseran name, a name so hated they might have killed him just for that. He'd told them his name was Hans Gerard Stoll-Becker.

The guard cuffed him across the face with a mailed fist, sending

Hans reeling back against the wall. "Put it on, you stinking stupid Kheld—be glad you still have your skin."

Not willing to suffer another blow, Hans obeyed. The tunic was coarse and ill-fitting, a slave's garment, but it was that or nakedness. A pair of crude sandals, hardly more than plank soles with loops of hemp rope, served as shoes. No sooner had he finished dressing than the guard grasped him roughly by the arm and hauled him out of the cell and down a long, poorly lit corridor. He couldn't even begin to guess where he was. He stumbled along with the guard as best he could into a wider space, almost a room. There the guard allowed him to sink down onto a stone bench along one wall.

All Hans could feel was pain. Not only from the Dekkora, his body throbbed where last night the guards had kicked him half-unconscious on the floor of his cell. He had passed out then—yes, that was when they had come back, taken his clothes and his *deiknya*, the only safety he had—and now they had come for him again. Dorilian hadn't helped him, not at all—had maybe given the orders.

I found him, just as Marenthro told me to. I found Dorilian, and he knew me. He looked at me and he knew.

Fear seized him then, the shadow of a thing he had been persuaded to forget. Like a child who had ignored a lifetime of warnings to walk upon thin ice, only to find it cracking beneath his feet. *Dorilian hated Stefan. Marenthro said it—I've heard nothing but that the whole trip here.*

And I am Stefan's brother.

Other footsteps sounded, coming from the corridor, along with other human voices and the sounds of a prisoner being brought in. Arne was flung onto the bench to join Hans. Hans grabbed at him protectively.

"No, don't touch me. Don't talk. They'll make it worse." Arne glanced toward the guards in fear. There were four of them, taking turns at rolling dice.

"I don't see how they could."

"I don't want 'em to try. My ribs." Arne clutched his side. "I think they're broke. I don't think I could take it if they hit me again."

Hans flinched at what the light revealed. Arne had been brutally beaten. His face and his limbs were purpled with bruises, his lip split, and one eye had swollen shut. Blood crusted his nose and mouth.

"My God, Arne. I'm sorry, really. I never thought it would lead to this."

One of the guards turned his head in their direction and snapped a warning. "Quiet, Khelds! If the Halia did not want your god-killing hides, I'd carve you for the practice."

But Hans had a question to ask, one which so far no one had answered. Maybe the reason Dorilian hadn't helped. "Please, tell me. The Hierarch," he inquired, "is he unhurt?"

The man looked at him in disgust. "His name should stick in your throat. After what you tried to do, the Mind of Leur is dead to you."

The man turned back to where his fellows had continued the game. At every throw there was an exchange of words and coins. Hans crumpled forward, his face in his arms. This wasn't at all what he had envisioned. Arne, too, slumped with defeat.

"What is this Halia?" Arne's whisper barely hid his despair. "Some kind of monster?"

Hans shook his head. "Some kind of magistrate, I think."

Arne nodded, but not as if it made any sense. The one blue eye that was not swollen shut opened wider still, with wonder. "That's what it's about, isn't it? That's what you came to Sordan for—to kill that bastard, Dorilian Sordaneon. That's what you couldn't tell—"

"Damn it, Arne! Are you trying to get us killed?" Hans looked around at the guards, but they were into their game, rolling dice and, mercifully, not listening. Most likely they didn't speak Khelda anyway. He grabbed Arne by the shoulder and shoved him back against the wall. The Kheld bit back a bark of pain but didn't struggle. "Think, Arne! This is Sordan. Don't mention him and killing in the same breath! And it wasn't like that. That's not what I was trying to do!"

"Sure, if you say so. But you ask me, it's a damn shame it didn't come off."

"You're no help. Just shut up and let me handle this, will you?"

Arne stared at Hans in disbelief. "You don't think you can get us out of this alive?"

"If I don't, it won't be for want of trying."

A door sounded far away, closing, alerting the guards. Soon footsteps echoed in the corridor and the guards hurried to stand at solemn attention as four richly dressed personages entered the chamber, their impeccable grooming at odds with the grimness of their surroundings. Three men and one woman, all tall and fair,

Staubaun beyond a doubt, studied Hans and Arne as if doing so offended their senses. To judge by the circlets upon their brows and the opulence of the embroidered sashes they wore, these were people of rank. The deference of the guards supported this. One silver-haired man turned to the captain and spoke to him in crisply enunciated Stauba.

"Are you certain these are the perpetrators?"

"Yes, Honored Ones." The soldier grunted his disdain. "Look at them bloody hard. They're Khelds, aren't they? We're not swarming with that lot."

The Staubaun man barely gave a glance. "Yes. Well. Bring them to the Halia so that we can get on with this business. I do not see any point in waiting until after the Coming. Secure them. Even when unarmed such animals are dangerous."

With hardly a backward look, the man turned his back on them and he and his three companions left the chamber, disappearing down the hall. Their jeweled backs and proud golden heads put Hans in mind of the elegance and flamboyance of exotic birds. *Staubauns.* Only now did he see in them an enemy he had not prepared himself to meet. As a child, he had met such men and women in great numbers, always in situations where his own status had been known and accorded respect. Now he had none of that.

Ezhno had been right about Sordan's many dangers, right to warn Hans—and be afraid for him—and Hans had been too single-minded to listen. *You wandered right into it, didn't you,* he berated himself. *You trusted blindly.* The guards took only a few seconds to clap him and Arne into heavy metal cuffs, then jerked them along in the wake of the departed dignitaries.

A wider passage, better lit and ventilated, led out past a massive door and a detail of armed guards. That corridor opened onto a walkway poised in the clear fresh air high above the city. Hans was not given time to see much except a soft gray dawn traced with pink, the lake serene beneath its blush of pearl—Sordan more than ever like a dream as day broke over the City of the Sordaneons.

The guards led their two prisoners through arching, light-filled halls where only echoes accompanied them. Though hurried along by the guard, Hans glimpsed secluded galleries, some solemn, some wonderous. One circular chamber opened to a waterfall of glass, thousands of tiny prisms, each as delicate as a chime, that sent forth mad swirls of color and sound with every breeze. In another chamber, a pillar of water roared loud as the sea, a raging tempest that hurled itself in all directions, churning at invisible walls, its primal energy contained by whatever principle held it captive. These were places of power which folk like the river dwellers, and even the dwellers of the city below, never entered. Sordan possessed heights to which even the loftiest of its citizens could not hope to aspire.

Sharp pain tore through Hans's shoulder when the guard jerked him around a corner and down a wide staircase. Behind him, Arne gasped and staggered against the railing, forced to keep up with the longer-legged man dragging on his cuffs. The stairs descended in broad, grand flights. By every indication, things were not going well. Either Dorilian had not recognized Hans after all, or he had concluded that Hans had been in on the plot to kill him. In that case, the tribunal might well be his answer.

Dorilian would not allow this. Hans wondered at his own certainty. *Not if he knew. Not if he remembers Permephedon.*

Something Ezhno had said came to him: *The Highborn cannot go mad, cannot forget, cannot believe a lie. If they did, so would the World.*

But what if Dorilian *wanted* to forget?

At the bottom of the stairs, they passed a pool of golden water punctuated with tall, graceful blue lilies and were steered to what looked like a great portal. Golden and gleaming, the portal's closed, ornate doors showed Sordan in glory, backed by a blazing sun. Guards opened a smaller wicket door in the lower right, then hauled their captives through a cavernous antechamber through another door into an immense assembly. A huge semicircle of dark wood atop pedestals carved as kneeling human figures—with wooden arms and hands raised in supplication—dominated the room. High-backed chairs, less ornately carved but bearing great authority in the gilded crests each bore, rimmed the table. On the wall behind and above the table, bathed in light from solar portals set high in the ceiling, presided an emblem of silver raptor wings bracketing an image of Sordan's citadel encircled by three loops: silver, green, and gold. Flanking that ensign were other banners: the emerald, black, and silver standard of the Highborn Sordaneons as well as the commanding royal blue, emerald, red, and gold standard of the Triempery with its emblems of crown and stars and sword. As the guards shoved him to the center of the room, Hans stared at that banner.

"The Triempery!" Hans could not keep the wonder from his voice. "He still honors it!"

"The what?" Arne did not understand.

About thirty persons stood around the table. Most were Staubaun or Staubaun-blooded Estols like Dern or Ezhno, tall and golden. Very probably these men and women were the leaders of the City. Shafts of light from the vaulted ceiling brightened the floor and walls as the captives were led forward and the solid door closed with finality behind them. At the head and center of the table stood the four stern-visaged persons who had visited the prison. Hans quickly surveyed the faces around the table and found them to be anything but reassuring. All looked ominously grim. Then he became aware of something else indicating that this scenario was ruinous: there was no sign of the Hierarch. Stunned, he wondered if Dorilian had turned them over to this tribunal... or if it was something far worse.

The tallest of the men from the prison, the one wearing an impressive sash of office, rested haughty golden eyes upon Hans, the more alert of his two prisoners.

"Khelds." The speaker as much addressed the congregation as the two men standing before him. "Last night in this City you attempted a most heinous assassination. By Leur's merciful hand, you failed. Thus, this day does Sordan decide your fate. The Haliasts will be seated." Amid a rustling of robes, the Halia took its seats. Hans and Arne remained on their feet facing the speaker with two armed guards at their backs. "I, Pallas Trophoneos, Speaker of the Sordan Halia, call this special meeting into session." Pallas's fine voice filled the chamber. "We have but one purpose in this meeting: to try, and dispose of, these Kheldish traitors. Scribe Yenardus will recite the charges."

Silence fell upon the chamber. A white-haired man rose from behind the seated Haliasts, unrolled a document, and began to read aloud a meticulously prepared series of complaints against the pair. *My God!* Hans looked at the council in total disbelief. *They must have worked on that all night!*

"...said Khelds did assist the aforementioned Mallogh, a Kheld of Amallar, in creating a sequence of diversions leading to the attempt on the life of His Most Highborn Grace, the Thrice Royal Dorilian Sordaneon, Hierarch of our City and its domains; that the Khelds did indeed affront the Hierarch and threaten him; that they be also charged with assault and intent to harm. That one of the Khelds has been multiply witnessed to have deliberately unhorsed the Hierarch in the presence of an armed assailant, thereby placing his sacred person in danger and exposing him to murder; that this Kheld did himself touch the Hierarch and for that act must lose his life; it is also noted and witnessed that each of the two Khelds herein named approached the Hierarch after his fall and that both carried weapons in the form of daggers..."

Hans could barely believe what he was hearing. Panic tasted like metal within his mouth. However circumstantial, the facts presented were damning. These grim jurists would never believe that the motives behind his and Arne's actions were not murderous. Even Arne did not believe it.

"Do the prisoners have anything to say in their defense?" Pallas spoke with flat indifference.

"Only that you are wrong, Honored Ones." Hans raised his voice to answer. Not a few of the Haliasts looked surprised to hear him speak High Stauba. "Rather than harming the Hierarch, my actions were solely intended to save his life!"

No comment answered him, not a word. The Halia had not convened to conduct a hearing. They had come to the chamber to sentence and execute, their minds already made up. That Hans dared to speak at all amused them.

Pallas eyed Hans and Arne with disinclination to suffer them further. "Truly," he said, "Khelds resort to the most preposterous defenses."

One by one, as the secretary placed the motion before them, the Haliasts raised their hands and voices to condemn the accused men. Hans looked at Arne who, already swaying with weakness and fear, had buried his face in his hands.

"This is a travesty!" Hans protested as soon as the vote was ended, before the Speaker could pronounce a judgment Hans was certain he would not like. "Where is the Hierarch's voice in this? He knows the truth of what I say. Let me speak with him!"

Laughter echoed from elegant floor to gilded ceiling as the gathered men and women exclaimed to each other and cast incredulous gazes upon the wretched pair standing beneath Sordan's proud emblems. The soldier beside Hans slammed a fist into his ribs to silence him as Pallas continued.

"Do you really think the Thrice Royal would be more merciful? We shall at least provide you with swift deaths, however little you deserve them. Throw yourself on the Hierarch's compassion and you shall find yourselves impaled in the Dekkora as warnings to future dissidents—just like the last Khelds to enter this City!" Having warned them sufficiently, Pallas took up where he had been interrupted.

"I hereby declare, as Speaker of this session and the last voice to pass judgment on you, the traditional method of execution for traitors and those who would spill sacred blood. By the ancient law of our Triempery and the Haliate of the great City of Sordan, you shall be first dismembered, then beheaded!"

"You shall do nothing of the sort!"

Two men stood just inside the chamber door. Attention naturally riveted first on the larger of the pair, a golden giant magnificently arrayed in the full regalia befitting a high lord and commander of armies. Alert and scowling, standing nearly the full height of the opened door and with his broad shoulders seeming to nearly fill it, he was by far the biggest man Hans had ever seen and certainly the most impressive. The man's right hand rested with clear intent on the grip of a great sword he had loosened in its scabbard. So awesome was that towering presence that the man at his side stood eclipsed—but not for long. The big man announced, in a voice as booming as his presence:

"His Thrice Royal Grace, Dorilian Derlon Amynas Valyoran Sordaneon ê Nemenor, Hierarch of Sordan and Sansordan, Prince of Caerdon, Bas of Kheshazen and Harad-Rebir, Archon of Katalderan and Warden of Tussah! All rise and be counted!"

The assembled Haliasts scrambled from their seats and hastened to the front of their grand table, where they knelt and bowed deeply. Hans noticed they did so without exception. Dorilian's long-strided footsteps echoed as he approached the table. Though Hans wanted to remain standing, he took his cue from the Haliasts and knelt. Arne, already at the end of his courage, dropped to the floor in a clatter of chains and threw himself to his belly at the entrance of the Khelds' greatest enemy. Arne had told Hans days ago that when in Staubaun lands the higher the lord, the closer to the ground he wanted to be. For this one, clearly, Arne would gladly have clawed his way beneath the stone floor.

Dorilian for his part looked as though he had just gotten out of bed—which, considering the previous night's events, was possible. He had dressed quite unlike either a monster or a royal, in dark sleek leathers down to his padded sandals, but he had taken the time for arms. No concessions had been made to Highborn splendor except for his sword, which remained in its silvered scabbard, but there was never doubt as to the respective positions of Pallas, the Halia, and their obviously irate ruler.

Dorilian strode to the center of the room and stopped when he stood beside Hans and Arne. The guards retreated several feet and dropped to their knees, swords placed on the floor in front of them and eyes cast downward, as the Hierarch stared down the Haliasts, all of whom had pressed their foreheads to the tiles.

Now that the man stood beside him, Hans was struck by Dorilian's sheer physical presence, a perception heightened last night by the image of horse and rider, heightened now by nothing more than his charismatic command of the situation. Standing at the far end of the room beside his towering companion, Dorilian had appeared smaller than he was. Tall and well made, with visible muscle beneath sun-browned skin, the Hierarch of Sordan would have towered over Arne, had Hans by a head, and only a few of the more purely Staubaun Haliasts could have looked down at him if standing. None would have dared to try.

"What does this misplaced assembly think it is doing?" Dorilian's dark, subtle voice conveyed emotion clearly. "These men were *never* handed over to your jurisdiction. They are mine! And *my* plans for them necessitate their keeping their heads. Since when has the Halia dared to presume ascendancy over my authority?"

"Thrice Royal." Pallas pushed himself onto his knees. His hands rested palm up on his thighs. His voice was deferential but also firm. "Sordan's Halia is legal body to Your Royal Self. The prosecution of all crimes committed within this City falls within our jurisdiction. In such matters we carry our own authority."

Heartened, Hans thought it might be a good time to speak up. "Surely there is some right of appeal, some *higher* authority?" He looked directly up at Dorilian, who stared back with surprise... or maybe annoyance.

Pallas, however, snorted disdain. "Appeal! How dare you! The scum of Amallar cannot presume to appeal to the Highborn."

"That is for me to say." Dorilian's reprimand carried a ring of censure. "Appeal is one of the privileges we have historically granted to men."

"Men? They are Khelds!"

"Yes. And according to Mallogh, *you* are sheep."

The Scribe, Yenardus, spoke up meekly from his place on the floor beside the Speaker. "Do you intend to grant them this appeal, Thrice Royal?"

"I already have."

An eruption of protest burst from several members of the Halia. The others followed.

"Thrice Royal!" One of the kneeling women spoke out. "These Khelds tried to murder you!"

The full force of the royal gaze fell upon her. "Did they? And how did you ascertain that, Honorable Aellea? Were you anywhere near the Dekkora last night?"

The woman averted her gaze and even her reply was chastened. "No, Thrice Royal."

"Of course you weren't. Not a person among you has the simple courage to show their head in a rainstorm, much less in a situation where they might have proven useful."

A small rumble of excuses filtered indistinctly through the room. Pallas, however, did not back off as easily as his colleagues.

"Thrice Royal, I appeal to Your Grace's respect for the ancient principle of citizen rule, of which you have been a staunch advocate." Still on his knees, he stiffly folded his hands in defiance upon his jeweled sash. "I advise Your Grace to consider his own position. It advances your policy to allow *us* to execute these barbarians publicly as befits their crime. The evidence is irrefutable. Numerous soldiers and members of the public have testified as to the events. These Khelds approached you with daggers. Their vicious accomplices, Mallogh Rassan and Achreios Gar, stated under torture again and again that these two Khelds had been recruited for the purpose of creating disorder and slaying you. A display of strong and immediate action in the form of a public execution is necessary if we are to discourage further subversion on the part of Kheldish insurgents."

"I will not allow it."

"Their crimes took place in this City, and not against you only. Their prosecution falls to us. For us to turn these men over to you would violate the language of the charter that established this body. Sordan is ruled by law, not whim. Even you must respect these limits."

Silence followed. Dorilian's expression changed from deliberate and regal to something almost feral.

"Must I? Then let us test those limits." Dorilian glared at Pallas as though he would publicly and personally behead the Speaker. He turned to the silent but watchful giant who had come all but unnoticed to stand at his side. "Tiflan," he directed, "Take these two into our custody. Remove them to the Serat at once."

Stolidly following his Hierarch's directions, the huge man relieved the black-garbed Citadel guards of their keys and stooped to unlock the manacles binding their prisoners. The rattle of loosened fetters falling to the floor clanged in the hushed chamber. Hans rubbed his freed wrists. Arne scrambled to his feet and gaped at his prodigious liberator in disbelief. Even down on one knee the man was taller than he was!

Tiflan had risen again to his feet, prepared to lead his charges away, when Pallas objected.

"Halt, Tiflan of Teremar!" Pallas's dark gaze looked past them. "Guards! Retain the prisoners!"

Having been unsuccessful at preventing the Hierarch's entrance, the Citadel Guard had resorted to standing at the doors to the Halia chamber. Several men moved forward to take control of Hans and Arne. They were within ten paces when Tiflan dispassionately drew his sword, a blade longer than some Kheld men were tall, and held it at the ready, facing the guards. To a man, they halted.

Seeing this, the Halia, which had so far granted Pallas silent support, turned to him with fresh alarm written on their faces. Obviously Tiflan intended to hold onto his unlikely charges against the entire Citadel garrison if necessary to secure their lives. The two guards who had brought the prisoners in remained kneeling; they neither stood nor picked up their weapons. Incensed by the outright contempt for his office, Pallas turned with stung rage on the man who had engineered his humiliation.

"We cannot endure this violation of our proceedings and prerogatives, Thrice Royal! Even you cannot overstep the Law!"

"And how do you propose to stop us?" Dorilian did not look the least bit worried. "Are you thinking to arrest our person?"

Gripped with fury, Pallas studied his Highborn adversary for a lingering moment, as though indeed he favored such a move. Hans detected the impulse, like a heavy current pushing at foundations of belief, a lifetime of mythos and directly experienced truths.

Perhaps Dorilian felt it too because his silver eyes narrowed. He lifted his left hand, upon which glowed that strangely bright ring.

"Try."

That single word cut through the chamber like a sword laid to their necks. Hans watched, fascinated, as the transgression Pallas had momentarily contemplated folded back upon itself, its hubris cut off at the roots. To lay hand upon Dorilian was forbidden. In any context. The Halia had strayed into peril and now confronted sacred boundaries that must be acknowledged and restored. Kneeling and head bowed, aware of peers watching what he would do, Pallas Trophoneos, Speaker of the Sordan Halia, reaffirmed his fealty to Sordan's very core.

"I beg leniency, Thrice Royal, for forgetting your birth. I would myself condemn the man who did so. It is not for such as we to question a Son of Amynas and Leur."

Relinquishing the humbled Pallas, Dorilian turned to Hans and Arne. No welcome met them in that hostile regard. Arne again gave way to terror. Only Tiflan reaching out to grasp the Kheld about the shoulders with a sturdy arm prevented Arne from falling to the floor. But Hans forced himself to meet Dorilian's gaze and for him it was that moment in the Dekkora all over again. His will froze, held fast by sudden and intimate awareness of another mind, the power of a thinking entity that rippled there, looking back. Then that contact shifted, shot out of reach, and Dorilian broke his stare first to concentrate again on the unfortunate person of Pallas.

"Who am I, Pallas?"

The question was silk, its purpose unkind. Pallas did not meet the gaze that bore down on him as he answered flatly, "The Thrice Royal Dorilian Sordaneon, Hierarch of Sordan... and lord paramount of this land."

Satisfied, Dorilian nodded. He looked around at the cowed faces of the Halia, some of which were discreetly approving. "Now that we have established who I am, remember this—I hold Sordan, not the other way around. The Rill is *my* bastion and this City is the jewel of *my* crown. I am ruler, not minion, of this domain!"

The Hierarch's message was brutally clear, and not for the Halia alone. Hans read his part in it. Dorilian's dominion was unassailable. The Halia could, if it dared, attempt to cite him for flouting, if not violating, certain laws—but they were powerless to enforce their judgment. Unfortunately for them, Dorilian fully realized his position.

"You may remove them, Tiflan. I will follow shortly. There are a few more things needing to be said to this assembly."

"As Your Thrice Royal Grace commands." Tiflan grinned expansively. He returned his unused sword to its sheath and attended to his charges, smiling broadly still. "Come on, lads."

Hand clamped upon Hans's shoulder, Tiflan steered Hans bodily along with Arne into the cool refuge of the antechamber, away from the subdued Halia and guards. Once they had gained the antechamber, however, Tiflan pulled them to a halt and seated them on one of the time-polished benches along the wall. The door into the assembly chamber remained partly open and provided a clear view of what went on within.

Tiflan directed that they should watch. "I think you both could benefit from a lesson in giving a royal tongue-lashing. He does it well."

Hans didn't have the least trouble imagining it. He had seen enough already to convince him what side of the royal temper—and tongue—it was wise to stand clear of. What he didn't know yet was the degree of his welcome, whether it was enough to have simply been saved from being beheaded.

He peered into the assembly chamber, intent on what was taking place there. Standing before the kneeling Halia, for all his plain dress the one to hold all eyes, Dorilian berated the highest court in his land. His voice rang bold and clear from portal to nave to the vault of the ceiling, even to the antechamber beyond, undiminished by the vastness of the hall, the calculated speech of a man accustomed to using words as weapons.

"I am not required to explain my actions, but I will tell you this: one of those two men you would have beheaded is of royal blood. Royal! Had you harmed him, I would have had you *all* impaled alive in Amallar and let the Khelds worry about honoring your dead bones. It is for me to say, not you, what is to be done with him!"

Hans caught Arne's quick questioning look, but he shook his head, indicating that now was not the time to speak.

From inside the room, weak protests floated up in answer. "But, Thrice Royal," they all began alike:

"...how could we know?"

"... they said nothing of it."

"... they look like Khelds, both of them."

Sunlight streamed through the high windows, silvering Pallas's pale hair and gilding Dorilian's disordered tawny mane. "You look like fools—should I condemn you for it? Could I but rid the world of fools, I would start with those who make the loudest noise!" Dorilian drew his sword, steel ringing in his hand, the blade slender and deadly, ablaze in the streaming sun of morning. "Unless, of course, we care to reach an understanding? Resume your seats."

No one spoke up in answer. They simply rose and filed back to their chairs. They seemed afraid to make any noise at all. Amazed, Hans marked how Dorilian maneuvered for effect, that his theatrics were skillful and convincing. Yet was it only show, or something more? Like the Haliasts, Hans didn't want to be the one to test that point. Instead he watched, transfixed, forgetting even his fear or that Arne watched him with astonishment, seeing the power this one man held over... everything.

"The time has come for you to remember that you are *Sordan's* governing body—not mine. If you are unwilling to do this, if you insist on monitoring the concerns of the Hierarchate and conducting unauthorized executions of crown prisoners—and you did disregard the strict orders I gave concerning those two men— then I shall be forced to act more strongly on the power of my position and birth. I am fully capable of placing Sordan under martial law. Military government! And I will do so, too, if cooperation from this troublesome Halia of yours is not forthcoming." Dorilian returned his sword to its scabbard, but the Halia knew it was not yet time to heave a sigh of relief.

"I expect you to respect the dictates of my office, to forgo second-guessing my instructions, to abstain from the Hierarchate's business except as it applies to your jurisdiction, and to refrain from your particularly unwelcome interference in my personal affairs. Above all, I expect you to finally start paying attention to administering this City. I rely on this body to keep this island and its affairs functioning smoothly. Instead I am devoting valuable time to straightening out Halia missteps and attending everybody's business but my own!"

Dorilian reached across the table and gathered several bound stacks of papers, tossing them back onto the table one by one, the loud reports of heavy documents dropping onto the hard wood punctuating a statement needing no words.

"Here! By looks, these reports have been cluttering this table for weeks! Requisitions, permits, licenses, petitions—nice safe things that should keep you out of trouble. There is enough work here for a solid two weeks of meetings. Since you have already gathered here for the day, I suggest you start now."

"But, it's the First Day of the Illumination," someone spoke up meekly.

Dorilian turned on the speaker with a ferocity that brooked no opposition. "Today! Now! Immediately!"

Deep silence. Pallas, who had remained standing throughout the entire tirade, wordlessly took his seat and picked up what was to be the first of many reports. The Hierarch stood by for several moments to bolster the Halia's resolve before turning on his heel and leaving them to their work. For the first time, Hans noticed that Dorilian had not come out of the previous night's adventure totally unscathed—one of his ankles sported a snug wrapping and his limp, while superbly controlled, could now be detected. Confused, not knowing what to say or do, Hans simply rose and stood. He tried to stand straight, to ignore his rough prison garments, the ill-fitting hemp sandals on his feet—to look like what Dorilian Sordaneon might expect a Stauberg-Randolph to look like. Like Marc Frederick's grandson. But upon seeing him, Dorilian merely glared purest exasperation. He did not stop but walked straight past, barely acknowledging either Hans or the others.

"I want to see you when you are through with them," he snapped to Tiflan.

Tiflan prudently clamped his lips shut and watched in silence as the Hierarch left the building. Dorilian mounted the smaller of two ivory horses being held near the Citadel steps, and the score or so soldiers attending there trailed in his wake as he rode away.

18

The private places of the Highborn are not cold.
Neither are they silent. The godborn are drawn to
beauty and music, their surroundings embellished
richly with all manner of color and sound. They do
this in places of great solitude, however, and few
outside their own circle ever see how they live.
The populace widely envisions them as inhabiting
open places and palaces as lofty as mountains.
Most do not stop to think that the Highborn are
human flesh and so dwell in human comfort.
—PRINCESS PALAISTEA, *BEFORE THE STORM*

"I don't like it, not one bit." Arne only spoke when Tiflan had left and he and Hans were alone in a suite of rooms high in an upper story of the many-leveled Serat. "It's as bad as that prison!" He looked again from the window he had deemed the most promising escape route, at the bluff that fell away from the walls, ledges of bare rock all the way down to the lake shore far below.

"That's what's known as a scenic view," Hans informed him.

"For birds, maybe. And what's with the maulers outside the door?" Arne's suspicions extended to the men Tiflan had left for their protection. "How do we know they're not there to keep us in?"

Hans sighed and wished Arne would stop complaining. He had spent the last hour trying to interpret what had happened to them and had yet to reach any conclusion other than that their situation had improved. In addition to the new accommodations, they'd been given jugs of water and plates of bread and meat.

"I think keeping us here is part of it," he explained. "I don't think the Hierarch wants us wandering about. We don't quite blend in, you know."

"Not me anyway," Arne agreed sullenly. He lowered himself onto the plush cushions that lined the broad ledge under the window. Neither of them fit in with the quiet elegance of this place where even the lowliest servants had the look of princes, wore silk garments and spoke with the gentle cadence of culture, where willowy Staubaun women with skin like pale rose petals and eyes like jewels turned away as though they had been somehow violated by Arne and Hans's mere presence. "But maybe you do."

"Maybe." Hans wondered how much he could infer from his change of surroundings.

"Who are you? I mean who are you, really? If you believe the Hierarch, one of us is royal blood, and it sure as all Madrock's hells ain't me."

There was no more point in keeping that secret. "Handurin Stauberg-Randolph." Hans met Arne's stunned stare with a guilty and apologetic smile. "Really, I am."

"I reckon you must be." That was all Arne said, but it was in the way he said it. The desire to believe warred with fear that he was being played for a fool. Stefan's brother? Here?

"I'm sorry I couldn't tell you before." Hans walked over to the window and settled beside Arne on the cushions. Beyond the window, boats by the hundreds dotted the blue shimmer that was Sarkuan. "I didn't think you would believe me. And even if you did, I was trying to travel in secret. I didn't want anyone else to know."

"I guess not. But it's true?"

"True as gold. My full name is Handurin Marc Frederick, after my grandfather. And I get the Kheld blood from my father, though he died before I was born so I don't remember him at all."

"His name was Erwan. Erwan Cedrecson. He was Thegn, and my great-grandmother's brother's grandson. You're kin to me."

"Am I?" Hans smiled. Kin ties mattered among Khelds, the usual question being not if a fellow Kheld was related—for that was a certainty—but rather to what degree. "I used to spend winters at Rhodhur sometimes."

"I don't reckon we ever met. My *kilth* hail to Eastmeary Brenna and that's where I lived until I was older. We're Thegn, but my mother had me off a riverman whose mother was Darm, so I'm not quite high clan like you are. I did see Stefan once, but you don't look like him all that much… except maybe a little."

"Just as well," Hans reflected, frowning. "He had a lot of enemies."

"And most of them right here in Sordan." Arne studied him somberly. "Hans, if you are who you say you are, then you should be up in Essera, trying get back your throne, not down here giving the Sordaneon a free hand to kill you!"

"What I told Ezhno was the truth, Arne. Marenthro sent me here. He said there was something here I needed and I would know what it was when I got here. I haven't figured that part out yet, but it's the right thing to do. I know it is."

"Not that I can say much about it being the right thing, being wizard stuff and all and seeing how's it turned out, with you getting me off that barque," Arne granted, "but most Khelds would like it a sight better if Marenthro would have dropped you off on Rhodhur's doorstep instead."

Hans had to agree. To the Khelds, this adventure wasn't going to look too good. "But what if I can come to them bearing an alliance with Sordan or something?"

Arne snorted. "If that's what you're after, nobody ever asked you to do it. Can't say they'd even want it, if you know what I mean."

"Well, we're not going to get anywhere right now, talking about what Amallar wants." The sun, having cleared the building, had begun to shine in Hans's eyes. Below, the waters of Sarkuan danced in a shimmer of white, hot beneath a cool northern breeze. "There must be some way to take a bath around here. I think we might be due for an audience later."

Arne looked up in dismay. "You mean with that Hierarch? What did I tell you—Dorilian Sordaneon's the worst news in the world! Now that I've seen him for myself, I don't like him any better. He means us no good, and I'd put money on that!"

Startled, Hans stared at his companion. "What are you talking about? He pulled us out from under a death sentence, didn't he? He could just as easily have stood back and let those men behead us."

Arne wasn't convinced. "Nice bit of grandstanding on his part, if you ask me. As soon kill a man as look at him, and then expect to be thanked for it. Just because he didn't want that bunch to make away with us doesn't mean he won't be looking for a better way to do it. Make it nice and secret."

Giving up, Hans simply shook his head and walked away. He was beginning to understand the enormity of the task he had taken on. He had to find some way to come to terms with the ruling Staubaun factions in the Triempery, which meant Dorilian and other lords like him, and he had to come to terms with the Khelds as well—and both of those parties seemed determined to oppose the other. A faint chiming alerted Hans to the chamber door, which had opened. A tall, fair-haired woman in flaxen robes, a golden disk affixed to her forehead, entered the room. She was followed by two youths wearing the house colors of the Sorda-neons. Each youth bore a wooden case.

The woman's calm brown gaze assessed Hans before she inclined her head in greeting. "I am Thuraya Lares," she said by way of introduction. "As physician to the Hierarch's household, I have been directed to attend your injuries."

"I thank His Thrice Royal Grace, Learned Lady." Tiflan had told them to expect a visit from a Sage and the proper form for addressing her. "I am honored. But please, my companion needs you more." Hans pointed to Arne, who had gotten to his feet and moved away from the window.

Upon seeing Arne, Thuraya Lares stiffened. Hans sensed that his own looks, however unclassifiable and tainted by Kheld blood, had been acceptable. It was possible, even probable, that she had been informed Hans was a Stauberg-Randolph and of royal birth. Clearly Arne, who was both shorter and had more obvious Kheld features, did not merit the same accord. Thuraya's patrician face placed her own aristocratic breeding beyond doubt, but her icy expression quickly changed to one of resolve. Whether because she remembered her duty, or maybe the temper of her Hierarch, she bowed her head.

"As you require."

She summoned one of the attending youths to see to the removal of Arne's prison clothing, then began a most professional exam-ination. Hans stayed near as the physician ascertained that Arne had indeed sustained two broken ribs and several less serious injuries as well.

"The Citadel Guard, for a change, has hurt itself a great deal more," Thuraya added cryptically. But Hans grinned at catching the cynical edge of her smile.

While Thuraya worked, Hans noticed that the two youths stole looks at him from the corners of their downcast eyes. One assisted the physician. The other had begun laying out fresh garments on the beds in the other room. From their curiosity alone, Hans understood that Khelds were not only unknown in Sordan—they were even less known in the secluded and privileged confines of the Sordaneon Serat. To these lads, the sight of Khelds was almost certainly akin to the appearance of some wild new breed of men, creatures to be regarded as dangerous until their ways were known. One of the boys, meeting Hans's gaze directly, ducked at being caught in the act of staring at a guest. Even so, Hans caught a flash of the youth's resentment at having to serve Khelds, a chore as much below his usual standard as would be the emptying of chamber pots for the Guard. Both youths were relieved to have only to lay out the clothes and explain the bath.

After giving Arne a pain-killing potion to ease the binding of his ribs, Thuraya turned to Hans to attend his injuries. Those were few, however, mostly scrapes and bruises despite the beating. Thuraya prescribed a long soak in the bath and left soon after.

Following a much-needed scrubbing with soap and water and a few hours of sleep, Hans took inventory of his situation. He and Arne were both alive and likely to stay that way. As far as he could tell, they were safe for the time being. They were also comfortable; the suite of rooms they'd been given was spacious and well appointed, far from the prison in which they'd started that morning.

And though it was too soon to know whether he would live to regret it, Hans had found Dorilian Sordaneon.

The sun had settled lower to the west and light poured onto the polished floor like a sheet of the finest beaten gold when a knock commanded their attention. A man Hans had seen Tiflan speak with briefly when leaving them here now stood inside the door. Brown and broad, with legs like sturdy oak stumps and the lined eyes of a mercenary, the man's expression had not changed at all in the long hours since Hans had first seen him. He nodded on seeing that Hans had awakened.

"Good. The Thrice Royal will see you now."

Thrice Royal, Hans reflected. The term was used for the Highborn alone, though he had yet to intuit the meaning.

He and Arne were given time to dress. The garments laid for them earlier offered little in the way of choice, although their sizes had been correctly guessed. Loose, pale chitons of fine cloth and excellent drape, with quilted hems and neatly embroidered borders, fastened at the shoulders with functional clasps and belted with soft leather. The sandals, too, were fine and well made but not fancy. In the end, Hans and Arne looked neat and clean but ordinary enough to pass unnoticed on the streets of the city below. Whatever their status was to be, they weren't being outfitted as royalty.

"I suppose it's good enough," Hans observed as they studied their reflections in the mirror of a large alcove that served as a wardrobe.

"He isn't in any hurry to make something of you."

"He may want me to make something of myself."

The main door abruptly opened and their mercenary-looking guardian reappeared. Without so much as a word, he motioned that they were to follow. After a moment's hesitation, and largely because the guards seemed to expect it of them, Hans and Arne did.

The long hall along which they walked was as cool as summer lemonade. Pale walls and glass-stone floors the translucent sheen of sunlit water framed furnishings as light in texture as they were in form, simplicity at its most elegant. The vast and airy passage was far removed from the back stairways Tiflan had ushered them along just a few hours before.

Hans studied their keeper, an ugly man, very nearly hideous, with craggy Estol features split by great scars that had once been terrible wounds. The man turned to Hans and Arne and gestured impatiently, "Come on, you two. I have orders to bring you, and so I am."

A sunburst door silently irised out of view. A second emerald door within swung inward. Beyond them gleamed a secluded, private world. A long antechamber filled with streams of golden light opened onto a pillared, cloistered courtyard and a sheltered garden of cool deep green, of shade trees and silence and the scent of lurking lilies. Here, footfalls fell softly, pleasantly muted in a realm of whispers. Beside a stephanotis-hung archway, a man stood in the shadows, awaiting them.

It was Tiflan of Teremar.

"I will take them now, Tutto." Tiflan gave a thin smile and handed over a small, tightly wound scroll of paper.

"Sure," Tutto growled, although he took the paper. "Now tell me what is going on here. All I get is the grand run around, first from His Most High and Mighty, and then on down the line. It's about time someone filled me in."

Tiflan shrugged his powerful shoulders with wonderful equanimity. "You were given a job to do, friend, and you've done it. Now it's time for me to take over from here. I cannot tell you more than that, and you know why. He will tell you himself when he's ready."

Tutto snorted and regarded Tiflan with dark, shrewd eyes. "I have a suspicion what this all is about, you know." To Hans, it was very like seeing a bulldog confronting a sleek wolfhound.

"And I know you will keep it at that."

When Tutto had gone and the great doors closed behind him, Tiflan led the way along the garden cloister. All was quiet behind these walls. From time to time a page or some other servant would be seen for a moment, only to be gone in the next. This was a private place, to be treated as such, and footsteps became their only company.

Just before they came to the end of the cloister, Hans cleared his throat to speak. He was more nervous than he cared to show. "When we see the Hierarch—"

"You will not see the Hierarch, at least not just yet," Tiflan informed him. "He is sleeping."

"Sleeping?" Arne squeaked, forgetting to be cowed.

"Yes, sleeping." Tiflan appeared puzzled by Arne's bemusement. "Kheldish rumors to the contrary, Dorilian does that sometimes."

"I guess we just assumed that it was he who had summoned us," Hans explained. But he remembered what the Halia had said earlier, about it being a holiday.

"No doubt he will later. But there are others with an interest in you now." Tiflan led the way under an open archway into yet another elegant chamber, this one with a center fountain and furnishings of some comfort, clearly a place of welcome. Tiflan walked to a doorway at the far end. "This way."

The apartment beyond was cool and understated and yet it was bold, a blunt statement of luxury so intimate that it had the force of personality. Walls shimmered with color, blues and greens. Floors glowed with stone patterns beneath ceilings of tiles set in gold. Eye-catching fixtures, sinuous and primal, emerged from the floors and walls at some places, holding aloft pale, smooth globes that at night would bathe surrounding areas in light. Here, in sumptuous simplicity, were the living quarters of a man unimpressed and comfortable with his nearly limitless wealth and inherited power. And perhaps with his personal power as well, for there were signs of it.

On some cushions piled in front of a wall-spanning arched window, seemingly poised in the very air above the lake and Sordan far below, a pair of young people looked up from a game of boards. Bright sun-gold hair crowned the head of the boy, and the girl's pulled-back tresses were the same deep honey brown as her eyes. Neither child looked to be older than twelve.

The boy bounded to his feet, and studied Hans and Arne with wide, gold-flecked eyes. His frowning companion also reluctantly stood, though she cast a less welcoming look their way.

Tiflan steered Hans and Arne over to the pair. "Prince Handurin of Dazunor, and Arne Anseldson, I present His Thrice Royal Highness and Heir to Sordan, Levyathan Sordaneon. And Her Exalted Highness and Princess of Sordan, Fahme d'Sordaneon."

Dorilian had *children*? A son and a daughter. Neither Marenthro nor Stefan had mentioned either.

To Hans's surprise, the boy broke at once into a warm smile. "Our welcome, Prince Handurin," he said in a clear, light voice. "May you find peace in Sordan. I am glad you have returned to your birth world—and my royal father is equally glad in his heart, though I am certain he will neglect to say so." Levyathan turned to Arne and welcomed him also, saying, "Any kin to Robdan Aelfricson is welcome in this house."

"Robdan?" Arne repeated.

"Am I mistaken? Tutto said that when the Eagle Guard asked about your family, you named him." Levyathan looked back to Fahme, who nodded.

Flustered, Arne said, "Well, he is my uncle, on my mother's side. I only said him because I got told he sits on the High Council. Those guards, though, said they never heard of him."

Levyathan's smile broadened. "That's because they do not sit on the Archhalia. Rest assured, Robdan is known to us. Our ambassador speaks of him as being fair-minded, which is much these days."

Hans found it a little dismaying that he had never heard of this worthy uncle. But then, there was a lot he hadn't heard about. He relaxed just a little at the favorable development. "Was it you who summoned us here?"

"Yes... and no." Levyathan gestured that they should be seated. They joined him and Fahme on the plentiful cushions, Hans sitting first and Arne following when it became clear standing just gave everyone a reason to look at him. Once his guests were seated, Levyathan cupped his chin in his hand and flashed a smile at Tiflan, who grinned back like a conspirator. "It may be that an order to postpone your audience was overlooked, or perhaps it failed to get passed on. I have wanted to meet you, Handurin, ever since hearing of you last night. And again this morning. Fahme thought I should wait, but..."

"I still think you should have waited," Fahme said.

A young page offered a selection of flavored, frosted beverages. Hans watched as Levyathan, then Tiflan, indicated one or another of three exquisitely colored liquids, to which the youth then added a fourth, blending the fluids to create a drink. When his turn came, Hans signaled for a color and strength on a par with what Levyathan had chosen. The drink was delicious—strong without being sharp, sweet without being cloying, faintly like sassafras.

"Ambrosia." Tiflan held up his glass, which was colored more strongly. "It does little for the body, but what wonders for the soul."

"I would have preferred for you to have had a better introduction to our City, Handurin." Levyathan spoke only after the page had left the room. "Such violence is far from usual, and this morning... was unfortunate. You were sent there in secret.

We did not foresee that the Citadel Guards would deliver you to the Halia. Or that the Guards would be so bold."

"I guess they thought they could get away with it, seeing as we were just a couple of Khelds." Right after saying it, Hans wished he had not. Rather than sounding grateful for being rescued, he sounded bitter.

"You are too quick to claim but one inheritance."

"One thing is certain," Tiflan said, "they are both Kheldish enough to have been beaten for it."

Hans assured them he was unharmed, aside from a few bruises. Arne's hand, however, dropped to his rib-binding. Fahme's brown eyes widened when she took a long look at Arne's purpling face.

"They did that just because you are Kheld?"

Arne nodded. "That, and because I had a knife."

"So do I." Fahme flung aside enough of her skirt to reveal a thigh—and the glassy dagger strapped to it.

"They are still Kheld hunting below in the Old City." Tiflan frowned at delivering that news. "Sordan's people do not take kindly to outsiders attacking their Hierarch. Three people are dead and several more wounded, and the damage to merchant stalls in the Dekkora was extensive. Many are total losses. All blamed on Khelds."

"But it wasn't Khelds," Hans began.

"We know that."

After long moments had passed, spent savoring drinks and bites of sweets brushed with nuts and honey, Hans asked a question. "Why did you wait until morning? I was known last night."

Tiflan and Levyathan exchanged glances. Fahme's steady perusal asked if Hans was really that dense. It was Tiflan who spoke.

"Yes, Dorilian recognized you. Yet I think you can understand the confusion that prevailed. The immediate aftermath was close to chaos. The Sordaneon Eagle Guard has only one duty, and that is to protect their Hierarch—and they were already unhappy that Dorilian had not allowed them to fulfill that duty fully in the Dekkora. Once they had him back in protective position, they were not exactly responsive to his subsequent orders to desist and returned him to the Serat, although they did obey his directive not to kill you and a follow-up directive that spared you from intensive interrogation."

"Torture," Hans interpreted.

"The Guard's imperative gives it extensive authority in investigations. Part of preventing assassinations is knowing where they come from. They wanted the two of you badly. Nor were they the only ones. Information obtained from the other two men did nothing to clear you. Dorilian listened until night was done to the arguments of advisers who tried to persuade him that *you* were behind the attempt. Knowing your identity but made the arguing more heated—and a motive more likely. Three times this city has apprehended assassins sent by your brother."

Stefan had tried to have Dorilian *killed*? Marenthro hadn't mentioned that either. What else had Marenthro not told Hans?

"I didn't know. I mean—" Would he have come to Sordan if he had known? He had thought all the hate directed at Stefan was due to rumors, exaggeration, like what Stefan had said about Dorilian.

"There was a lot to sort out. When we found Achreios Gar's 'dagger,' we knew it was not intended to kill, but to accomplish something much fouler. Nothing any Kheld would conceive. And then there was this—" Tiflan reached into his belt, then extended one broad hand. Nestled in his palm was Hans's *deiknya*, dull now and lifeless but recognizable by its markings. "We found this among your possessions, courtesy of the Guard. Your other belongings were less interesting."

Hans took the item into his hand and watched the medallion warm again to full color. The crown and sword; the winged horse upon a field of stars.

"The *deiknya* still retained traces of color when the Guard first took it from you, so we knew it was valid. Identification enough under the circumstances. As Dorilian had detected no malice on your part—and said, rather, you looked scared to death—it was possible, though just barely, to surmise that you might have been caught up in the unholy situation by purest chance. Stranger things have happened. In any case, it was nearly dawn before matters could be put to rest. Much earlier in the night, Dorilian had pulled the Eagle Guard and transferred you and your companion to cells in the Citadel with full orders for your protection. He did not tell the Citadel Guards who you were, only that you were Hierarchate prisoners. Someone else must have told them you had been involved in an assassination attempt. *We* had ceased to label it such."

Hans sensed the underlying rationale. The Sordaneon Eagle Guard, aware of his identity, might have acted on its own, individually or as a unit, to remove a perceived threat to their ruler. The Citadel Guard would want to preserve their no-name prisoners for the Hierarch's justice.

"But that put us in reach of the Halia," Hans finished. He closed his hand over the medallion and wished his new garment had pockets.

Tiflan nodded grimly. "An unforeseen complication. You were there as Hierarchate prisoners, not theirs, and Dorilian had issued explicit orders concerning you. As Lev here said, we had no way of knowing that the Halia would defy those orders or seek to make examples of you on the spot."

"I'm just glad you found it out before they killed us. It was close."

"It was almost closer. Once Dorilian had ensured the Eagle Guard could be trusted, I was ordered to transfer you to the Serat. You are lucky I decided to implement my orders immediately and went to see how you had spent the night."

"We didn't sleep," said Hans.

Tiflan resettled onto his share of the cushions like an indolent, well-satisfied cat. "Actually, lad, neither did I. I became alarmed when I found you gone from your cells. I have heard of Kheld trials. Now we know the Halia has a number of Citadel soldiers on their payroll—a number which, by the way, has been significantly decreased. As soon as I found out, I wasted no time. My authority with the Halia is… none at all. I got hold of Dorilian, and the rest you know." Tiflan grinned at Levyathan. "You should have been there, lad. Pallas finally bit off more than he could chew, and Dor made him swallow every bit of it. Sad to say, but the Halia thought it was doing him a favor! I will have to inquire after the Haliasts' digestions tonight, and what a pleasure it will be." His eyes twinkled and he laughed again. "Although I really do hate to ruin a Feast of Coming."

By the way Levyathan and Fahme had quietly smiled through Tiflan's tale of the events, both youngsters had heard it all before. "That is the way of it with Tiflan," Levyathan said to Hans. "He is always there for us—at the right place, at the right time."

"Your sire might not agree with you, son." The big man chuckled agreeably. "He was calling me a rare nuisance, last I heard."

"That's because you got him out of bed barely half an hour after he had gotten in it."

"For which he should thank me! I spared him from a lifetime of having to explain to people how it happened that Prince Handurin came to Sordan and lost his head." Tiflan stretched his long legs all the way across the floor between himself and the others.

"See what I mean?" Levyathan said, as together they all laughed with him. Even Fahme cracked a grin. Tiflan had definitely been in the right place that time.

A sudden hush and the sight of Arne's face going white provided the first warning. The page serving nut-stuffed rolled pastries glanced up and abruptly joggled his tray, sending three pastries to the floor. Hastily, he stooped to gather them up again.

Hans looked up at Dorilian, who pointed to him and Arne.

"Does no one in this City obey me anymore? What are *they* doing here?" Still wearing the somber garments of that morning, Dorilian looked every bit as threatening as he had before the Halia. Only the sword was missing.

Tiflan rose respectfully to his feet. Hans and Arne followed his example. "Tutto brought them," Tiflan explained. "Someone must have forgotten to let him know of your, uh, change in plans."

But the Hierarch plainly did not believe that explanation. He frowned down at Fahme, who met his gaze directly with no fear whatsoever. "Lev wanted to meet them," she said, then went back to setting up the pieces on the board.

"I thought as much." Dorilian gestured to the still-present page. "Leave us. Find Commander Rebiran and tell him I want him."

"Yes, Thrice Royal!" Looking relieved at having been dismissed, the page darted from the room.

"Legon?" Tiflan sniffed indignantly. "What under the sun of Leur could you possibly want with him?"

"I should think that perfectly obvious. I need someone I can trust to actually *do* what I tell them." Thus reprimanding Tiflan, Dorilian set his sights on more passive game.

Hans did his best not to look like a scared rabbit. He should have guessed that his welcome had been too good to be true—the lovely setting, the pleasant company, the friendly young Heir. Dorilian's personality sucked the life out of the room.

"Well?" Dorilian prompted after an appropriately uncomfortable interval. "What am I supposed to do about you?"

Taken by surprise, Hans jerked to attention. The question had been put to him expectantly. "I don't know," he stammered. He was quite amazed he could speak at all. "I—I thought maybe you would know what to do."

His stare withering, Dorilian turned to Tiflan. "This is ridiculous. Are you absolutely certain Marenthro did not leave instructions pinned on him?"

"We found none. I think he is intended to speak for himself."

Hans had lost ground already before he had even begun. Small wonder, when he had allowed himself to be caught off guard, to speak without thinking. He struggled to recoup the loss. "Your Thrice Royal Grace"—it was probably safest to deploy the style used by the Haliasts—"I have come a long way and through no small hardship, as you know, to see you. I did not know what I would find in Sordan, or what would find me. I nearly lost my life because of it. But I thank you for what you did at the Halia this morning. I promise I shall cause no more trouble for you."

"My honor is equal to the debt; there is no need to speak of it," Dorilian informed him curtly. "As for being trouble, do not make promises you cannot fulfill. Your family was born to cause trouble for me. What surprises me most of all is that you came to Sordan knowing, as I am sure you must, about my quarrels with your brother."

What could Hans say? "I want to mend that rift, if I can."

"Did you seriously think I would welcome you, given your family?"

"That is for you to say. I believe you have a mind to it."

"You are either the boldest Stauberg-Randolph that ever lived or a fool." But Dorilian had distanced himself once more. His expression was even less welcoming and far more calculating.

Tiflan spoke from behind Hans. "Boldness runs in his family."

"Not in every instance. And the Stauberg-Randolphs have had their share of fools. Be that as it may, birth did not place Handurin in Sordan. He came, unheralded and uninvited, and I would know why. I strongly suspect Marenthro's hand in this."

The *deiknya*, of course.

"You could talk to Marenthro," Hans suggested. That sounded like the best idea he had heard so far. "This City is marvelous. It's advanced. Surely there must be some way—"

But Dorilian refused that course utterly. "I have no wish to speak with him. By what argument did he bid you to come here?"

"He said I needed allies, and you would be the best one to get."

That earned a scornful stare. "And you believed him?"

"Why shouldn't I have? Marenthro isn't a liar."

"No, of course not. But did he tell the whole truth? And for that matter, do you?"

"What more do you want?" The words leaped out onto Hans's tongue and from there into the frosty distance between them. "You know far more about me than I know about you. You know who I am. You even know where I've been all these years. Marc Frederick surely told you about where he—"

"Stop while you can." Dorilian's face hardened, every muscle rendered bloodless by some powerful emotion. Each word he spoke was edged with ice. "You know nothing of what we talked about or what he might have told me. Do not bring him into our conversation again."

"He was my grandfather."

"Yes, and don't think I have not remembered that."

Hans felt Tiflan's huge hand squeeze his shoulder, warning him not to say more.

Dorilian possibly noticed the gesture, for he turned away. "This is a bad time for conversations."

"What is to be done with them?" Tiflan asked.

"The same. I gave you the orders this morning."

"Are we to be prisoners, then?" Hans asked stiffly. Beside him, Arne, pale and bruised, gave him a look that clearly said *I told you so*.

"No." Dorilian ran a hand across his jaw and it seemed to Hans that some of the anger left him. "I will be more generous than your family has shown itself to mine in the past. You are to be accorded hospitality, with privileges to be defined but not unduly restrictive, and no liberty beyond this Serat. Your safety remains our greatest concern. You will find that the Serat and its grounds are extensive and not without its share of wonders. But under no circumstances are you to wander about the City." He moved over to the window, away from them. "I will decide what to do with you later."

Hans knew this time that it was best to remain silent. *How much later?* he wondered, his gaze following the darkly clothed man he both knew and did not know at all.

Dorilian turned his back on the city below. "My grandfather,

Labran Sordaneon, was your grandfather's 'guest' for thirty-five years at Stauberg. He died there." Dorilian watched as the color drained from all their faces, even young Fahme's, then smiled contemptuously. "You will not languish here so long as that. We will talk, but I have not now the time for it."

The tension abruptly shattered as a man came into the room to join them. Hans recognized him as the nobleman from the Dekkora the night before, the Eagle Guard commander who had attempted, without success, to deal with Mallogh. Hans found himself thinking of a knife, thin and keen and colorless. The man's pitch-dark eyes seemed never to have seen the light of day.

"This is Commander Legon Rebiran. He will show you to your quarters now," Dorilian informed Hans. "There will be more time for you later, after the holy days. Indeed, tonight is the Feast of Coming, and all my court is to attend—those, that is, for whom such things matter. You may attend, Handurin, if that would be of interest to you. If so, Tiflan shall see to it."

Sunlight streaming from the west blazoned signatures onto the flaxen carpet, signaling the sinking day. Legon wordlessly led Hans and Arne to the door. As they left, Hans heard Levyathan address his father.

"Dor, are you sure?"

"I am sure." Affectionate firmness was followed by admonishment. "What manner of foolery was this? You could have met with them in the garden. You knew that I would find you out if you brought them here."

As the heavy door closed behind them, bringing them once more to the courtyard and cloistered silence, Hans thought he heard Levyathan laugh.

19

When Amynas found the Leur dwelling in the
Nemen lands, he was overjoyed, and the pair feasted
much upon their reunion. The Nemen folk at first
wished to slay Amynas, for they hated his Aryati
kind. "World Destroyer," they said, "Tell us why
we should spare you." To which the Leur said,
"Destruction is the Father of Creation. And who
among you would slay the World yet to be born?"
—CIBULITUS, *ANNALS OF THE RETURN*

Ignoring Arne's protests, Hans elected to attend the Hierarch's party. Everything about Dorilian so far told Hans he was being tested. Now was not the time to show reluctance to take on new situations. *Everything* he did anymore was a new situation.

Plunging into Sordan was not so very different from plunging into a new semester at the university—or through a gateway.

If nothing else, Sordan was beautiful. Hans stood in a room of pale walls the gentle hue of misty moonlight, upon a floor inlaid as if with veins of ice. Luminous and vast, the Serat's Celadon Hall overarched and surrounded a thousand people as if they were but a few. Mere mortals did not do the room justice—it waited upon gods who would never return.

Once, long ago, those gods *had* returned.

Hans remembered the story from his childhood. There had even been a book with pictures. Amynas Malyrdys and an immortal being called the Leur had journeyed from their refuge in one of the mythical pasts to see what remained of the Creation—and they had found it in Sordan. On the First Day they had come and partaken of the new World's gifts, learning it would sustain them. On the Second Day they had reveled. On the Third Day they had magically conceived the Three and gifted the Second Creation with a union between the gods and humankind.

And here in Sordan these things had been repeated in reverence for two thousand years.

Tonight was the Commemoration of First Day, the Feast of Coming.

Everything in the glittering hall was gem-strewn silk and bright crystal, colors clear and new. The floor, pure gold with diamond veins, reflected every movement while overhead, curtains of flowers floated like fragrant clouds. Even the walls were draped with brilliant heraldry, the banner of every royal and noble house present displayed for all to see. Lofty personages of many lands, their names as renowned as their ambitions were high, proclaimed their standing and wealth with finery, while their consorts, creatures every bit as resplendent, fraternized over politics and fashion. Invitations to the Sordaneon court might be coveted but, from the number of persons present, they obviously were not rare.

Hans would have gladly turned tail and fled from such a gathering had Tiflan not been in secure possession of his right elbow. At least his clothing was up to the occasion. From leather sandals with large golden medallions on his feet to a cobalt blue long tunic of finest silk, from the embroidered belt to the simple but elegant circlet upon his head, Hans had been transformed from a common deck-hand to rich respectability. Tiflan guided him into the Celadon Hall's grand atrium and the company of several determined members of Staubaun gentry, who paid Hans scant mind in their efforts to gain the attention of the ruler of one of the Triempery's more eminent domains. Before long, Tiflan had become so much of a public property that Hans was squeezed out of his company entirely.

As people moved around Hans, snatches of conversation drifted his way. Not one Denizen of the Seven Houses had been invited. No one, in fact, from Essera. Jooar of Lahgael would not be present this year; the Elector of Trongor was unhappy with Dorilian's latest trade proposal; the Brotherhood of Shipbuilders had petitioned the Hierarch to provide funds for a new shipyard at Rubyan. Adrift in the Hall and not really understanding most of what he overheard, Hans sought the company of a broad-leaved plant near the night-darkened windows.

The sight of a stocky, scar-faced man stomping toward him nearly startled Hans from his niche before he realized that he was not Tutto's target. Instead, Tutto took hold of a tall young man attired in noble rank, then maneuvered him to one side, nodding curtly to other guests until they were sufficiently out of earshot. The plant and an angle of pillar hid Hans from view.

"Anything I should know, heh?" Tutto growled.

"Odd you should ask," the young man answered lightly. "But then, you probably already have heard my news."

"Heard what?"

"Just this. I came up from Va-Bakkeba this morning, on an Ardaenan ship out of Amroset."

"That's nice." Tutto did not sound very impressed.

"It was flying the royal ensign." The young nobleman employed a tone even Hans behind his potted palm could construe as meaningful. "And, although I did not see him myself, I should guess that it is an unannounced visit."

"Gsch!" Tutto sounded genuinely alarmed. Hans wondered what visit could arouse such unconcealed dismay in a hardened mercenary.

"Should liven things up a bit," the other said.

"Things are lively enough as they are." Hans could imagine Tutto fingering a sword as he said it. "The Hierarch got it in his head again last night to go out among the people. Held back his guard and fell into a bad situation. He's touchy enough after that— Leur only knows he was close enough to it. He gave hell to the Halia this morning over nothing at all—but now he will have every reason for a real show of temper. That Endelarin has a perfect sense of bad timing!"

"It does seem so. Wasn't he thrown into the harbor on his last visit?"

"He was. And well deserved it too, the heathen. He looked like a giant jellyfish as his sailors pulled him from the water still wearing royal purple."

"What was it again that caused his embarrassment? Surely not a woman?"

Tutto snorted as they began to move away, back into the

mainstream of guests and gossip. "*A* woman? Say several. And what's more, they all agreed to it."

Once more alone, Hans gazed out across a mass of color and confusion and unfamiliar faces, hearing music he had never heard before, names he did not know. And one that he did. Endelarin Nemenor, King of Ardaen, even if he had not been the subject of such interesting gossip, was a person of note. Among other things, Hans remembered Marc Frederick claiming Endelarin had a hundred wives—an accomplishment which, as a child, Hans had thought completely awesome. He remembered too that his grandfather had valued the Nemenor king as an ally because of his ships. The Ardaenan seafolk who ranged the oceans in their red-sailed vessels could strike swiftly at offending fleets or effectively blockade an enemy port. In any port but Sordan, Endelarin would have received a royal welcome. But Sordan had its Rill and its dominion, with no fear of a blockade by Ardaenan ships—and Highborn Dorilian was powerful enough to like whom he pleased.

With a sigh, seeing now what could be gained, Hans decided that he would mingle. He needed useful information and talking to other people was a good way to get some. After just a few steps, he remembered why he so hated this kind of occasion. Though he drew glances from men and women alike for being well dressed and rumored to have arrived in the company of the Bas of Teremar, nothing else about Hans stirred more than a handful of token nods.

It didn't help that Hans could not begin to contemplate an introduction. *Hello, I am Prince Handurin. Yes, that Handurin. Remember my brother Stefan?* That wouldn't go over very well. He had just found himself boxed yet again between groups of strangers when he heard a familiar voice. Pallas and several of the Haliasts had gathered not far away, stiff collars of rank standing up about their necks and their voices speaking words Hans immediately decided were worth overhearing. He edged closer.

"There *was* no way to stand up to him. I wanted to! I tried! I had sense enough to stop—in the mood that was upon him, he would have hewn me down without a second thought. I have seen enough of that man's willingness to use a sword." With a bit of violet cloth, Pallas dabbed at a trace of perspiration on his brow.

"Our Hierarch is not that rash." This speaker, a woman, begged to differ. "What puzzles me most is that he became so upset over these *particular* Khelds. We have done much the same with a multitude of others and not once did he express so much as a wish to delay the proceedings. Either something very different happened at the Dekkora last night than we surmise, or those two were not what they seemed."

"He said one of them was royal," the man at her side recalled. "Is it possible the one is that Esseran boy nobody knows how to find?"

"Preposterous!" Pallas huffed. "That one is probably already dead. No. One look at this misordered pair and you could see they were Khelds. Blue-eyed, shaggy, filthy Khelds! One possibly had Staubaun blood, but so does every whore's son along the Dazun or in Leseos. The Sordaneons have never recognized the existence of a Kheldish nobility, not in six hundred years have they done so, and now all of sudden Dorilian changes the game and promises us a heathen death if we harm the runts!"

"You don't suppose, do you, that the Hierarch is considering an exchange of diplomats? Or an alliance? He implied that these Khelds were of use to him." The woman seemed intent on establishing a rationale.

"If he is thinking of that, it will be his ruin!" Pallas's words carried all the force of a vow. The other Haliasts exchanged glances.

"Oh, come now, good Pallas," a fourth member consoled his colleague. "Such talk is premature. And also ill-advised. The last sniff of a Kheld alliance was years ago, and that died with Marc Frederick. Once Stefan took the throne, he killed even the possibility. Our Hierarch regards Khelds with the utmost contempt. They own nothing he wants and cause him nothing but grief. If you ask me, this whole thing is quite strange and not worth the crossing of him."

Three sharp raps and a burst of mellow fanfare interrupted them, bringing all eyes to the main stair at the palace end of the Hall. There, a royal-robed chamberlain called out the Sordaneon names and titles, announcing the arrival of the Highborn rulers. The room's population arranged itself according to rules of conduct Hans had yet to grasp, forming a gallery several persons deep the length of the Hall. Hans found himself pressed into line beside some of the Haliasts and was thankful that the Hierarch's timely arrival commanded all eyes.

With reason. Hans gaped in amazement. If he became Essera's ruler, would people expect him to dress like *that*?

Each item Dorilian wore had to be worth a princely ransom. Gone were plain leathers, replaced by a chiton of lustrous white silk. A breastplate of silver eagle wings, each metallic feather a perfection, spread across Dorilian's chest and shoulders, sheathing him with the magnificence of a god-ancestor. A milky green dagger glimmered like a claw in the golden talons of his belt. In addition to the brilliant blaze of the ring on his left hand, Dorilian wore a crown like no other: radiant sunlight-hued metal clasping a green center stone and a circle of seven points with emeralds that blazed verdant fire.

No one Hans had ever seen in person or in books—not even the Sapa Inka at his coronation, dressed as the Child of the Sun—had looked more resplendent.

I will never pull that off, he realized with dismay. He couldn't even pull off what he was wearing now.

Both Levyathan and Fahme walked behind Dorilian and were exquisitely attired. Levyathan was clothed in his family colors, which had the effect of making him look alarmingly adult, whereas Fahme wore an airy ankle length silver gown that highlighted her youth yet left no doubt she would in just a few years become a beauty. Both young people wore regal circlets.

As the Sordaneon entourage made its way along the gallery, men bowed and women curtseyed as low as the floor and their pride allowed. All the while those downcast eyes stole glances, an undulating wave of human motion looking to see who got noticed.

Hans wavered. In all the confusion of information, Tiflan hadn't told him just what his standing was supposed to be. Although Hans was a guest of sorts, he was foremost of all a son of a royal house, nominal prince of a domain, and king designate of Essera—yet he had no idea at all of what the protocol might be. The last thing he wanted was to appear presumptuous in front of Dorilian's own court. He decided it would be prudent to bow along with those around him. When in Sordan...

It had been years since he had bowed to anyone, but he did so neatly. He thought. Unfortunately, his golden circlet, to which he was unaccustomed, slipped a little and, as Hans put up his hand to steady it, fell inelegantly from his head. Though he caught the thing, a rustle of interrupted movement and a silence so deep it became embarrassing told him that he had been noticed. He looked up, circlet in hand.

"Handurin." Dorilian recognized him by name, shocking not only Hans but also the greater part of the gallery. Heads snapped in their direction with unequivocally interested stares. "You have been snared again by our Halia, we see." Dorilian's gray gaze relinquished Hans and moved to a point past his shoulder, the court following that direction as hounds to the scent. "Our Lord Pallas," Dorilian identified his quarry. "You, too, surprise us. Have you finished the work we gave you to do this morning?"

Hans barely kept himself from jumping when Pallas replied from just behind him. He had not known the man was so near.

"No, Thrice Royal," Pallas managed politely, though his voice sounded strained. "There is much yet to do."

"A pity. Tomorrow is Second Day, and you and all your friends at the Halia shall have to miss it. The Third Day, however, is set aside for the Law." Dismissing Pallas, Dorilian returned his attention to Hans. "Come, Handurin," he directed, gesturing him into line with his entourage. "It appears we must take you upon our self."

Resettling his circlet, extremely conscious of the many hundreds who watched him, Hans stepped from the gallery and joined the Sordaneon party. He was not prepared to handle this much attention, and he began to feel, in turn, faint and sick. But a touch on his arm, a sudden strengthening warmth, brought his head up and he looked into Levyathan's discreet, boyish smile of welcome. Fahme extended her hand and drew Hans to stand at her side. His stomach settled as he realized all was well, although he knew better than to think it would be so for long. Already there were whispers, portent-like, rising from the gallery he had left behind.

His presence in Sordan was out.

There was no more time for conjecture on his or anyone's part, however, for there burst into the Hall in a blaze of scarlet an apparition the like of which Hans had never seen. Even Dorilian froze, his entire court at his back, as a man dressed head to toe in royal crimson and glittering almost painfully with diamonds and rubies in gaudy array barreled into the room and approached without so much as an introduction. Guards, led by Legon, moved quickly into place, but they did not appear to anticipate an attack.

Although shorter than a Staubaun, as short as a Kheld might be, the man managed to appear like he ought to be bigger. He was ordinary-looking but not quite homely, with pitch-black hair silvering at the temples. His wind-tanned face sported a toothy smile, topped by a large, noble nose and eyes of lively ocean gray. He flung open flounced, be-braceleted arms in greeting.

"Dorilian! Dear *cousin!* How marvelous to see you again!" He bounded forward, stopping short as the Eagle Guard closed ranks. Hans was not at all surprised to see Dorilian regard the man with a disdainful glare of the sort usually reserved for offensive suggestions.

"I thought I told this molting sea snake to stay away from Sordan," Dorilian said to Legon, who now stood beside him.

"You did, Thrice Royal. You told him twice."

"Must you always make me feel unwelcome?" the bejeweled sea snake admonished. "I deserve better than I get from you—but then most people do. Indeed, the ugliness of our last parting threw me into such melancholy that I was forced to take sixteen new wives, one for each day of my indisposition. Nonetheless," he punctuated his chiding with a deep sigh, "in view of our common ancestress, I forgive you."

"Spare these attempts to repair your welcome here."

The man ducked and peeked between the guards. "Only if you invite me to supper. After all, I *am* a royal cousin of yours."

Dorilian condescended to look at him. "My most vexing problem at the moment, Endelarin, is a preponderance of highly questionable royal cousins straining my hospitality by unexpected appearances."

"But *I'm* not questionable! I'm documented!"

Dorilian fixed him with a look that would have driven a lesser man from the Hall. "What you are is uninvited. Unfortunately, the harbor is too far away for even Tiflan to throw you. As it is First Day, courtesy demands that you not be turned away unfed from the hall of any blood kin. So stay, Endelarin, but *not* at our invitation."

Before Endelarin could protest anew, Dorilian had turned his back on him. The gallery, no longer required to show attendance, dissolved into its former exotic shapelessness. Even so, Endelarin remained with the Sordaneon party until it reached the raised dais where they would be seated for dinner. He stood at Hans's elbow as though he belonged there, mingling with the others.

"Hello." Hans wished he felt surer about how to phrase his greeting. "Are you *King* Endelarin, of Ardaen?"

"Yes. Though one would hardly think so by my reception." Endelarin gave Hans an up-and-down glance, acutely interested. "Who are you?"

"We've never met. You knew my grandfather, though, and my brother."

Endelarin perked. His broad smile returned. "Oh? I can't imagine where. Maybe you have met my heir, Andralldi. He went to school at Permephedon for nearly four years. Until that dastardly deal of death and destruction took away some of the school's respectability. Most of the Highborn folk and their heirs besides! Dreadful affair, wasn't it?"

"I would rather not talk about that." Hans looked nervously toward the Hierarch.

"Nobody who knows anything ever does. Dorilian, for instance, once drew a sword—and seriously too—upon my curiosity!"

"Did he really?"

"Well," Endelarin chuckled at his gullibility, "he wouldn't have used it. Really not a man of regicidal habits despite his reputation." The sea-colored gaze upon Hans took on a darker, shrewder, glint. "Tell me, which of the questionable royal cousins would you be? You look vaguely familiar, somehow, but I have never seen you in Sordan before. Or anywhere else, for that matter!"

"I am, ah, Handurin Stauberg-Randolph." Hans felt a twinge of alarm at actually saying his name aloud and in public. Nervously, he extended his hand as he was accustomed to doing upon a formal introduction—until he saw Endelarin simply staring at it, and he remembered belatedly that among Staubauns an armclasp signaled kinship, and Endelarin Nemenor was neither kin to him nor Staubaun. Consciousness of the blunder caused Hans's face to burn red as he retracted the offer with the best composure he could manage.

"Oh, ho, ho!" Endelarin, delighted, raised his eyebrows. "Handurin, is it? *Stauberg-Randolph*? Don't tell me you're Stefan's brother!" No less than half the room turned toward them, frozen-countenanced, their stares cold and sharp as the ebullient man continued to voice his amazement. "Stefan's brother! Well, who would have thought? Who, indeed! My trip is already made worthwhile to find you here. And not, I might add, moldering safe in Dorilian's deepest dungeons."

"My welcome is more for my late grandfather's sake than my own, I think." Hans felt another rising wave of sickness as conversation to every side of them dulled and then dropped into silence.

"Probably. You certainly cannot thank your brother for it!" Endelarin, unfazed by the multitude's reactions, threw a protective arm up on Hans's shoulder and led him away from the hostile circle into a part of the room that had not yet heard the news. "Don't mind them. They won't dare tread on Dorilian's toes over such a small morsel as you, seeing as he himself has seen fit to let you be. So, you have returned! How excellent! People have often lamented that Stefan was not sent to the netherworld instead."

Hans relaxed enough to grant his rescuer a crooked smile. "My reception thus far has been, well... ambiguous, at best."

"Oh, you mean *him*?" Endelarin gestured toward Dorilian, who was standing not far from them and greeting a line of ambassadors. "Judging from past experiences, this counts as a rousing reception! I can personally testify that if Dorilian had a mind not to welcome you, he is perfectly capable of throwing you into the cold waters of his wretched harbor. Two years ago I had just such a reception, which left me with three months of head cold and no apology."

A panoply of silver-throated cornets filled the Hall with the clear sweet call of nightbirds. Golden trumpets burst forth to herald the rising of the virgin moon—newly full and brilliant. Hans heard the hollow taps of order and felt rather than saw a movement to the table. He followed Endelarin to the dais, where the chamberlain escorted him to his place. Hans took his seat at Tiflan's left and noted that the chamberlain had Endelarin sit beside Hans, as far from Dorilian as it was possible to be and still be at the royal table. Tiflan leaned his large frame forward and peered past Hans with placid, almost bucolic, inquiry at the Ardaenan king, who waggled his fingers in greeting, each massive ring thereon winking in turn. Tiflan looked about to say something but was forestalled by a stir at the opposite end of the Hall which drew all eyes and attention to the staircase there.

Two men in apricot livery, white geremant feathers flowing

winglike from jeweled caps and themselves fairer than Sordan's native sons tended to be, cleared a path for a lady just now arriving. Tiflan muttered something in a low voice that Hans did not hear. His mind was taken with wondering what benign goddess had bestowed upon that lady the moon-gold splendor of her hair. From beneath a circlet of pearls, her tresses fell in a bright curtain about her bare shoulders. She was Staubaun slender and graceful, her gem-laced skirt flowing mistlike about her form as she descended the stair as though down stones into her private garden, her birth like a star upon her brow. Those standing bowed and curtseyed as she passed, and those sitting stood and did the same from their places. Only those seated on the dais, and the royal children at their own table, made no move but that of watching her.

"Who is *she*?" Hans asked Endelarin urgently.

"Down with your flag, my boy," the king cautioned, though he looked quite like a starving man at a fruit stand himself. "That vision of heavenly delights is Melenthas, a princess of Merced, which is an island nearer to my country. The beauteous creature has designs to become a Hierarchessa."

Hans recalled one of Tiflan's revelations: Levyathan's mother was dead, the Hierarch unencumbered by a wife. He watched enviously as Melenthas curtseyed to Dorilian, who stepped forward to greet her and, in full view of the Hall, extended his arm so that Melenthas might place her claim upon it. When Dorilian ascended the platform again, she was at his side. He led her to sit in the chair beside his own.

Tiflan snorted and said, none too quietly, "About time!"

The lovely Melenthas, unruffled in her queenly grace, ignored the noble Bas of Teremar and sipped nectar from her crystal goblet. Enchanted even by that simple gesture, Hans thought he discerned Melenthas's gaze, in meeting his among her neighbors', pause and linger for an instant before sliding to attend her royal partner once more.

I should have smiled, Hans thought, encouraged, *then maybe she would have.*

All in the hall were now seated. Dorilian alone remained on his feet, standing as at the center of a stage. He took up and held aloft a great curved vessel tooled of silver and traced with fine veins of clear green glass.

"This night we partake of the Feast of First Day, the Feast of Coming, when the old year passes and we stand upon the threshold of the new." Dorilian's sure voice rang out across a reverent silence. "This is the cup of our ancestor, Amynas, who drank from it by moonlight and broke bread beside it, thus consecrating the First Day of a new Age. The wine ever flows from this cup, for he did pour his very blood into the years that were to come, and are come, and are yet to come. Raise high and drink deep, for this night Leur dwells again in the Citadel of Light."

As one arm, the hall lifted its goblets in answer, then followed the Hierarch in drink. The cup was passed to Levyathan, who also drank from it. It went no farther. Only the Highborn, descended from Amynas, could drink from that holy cup. Not even Marc Frederick at the height of his reign had dared to breach that age-old sanctity.

The feast proper commenced upon that note. Hans accepted the first light course as it was set before him and pondered his meager education in Highborn mysteries. He heard Endelarin speak up at his side.

"A very proper priest, wouldn't you say?"

"Who?" Hans asked distractedly. "Dorilian?"

"Why, of course Dorilian." Endelarin looked surprised that he could think otherwise. "Who else? He just gave us his benediction. Not a bad job, actually, as such things go. Deben used to get rather pompous with his."

"I guess I don't think of him as a priest." Upon reflection, the idea seemed less ludicrous than it should have.

Endelarin prodded skeptically with his golden fork at a plump, juicy prawn. "Oh, yes. All the Highborn are priests. One of their prime functions in life is to uphold their own divinity. They can get quite touchy about it. Fanatics, the lot of them."

"I wonder how much of it Dorilian really believes." It occurred to Hans that Highborn descent from both a human god and a Leur one probably formed more than just the basis of the Hierarch's rule. It very likely permeated Dorilian's psychology—and his politics.

"I don't think you should ask him," advised Endelarin.

"Oh, not yet, anyway," Hans assured him.

Endelarin twiddled the speared prawn in his direction. "Well, be sure you know what you are about when you do." He punctuated his warning by popping the prawn into his mouth.

The feast was certainly living up to that designation. Servers balanced great trays of dishes, each course swept away to be replaced by another even more delicious. "Does all of Sordan eat as well as we do here?"

"We don't eat as well as this at my court in Amroset!" Endelarin enthusiastically dug into yet another plate of delicacies. "You don't think I came here to visit Dorilian, do you?" He chuckled upon seeing that Hans was being more serious than he. "You need not worry. I am certain that the inhabitants of this fine city eat well enough. You might have noticed that the town is prosperous. Rill revenues, you know. And thanks to their Entity's exceptional utility, they get food from all over! If Sordan's inhabitants don't eat well, I can see no excuse for it."

"A wealthy city might prosper at the expense of its people."

Endelarin stopped in midmotion, his balanced fork half-lifted to his open mouth. "What manner of philosophy is that?"

"I mean that I see a lot of nobles. Everyone in this hall is rich. Perhaps Dorilian should give such a banquet for the common folk."

"Oh, I think he would—except he has no need to put the fear of his god into *them*."

"I don't understand."

"You really must learn to be more observant, my boy. Dorilian traffics in perceptions; all the Highborn do. They know where the truth lies. Take the sea. If you just looked at the surface, you would think it held only water! Now, take this fine party—" Endelarin indicated the room before them, the tables and milling servants. "By this grand display, you would probably think that Dorilian regards all of these noble lords and ladies as the creme of his subjects—his most favored, the most deserving of his high regard."

Hans nodded. That thought had crossed his mind.

"Then you would be wrong, my boy. As wrong as the sun setting in the east—which it never does, by the way. I can assure you that, but for a sacred few, Dorilian regards every soul at this banquet with the profoundest contempt. Us included."

"He hasn't been too… disrespectful." Hans still clung to hope of his situation improving.

"He's being careful. But make no mistake, he will find opportunities to torment you, on account of the family feud. And me too, for all that I am a king and my country considers him the very definition of an excellent return on a risky investment. I do love a consummate bastard!"

Hans cast a hasty glance at the table's enthroned center. Either Dorilian was not yet aware of Endelarin's presence at his table, or had chosen to ignore him. At the moment Dorilian was involved in conversation with the man to his right, who Hans had been told was the Bas of Suddekar, another royal kinsman. The two men looked a lot alike—but one was Highborn and the other not. Had he not already known that fact, Hans could not have told it just by looking.

"Well, I don't have to agree with him."

"And there you have it. If Dorilian's opinions are troublesome, it is because people attach importance to them." Endelarin appeared genuinely unconcerned with the Hierarch's low estimation. "I don't let his opinion bother me, and I don't see where his churlish insolence to my good name has done me any real harm. If anything, I do believe I have taken on a certain luster! After all," Endelarin reasoned, "at least he notices me."

That was certainly true. And Hans had to admit that Sordan's Hierarch most likely did view his noble subjects with subtle disdain. But was it contempt Hans saw behind the studied expression he encountered every time his gaze met Dorilian's? Or was it something even more frightening—that possibly Dorilian deemed Hans unworthy even of his hatred? Stefan at least had earned that.

"I don't know how I am going to do this." Hans had spoken his frustration aloud before he realized he had done so. He decided to explain. "I—I've been away for a while. I don't even know where to start."

"Nobody ever does," Endelarin said by way of consolation.

Tiflan had been listening to the conversation and he frowned at Endelarin before turning to Hans. "You can start right here, if you want to. I have watched the way you look at Dorilian. It is not like you're looking at a man at all, but at an obstacle to be overcome. If that is the way you are going to be with him, you will be no different from all the other fools he must bear. Let him reveal himself to you before you decide what he is. Never forget that he is Highborn and the world is as he perceives it." When Hans tried to protest, Tiflan cut him short with a glance. "If you are afraid of him, lad, he will respond to that—and that will be the shape of your world. Yours and his. Get rid of your fear before it drags you both to ruin."

"Afraid of Dorilian?" Endelarin peered around Hans. "Well, I suppose Stefan was. I suppose a great many people are—because he is unpredictable. Nobody ever seems to know where he stands or what he is going to do."

"That is not necessarily bad," Tiflan countered.

"Who said it was bad? Not I." Endelarin placed his hand on his own jewel-encrusted chest. "His father now, the late and unlamented Hierarch Deben—the Fourth, wasn't he? He was as predictable as a mountain: one always knew *exactly* where he stood. He never seemed to move, either, come to think of it. Old Deben just did whatever people thought he should do, and he was an absolute failure at everything he did."

"What has that got to do with Dorilian?" Tiflan patiently buttered a slice of sweet bread. But Hans noticed that he did not refute Endelarin's statements about Deben's failings as Hierarch.

"You are an obtuse ox, aren't you?" Endelarin persisted. "I just provided you with the most amazing insight about why Dorilian is considered unpredictable!"

"You did?" asked Hans.

"Certainly." The sea king used his salad knife to gesture at the crowded tables of noble guests below and in front of the dais. "Because of them! Deben was considered a paragon of predictability simply because he did the things people thought he should do. A surer road to failure has yet to be found. Most people base their expectations on what other people expect, and when they say everybody can't be wrong—well, they're wrong. But Dorilian resists that kind of direction. There is in him more perversity than is good for a man who would be a god. You see, just when people think they know what to expect, he does something else, and it alarms them. In fact, it unnerves them terribly to think he might do something they might not have thought of first. People dislike most those things they cannot control."

Tiflan cocked his head to the right and eyed Endelarin with an oft-hidden shrewdness. "You know something, Your Majesty? You are not so dumb as I thought."

"Yes, I know. I wish you would inform our cousin over there— he is quite convinced of my inability to reason."

They all three looked across a gaily discoursing Melenthas to find that Dorilian was looking their way with a puzzled frown, as if he knew that they were speaking of him and was curious as to the reason. A tooth-baring smile from Endelarin prompted Dorilian to return his attention to Melenthas, who had not noticed the lapse in concentration. The minstrels led into another gentle tune suitable for courtly digestion.

"I really don't know what he sees in her." Endelarin mumbled his aside once Tiflan had turned away.

Hans stole a covert glance at the Mercedan princess. Melenthas was as entrancing in her nearness as she had been from afar. He sighed and wished that he could have such a beautiful dinner companion. Endelarin was entertaining, but....

"Maybe he's in love," Hans replied absently. "Maybe he intends to marry her."

Endelarin did not appear to notice the note of longing in Hans's voice. "Love her? Marry her? I would not wager on it. I cannot see that Dorilian intends to marry anyone, at least not soon, although he really should."

"What do you mean?"

"Well, heirs, for one thing. Siring offspring is somewhat of a dynastic obligation."

"He already has a son and a daughter too," Hans pointed out. "There are other reasons to take a wife."

"Something I know well! However, I can see you don't know much about his first marriage." Endelarin leaned near, the better to confide juicy details. "If you did, you would not be treading there. No one ever talks about that either. It was a scandal of sorts from the very first vow. Things began badly and ended worse. It's shocking how many people have forgotten—though I don't think we ought to go into that." Endelarin finished in a flurry, nearly tripping over his own tongue. From his proximity just to Hans's right, Tiflan was scowling ferociously.

"I think I can safely tell you this much." Endelarin resumed confidences in the barest of whispers no sooner than Tiflan had returned his attention to the Hierarch and the other guests. "Dorilian has no patience for mating games. A dozen noble houses at any given time are trying to wed their daughters to him, but he will have none of it. He has been burned, badly, and... well, there is a limit to how far a man will go to play with fire, no matter how lovely. Sometimes he comes to the decision that such games are not worth the aggravation. Still, the ladies are persistent with their advances. Personally, I question their taste, although it is only Dorilian's personality that is disagreeable—his pedigree is beyond reproach and he is not without aesthetic value. The royal blood-lines came together rather nicely in his case."

"He is... handsome enough, I suppose." Hans felt only awkwardness at the admission.

"Yes, he is," Endelarin concurred with something close to pride. "The Highborn run to good-looking males. Especially so since the Nemenor infusion. Before we contributed a few good measures, the Sordaneons were a pale, Staubaunish lot. They looked anemic, whereas now they at least look healthy."

The main course arrived on the arms of waiters wearing gilded mail designed to look as though they were clothed in scales. Hans realized for the first time that only seafood was being served, that he had not tasted a single morsel of land meat throughout the day or this evening. Fish, Endelarin informed him, had been the food on that First Day of All, caught in sorcerous golden nets cast onto the first waves that touched the Leur when he stood on Sordan's silver shore. Another myth reenacted.

"There sure is a lot of food," Hans mentioned again as a whole lake eel, as long as three tall men, was set before the table and sliced with golden lances.

"Well," Endelarin conceded, "tomorrow is Second Day, when not a crumb of food is to be eaten in Sordan from the crack of dawn until the sun rises on Third Day. Not long as fasts go, but it pays to stock up!"

"Isn't that the day of revels?"

"If you care to call it that. I call it chaos. You can do anything but eat. They get drunk as lords around here on empty stomachs. And of course, some will start tonight." Endelarin gestured to Tiflan, who—his face slightly flushed with good Teremari wine—was smiling broadly at nothing in particular.

The meal had ended and the table cleared of all but pastries and fruits and goblets of light sweet wines when Tiflan pushed his chair back and rose to go speak with Dorilian. Hans saw that the Hierarch was standing near the side door where Legon and a man in the emerald and black livery of an Eagle Guard courier were reading from a piece of parchment. The soft background music had become bolder and livelier and many guests had left their places to mingle as the tone of the evening turned festive. Hans wondered that he had not even noticed Dorilian leaving his place, but as he watched Tiflan amble somewhat carefully away from the table, he caught hold of two of the most luminous golden eyes he had ever seen.

Princess Melenthas smiled at him across Tiflan's empty place. "At last we are given a chance to make acquaintance before this evening is ended," she said. Her voice was as clear and free of clouds as spring skies.

Wondering at his good fortune and determined to make the most of it, Hans responded with all the hope and warmth he had felt toward her all evening. "Nothing could please me more, Your Royal Highness."

The crested neckline of her dress, stiffly elegant, rustled as she inclined her head to study him with slightly more than casual regard. An earring, falling across her cheek, glittered like a trail of stars. "I heard from someone," she smiled coyly, "that you are Handurin Stauberg-Randolph."

Maybe, if she liked her men royal, a future king of Essera would be of interest. There might yet be an upside to this adventure. Hans relaxed into a smile. "I suppose I might as well own up to it."

"While you can." Softly voiced sharpness sent a warning singing through Hans.

His mouth went dry. What had she heard, sitting at Dorilian's left hand? "Excuse me, but do you know something I don't?"

"Simply your family's reputation, which precedes you. From what I have heard, you are not welcome."

Newly alarmed, Hans shot a glance across the room to where Dorilian and Tiflan still stood in consultation with officers of the Guard. "In truth, Princess, I do not know what you have been told."

Melenthas, following his gaze, smiled carelessly. "You may be sure that Dorilian told me nothing. He plays a game with you, the same Highborn game he plays with us all—and all of them." A gesture of her chin directed Hans to look out at the crowded hall. "We are all pieces on his board. A few are pieces of rank. You, however, are but a pawn. A deluded, Stauberg-Randolph pawn, as your brother was before you. You should never have come here, where you are not wanted for so much as a word or a dance."

Hans felt as though the floor had fallen out from under him. He had not expected to meet with disdain. Though it hit the mark, Melenthas's venom stood in sharp contrast to Dorilian's calculated coolness or the ignorant enmity of men like Pallas. What he could not tell was whether he had wandered into a provocation or a trap.

"I have been received by the Hierarch with no less than perfect civility and honor." He delivered the reminder, though the calm with which he made that claim was forced. Dorilian's civility had been less than perfect at times, but only in private.

Melenthas's fingers teased the golden rim of her wine cup, her eyes watching above it and the smile sweetly curving on her lips. "Tagtail relations will always step up out of the gutter to press claims to what the rightful heir should have and, lest they cry foul and raise their unwashed minions to the cause, must be treated with feigned welcomes and fine words. The Stauberg-Randolphs have poisoned Essera long enough with their bastard line. You should take your Kheldish blood and half-breed ways back to where you came from. Sordan has nothing for you, as you will soon learn."

Her scorn stung Hans in places he had not even known were tender. Childhood barbs and wounds that until now he had put aside welled up and clamored to be heard again. *Little half-breed... bastard... usurper brat... pretender.* Always whispers interrupted, veiled glances, snickers—telling him that he and his brother were less than others for their father being Kheld. That their mother was half Kheld. Marc Frederick, too, had Kheldish blood. Had that been part of what had destroyed Stefan? Had Staubaun arrogance hardened and twisted him? Hans had not envisioned that he might need to stand against people so far removed from recognizing other people as having worth that they could reject every hint of impurity. Maybe that was what Endelarin had meant, the reason Dorilian disdained even the most noble of his subjects—who would, if they dared, have disdained him.

Impurity! Hans wanted to toss back at her. *Ask your Highborn lover what it is to be impure—he with his Nemenor-tainted blood!*

But he bit those words from his tongue before they ever departed. If Dorilian did not boast of his Ardaenan blood, neither did he attempt to disown it. And not even once had Dorilian slighted Hans about *his* birth. To aim barbs at him would be inexcusable. This woman, however, was another matter.

"Lady," Hans said, keeping tight control of his anger, "our blood-lines are not ours to choose in this world, and I am not ashamed of mine. Actions matter more to me than ancestors. But Mormantalorus, I have heard, is stepping up its breeding program—and I think you are just the kind of pedigreed bitch they are looking for."

Melenthas raised her hand to her mouth but failed to bite back a furious exclamation. Though blood rushed to her cheeks, she had no time to launch a stinging retort. Endelarin, who had been looking on and listening as well, chortled his appreciation of her embarrassment.

"Bravo, lad! Bravely said!" The ruby crown on Endelarin's head slipped to one side, his warm complexion positively glowing as he waved a goblet of amber wine in sloppy salute.

The entire room came to a standstill. Conversation died to a whisper and then not even that.

"Endelarin!" Dorilian shouted a warning.

"But... but—truly—it wasn't me!"

As Dorilian strode up to him, Endelarin made an undignified dive out of his chair to avoid being grasped by his velvet-padded shoulders. Tripping over his own chair he waved his arms for a moment as if to take flight, then tumbled in the most uncourtly manner possible down the dais steps and rolled into a side table bearing flagons of red Teremar wine. Jostled, the flagons fell over and a few crashed onto the hard floor all around him, spilling their contents like fountains. Spouting with wronged wrath, wine still raining down upon him, Endelarin assailed Dorilian with all the sputtering pride he could muster.

"Dorilian, you ingrate! You are a vile-minded bully, and I... I disown you!"

With Princess Melenthas standing at his side in a mixture of bright-eyed outrage and nervous hand-wringing, Dorilian looked down from the dais steps. "Do it. And while you're at it, take the next ship off my island. At long last perhaps I shall succeed in clearing Sordan of vermin!"

"Not unless someone has the presence of mind to throw you into the hold along with me!" Taking care to avoid pieces of broken glass, Endelarin rose to his feet and began to squeeze wine from his sodden garments in wringing handfuls. "You have assaulted an innocent soul, you blackguard!"

"You deny affronting the princess and our hospitality?" Across Dorilian's chest, caught in silver brilliance, the Sordaneon eagle spread its wings, talons poised as if to strike.

"Deny? What's to deny? I heartily avow my innocence of even so much as an ill-placed thought in regard to your pretty plaything!" Endelarin recovered his ruby crown from the hands of a helpful page and settled it firmly over his wine-plastered dark hair before stalking back up the steps. "She is much too hard for my taste. I'm surprised you haven't broken a tooth on her."

Bemused, Dorilian turned a curious frown onto Melenthas. She twisted the opaline ring on her finger, unable to look either man in the eyes. At last she pivoted and pointed at Hans, accusing him of her displeasure.

"It was him! He is vile, utterly vile—a barbaric, uncouth son-of-a-Kheld and—and—and he said the most dreadful things to me! I have never been so insulted in my life. King Endelarin said naught, but he laughed at my discomfiture and thought it all a fine joke. You should expel them both, Thrice Royal, for their ill manners. And to spare your guests their loathsome insults."

Dorilian ignored Melenthas's outburst and eyed Hans with frank interest. "What could you possibly have said to bring all this about?"

In front of Dorilian's guests was hardly the time, or the place, to thrash out the matter, so Hans simply answered with as much dignity as he could. "If it may please Your Thrice Royal Grace, I will tell you later."

He had the distinct impression that if the gathering had not been present, Dorilian would have dragged him out bodily and shaken it from him. Instead, Dorilian simply frowned and faced Endelarin, who stood glaring up at him expectantly.

"Whatever disgrace has befallen you, Endelarin, you will deserve it before the night is out." Dorilian turned to address the guests crowding the dais, eaten up with curiosity and desiring an explanation. "This matter is done. Return to your revels."

Endelarin grabbed Dorilian's arm as he moved to depart. "Surely I should receive an apology, cousin! You were most impetuously unfair!"

"And you shall receive your apology," Dorilian assured him, guiding him back to his place at the table, "as soon as you are on your flagship sailing a straight course back to Ardaen." With that, Dorilian returned to his guests.

Not quite content but unable to pursue the matter further, Endelarin took his seat and glowered into a dish of flavored ice placed there at Tiflan's request. He smelled distinctly of wine and was more than a little sticky. Tiflan grinned at him across Hans's nose.

"Your perfume is getting stale, Your Majesty. Perhaps you should seek out your chambers for a bath and a change."

"An excellent idea," Endelarin agreed woefully. "Do I have chambers?"

"I arranged some for you."

Endelarin refused to leave until he had finished every bit of his ice, his favorite flavor. Then he and Tiflan strutted from the crowded hall, both chuckling heartily as they left.

A period of dances followed the dinner. Joyful music born of flutes and strings accompanied pairs of lords and ladies in the often-intricate figures of Staubaun dance. Traditionally all persons participated in the first dance, which was led by the Hierarch and his consort. Dorilian, as capable in this as he was in all things, went through the movements of the dance with a controlled, masculine grace as haunting as the music, Melenthas following like a glimmering golden shadow. The entire Hall seemed captured in swirling focus about that prime pair as they moved to a melody as ancient as Sordan.

Hans felt someone move to stand beside him and turned to see a woman somewhat taller than himself and probably several years older, with summer-gold hair and lively brown eyes. She smiled at him.

"Ask me to dance, Your Royal Highness, and we will both blend in far better."

"I don't believe we have met."

"Let's become acquainted while we dance."

Hans, unfortunately, did not know this dance at all. To him, the movements possessed an alien strangeness that little resembled dances he knew. He had, however, taken a ballroom dancing class at his moms' insistence and found that feigning a waltz worked fairly well.

"There. Now people have even more reason to watch you. I am Asphalladra, once Archessa of Heddros," she said. "I knew your brother."

Hans relaxed a little more into the dance. "Not many people would admit to that."

Asphalladra ducked her head slightly but did not deny it. "I don't usually mention it. Stefan and I were not especially friendly. He was my husband's friend."

"Oh. I—"

"Cullen Brodheson. Stefan ennobled him. Archon of Heddros and Enlad of Wyre. Your regent, Erenor, executed Cullen after Stefan died."

Hans nearly stopped dancing. Only Asphalladra's body filling the crook of his arm and the movement of other dancers through the room kept him moving as well. Stefan and Cullen had been friends from boyhood, as close as brothers. Hans remembered a smiling young man with freckles. He also remembered Stefan saying that Dorilian had deliberately broken Cullen's leg.

"I knew Cullen. I mean, I met him a few times. I didn't know—"

"That he was married? Or that he is dead? There's a great deal you don't know. You have been gone a long time." Asphalladra pressed closer and molded her body to his. Hans noticed it was in approximation of the dance, and made it easier for her to speak privately. "Erenor would have killed our children, our son and daughter, had I not fled Essera with them. They are—were—heir to Cullen's title and estates. *My* family… well, my father and the Regent had lined up another husband for me. I feared that man even more. Sordan was the only safe refuge."

"I'm sorry. I—"

"I'm not asking you to do anything about it. You will learn soon enough that Essera is a hideous fabrication, stitched together by broken things."

"Are you saying I shouldn't return?"

"On the contrary! I think Essera needs you."

The music sped up to a lovely crescendo. Hans spun Asphalladra around a few times and she somehow flowed with him, her skirt delivering a silky caress to his legs. He was fairly sure they made a pretty presentation. Asphalladra turned so her lips were near Hans's ear, her voice confiding and warm.

"I have a message—your mother is happy to know you are safely in Sordan. Dorilian told her. He may not tell you. He has more locks than any vault."

"But he told you?"

"Oh, no. Your mother did." The music stopped and, with it, the dancers. Asphalladra smiled and curtseyed. "Thank you for the dance, Your Royal Highness."

Hans had barely murmured his thanks before she stepped away and blended easily into the background again. Asphalladra. He must remember that name. Hans was less sure what to think about his mother. Of course it was only natural that his mother would want to know if he was safe, and he was glad to learn she did know. Writing a letter had crossed his mind but his room had proved devoid of paper or writing implements and he did not yet know how restrictive Dorilian would be about correspondence. Emyli herself might be one of many hidden forces pulling strings about which Hans knew nothing. Dorilian so far had not talked about her.

Though Hans had danced with Asphalladra, Melenthas's taunt proved prophetic and he found no other partners forthcoming. Alone again, he wandered near the terrace windows, only to see Dorilian cornered by a stocky, soberly garbed man and several other nobles drawn by the Hierarch's accessibility. Hans was trying not to listen when he noticed that the exchange was not casual and that it involved him, if only indirectly.

"Look, Herberth, I do not discuss these things at State dinners." Dorilian's tone was resolute, but the stocky man confronting him was not easily put off.

"Why the Leur not?"

"Because," Dorilian explained with obvious exasperation, "if I do, nobody gives me any chance to enjoy myself—and I do not like these affairs very much to begin with."

"This is important. Handurin—"

"Is not a subject for discussion."

"At least tell me what he is doing here!"

"Eating my food. That is the end of what I will say about it, Herberth," Dorilian warned. "Now you will kindly cease to bother me else I will find it necessary to avoid your company for the remainder of your stay here."

Herberth. Hans had heard that name a few times this evening, so he knew the man was the Elector of Trongor. He had heard a lot about Trongor on his journey upriver, and Arne had told him more. Trongor held the tenuous position of being one of the few countries that maintained ties with both Sordan and Amallar. That its leader had attempted to force an audience spoke well for Trongor wanting to hold that relationship.

Herberth backed down before Dorilian's threat. He valued his own ally well enough to know how far he could press an issue—and for the moment, Handurin Stauberg-Randolph was not an issue to be forced. Talk turned instead to an older white-haired Bas named Terveryan, who recited the virtues of his nubile daughter.

A flurry of activity on the main floor drew all eyes and brought the room to silence. Hans looked over just in time to catch the grand reappearance of Endelarin who, not to be kept from the best part of a party, had returned to the gathering in a fresh set of clothing as flamboyant as the first. This time, Endelarin had chosen for mischief, for he brazenly imitated the Hierarch's splendid attire, including an Ardaenish cock blazoned across his chest. The stunned nobles watched Dorilian covertly as they gaped, some aghast at the sea king's audacity, some struggling with laughter and wondering if they dared let it loose.

"Dorilian! Cousin!" Endelarin waved. "Do look at me, we match! Now the ladies will have no excuse for preferring you over myself, as they so often do."

Dorilian stood for a long moment and simply stared at this parody of him. Hans found himself wondering along with the court if Dorilian was about to create a scene. Instead, he tilted his head and one corner of his mouth turned upward.

"Endelarin Nemenor, one of these days you will succeed in going too far."

"Ah, ha!" Endelarin chortled. "I made you smile! That is a good sign, a very good sign. You are not lost to humanity, Dorilian, only misplaced!" Having succeeded in tweaking his royal cousin, Endelarin turned to gloomy Terveryan, the Bas of Anit-Rebir. "Your daughter for the next dance, Most Noble? Thank you."

The elderly man went almost purple with rage as Endelarin led his favorite child into the swirling movements of a lively roundel. "Do something, Thrice Royal!" Terveryan demanded. "That libertine has my daughter!"

"She will not lose her maidenhood on the dance floor, Bas Rebiran." But Dorilian continued to watch Endelarin with a sort of keen anticipation and surreptitious delight.

Endelarin could very well end up in the harbor again tonight if he was not careful, Hans knew, but somehow he doubted it. While he tried to unravel what he had just witnessed, Melenthas once more claimed Dorilian's partnership in a dance. Hans sighed, beginning to believe that between the demands of Sordan and the Mercedan princess, he would never get a chance to talk with his host. He wished he had some of Endelarin's... insouciance. But he didn't.

Neither his moms nor his education had prepared him for this.

Now that he had met Dorilian, he was at such a loss that he could think of neither anything to say nor how to say it. He had heard that Dorilian hated Khelds, had hated Stefan... was someone Stefan had sought to kill. Yet Asphalladra had told Hans that Sordan had offered refuge for her and Cullen Brodheson's children, had been the only possible refuge, and Dorilian had to have been party to a decision like that.

Who *was* this man?

Hans wandered out onto the terrace in search of a view and to clear his head. Taking deep breaths of cool night air, he stood next to a parapet and gazed out across the World. The stars, a bright river against the night, seemed to reflect the City that burned as brilliantly below. Last night had seen such violence; this night seemed to belie those events. Music filtered through open doors, tired chords strummed by weary fingers, to mingle with human laughter and the sweet rustle of leaves on the velvet voice of night. Below, sharp hoofbeats sounded along a winding road, vanishing around a bend. A slight breeze from the lake touched his face with swift warm fingers, ruffling his hair and brushing his silken tunic against his skin. A sense of recognition seized him, something powerful and clean. Perhaps Hans didn't belong here in this corner of the World, but he felt a kinship with Sordan, a City the rivermen celebrated in song for having shrugged off decades of Esseran domination.

Hans dropped his hand to trace the seamless stone of the rampart as he walked its length. His eyes drifted again to the show of lights below and compared that delicate beauty with the raw might daylight would reveal. Somehow the comparison was not as sharp as he had thought it would be. This display of lights against the darkness was a statement of greater might than any vista of towering battlements—and he had only to look behind him to see proof of why Sordan was called the City of Light.

He had reached the end of the terrace. Though Hans didn't really want to return to the Celadon Hall and an evening of public shunning, it hardly made sense to hide out here for the rest of the night. He was being watched, assessed, by a man he needed to impress. With a sigh, he turned around and began to walk back along the terrace, its broad expanse and elegant balustrades streaked with patches of light from the tall windows that faced it.

It took him but one breath to realize he was not alone.

20

The race of Leur is long-vanished, but three of the
Five Cities they gifted to us remain. Though these
cities were built for mortalkind and serve us well,
they yield little in the way of answers. For thousands of years, they have existed in splendid stasis,
maintaining pure air, perfect temperature, water
hot and cold according to need, lights glowing into
the night and dimming by day, lighthouses to a
dark Creation.
—Patroculos, *Journeys to Many Lands*

For a heartbeat, Hans's only thought was to avoid Dorilian. To judge by the stillness with which he leaned against the rampart, gazing into space, Dorilian was deep within his own thoughts. Hans had no wish to disturb his solitude. The man had probably come out here hoping to get a few moments to himself. On the other hand, maybe Dorilian had maneuvered just this time and place for speaking with him.

He expects me to doubt him. Because of Stefan. And he doubts me too, for the same reasons.

Hans had crossed half of the distance between them when he stopped, uncertain of whom he approached. As he gazed out over his luminous city, Dorilian appeared so changed that Hans entertained for a moment the notion that he had been mistaken all along, that he had somehow met the wrong man. Not in all his imperious airs of the last several hours had Dorilian looked so regal as he now did, lost in thought, with the moonlight full upon him. Only when the inevitable moments had passed and the Hierarch turned very slightly to acknowledge him did Hans walk to join him at the parapet, fully expecting to see the familiar coldness return. But the warmth remained as Dorilian gazed out once more upon Sordan's sprawling lights. Hans thought Melenthas would probably sell her soul to be the recipient of a look like that.

"So, Handurin," Dorilian said. "What do you think of our prison?"

"A prison?" Hans tried to guess what Dorilian meant by that, and his heart sank.

"It doesn't look like one." Dorilian's rich voice, shaded with darkness, matched the night. He pointed to the city below. "From down there," he said, "men look up and think upon what manner of beings are so exalted as to dwell in such extravagance." He turned a sardonic smile upon Hans. "When I look down there, at the little lights, so many of them, knowing that there must be in attendance at least one person and maybe more, I wonder: who are they? Who are those uncounted souls who watch my every move? And when I look at you, you are like one of those lights—a small fire... or maybe a great one—but still too far away, so that I must wonder not only who you are but also whose supper you might be cooking."

They did not speak for a long while. Hans had no clear answer as to whose purposes he served, whether his own or Marenthro's or those of the Khelds he had yet to meet, much less win over. An unexpected burst of laughter drifted their way from the bright windows that poured radiance in molten bars onto the terrace at their backs. At his side, Dorilian had assumed again his distance and was unapproachable. They were like creatures of the night met at some forest glade, eyeing one another across the shallow water of their drinking hole, each knowing himself to be both hunter and hunted, the seeker and the thing that is sought.

"You are good at silence," Dorilian said at last. "That quality is rare enough to be admired when it is found. But I think we ought not overdo it."

"What do you want to know?"

Dorilian shook his head as though he were already weary of a problem that had not changed its aspect since they had met earlier. "Everything... and more than you can tell me." He sounded resigned. The crown upon his head shone as brightly resplendent as the moon itself. "Marenthro sent you on this errand—this I would know even if you had not told me—and I can guess his purposes, which are as blunt as the means by which he hopes to gain them. But you, I know less well, and I cannot guess your purposes, as guesswork is an art to be practiced only by the well acquainted. Or the desperate, which I am not yet. About your wizard, I can do nothing. Like the wind, he will have his way: go over walls or around them or blow them down as he sees fit. I do but watch the way the wind blows. But you, Handurin, are another matter." Once more Hans suffered a piercing scrutiny he found unnerving. "About you I can and must be certain."

Hans could think of nothing to say. The man was quite beyond him.

After a few moments, Dorilian looked away. "Again, you practice silence."

"What could I say that would convince you? I'm not a mind reader and I don't come with references."

"Except Marenthro's."

"I have a feeling he's just hoping for the best."

"He might be, at that. But wishing, even his, goes no further than the deed that carries it forth. You are here, where he would have you. And I have seen to it that you cannot be kept secret. That is as I would have you. Your reliance on my protection ensures a dialogue."

"With me?"

"With everyone."

"You come right out with it, don't you?"

"I would have you understand me."

"That's asking rather a lot." It seemed to Hans that understanding Dorilian was like understanding quicksand: it didn't really help.

"Surely you did not come to me expecting to be welcomed as a friend?"

"I wasn't sure what I would find, but I had not thought I would end up finding an enemy."

Hans wanted to strike a nerve, any nerve, even one of hostility. But Dorilian merely said, "Do not be too quick to judge your situation."

That mild rebuke signaled a subtle change in position. Somewhere between that very afternoon and this moonlit meeting, Dorilian appeared to have granted him a modicum of respect. Hans suspected it had something to do with his confrontation with Melenthas.

At the moment Dorilian looked too thoughtful to risk provoking him again, so Hans sank once more into his well-practiced silence and watched along with him the play of lights below. From this vantage, they looked down at not only the Dekkora, its openness defined by lights and shadows, but also the abstract, unsettling curves and lines of the massive Rill corridor. As Hans watched, he detected a low whine that cut to a higher pitch, then another, repeating in building cadences until something—brilliant, silver—burst from the terminal in a spear of light, shooting away from the city, gone almost before he could see it. A lingering thrum died only after it was gone.

"Can you tell me about that?" He pointed to the Rill. "Do you know how it works?"

"It is a god. It does not matter how it works."

Hans sighed at the answer. Apparently he would have to get used to having advanced technology go unexplained. But Dorilian had not said he did not know. Hans glanced at him, perplexed. Something about his question had raised Dorilian's defenses again. Or maybe it was something else, something in the scene below, the dancing, flickering parade of torches that moved upon the road toward the Dekkora. Not troublemakers this time, but a growing flood of pilgrims, the first celebrants of the coming day, for they stood on the doorstep of morning.

"It would be ill omened, whatever I should choose to do," Dorilian murmured, speaking to himself. "No path can be divined aright through so much darkness."

The change in mood poured over Hans like a sharp, drenching rain.

As though awakened to Hans's company, Dorilian gestured down to where the revelers gathered. "No good thing ever comes of Second Day. Look at them. It is not yet dawn and already they dance for the setting sun to set loose all the demons of a thousand hells to consort with mortal folk, openly and welcome, so that they and all excesses might be exorcised. Would that it was so easily done! Yet people do strange things on Second Day, and in the name of a universe they do not understand, they dredge holy madness from the pits of their beings and will dance until they believe that they are gods themselves. What happens on Second Day no man cares to explain after."

"I thought it was a celebration, a happy time."

"For some, maybe."

This time, Hans let his questions lie unanswered. Had Dorilian wanted to expand upon that statement, he would have. Clearly, however, Sordan's Hierarch took no joy in the celebration of Second Day, even though his entire court and every house in his capital was this night happily anticipating the revels. Something was so terribly wrong that even Hans could scarcely miss it. Wanting to keep alive the fragile contact of their meeting, the first real conversation between them, Hans attempted a diversion.

"The Khelds say that Sordan was built by Faery folk, you know," he said.

As he had hoped, Dorilian took note of the remark. Sordan was a subject that naturally sparked his interest. "Faery folk?" He snorted, casting his opinion. "That is a fanciful way of putting it. Those little knock-kneed creatures they think they catch peeking out from under the local fungus?"

Although he found Dorilian's acquaintance with such strictly Kheldish denizens surprising—Staubauns, as far as Hans knew, had little knowledge of Kheld lore—Hans decided it wouldn't hurt to educate him further on the subject. "Oh, no," he said. "Those are something else. Those are little people, forest sprites and the like. They are mischievous but not truly powerful. I am talking about the Faery folk, who lived in the Bogs long before people like us ever came to the World. According to what Kheldish tales say, when people did come, they employed a trick to get the Faery folk to build the Five Cities for them."

"What manner of trick?" Dorilian's interest, as elusive as his regard, had quickened.

"I don't remember," Hans confessed, feeling like a fool having to admit it. Not only had he demonstrated an appalling unfamiliarity with Staubaun traditions and mythology, but now his knowledge of Kheld lore was proving just as lacking. And just when he had gotten Dorilian interested in what he was saying. "I think the humans promised them they would not watch, but they did watch and learned the secrets of the Faery folk," he remembered a bit lamely. "When they found out about it, the Faery folk took away one of the Cities and all the land where it stood. But men already knew more than was wise. They became sorcerers and created a golden, beautiful race to serve them, and they destroyed one City in a war. Ever since then, there have been but Three Cities—and you can see for yourself that gold-haired people still hold them."

"I would not credit that entirely to having tricked the Faery folk." Despite the warning, Dorilian looked like he might be amused. "And it may be that your Kheld barbarians, like we, remember by such tales the forgotten history of the World before Exile."

"I suppose it might have been a Staubaun myth to begin with."

"It would seem so." Dorilian turned away from the lights of his city far below and, taking a seat upon the wide parapet, peered upward through the darkness at the soaring planes and spires of Sordan's Citadel. "Sit."

Having been given permission, Hans sat upon the parapet and looked up. Brushed by the moon's gentle glow, the silver towers of the Citadel seen above the frosted balconies of the Serat mirrored forgotten visions of misty legend. Who had built those ethereal towers? Tossed those walkways into space?

"You can still see the Light of Leur within her," Dorilian observed quietly. "Even the memory of Leur is fading, if ever memory there was. Only legends live on, past truth and past knowledge, outliving all else but these Cities they left behind. We can but look at their creations and let our hearts be broken, because something that was great in the World is gone from it forever. But this night we celebrate an elemental truth. Here it Began. Here it Ended. Here it Begins Again."

"Here what Began?"

"The Creation. The World That Is."

"I wish I could say I understand you."

"You will in time, if that should be granted you. Sordan is a place for beginnings and endings. Which it shall be for you remains to be seen. But this is the reason Marenthro had you come here. You are being thrown into our vicious circle, Handurin. It might have proved better for you if he had kept you out of it."

"I think he wanted to. I think maybe he tried, but the situation was one I don't think he could control."

"More than you would know about." It was odd, Hans thought, the way just talking about Marenthro put Dorilian on edge.

"Look, I know people around here think Marenthro is all-powerful," said Hans, "but he's not. He's immortal, maybe, but he's not infallible—and he's certainly not omnipotent. He can't be everywhere or do everything. In fact, he told me outright that there are certain things he cannot do."

"Or will not, you mean. I have seen for myself the deaths that monster considers acceptable. But I will not recount those horrors." Dorilian closed his eyes and turned away. Hans could guess against what memories. "Not to you."

But I know already. It took all his restraint for Hans not to say it. *I, too, was at Permephedon. I was behind your eyes, and you never knew it. I saw the way Marc Frederick died. I saw what Nammuor did.* Again he looked down at Dorilian's left hand upon the parapet, the Rill Stone—Tiflan had explained that too—burning green and strong upon his finger. That finger and the one next to it should have been missing but were not. Were they real, flesh and blood, or merely marvelous prostheses?

Maybe Hans didn't have to tell Dorilian what he knew. There was another way to talk about that day. "I have some idea. As a child I had bad dreams about my grandfather and the way he died. Dreams so bad I… that's why they sent me away," Hans ventured. He watched Dorilian's reaction closely, noted the way the Hierarch's jaw clenched, his body tensed. Defensiveness wafted off Dorilian so perceptibly that Hans knew better than to say more. "Marenthro explained it and he warned me that whether I returned to this world or not, there was something powerful and terrible—an enemy—who was going to be a problem."

Dorilian shot him a look. "What enemy?"

How much could he safely say? "I'm not sure."

"But you would hazard a guess."

"So would you."

Suddenly, Dorilian lunged onto his feet and loomed over Hans, who shrank away from him only to realize he sat with nothing but a free fall into darkness at his back. Dorilian's body crowded his. Too alive and unpredictable—and near. Hans's heart leaped into his throat as Dorilian's voice dropped to a vicious whisper.

"Oh, yes, now we're getting to it, aren't we? It certainly took you long enough! What are you not telling me?"

But Hans was finding it hard to appreciate just what his lack of openness had cost him. "Please," he pleaded, his mouth suddenly dry. He curled his fingers against the front edge of his seat to prevent himself from being pushed back further. "I don't want to fall." He didn't look away from Dorilian, afraid that if he did, he would lose his grip.

To Hans's horror, Dorilian was in no hurry to release him from his dangerous perch. "The hell you will fall. You are going nowhere until I am finished with you."

"I don't know what you're talking about."

"Make no mistake, Marenthro sent you here to save your life. My guess is that he was forced to move ahead of his plan, with little time for preparation." Dorilian's dark voice lowered even more and he moved a fraction nearer, pressing Hans even farther toward the brink over which he hung so precariously. "It wasn't just the Archhalia—he knew you would be hunted. Your enemies have joined ranks and you would not stand a blind man's chance in a wolvern's lair. And that is why you came here, with your tattered little hanger-on, looking for a nursemaid. A prince in naught but name, with precious little to offer, who does not even know what to ask for. For all your talk of Amallar and Khelds, you bear no proof of backing and I doubt you are even able to name your supporters there. And any other support you might have hoped for will hardly view this excursion of yours without questioning either your motives or your sanity. You will be very lucky indeed if you do not lose your Kheldish friends by it. And to make matters worse, you are already too well-known in *this* land to make free of it without my help. No matter that my helping you might well cost me alliances that I sorely need and gain for you more grief than honor. In short, you are alone and stranded in a strange land. Your prospects, on the whole, are rather bleak. But you are alive, which will serve to let Marenthro off the hook with your mother!"

Dorilian eyed Hans with unconcealed exasperation. "My ambassador to the Archhalia attempted to contact your wizard personally, regarding your *deiknya*. It occurred to us that he might want you back. He was—how shall I put this? Oh yes, unavailable. But then I do not suppose there is anything he can add to improve our situation, do you? Every sorcerer has his cauldron—and we *are* in a stew."

"He would have talked to *you*," said Hans, trying to justify Marenthro's vanishing act.

"I am sure he would have," Dorilian agreed. A perverse sort of satisfaction played at the edge of his smile. "But I'm not biting."

"Why are you so set against him?" Although earlier conversation had hinted at it, Hans found Dorilian's antipathy unsettling.

"Marenthro? Ours is a private discord."

"Not if it includes me," Hans pointed out. His muscles had tightened, his breathing shortened, as the strain of leaning backward began to take its toll.

"Very well, then," Dorilian relented, "as it is common knowledge hereabout, and I should think elsewhere, that I cannot abide him. More even than the deaths he has countenanced and the ruin he does not deign to prevent, I dislike the way he plays with people's lives. Mine, for instance"—he mockingly regarded his cornered companion—"and yours."

"He's not playing games. He's trying to help!"

"Are you truly that naive? Perhaps you are. We are worlds apart, Handurin, you and I, in ways you cannot begin to imagine."

Night's erratic breeze quickened its cool caress and music filtered upward from the streets below—muted, brassy notes—a different breed of music, harsh and loud and slightly drunken, refusing to be bound by walls. Hans felt its beat pulse in his blood and under his ribs. Dorilian shook his head slightly and turned away from the music. To his eyes the haunted look returned full force.

Though Hans hadn't been thinking of physical danger, the image of falling forced itself into his brain. Once there it settled like a spark and began to burn until the night blurred to a crimson sky. In a nightmarish vision, the flagstones below suddenly flew upward, rising to meet him—somewhere, someone screamed.

Brutal pain shot through Hans's arm as Dorilian grabbed him and hauled him from the edge and back onto his feet. "Fool!" he berated. "Are you trying to ruin me? I told you I would not let you fall!"

Hans found his balance. What had just happened? "I'm sorry. I must have been daydreaming… or something."

"It is not a place to be sitting, in any event." Dorilian released him and abruptly Hans missed the sharpness of that physical contact: brief as it had been, there had been something powerfully alive about it, a warm—alien—reality.

"Thank you," he said, though he did not completely mean it. Dorilian had made him sit there in the first place.

Dorilian, not one to miss an inflection, granted a thin smile. "For the time being, I am satisfied. You have the honor of my House, Prince Handurin, for so long as my name protects you."

Hardly a heartfelt welcome. But it was a statement of protection, just the sort of acknowledgment Hans had been searching for all night. Though he had dared to hope for more, Hans knew by now to be content with what was given. He bowed formally to Dorilian and responded in turn.

"I thank you, Thrice Royal, for your hospitality. Perhaps I shall yet prove worthy of it."

"Your presence suits me well, I assure you," Dorilian said, his meaning hidden in the knowing line of his mouth. "I have got everyone properly in turmoil now, haven't I?" Unreadable, he looked over his shoulder at the lighted hall and the shadowy figures within. To Hans he offered nothing more, not the armsclasp of kinship nor the courtesy due an equal, as yet assigning him neither stature. "Come," he said. "We must return to the festivities, and I to the demands of my position. We shall do so together. I would emphasize your standing. There are more than a few in Sordan— and beyond—who would seek your death if they thought I would overlook it."

Glass doors swung open onto the terrace. Only then did Hans notice Legon Rebiran. As Hans and Dorilian walked past, Legon silently relinquished his post in the shadows, permitting the party guests to stroll once more across those lovely flagstone courts into the night.

21

The Highborn mythos embedded itself in
Staubaun society through ritual worship and
ceremonies that commemorate key events
surrounding the Return. These acquired broader
meaning as the events became more distant in the
populace's memory. The Esseran Feast of Imenos
barely resembles the Return of Amynas and Leur,
which it celebrates. The ceremony that retains the
purest links to Malyrdean myth is the annual
celebration in Sordan. The three-day cycle of the
Illumination re-enacts the entire myth.
—Patroculos, *Journeys to Many Lands*

Second Day dawned like any other. Tiflan's early arrival was the first indication that something different had been planned. On what could be assumed were Dorilian's instructions, the Bas of Teremar spent most of the morning seeing Hans and Arne properly outfitted for the upcoming celebration. When he finished, they stood draped in an arsenal of finery that would have put Endelarin to shame for sheer gaudiness. If First Day and the Feast of Coming were for the showing off of one's status, Second Day was for simply showing off. Good taste flew out the window along with every other rule of fashion.

Hans had to give Tiflan credit—the man had a certain robust flair. He had decided that Hans was to wear a suit of silken tatters, blue over red over gold, the colors showing through as he moved. Hans protested briefly when Tiflan placed a golden crown on his head—for all that it was glitter and paste and not real—but Tiflan overruled him.

"We can't let him out-do us, now, can we?"

"Let who?" asked Arne. He stood nearby in his own costume of white and black satin, with a cloak showing white horses printed on a black background, and a great white horsetail floating down from the crested silver helm on his head. Hans could tell Arne liked that the helm had a visor that could be dropped to conceal his eyes.

"That blasted Endelarin, who else? He always steals the show—and the honors for best costume. It has gone to me for the last two years, but then he was not around to spoil my fun."

"But I don't want to stand out," Hans protested. As he looked in the mirror, he thought that the crown looked more ludicrous than anything else.

"You will stand out if you don't stand out, lad." Tiflan gave Hans a dusting off and stood back to survey the result. "Not bad," he said. "You are fitting company for such a fine fellow as myself." His great shaggy head fell back as he roared with laughter. He had chosen sky-blue rags and bright orange stockings for his dress as a wandering musician. Across his broad shoulders he had slung seven silver-stringed gitars. Pan pipes hung down upon his chest like golden hands, and flutes and clackers adorned the many rings upon his fingers. Even his boots were laced with tiny coppery chimes.

It was late morning by the time they made their way from the quiet, shaded ways of the Serat to the milling openness of the Dekkora. All evidence of the fires and chaos of the nights previous had been removed or covered over. Walls and buildings shone in clean, white splendor and the crowd, swollen by pilgrims from far-flung provinces, all wore colors and masks. According to tradition, colors confused the demons and masks served to conceal the identities of the wearers, protecting them from harm. Hans tugged at his own mask, glad of the anonymity it offered.

As cousin to the Hierarch and ruler of a great domain, Tiflan had no need to battle for space in the crowded square. He and his guests occupied one of the elaborate tents set up on the second of the three landings approaching the Rill terminal, from which vantage point they could watch the games and performances in comfort. Dorilian's tent dominated the center of the landing, of course, and stood next to theirs. Hans had seen already that Dorilian, while in attendance, was not in costume. Neither were Levy-athan and Fahme, who occupied seats of honor. The royal tents looked directly down on the lowermost landing, which was clear of crowds and set up as a stage. Tiflan had barely gotten Hans and Arne settled in when Endelarin bounded into the tent and rapped Tiflan on the head with a jangling wand, setting the bells in the taller man's hair to jingling.

"What a pair we make!" Endelarin crowed. His broad, toothy grin looked disturbingly diabolical beneath a pair of magnificent, curving ivory horns, each laid with gold leaf and precious gems wound about like cords from base to tip. "Lovely, aren't they?" Endelarin patted his strangely wrought treasures. "I got them off an idol."

The rest of Endelarin's costume was no less flamboyant. He wore a short gown of gold silk embroidered with emeralds to look like green scales, and great golden ring-claws, set with rubies about the tips like blood, capped his fingers. From his belt dangled an astonishing assortment of trinkets, from little lifelike figures of men and women in the most suggestive of poses, to bags of glitter dust and polished bones, and moons of various phases and sizes. Only his trident, however, looked dangerous.

"That's... a wonderful costume, Your Majesty," said Hans in genuine admiration.

"Well, I don't want the demons to carry me off, you know." Endelarin swirled his floor-length cloak to half cover his face and glared sinisterly above it. "Do you think they will recognize me?"

"Probably," Tiflan concluded. "But if they haven't carried you off by now, I would not worry about it."

Arne tugged on Hans's sleeve and whispered into his ear. "Who's that?"

Hans whispered back. "Endelarin Nemenor. He's King of Ardaen."

"Him?" Arne looked doubtful. Amallar was the Esseran domain nearest Ardaen, though tall mountains divided the two countries, and Khelds had even less contact with their seafaring neighbors than they did the folk of Sordan.

Brass trumpets sounded across the Dekkora, high above the noisy crowd. In swirls of color, masses of people pushed nearer the landing as actors took places upon the stage.

"Now we are in for it," Endelarin said in a low aside to Hans. "The play takes hours."

"The play?"

"The Illumination. The story is a bit dated and players tend to stray into melodrama, but the masses love it."

On the stage, a black-robed celebrant raised a sword over his head. Hans gasped along with the crowd as the man brought the weapon down point first, plunging it deep into what looked like a human form upon the stage. A shocked cry broke from the lips of the audience, many of whom had never seen the play.

"Thus you are wood, who would have been master!" the man shouted above the corpse. *"Fit to burn, he who started the fire!"* With that he ran offstage and was gone.

On the stage, the sword stood upright, a shining exclamation.

Another man, richly dressed, ran onstage. Discovering the body, he began to deliver a soliloquy on the Devastation and he who had caused it.

"Grab the sword, man, and run!" Endelarin murmured impatiently to Hans's right. "This is all introduction, anyway," he explained. "The really good stuff comes later."

As Hans watched, the man, revealed to be Amynas, took up the sword and swore upon it to Return, then fled. Endelarin toasted the occasion with a round of Ardaenan mead, strongly flavored with honey and malt and brewed, Endelarin avowed, in the empty skulls of all the wise men to be found in Ardaen. Although Hans choked a bit at that, he had to admit that the liquid practically flowed down his throat without needing to be swallowed.

As the hour passed and both Tiflan and Endelarin started roaring with laughter, Hans stole nervous glances at Dorilian, wondering just how far they could go with their irreverence. It was the Hierarch's ancestor, after all, being celebrated. Dorilian, however, seated with Levyathan and Fahme, and isolated by the icy white of his robes, seemed to be totally absorbed in watching the performance. In truth, when Hans took the time to watch, he could tell that the actors were very good. Maybe he really was drunk on the liquor of wise-men's skulls—for the play took on a rich pseudo-reality wherein the Passionate Truth became all at once very clear.

Illumination.

Hans peered into the mind of Belief and found what it was that so many clung to so fervently. His heart throbbed as Amynas Wanderer, his anguish having driven him to seek his ruined world, knelt before the light-crowned Citadel on Sordan's holy shore, his promise to Return fulfilled.

Bowing to the Hierarch's tent, the actor ascended the steps, holding the sword out before him as an offering. Dorilian too had a part to play. He descended to meet the portrayal of his forefather, Amynas Founder, and took up the sword. He brandished the weapon to the crowd, which had fallen silent, then pressed the blade to his forearm and slowly drew the edge across his flesh. Blood welled and dripped along the blade, which Dorilian handed back, red-tinged and seemingly ablaze with the fiery last light of day, to the triumphant actor.

The crowd cheered. With a grin, the actor took up the god's sacred sword and flung out his arms as Amynas's statue in the fountain would portray him for eternity and shouted in triumph:

"Now shall all foul things flee before me!"

A collective cry answered from minds enraptured—a full, raw animal howl of mingled joy and hope and despair—as the crowd, caught in the silver web of the actor's performance, half-believed that the world, indeed, stood on the threshold of rebirth. The celebration had just begun. From tongue and lip and throat the chants poured forth in wild adulation. From hands and feet the clapping and stamping began the wild dance. *Amynas'Sordanaeyi! Amynas'Sordanaeyi! Malyrdys'Sordanaeyi!*

Dei'Sordanaeyi!

The god is in Sordan!

In wonder, Hans observed an aeon compressed into the last few hours of the year. The crowd hurled itself almost as a single creature into a new, writhing form. Groups of hundreds coalesced into mad processions. Representative factions from each village and town got their chance to perform on the stage from which the magic of the Illumination had not entirely vanished, their flying feet and waving arms calling always for more dancers, more movement, more outpourings of joyous fervor. *The god is in Sordan!* Pipes and drums and brazen horns filled the space between worlds, for this World would die with the setting of the Sun—and the new World would not be reborn until the rising of the Sun in the morning.

Although Hans did not believe that the World was ending,

something about these vibrant dances, these colorful and eager dancers, drew him powerfully into their sway. His flushed face and hungry eyes gave him away, for Endelarin said, "You want to join in, don't you?"

"Yes," Hans said. Beside him, Arne gaped and looked horrified.

"I don't think you should," Tiflan said doubtfully. "Dorilian would not approve of it."

Endelarin blithely waved him off. "Dorilian be damned!" The remark bordered on blasphemy considering all that had just taken place. "He took part in the dances himself once. Why should he spoil everybody else's fun? Come, lad." He tugged at Hans's sleeve. "What harm can there be in it?"

Endelarin bounded to his feet, drawing Hans with him as he ran around and behind the pavilion's silken walls. Left behind in the tent, Tiflan had been less quick on his feet and missed them as they fled around the corner.

Hans was out of breath by the time they reached the lower ramparts of the Citadel where its ramps sided on the Dekkora. They had run the long way around, since traipsing down the steps would have drawn too much attention. Endelarin for all his unathletic build ran remarkably light on his feet. They stopped beside the wall to catch their breaths as the sinking sun touched the thin low clouds over the lake and turned them glowing orange, then dying red. The running had cleared Hans's head a little and it started to dawn on him just what he had done. If Tiflan did not end up killing him, Dorilian probably would.

But when he turned to Endelarin, thinking to ask him to go back, the sea king's eyes sparkled merrily behind his Sorcerer's mask, and with a crazy whoop and laugh he bounded off into the crowd.

Hans's only thought from that point on was that he must not lose him.

The red and bloated sun touched the mirroring surface of the lake so that it shimmered like something molten. A shrill howling broke from the throats of the crowd as twilight deepened to darkness. Hans couldn't tell how much time had passed. An hour? Two? It might be more. Torches flared and great bonfires set the Dekkora itself aglow. The partying would continue on into the night, people celebrating until the New World was born again with the dawn.

Endelarin, however, had no taste for night dancing. "It isn't demons I am worried about!" he informed Hans as he hurried him across the torchlit Dekkora to the steps, magically aglow beneath the three wondrous lights Hans had noticed on his first night in Sordan. Like new-risen moons, they hung supported by naught but their own celestial perfection. Hans wondered how it was possible the orbs had not burned out in many thousands of years. Or how the mechanism for suspending them had not failed.

"Magic," Endelarin informed him. "You won't figure it out, no matter what mathematics you use."

The Hierarch's pavilion was empty and in the process of being taken down, but Tiflan awaited them under the Teremar silks, still seated where they had left him. Most of the other nobles and their households had retired to their lodgings so that they might purify themselves for the more solemn ceremonies that would begin after midnight.

"At least you had sense enough to bring him back with you," Tiflan grumbled upon seeing them.

"It was good for him." Endelarin plopped onto the scattered cushions and helped himself to the wine. "He's young; he needs the exercise." He poured a cup for Hans but Tiflan took it from him.

"No more wine. He's fasting, and I want him in some sort of shape for Third Day."

Hans looked around, half-expecting to find Dorilian standing nearby, ready to lay into him. But only Arne was there, looking nervous and tired and very obviously relieved to have him back. In fact, he looked so relieved that Hans felt guilty at having left him. Other than the young Kheld, only guards and a few retainers stood nearby in case they were needed. He accepted, gladly, the horn of water Tiflan handed him.

"And what did Dorilian have to say about it?" Endelarin asked, bringing up the question most on Hans's mind.

"Nothing."

"Nothing?" Hans asked. "You mean he didn't mind?"

Tiflan frowned, his expression grim. "I mean he never noticed.

If he had noticed, he would have minded very much indeed. However, he left around the same time you two pulled your vanishing act."

Endelarin arched one eyebrow at that but said no more. Instead he poured himself another cup of wine.

"Why did he leave?" It seemed to Hans that the Hierarch of Sordan would have stayed for that final moment, the setting of the sun, which the god Amynas himself had witnessed. All of Dorilian's actions up to that point had been consistent with conscientious observance of his caste's religious function, if not his actual godhood. But then, Hans had to admit he didn't know everything about that.

"It has little enough to do with you, son. He would have left in any case." Tiflan glared at Endelarin, who made a show of sipping his wine in an effort to escape his friend's displeasure. "The point is, had he known you were out there, he might not have."

"You wanted him to leave?"

"If that is what is best for him."

"You might as well let him know," Endelarin spoke up. "Everyone else does."

"Know what?" Hans looked from one man to the other.

"The reason Dorilian never stays for the revels."

Is that all? By now, Hans had acquired a good grasp of his host. *Why such a big deal? He probably just doesn't like them.*

Tiflan sighed. "Twelve years ago, Dorilian danced this dance. He danced the Sorcerer."

"The Sorcerer?" Hans asked. Endelarin's part? The more he thought about it, the more he saw the implications. One of the Highborn as Sorcerer....

"Yes. It was a bit out of the ordinary, as you can imagine. His father was still alive, of course, and consecrated the Illumination that year, but the impact was tremendous—unforgettable. The descendant of the god *as* the god. But that isn't the point, either. What you must understand is that he was dancing the dance, *that* dance, with that music and the crowds and the whole crazy thing, when—" Tiflan paused, struggling to go on. His voice shook when he continued. "Levyathan died. The *first* Levyathan—Dorilian's younger brother. He fell from the Serat terraces, a terrible fall, to the courtyards below."

Another memory slipped into place: of hushed conversations and Emyli, Hans's mother, saying a child had fallen from a great height. All at once he understood. Last night, on the terrace, the feeling of falling; it suddenly made terrible sense. "Dorilian saw."

Tiflan swallowed, then his eyes closed. "Worse than that. He *felt* it. The Highborn feel each other's deaths. And he was wide open—in the dance, with the drink—he had no shields. It was as if he died too."

Startled, Hans grasped something more. "Are you telling me… he experiences when his own kind *die*?"

Endelarin paused in pouring another cup of Tiflan's wine. "That and more. The Highborn are empaths. They feel and wreak havoc on all kinds of things. Has no one bothered yet to tell you that?"

Marenthro certainly hadn't. No one had. And yet it explained so much—like why being around Dorilian was so fraught with obstacles.

Horrible as the image of the fallen boy was, Hans's mind flooded with images more chilling still, of blades carving open the throats of helpless, glassy-eyed men until rivers of blood flowed in nightmare patterns across Permephedon's pristine floor. The way that blood had stained Dorilian's hands and pooled around his knees. Blood and fire and pain. How many Highborn princes had Dorilian watched Nammuor slay that day? *Dozens.*

But worse—Dorilian had felt every one of them die.

22

Amallar divides the Staubaun lands as surely as a
mountain range. It occupies the forested expanse
between two nations as distinct as loam and sand.
If the Rill had not served to bind those nations
across immense gulfs of distance and culture,
Essera and Sordan would have been enemies and
Amallar a prize for which both contended. Because
of the Rill, however, Amallar was left in peace,
unspoiled and uncoveted, passed over as surely by
politics as it was by the Staubauns' silver Entity.
—ROBDAN AELFRICSON,
THE STAUBERG-RANDOLPH SUCCESSION

"Handurin is *where*?"

Erenor, the Prince Regent, removed his cloak
and flung it across the room at his front hall servant.
The boy scooped the garment into his arms and hurried away.
Before turning to face the representative from the Seven Houses,
Erenor wiped his expression clean of surprise. Handurin wasn't
supposed to be anywhere except at the bottom of the ocean.
Handurin was supposed to be *dead*.

"Sordan, Your Grace." Pearls in intricate designs beaded the
collar and hems of Iphithus Kheprion's rich robe of marigold silk.
"Two separate communications arrived last night by way of Rill.
One was directed to Merath by array, addressed to Princess Ionais.
The other was from the Elector of Trongor to his Archhalia
ambassador. Both stated to have seen Handurin Stauberg-
Randolph at the court of Dorilian Sordaneon."

Outside the expanse of clear-paned windows, the Rill lifted white arms above Dazunor-Rannuli's golden palaces and murky canals. Erenor stared at the thing. "A sighting without confirmation," he opined.

"No, two *independent* sightings by men without sufficient imagination to think of such a thing themselves." Iphithus considered Erenor a moment too long, then frowned. "Other communications have arrived this morning bearing the same news. The Seven Houses would appreciate your looking into this matter. We are not at all pleased by this development. Or the variables it introduces into our relationship."

You arrogant mouthpiece. Erenor barely refrained from saying it. Iphithus was not merely a minion; his presence delivered a subtle insult along with the news. As Regent, Erenor was Essera's defacto king and deserved a visit from one of their Denizens. He took what satisfaction he could in knowing that Essera's cartel of Rill merchants was even more helpless than he when it came to gathering information on the Sordaneons. Dorilian had purged all relations with the Seven Houses after they had collaborated with Stefan on seizing control of Sordaneon holdings in Dazunor-Rannuli, including the fabled Rillhome Palace. Although the cartel deployed a spy network that surpassed his own and were known to have contacts within the Brotherhood of Epoptes, Erenor relied on his own carefully cultivated informants to provide superior insight into the Hierarch's designs.

"Sordan's Hierarch has no formal relationship with this Regency," Erenor reminded Iphithus, who would carry the underlying message of cooperation back to his guild's cursed Customhouse. "I will make the appropriate inquiries as to Prince Handurin's status and prepare a report to the Archhalia. You will receive a copy in advance."

Erenor watched the man go, then cursed out loud when he was certain no one would hear. "Damn that Kheld-blooded bitch!"

Emyli Stauberg-Randolph had played him, of that Erenor was now certain. One domain's ambassador might be mistaken; two would not be. Handurin was in Sordan, and by evening Erenor would face an antechamber full of emissaries clamoring for an explanation.

The timing could not be less in his favor. In just two weeks, the

Archhalia would meet to decide whether to issue a writ of contempt against the Princess for failure to return her son to his government. On the heels of that writ Erenor had planned to introduce a petition to expand the authority of his regency by taking over the vacant Principality of Dazunor. He foresaw now that the representatives would be thrown into disarray by this news and far less likely to demand that Emyli surrender the domain to Erenor's authority. They would be even less likely to consider his petition now, with the actual Heir known to be alive and in Sordan.

Movement caught Erenor's eye, the passage of a Rill charys entering the city in a long, graceful glide to the mount. Though the sight never failed to awe, it did nothing to warm him now. Just weeks ago he had been at Aral, putting the finishing touches on his campaign to smother the insurgency in Dannuth. When Nammuor had promised to use sorcery to dissolve the *Ariande* in unquenchable flame, the ship reduced to nothing within moments, Erenor had felt a joy that bordered on physical ecstasy. For a few hours, he had imagined himself unburdened, free to present his case to assume Essera's crown. Until Nammuor had summoned him.

On a palisade overlooking the sea from which *Ariande* had vanished from the World, Erenor had faced a man who was wearing a crown filled with Highborn blood.

"Your information was false. I put watch ships along the Rift line, myself at this one, which your agent said Marenthro would use." The Sorcerer had regarded him coldly, the Diadem like a fiery corona upon his head. *"There was an event. The Rift opened, but not here. Zepheron was a decoy."*

"But the message—intercepted from Princess Emyli—"

"A ruse. She's Marc Frederick's daughter, Marenthro's pupil—and she is desperate to save her cub. He was not on that ship. I am more suspicious than you. I devised an array to monitor the Rift that would alert me should a Gateway be created or revived. One did revive. I saw him for just a moment before I destroyed that portal: a young man with Stauberg-Randolph eyes."

But the Sorcerer had not been able to say for certain what Handurin's fate had been. "If he is alive, he will not stay long hidden. Let me know when you find him."

Still, Erenor had clung to hope that the nuisance prince had perished. He had left Aral the next morning to attend the Coming in Dazunor-Rannuli. To be near the Archhalia and the Rill. To rid himself of the image of Zepheron sacrificing himself and his ship in a blaze of unholy fire. Erenor was still confronted by a bedrock of support for Emyli's son, the rightful Heir of Stefan and Marc Frederick—and, through the latter, of the extinct Malyrdeons. For the sake of that bloodline and the Wall Entity, men like Zepheron were still willing to plot behind Erenor's back, even throw away their lives. He would not be safe until he had eradicated them all.

At least he could now tell Nammuor that he had found Handurin.

With a sigh, Erenor walked to the window and surveyed its view over the courtyards of privilege. From the palace's waterfront facade, he looked out at alabaster villas with rooftop gazebos, splendid palazzos of golden sandstone, magnificent porches fronting the water where noble punts bobbed, tied to gilded posts. There had been a pageant earlier along the Upper and Lower Canals and those waterways now streamed with activity, barges and boats by the hundreds, mounded with blossoms and merrymakers. Petals, scattered during the festivities, floated in colorful processions upon the water. Today was Second Day, when Dazunor-Rannuli celebrated the coming of the twofold god, Amynas and Leur, and the death of the old year. Tomorrow would usher in the new. Sordan would have a more important celebration, of course. The actual Consecration, Highborn Dorilian enacting his singular claim to godhood for all the world to see.

And now Dorilian had Handurin, his rival for Essera, in hand. It was almost too rich. The Hierarch's hatred for Stefan had been deadly enough, with consequences ruinous to both. Who knew what old scores Dorilian might address upon Stefan's heir?

Perhaps Nammuor would not be so unhappy after all.

23

Godhood was never the goal of the Highborn
experiment. Their race had been created to
overthrow false gods. That they succumbed to
being made gods themselves was a flaw of the
original paradigm.
—Zamenes,
On the Natures of Gods and Men

The Highborn feel each other's deaths.

Even now that he and Arne had returned to their rooms at the Serat, Hans continued to recoil at that revelation. Dorilian was a far more complicated puzzle than he had imagined. *An empath.* More than that—as Tiflan had explained on their return to the Serat—Dorilian was a projective empath. When gripped by strong feeling, he hurled his emotions as if in battle. No wonder Hans had so often felt as though he were under assault.

Maybe Marenthro should have warned him about that too, that he would be meeting up with a man not merely scarred by death, but warped by it. Not just Marc Frederick's death, but those of all the other Highborn princes who had died that day and since. And now Hans had just heard about Dorilian's brother, who had died in front of him on Second Day, fallen from this very Serat. A brother after whom, barely a year later, he had named his son. Everything about Dorilian was wrapped up with madness and myth and the End of the World.

And I risked compounding it when I ran off.

Sick with guilt over having let Endelarin cajole him into taking part in the street celebration, Hans vowed to himself that he would conscientiously observe the remaining hours of the Coming. Now that he knew what kind of pain he might awaken, he would never reveal to Dorilian anything that might recall his experience of the Demise. Marenthro had warned him—sort of—but not nearly enough. Why? Because he hadn't wanted Hans to approach Dorilian believing what Stefan always had—that the Highborn prince was something other than human?

Demon-breed.

"Told you so," Arne had muttered under his breath when Hans had confided what he'd learned. "Damn witches, they are. Stefan had the right of it." It irritated Hans that he lacked enough information to challenge what his brother might have thought.

Participants in Third Day rituals were required to purify themselves, so Hans and Arne dedicated their night to doing so. They had already fasted. Now, making use of the large pool in the center of their bathing chamber, the water of which was warm and sweetly scented, they scrubbed away every trace of dirt and sweat. Tradition dictated that the last vestiges of the past year must be removed, even impure thoughts if one did not want to carry those over. Everything leading up to the Third Day of Coming, the Consecration of the Three, was designed to prepare the World and the humans in it for rebirth. Predictably, Arne wasn't too happy with the process.

"It's bad enough they got us smelling like we're covered in flowers, but there's still no speck of food. I'm all starved out," Arne complained. Bruises still marred his limbs and torso. He had wrapped his hips with one of the several thick, soft towels provided by the stealthy staff and used another towel on his hair, tousling the dark curls. "I ain't had nothing to eat for over a day now, just wine and water. One makes me sick and the other makes me piss. It's not natural."

"Drink the water and you'll be fine. You can live for a few more hours without eating." Hans could have argued that fasts were standard religious fare everywhere save Amallar, where food *was* religion after a fashion. And he genuinely sympathized. His own stomach had been growling vigorously for most of the night. "Think of it this way: it doesn't make any sense to eat when the World is ended," he reasoned. "If there's no sun, there's no food.

So we just have to wait until Dorilian brings it back in the morning."

"He can't really do that, can he?"

"Do what? Bring the sun back? I suppose he can. Symbolically." Seeing Arne's eyes widen with alarm, Hans added to ward off more talk of witches, "The sun isn't gone, Arne, not really—no more than any other day."

"I reckon not, being the sun and all." Arne pondered, then said, "But there's got to be some truth to it. They miss that in the north, in Essera. Folk up there long for the days they had rulers who could do things like blast armies to hells or make mountains bleed stone."

"God-avatars are pretty much the standard order for rulers, Arne, no matter where you go. What are you worried about? Dorilian isn't going to really do anything. It's just a ceremony; a reenactment, that's all." Hans finished toweling himself and walked into their adjoining bedchamber. Clothing had been laid out on both beds.

"Aw, Madrock's hells. Look at this." Arne held up a sleeveless chiton of white linen. It was so short it might not even reach his knees. "This thing won't cover a baby! Everyone will see I have hair on every inch."

"You don't have *that* much body hair." Hans held up his garment and found it to be nearly the same thing, just barely knee-length.

"I have plenty of hair. And mine's dark, so it shows more. You don't have my problems. If it weren't for your eyes, you could pass for something besides Kheld."

Having no other choice, Hans donned the white garment and noted that, while the fabric buttoned at the shoulders, the side panels were open, not stitched at all. Simple and almost primitive and most definitely ceremonial. He scanned the room, looking for something. "They didn't give us any shoes."

A tone from the door preceded entrance of Tiflan, arrived to escort them to the ceremony. His white garment merely made his honed musculature more impressive.

"Problems?" he asked upon catching the look on Hans's face.

"Yes." Hans pointed to his feet. "No shoes."

"Ah. I forgot to mention that. We go barefoot to acclaim the Birth of the Three and witness the Rebirth of the World. These hours are sacred, and Tur-Ahraean is consecrated ground. Even

Amynas went unshod on the Third Day. In fact, he was naked." He laughed at their expressions. "You will not be. We can all thank the gods the myth is not reenacted in its entirety."

Of all the celebration and ceremony of the Coming, Dorilian most disliked Third Day. At least on First Day he could feast upon the finest creations of the best cooks to be found in his corner of the Triempery. On Second Day he could appreciate the artistry and poetry of that year's production of the Illumination, after which he would mercifully leave before the music and clamor ate away at his brain. But Third Day...

Third Day meant walking barefoot on a path of icy, albeit swept smooth, stone. It meant being cold and feeling the bite of a chill spring predawn. It meant standing in front of a multitude of his subjects and foreign dignitaries while wearing next to nothing, a state of vulnerability that rendered him unhappy and paranoid and angry at being that way. At least his singular status as Hierarch permitted him to wear the Rill Stone—the device held a living piece of Derlon, whose sacred birth they were celebrating.

The Rill Stone, however, did not enable Dorilian to translocate or cast a defensive shield. He could use it only to collect and hold Rill energy, though he had not yet tested the full limit of how much. Wielding Rill energy presented great risk.

His uncle Delos had burned his body beyond repair by summoning Rill energy through one of the greater enhancers.

Dorilian had mastered his gifts well, but he still needed to be careful and not take unnecessary chances.

"Dor? Are we ready?"

He looked up. He and his retinue occupied a courtyard attached to Sordan's Citadel, the massive struts and arches of which possessed enough warmth and residual arcane brightness to provide a comfortable space in which to wait. Levyathan stood before him clad in a two-panel white chiton such as every participant in the mountaintop ceremony would wear. Fahme, standing nearer the doors that would lead onto the road, had bound back her hair and looked more eager to begin as she talked with Tiflan and his two charges: Handurin and that Kheld of his.

Dorilian frowned. He should not allow the Kheld. Strictly speaking, no Kheld could possibly have attended the first Consecration. Then again, neither could just about any person but a Leur or an Aryati—and, as far as Dorilian knew, only he and Levyathan fit those criteria.

He grimaced. "Almost." The Sages would have told him if he risked missing the dawnbreak.

Levyathan glanced back at where Tiflan was speaking with Handurin. "He is uncertain about us."

"Handurin? He is uncertain about *me*."

"Mostly about you. He senses your ambivalence."

Dorilian barely smothered a laugh. Levyathan always knew where truth would be found. "Perhaps he does."

"And so does everyone else." Narrow trees and hanging curtains of flowering vines gathered at the base of the graceful arches at Levyathan's back. He looked so young, very much a child, and called to mind the ancestral statue of the boy-Hierarch Dares. Levyathan took a seat on the bench beside Dorilian. "What will it take to put this uncertainty behind you?"

How unusual. Lev knew better than to advocate for someone with whom Dorilian might have... issues. "You like him, do you?"

Levyathan ducked his head, then smiled back. "I do. I feel nothing evil in him."

"People do not have to be evil to be dangerous to us." *Remember Ermenthalia... and Stefan.* They shared that thought along with the silent litany it awakened. *Marenthro. Emyli. We cannot trust their designs.*

"Do you fear Handurin is plotting against us?" Doubt dulled Levyathan's inquisition.

Dorilian gazed across the room. The Stauberg-Randolph prince was standing next to that Kheld of his and at least pretending to be interested in something Fahme was saying. Although Handurin's resemblance to Stefan could be unsettling—the same cheekbones and chin and that thrice-cursed warm smile, so friendly in him and in Stefan so false—he didn't look dangerous.

"Probably not. Frankly, I don't think he has the sophistication."

It intrigued Dorilian that Handurin had arrived on his doorstep armed with so little foreknowledge. His memories of his brother were those of a child and, as such, were useless. His current knowledge of Essera and the World hardly surpassed that of the

Kheld. Still, there was something almost welcome about that. Neither Emyli nor Marenthro had accused Dorilian of killing Stefan and Handurin appeared to be of like mind. Indeed, Handurin believed Marenthro had sent him to Sordan for conciliation.

He said I needed allies, and you would be the best one to get.

The *best* one. But not the *only* one.

If Handurin were plotting against Dorilian, he was doing a damn poor job of it.

Dorilian tapped Levyathan on the knee to signal it was time to go. "I need to know more—about him, about his purposes. I must find out once and for all just what I am dealing with."

Together they rose to join the rest of their party. Sages and Epoptes had lined up to form a procession ahead of them on the Path of the Ancients and would lead the way to the Standing Rock that stood between the Dead World and the New.

"He is not our enemy, Dor. Please don't turn him into one."

"Go, join Fahme." Dorilian was to walk alone. Gift-bearer. Derlon's Heir. In the days before Marc Frederick and Stefan had come to the throne, Sordan's Hierarch would have been accompanied by the bearer of the Wall Stone and by the King of Essera, wearer of the Leur's Ring.

Whatever Handurin might prove to be, and whether Marenthro had thrown Dorilian a gift or a curse, was a matter that could be unraveled later. Intelligence had reached Sordan from agents in Erenor's court about a failed plan to intercept and either abduct or kill Handurin at a Rift point in the north. Consequently, Essera's foremost admiral—Marc Frederick's friend and a man Dorilian had known—was now dead. Yet another possible ally removed from the game board.

Erenor was not to be trusted. Essera's domains were divided. Their returned Prince was effectively neutered, his support eroding. And Nammuor's power in Essera increased by the day.

Things could hardly be worse.

But at least, for today, the Consecration's ritual clothing requirement provided Dorilian with a bit of protection: they made weapons all but impossible to hide.

When Hans saw Tur-Ahraean, his first thought was to wonder what had broken the mountain's back. Predawn silver etched the mountain against the vault of the sky, its smooth line broken by a vertical cleft that plunged downward, perpendicular and sheer, only for its meeting with the ground to be hidden by a towering pitch-dark monolith. Torches borne by thousands of congregants lit the ominous cliff faces to either side of that monumental structure, but no flames reflected from the monolith's featureless surface. More than anything, Hans thought the Standing Rock resembled a yawning portal into the underworld.

"Looks like the Dread Door," said Arne. "The hole in the mountain where old One-Eyed Bess led Alm when our folk walked through to the Bogs." He had never seen the Dread Door, of course, a product of folktales that persisted only in retellings.

All Kheld children knew the story of how the god Lud had guided the Kheldfolk out of their home world, from which they had been driven by a merciless enemy, through a supernatural Door into a new world, this one, where they had immediately set about trying to seize a bit of land for themselves. The local Staubaun lords and princes had not taken kindly to being invaded and relations between Staubauns and Khelds had remained unfriendly ever since.

Hans noticed that Dorilian and Levyathan now stood apart, father and son outlined in white against the Standing Rock. Behind them stood two groups of what were probably dignitaries in formal attendance, their foreheads marked by shining ensigns. Large gold circles glowed upon the brows of one group of twelve men and women. The other group, all men, were similarly marked: glowing, silver wings burned upon their brows.

"Sages and Epoptes," whispered Fahme, who had noticed Hans's stare. They along with Arne stood to one side, watched over by Tiflan and Tutto.

"Epoptes?"

Fahme cut him one of her looks of censure. "Mages," she explained. "They study arcane arts like waterglobes and crystals and know how to talk to the Rill." Her face turned wistful.

Seeing her expression tugged at Hans's own childhood dream of someday flying airships. "Do *you* want to talk to the Rill?"

"Yes!" Fahme's eager gaze locked on his. "Don't you?"

Hans paused to consider the question. "Until this moment I had no idea it could be talked to."

"It might not listen to you anyway." At a finger to his lips from Tiflan, Fahme lowered her voice. "I want the Entity to hear me, and for me to hear it. I think... it will have a lot to say. It has lived two thousand years!"

Three celebrants ringing handbells approached the large sunken space in front of the Standing Rock. They were followed by a single figure clad in black. Head to toe, hooded and veiled, the person appeared sinister amidst so many pale attendants. *Thaa*, Hans thought—though he knew somehow that it wasn't. With a strong voice, the figure stood at the edge of the depression and spoke.

"Behold the World in Darkness! The wind whispers the names of the Lost.

"Where are the Rannui?"

To every side Hans heard people answer as one voice: "They are gone."

"Where are the Laceni?"

And the people responded a second time: "They are gone."

"Where are the Urrai?"

"They are gone."

The litany continued and it dawned on Hans just what he was hearing. They were recounting the List of the Dead. He had heard Marc Frederick speak of it, how those who had Returned had compiled a list of those peoples who had perished, entire nations swallowed by the Devastation of Arya. The names no longer held much meaning to the hundred thousand who invoked them; even the language being used sounded obscure, perhaps an ancient dialect of Stauba. Though it sounded familiar, he barely understood it.

As he murmured with the others, Hans could not keep himself from stealing glances at the bowed heads of the crowd, observing their participation. Endelarin, for once completely sober and not flouting the prevailing rules of dress, was present with an Ardaenan delegation, giving witness that his people had survived where others had not. In the drone of so many voices, it seemed real ghosts haunted the darkened World. Hans could feel them congealing in the thin cold breeze that seemed to touch Tur-Ahraean with a lingering dark hand each time an ancient name was spoken.

Among Sordan's Haliasts, the Speaker Pallas stood with head bowed and hands folded with devotion. Tiflan, too, spoke in hollow tones as though from the graves of the fallen. Only Fahme's voice sounded unburdened, young and true and perhaps less understanding of what was being remembered.

Hans noticed that Dorilian and Levyathan stood at the perimeter of the sunken space, unprotected. Exposed. The thin garments they wore revealed that they were both unarmed, but also that they were human—vulnerably so—in every visible way identical to the thousands surrounding them. Barefoot and penitent in a darkness of which they were part.

"Where are the Aryati?" the black-robed speaker asked.

"They are gone!"

"Into Darkness they are gone!"

As one, the Sages and Epoptes extinguished their torches. Attendants ringing the ceremonial circle did the same and darkness claimed the mountainside. When Hans lifted his gaze, he noted that the sky above the cleft had lightened to a gray like dull silver. He blinked when a brighter light abruptly spilled onto the cliff faces in front of him, illuminating the darker-than-dark surface of the Standing Rock. *What the—*

Dorilian had walked toward the Standing Rock and now stood before it with his left arm extended—and his open hand enveloped by a ball of brilliant light.

The Rill Stone. It could be nothing else. A piece of a god.

Hans looked at Arne in time to see the Kheld silently mouth two unmistakable words: *Fuck. Me.*

With ceremonial solemnity, Dorilian strode up to the black shape of the monolith. He reached out his left hand. He touched the left side of the stone and upon its surface a bright design burst into glowing being. Dorilian walked three paces to the right and touched the stone again to call forth another fiery mark. He returned to the center and placed his palm flat upon the stone. A third brilliant sign appeared. All three glyphs blazed with clear light, their shapes apparent—a star crown, a sword, and the now familiar ellipse and hyperbola symbol associated with the Rill.

The monolith—no longer black—bloomed with pinks and golds, its new symbols burning in a translucent matrix. Light tipped Dorilian's upraised hand with fire and spilled down upon him, clothing him in an aura of dawn. Shining, he stood forth like a beacon on the edge of a World Reborn.

Turning around to face the masses, Dorilian spoke to them.

"As Darkness ever yields to Light.... go! And remember whose Children we are. This is a World Reborn, Twice Created, and beloved of Leur. Care for it well, for it cannot be made again."

In great rolling waves, guided by people newly arrived and clad in yellow robes, celebrants formed lines that would take them to the foot of the Standing Rock, where they would be allowed to step into the first light of a new dawn to touch it and thereby fulfill their pilgrimage. Legon made his way from the crowd to escort Fahme to rejoin her father and brother at the fore of that procession.

Tutto departed to secure their return. "The years have imprinted holy writ on my fingertips. This day needs me for other things."

Hans and Arne remained with Tiflan among the first rank of pilgrims. It surprised Hans only a little to see Endelarin sidle up to join them. Endelarin was a king, after all, though without his finery he could have passed for a well-scrubbed and laundered dockworker. Being royal and kin to the Hierarch, they stood in line behind only the Sordaneons and the eminent Sages and Epoptes. Very little time passed before they stood in front of the newly wrought Sign of the Three. Tiflan demonstrated the accepted way to touch the Standing Rock's misty, apparently insubstantial surface. Now that the sun had emerged behind it, daylight poured through to fill the bowl of the mountainside with pinkish light.

Following Tiflan's example, Hans pressed the tips of his fingers to the stone. He felt a cool, palpable presence—and what felt like solid rock. Although clearly there, the surface he touched was not completely inorganic. He had encountered things of this nature before. *It is like Sordan's Citadel, or the Leur's Ring—a living thing.* As he pulled his hand back, he wondered what science could explain the monolith's properties, or whether he was, indeed, in the presence of magic.

Hans looked at Arne to do as he had, but the Kheld shook his head.

"I don't think I ought do it." Arne's gaze flicked to the knot of Epoptes and Sages who had taken to standing in attendance nearby. There was no mistaking the reason for Arne's nervousness: even the two women among the Sages fixed him with stares that promised murder.

Hans resented the silent coercion. "Don't let them intimidate you. Do it anyway."

Arne shook his head. "It's bad enough *you* did. They were looking at you that way too."

Except against Hans they would be reluctant to make any move. Against Arne, they might be willing to test their Hierarch's entrenched antipathy toward Khelds. Though Hans knew Arne would do whatever asked, it might be dangerous to press the matter; Dorilian had bestowed protection on Hans, not Arne.

To Hans's relief, Endelarin chose that moment to walk up, placing his body between his companions and the onlooking stares. He leaned near each symbol to get a better look. "Yes, there they are, no mistaking them. Clear as day and twice as bright!"

"What are they?" The symbols burned white-gold, orange, and blue within the mysteriously transparent monolith.

"The Signs of the Three, which they wrote themselves onto this stone." Tiflan spoke before Endelarin could answer. He pointed at the glyphs one by one, from star crown to Rillsign to sword. "Erge-iron. Derlon. Amarantos."

"Born right here, the three of them," piped in Endelarin. "Or so legend says."

"This very spot?"

"Well, more accurately… there." Endelarin turned to point at the strangely smooth and metallic, glyph-inscribed depression just behind and below the ledge on which they stood. He looked at Tiflan and shook his head. "Clearly you are falling short in the myth-telling arena."

Tiflan glowered. "I am doing well enough. There is a lot of myth to cover. He will learn the rest as needed."

One of the eagle-emblazoned Epoptes stepped forward. "Royal Ones."

They were holding up the queue of pilgrims. Endelarin, Hans noticed, was standing with hands clasped behind his back and had not touched the Standing Rock yet. Though Hans made an effort to alert him while still near enough to do it, Endelarin lifted a forbearing hand to dissuade him.

"I don't meddle with magical things. What if something should go awry? Can you imagine the spectacle? Dorilian might execute me for offending his ancestors!"

As they skirted the remaining crowd along a secured and guarded perimeter that would take them back through the Citadel to the Serat, soldiers of the Eagle Guard fell into line ahead and behind to escort them.

"Sorcery scares the blood out of me too, turning rock to air and writing in fire," Arne said. Hans noticed his friend had begun to feel comfortable enough around Tiflan and Endelarin, at least, to speak.

"It wasn't air. The rock, I mean. And it isn't sorcery," Hans said. The word felt... wrong somehow, though he could not articulate why.

"What is it then?" Endelarin challenged.

"Some application of the physical sciences." Hans had no sooner spoken the words than he realized he had raised an argument he could not win. His university courses in the physics of an archived past were insufficient to develop plausible explanations for what he had just witnessed.

"Which of the sciences?"

Hans flushed. "I haven't figured that out."

"Well, there you go. Neither has anyone else—and believe me, people have tried. Science is no better an explanation than a supernatural phenomenon so I don't see why we can't just leave it at that." Endelarin sidestepped a stone that had fallen or gotten kicked onto the path. "Sorcery is such a fraught word anyway. Wizardry is a better word for this sort of thing, don't you think? The Children of Amynas and Leur are not subservient to other forces, the way sorcerers are. They are quite independent."

And Nammuor, Hans knew from what little Marenthro had told him, was a sorcerer. There was sorcery and there was... whatever Dorilian was. Hans no longer needed to ask how much of his own godhood Dorilian believed.

They met with Levyathan and Fahme again inside the pleasant and now sunlit Court of First Dawn where they had gathered before the Consecration. Tiflan immediately hauled Endelarin aside for what was probably a heated discussion. Hans and Arne joined the royal children beside a long, narrow pool graced with a floral mosaic of water-blooming plants that, when viewed from the elevation of the entry, showed a woman dancing.

Yet another myth, no doubt, about which Hans would need to learn.

"That was quite… amazing," Hans said. Levyathan and Fahme exchanged silent laughs, which told him they had probably wagered on his reaction.

Fahme snickered. "Father knows how to put on a show."

"Do you know how he does that? Make light in his hand?"

Another shared look, this one shaded by warning in Fahme's frown.

Levyathan ducked his head. "I think that is something Dorilian is best suited to explain."

Probably, though Hans would rather find things out from other people. "Well," he said, "now that I have gone through the whole myth cycle of the Coming, I can say I learned a lot. Like today, I learned that the Three were conceived—or at least born—right in front of the Standing Rock. Endelarin told me."

Levyathan nodded. "We don't know exactly where the glorious occasion occurred, but after Amynas brought the People back from Exile to Sordan, he showed them the Standing Rock, and the Three performed the first Consecration, it is said, on the site of their creation. It is the only suitable place to commemorate the event."

"Leur… and human."

"As births go, it was momentous. Mortal with immortal, entirely intentional. Amynas had to become immortal for it to happen."

"How did he do that?"

"No one knows." Levyathan looked away. Hans followed his gaze. Dorilian stood near the entry, his guards now many times more numerous and standing in formation at his back. He wore some sort of crown again, golden and tipped with silver. Facing him were several Epoptes, the eagle signifiers on their foreheads sparking bright points in the building's shadow.

"What is that about?" Hans asked. The men confronting Dorilian looked tense and their orange- and purple-cloaked leader was gesturing forcefully—probably the reason the guards had just moved forward.

"The Epoptes and my father are currently at odds."

"Heretics," muttered Fahme.

Hans had yet to fully grasp the relationship between the Epoptes and the Rill. What he had heard so far suggested they were somehow in charge, that they talked to it or ordered it about. Yet every time the Rill or the Epoptes were mentioned or as in this case, present, Dorilian was proximate. The Hierarch was himself part of some bigger picture of the Rill itself.

Stefan had harped on the Highborn and their Entities for a full season, the year he and Hans had spent in Amallar rather than be anywhere near Sordan's hostile prince. Stefan had also said something else—that Dorilian had invaded Amallar, that he had tried to kill Stefan there. And he had said Dorilian could not be punished because of his family's connection to the Rill.

Marenthro had warned Hans that he would be dealing with ghosts. He hadn't said a word about dealing with Entities.

24

Few people have ever really wanted to know me—
and fewer have ever wanted me to know myself.
—DORILIAN SORDANEON

"Why are you telling me this news? Do you think I care?"

Dorilian was accustomed to his grandmother's acerbity. With Third Day safely arisen, Ermenthalia ended her Second Day fast by sharing a small repast of fruit and sweet pastry knots with him. Aside from this annual tradition, Dorilian seldom visited.

"I like to hear myself talk. It's why I visit you at all." He had not thought for a moment that Ermenthalia would care about Handurin's reappearance. It impacted neither her welfare nor her comfort.

The old woman's gaze narrowed. Sometimes Dorilian could almost believe she had grown fond of him. "I am surprised you have not had the Stauberg-Randolph bastard killed and sent his corpse back so they could pop a crown on its head and install it as king."

An apt image. For as long as Dorilian could remember, Essera had gone to ridiculous lengths to prevent having a Sordaneon on its throne. "I find it fascinating how my *failure* to kill Handurin is what has taken everyone aback. I'm treating him like a minor noble."

"Given his uncouth background, you can be sure he does not know the difference. Besides, you like testing people."

"I like catching them off guard. Better yet if I can catch them spouting hypocrisy."

"Do tell." The pink cup Ermenthalia lifted to her lips showed delicate fern frond shadows, like curls of smoke. The Devastation's wild energies had wrought some wondrous things, and vitrified ghost casts were among the finest.

"They would rather kill Handurin themselves. At this very moment, I assure you, half of Essera is trying to unravel what might entice me to turn him over." Dorilian selected one of the glazed knots of sweetened bread upon the pretty platter in front of him.

"The Khelds want him."

Possibly. *Probably*. To have made that conclusion, Ermenthalia had not needed the limited correspondence Dorilian currently allowed her. The way she framed her statement, however, hinted of subtle shading. She sought to stoke his insecurity.

"They will have to wait."

"And wonder?"

"And wonder." Dorilian picked up and ate another of the two remaining sweets on his plate. As ever with his grandmother, he had brought the food and drink—indeed, he had brought the table settings. Tollenberg silver. Nathiri glass. Everything. Ermenthalia's prison was secure, and Legon had made certain there would be no weapons, not so much as a hairpin, but Dorilian did not trust her for even one moment not to poison him.

He chose another avenue of conversation.

"Would you like a new book to read? Zamenes has written another discourse. This one is about whether gods can be mortal. Or you might prefer the Gracious Princess Sapphia's treatise on marriage."

"The only thing I would like is to hear news of the boy."

A desire to see and speak with Levyathan was Ermenthalia's sole consistent request and her obsession gnawed at Dorilian's patience. Much as he wished to believe that she would never betray Lev to Nammuor, shreds of doubt remained. Her ties to Mormantalorus had emboldened Ermenthalia to strike at Dorilian and Levyathan before. At least she no longer brought up the particulars of Lev's birth. Perhaps, like much of the population, Ermenthalia had finally forgotten the name of the unholy bitch who had conceived Dorilian's Heir.

"Levyathan is well. He is progressing in *Leur'alta*. He likes languages."

"You tell me nothing I cannot already infer. He is Sordaneon. How *else* is he to ever commune with the Rill? Do you still dream that someday the Epoptes will let you near it?"

"No. I know better than to hope for that."

"I received a letter from your esteemed cousin, the Princess of Merrydn. She has once again offered that I might stay with her and be rescued from your unkindness."

"My kindness is that you live. What else did my dear cousin have to say?" Ionais's reasons for reaching out to Dorilian's perfidious grandmother had little to do with kindness and more with Ermenthalia's frozen Rill portions. He had noticed Ionais was amassing assets as well as alliances.

"Only that your continued holding of the Archessa of Heddros is obscene. She asks if you are fornicating with her." Both silver-white eyebrows lifted. "Are you?"

If Dorilian could have said "yes" he would have, if only to send Esseran minds racing for the gutter. They had been wallowing there for weeks already. "Not yet."

"Hah! You abandon all sense of propriety if ever you sleep with that creature."

She was doing it again, sheathing insult within insult. Dorilian would rather gaze into a chamber pot than at this woman who so resembled his father. *We take the race of our mothers*, he reminded himself. *She is Deben's—not mine.* A painting of Dorilian's mother hung in his personal library, reminding him daily that he had Valyane Teremareonea's gray eyes and honey-toned hair, even the sun-browned tones of her skin.

He knew what Ermenthalia saw when she looked at him. He had shown her enough of his Highborn gifts to earn her acknowledgment, but the shallowness of their conversations precluded her from drawing informed conclusions, as she proceeded to prove.

"Rumor is rife that your grip on reality has slipped. You spend too much time alone." With a dismissive hand, she pushed aside her plate, upon which three knots glistened uneaten.

Though tempted, Dorilian ignored the sweets. He would leave them for her.

He rose to take his leave. "Reality has a firmer shape near me than away. You might remind Ionais of that should you get another chance to write to her. She is much nearer to the heart of madness than I am. Or you." He signaled to Legon, who had been standing in the archway between the courtyard's sunny eating alcove and the rest of the apartment. Moments later Dorilian's escort had reformed. "Be careful, Grandmother. There are lives in this world with which I take no chances. Yours is one of them. I believe I have reached the limit of my ability to trust you. No more letters—to Ionais or anyone. I need Essera in darkness, and you shine too much light."

"I respect your concern," Quirin Chrysolemnos responded to Chyralane, the Denizen of Phaer. He made a point of adjusting his sash of high office, gold thread on purple silk, where it angled beneath the black and orange stole of his Order. "But nothing about the threat has changed. Dorilian is caged by caution and diminished alliances. This is as we wanted—and continue to want—for the Rill's safety and ours. Travel aside, he has no contact with the Rill at all."

"Perhaps not, but his ambitions wander north." Chyralane walked at Quirin's side, albeit slowly. Because of her advanced years, people accommodated her.

"Handurin? Emyli's son changes nothing. Do we know for certain that the boy in Sordan is truly the prince?" As far as Quirin had heard, Emyli had not made a statement.

"Dorilian has proclaimed him so. He could not lie about such a thing."

Quirin frowned, and not only because that assertion was true. His informants also claimed that the youth had, upon apprehension, produced a *deiknya*. Only Marenthro created such devices. Quirin possessed one himself.

Sunlight spilled past the square pillars that framed the sight of Dazunor-Rannuli's Rill platforms and set aglow the long gallery's flame-colored floor. Beyond the portico sprawled a view of the Mount's three monumental runs, each crowned by massive rings and dawn-tinged arches. Although Permephedon's and Sordan's Rill complexes were larger in terms of numbers of runs and primary structures, only Sordan, with its connection by river to the sea, handled more traffic than Dazunor-Rannuli. Because Sordan already was home to the main terminus and Temple of the

Inception, the Brotherhood of Epoptes had built its lofty College in Dazunor-Rannuli to serve as the Order's stronghold. From it, they celebrated Derlon's Gift and oversaw the many factions of Essera's powerful Dazun River commerce.

The teeming city was also ideal because the location removed the Brotherhood—and through them, their oversight of the Rill— from the pervasive influence of the Sordaneons. That did not, however, eliminate the need to monitor the Entity's descendants. When it came to Rill operations, the Sordaneons were more often impediments than allies. Neutralizing them had been Essera's goal for the past century. Quirin faced Chyralane again.

"We see no reason to alter our approach. The Rill is not affected by any of this. The last disruption of the system was on the day the Malyrdeon princes were slaughtered—and all the world knows what caused that."

To that Chyralane could but nod. That day, the Rill had been reacting to the Wall, not Dorilian. Still pensive, she caught Quirin's attention by raising a finger, the nail of which was tipped with gem dust.

"Is there a way we can restrict the Hierarch's travel? Prevent future unannounced visits to Essera?"

"Not without breaking the Covenant. Dorilian wields the Rill Stone. All other ramifications of that device aside, the Charter stipulates that a Sordaneon cannot be refused travel. We can, however, delay matters, be less prompt. For the time being we have made his travel... inconvenient. He travels very little as it is."

They stopped to watch the slip nearest the windows spin a charys out of but air. A gleaming spindle of light elongated into a tube massive enough to carry several barges' worth of grain, wool, or lumber, in addition to hundreds of passengers. Light transformed to a useful, opaque shape neither metal nor glass but something with the qualities of both. On the side of the run facing the College, machines seamlessly initiated loading operations. Quirin watched with pride. His Order oversaw the welfare of nations, the might of vast economies—indeed, the very machine of an empire.

A tall woman, Chyralane looked down at Quirin, smug warning on her lips. "Do not provoke him unnecessarily. Dorilian is quite prepared to be your enemy. He has already declared himself mine. He is a greater danger than that creature in Aral."

Quirin snorted. He needed no warnings. "Nammuor has not threatened the Rill that I know of. Have you heard otherwise?"

"No. But the day will come when he wants it. My wager is he wants it already. Only a simpleton would fail to see that Essera is but a new road by which the Mormantaloran hopes to reach his enemy. We must do all in our power to keep Dorilian from Nammuor and Nammuor from Dorilian. The day those two men engage in war will be the end of all we hold dear."

Quirin felt the bite of those words. They lunged from the grave of a past drenched with peril: mage arts as now practiced by his Brothers were but shadows of the vast power the Aryati had harnessed. To defeat those powers, the Children of Amynas and Leur had shattered mountains and raised Entities. Rumors that Dorilian might possess the latent abilities of his legendary forefathers were rampant, whispered by the fearful though unsupported by evidence. Nammuor's talents, in contrast, had been known for a decade, trumpeted by his subjects and informants alike. Marenthro had said once—and only once—that Nammuor, not Dorilian, had unleashed the tower-shattering energy of the Demise. Nammuor had never claimed the deed, however, and many refused to believe it. Dozens of reports placed him in Mormantalorus at that hour.

But if the rumors were true—if Nammuor had somehow unearthed the Undying Crown and fashioned a way to wield its power—the risks to the Rill were enormous. To Quirin's relief, Chyralane raised a different concern.

"What about the redirections? Those threaten the Sordaneon's plans. If he should intervene—"

"Dorilian was never instructed in Rill magery. The Hierarch Labran was held captive at Stauberg and what little he knew he taught to no one. The Archmage Sebbord, who did possess such skills, made a solemn vow not to divulge operational controls. He petitioned three times for us to instruct his grandson and we denied those requests. Dorilian knows only the same as any of you: how to use a tonal panel to send and receive communications."

"Hah!" Chyralane sniggered. "You do not even allow him access at that level."

Quirin met and held the scornful look in Chyralane's snakish gaze. "We would be foolish to do so. Believe me, he has neither the physical access nor the tonal training to reverse load directions."

"A good thing for you as you conspire with Erenor Tholeros." Though aged, Chyralane's eyes remained bright and unclouded between lined lids. "I fear you indulge too far a man who dances with so many partners."

It was only a short distance farther to the chamber in which they would meet with other members of the Consignation Quorum. Representatives of the many offices charged with maintaining Rill norms and policies, the Quorum had been summoned to deal with Dorilian's charges of shipment diversion. They might also discuss Erenor's petition that the Stauberg-Randolph Rill slots, formerly controlled by Stefan and currently held by Emyli, be placed into the Crown Trust overseen by the Regent. Doing so would render those slots unavailable to Handurin, who had yet to be repatriated, until—and if—he became king. Although the boy was going to be a problem, he was not yet one the Quorum need address.

Quirin looked at the door to the chamber. Upon that signal Chyralane fell into step beside him.

"I dance with far more partners, Denizen. I dance with the Sordaneons and Permephedon and the lingering prophecies of the almighty Wall. But above all I dance with the Rill."

25

If Hans had hoped he might learn more about Dorilian while in Sordan, he was mistaken. On the morning after Third Day, before they had so much as finished breakfast, Tiflan entered the suite Hans and Arne shared, tossed them two bags, and instructed them to pack.

"Hierarch's going on retreat. You're going with him."

As Hans and Arne owned nearly nothing, it took no time at all for them to be packed and ready to go. Before the sun had cleared the City's Citadel they were mounted and on the road.

While the Sordaneon Serat was the official and best-known residence of the Hierarchs of Sordan, there were others. Dorilian preferred his estate of Rhondda on the southern shore of Sordan island, a place that provided the privacy Sordan itself could not afford him. In addition to Hans and Arne, Dorilian brought an army of nobles and retainers to fill his sprawling palace there. Levyathan, and Fahme also, remained in Sordan.

From the moment he first saw Rhondda, Hans knew that Dorilian must love it, that it was as much a part of the man as Sordan's steepled splendor. That insight reassured him. From its cliff-hung gardens overlooking the lake, the royal estate shone with a patina of quiet dignity. The palace itself was archaic and beautiful. For centuries it had been carefully and lovingly preserved. Glazed wall tiles offset antiquated water spouts, and arcades overgrown with dense mats of trailing creepers and vines formed perfumed passages between the villa's far-flung wings. Restful—with shaded halls, abundant pools, and scented arbors—Rhondda presented a deliberate contrast to Sordan's regal vibrancy.

It wasn't long before Hans glimpsed facets of Dorilian's character he had not seen only days earlier. Even Arne, as obstinate in his own way as the Hierarch, had moderated his opinion to something that, although it was not kind, was at least diplomatic. Still, even though Hans was a guest in the man's house and welcome at his table, with all the luxuries of royalty freely provided for the asking, he met with Dorilian only occasionally. When he did it was always in the company of others at dinner or when guests were invited from surrounding estates and villages. At such times Hans knew his presence was less required than simply included, a matter more of indulgence than interest. Having proven Hans no threat, Dorilian seemed content to tolerate him. Hans spent hours wandering the royal estate, looking for reflections of its owner.

One bright midmorning, Hans came to Rhondda's exercise yard. He'd seen the small arena that occupied one side of the villa's extensive baths, but never while it was in use. None of the several men in the amphitheater appeared to notice him when he entered, but after a while Tiflan waved him over. Hans maneuvered around men who had lazily draped themselves upon the steps and took a seat beside Tiflan.

"A bit overdressed, aren't you?" Tiflan made a point of Hans's attire without once taking his eyes off the wrestlers in his corner.

"I'm just observing." Hans did feel out of place. Tiflan lounged like a great golden animal, rippling muscles forming landscapes under expanses of flawless suntanned skin, with only a white loincloth to preserve his modesty.

"You should do some wrestling." Tiflan looked Hans over. "You look good for it."

"I used to work with weights." Hans had never been able to build up the necessary weight for competitive wrestling. Tall enough, but light for his size, he had always found himself matched against much smaller boys until he had finally dropped out from sheer embarrassment. But he had not looked skinny and lifting weights had improved his strength.

"It's not the same."

"No, I guess not." Hans racked his brain for a more impressive response. "I run, sometimes."

Tiflan nodded. "Dorilian runs."

"He does?" For some reason, this surprised Hans. He had never thought of Dorilian engaging in physical exercise. It seemed so... ordinary. "When?"

"Early morning. On the beach."

"Alone?" That, too, seemed improbable.

"Mostly. Legon goes with him on occasion. Why the sudden interest?" Understanding teased the very edges of Tiflan's smile. "Are you going down to the beach tomorrow?"

"Maybe. I don't know." They watched a burly blond toss his opponent to the floor and pin him there to the sound of shouts and whistles from the gallery of seated onlookers. The man wore a headband of snakeskin leather.

"Damned Suddekan," Tiflan grunted. "Built like an ox. I'm a fool not to wager on him."

"Why don't you, then?" Hans asked. The Suddekan was big and heavily muscled. Even Tiflan might have trouble with him.

"Wouldn't give him the satisfaction." Tiflan snorted. Another man, probably himself a noble, fair body golden tan from the sun, approached and stood by as Tiflan acknowledged his wager and agreed that the match had been worthwhile. It was the sort of conversant pleasantry Hans had come to associate with aristocrats. They appeared to prefer their relationships to be little more than ritual, like nods between strangers. Such suspicious ground fostered few friendships.

As they made their way from the arena to the baths, Tiflan decided to drop another bit of news. "Seeing as Tutto has been left in Sordan to protect the Heir, I have been directed to instruct you in the basic and necessary art of swordplay," he announced. "Have you ever handled a blade?"

"Well—" Hans had held swords, of course, when he had lived at Gustan as an eight-year-old. A boy's weapons, child-sized and blunt. He wasn't keen on learning how to use one for real. Real swords were sharp—and he disliked the purpose to which they were put.

"They come in handy sometimes."

"I suppose so," Hans admitted unhappily.

"Like good wits, you know."

While Tiflan stripped and immersed himself in the warm swirling waters, Hans resolved to start running again in the mornings. It would give him something to do and the beach was quite pleasant on this part of the island.

Besides, one never knew who one might meet.

Hans left the villa early along the wooden walkway leading down the cliffside to the beach below. Predawn silence made bird calls sound shrill, waves slap instead of slither. A light breeze, lake-scented, rustled the palms, lending subtle music to the first evolutions of day. His footsteps beat out an accompaniment of creaking boards. Dorilian was on the beach, his white garments clashing with sky and water.

Alone.

"Hello." Hans delivered the greeting with as much cheerfulness as he could convey. When he received no answer, he began his limbering exercises anyway, not asking for permission as Dorilian stood by, watching him with critical interest.

Under pressure from that scrutiny, Hans noted diverse details of the other man. The smoothly muscled legs, unscarred, pampered, but hard. The way his bare feet pressed into the sand. How very casual Dorilian was, at ease, the lake wind ruffling his precisely cut hair, his loose white togs. That look of someone annoyed by having his routine interrupted. Hans only then fully realized the challenge implicit in his coming here, uninvited, altogether too presumptuous of his right to a Highborn prince's company. To *this* man's company.

I have a right, don't I? He hasn't called down the guards yet.

As though he caught that thought, Dorilian frowned and glanced back up the bluffs at the villa. Who watched from those windows? Hans knew Dorilian would risk no falling out in front of them.

"Well, let's go," Hans urged. "Before it gets too hot." At this early hour, the sand was still cool. He pushed himself onto his feet and glanced at Dorilian, whose faintly affronted expression at last gave way to resignation.

Dorilian set an easy pace and settled into it, Hans matching his speed. They kept to the edge of the surf, letting cool waves rush in to lick at their feet as they left behind footprints to be obliterated along with those of waterfowl and tiny mammals. Golden sand lay strewn between the blue lake and towering cliffs of green like some royal road, a carpet so fine it was like dancing on velvet. Hans rejoiced at the feel of running barefooted, a sensation he had seldom enjoyed. *You don't wear shoes in his presence unless he does*, Tiflan had warned, *lest you tread upon his footsteps*.

So good did Hans feel that he began to consider picking up speed. It had been a long time since he had last raced. But this was no race, and to turn it into one might merely give Dorilian a new means by which to humble him. Hans began to think that Dorilian intended to run all the way around the island, that they would soon pass Sordan on their way back to the villa, so far had they come. But Dorilian pulled his pace when the sand turned to pebbles and the cliffs at last crowded the beach into nothing. Gentle waves surged between huge outcroppings of rock jutting out from shore. It was toward one of these lonely outcroppings that Dorilian, turning his back on Hans, slowly walked. Resolved, Hans trotted over to join him. With fierce suddenness, from nowhere, Dorilian spun around and, with his fist, struck Hans full and hard in the face.

What the hell?!

The force of that blow slammed Hans backward against the rock. Another blow came at his head, but Hans dodged it and threw his shoulder into Dorilian with all the muscle he had, carrying them both to the shallow, stony beach where they grappled as the waves rushed in. With feral quickness, Dorilian used his greater height and weight to advantage and pushed to his feet. To Hans's surprise Dorilian made no new attack but backed away, dragging a bloodied hand across his mouth. Strangely enough, he was laughing.

Hans didn't think it was funny. None of it. His bleeding nose hurt like hell and his mouth felt as though it had been smashed in with nails. "Wha's godden inu you?" he demanded. His words sounded garbled. "Wha wuz *dat*?"

Leaning on the rock, Dorilian looked down on Hans. He shook his head in disbelief. "The first accomplished what I sought. I apologize for the second one."

Hans bent his face into his cupped hands to catch the blood pouring from his nose. "Second one? Who cares 'bout da second one?" His words continued to sound slurred through his woven fingers. "I wan' to know why you frew the first!"

Dorilian pushed away from the rock and knelt in the shallow water beside Hans. "Tilt your head back," he directed. He used his fingers and some water to clean away most of the mess. "Handurin," he said, "I tell you this truly—I did not know you would bleed so much." He applied pressure on each side of Hans's nose to stop the bleeding.

Hans couldn't believe this was happening. "What did you hit me for?" he asked again after another minute had passed and his nose no longer bled freely. "I didn't do anything. Did you just want to see if I would bleed?"

"Something like that." Dorilian bent over to wash his hands in the cold lake water.

"Are people even *real* to you?"

"Some more than others."

Hans watched Dorilian calmly scrub at a tiny spot of blood— Hans's blood—that had gotten on the royal garment, as if that was his only concern. "Are you even listening to me?" he cried in frustration as Dorilian pushed to his feet again.

"I am waiting for you to grow up."

Still furious, Hans saw his chance and took it. He sprang and this time his fist landed, mashing flesh against bone. Dorilian tumbled back onto the pebbled beach. "Bastard!" Hans shouted angrily. "I've had all your bullying I'm going to take! You can't push me around like you did Stefan!"

He never saw the return blow. Something—a fist or a foot— caught him beneath the ribs and something else swept his feet out from under him. He landed, hard, upon his back, Dorilian atop him. A knee was in Hans's gut, a previously concealed knife to his throat.

"Shall I kill you, Handurin?" Storm-colored eyes, murderous now, bored into his. "It would save us both a lot of trouble."

"Why don't you?" Hans barely managed more than a croak. Dorilian was solid and strong, and there was nothing Hans could do to stop him.

"You tell me."

He would have killed me already if he did not mean to spare my life. But Hans knew he required a different answer, one that would advance him. "You need me," he gasped, "as much as I need you."

Dorilian rose to his feet and glared down with grudging confirmation. Hans got himself up only as far as his elbows as he coughed and struggled to catch his breath.

"If you attack me again, Handurin," Dorilian said, "I will disembowel you with one kick."

It was not an empty threat. Dorilian Sordaneon, of all people, had surely trained to defend himself. He ran barefooted on the beach to keep his feet strong, his balance sharp. Hans didn't like to think of what other skills this man must have honed to survive, how many attempted assassinations he might have foiled on his own. That he had killed was certain. That thought cooled Hans completely—he hadn't actually meant to harm Dorilian. His attack had been one of anger, wholly unplanned. He pushed to his feet and carefully dropped his hands to his sides. Things had gotten too far out of hand already.

"I... I don't want to fight you." Hans continued to look his enraged adversary in the eyes. "I never wanted to fight you. But I won't just sit still and let myself be attacked without provocation!" No Dominioner would. He lifted his chin defiantly. "If you hit me, I'm going to hit you back."

Nodding slowly to himself, accepting that, Dorilian relaxed, though not completely. After sliding his knife again into a sheath at his hip, he bloused his tunic to cover it. "Then I will wait for provocation next time. But be forewarned, Handurin: if you ever lay an angry hand on me again, I shall kill you without a shred of remorse. And if I do not, there are others who will gladly do it for me."

It was clemency of a sort. Under other circumstances, Hans would have been slain on the spot. Luckily for him, there had been no one around to witness his infraction. Dorilian exhaled with a muted curse and gingerly touched his reddened, oozing lower lip. "On second thought, I might have to kill you anyway," he said. "How am I going to explain this to my attendants?"

"You're the godborn one around here, remember? You don't have to explain."

Dorilian grimaced. "Is it as obvious as it feels?"

"Yes," Hans was forced to admit, though he smiled inwardly.

"Then I shall certainly have to explain it." Dorilian knelt at the waterline and rinsed his mouth with lake water until it came clean. "Come," Dorilian said when he had returned to standing. "We cannot stay here all morning. Already this choice of outings has proven ill."

The sun was bright as they walked along the beach back to the villa. Light glanced off their faces with friendly warmth but was not yet hot enough to fully dry their hair or their sopping clothing. There would be some explaining to do when they returned.

"We could say we were shipwrecked," Hans offered lightly, hoping to crack the thin, awkward shell of silence between them.

"Wonderful. Now we must also explain the loss of the nonexistent boat."

"We went swimming, then."

"In full clothing?"

"People do."

"Yes. And they also look as though they have come from street brawls, usually after they have been in one. My courtiers are not blind, Handurin, nor are they stupid. You could have helped matters greatly by not bloodying me."

"But you...." Hans trailed off, leaving well enough alone. Remnants of bewilderment and anger firmed the corners of his mouth.

"That is all beside the point. My people don't care if *you* get damaged." After a drawn-out pause that visibly eased his irritation, Dorilian asked, "Why did you seek me out this morning? And do not pretend you came by chance."

"I was only trying to break the ice." Hans decided that the truth, for all its insipidness, would have to do. "I never was fond of guessing games as a boy, and I find I like them less now. I want to know where I stand. And I do like to run," he hastened to add. "At school in... the place I was... I was considered good. Very good. I even trained for competition."

"You should continue, then."

"I intend to."

They stopped to watch a red-sailed ship appear around the far bend of the island, coming from Sordan. It had already been cleared by the Sordaneon warship patrolling the approach.

"Damn," said Dorilian. "That is Endelarin's vessel or I do not know the set of its sail. He said he would come when he had finished his business. I had hoped he would take longer."

"You really don't like him, do you?"

"What is there to like? My grandmother wore not half so much jewelry, and she was the height of bad taste in her day. At least she did not swagger." The dark-hulled vessel cut waves on its way to Rhondda's dock, its red canvas sails rippling in the light breeze. Very little was needed to imagine Endelarin Nemenor waving at the rail. Indeed, Dorilian's gaze narrowed as though he could see him. "Surely you have noticed by now that he is not the fool he feigns to be? You were with him long enough to have seen him sharp upon the point when it suits him. Such a man is not to be trusted until it is known which side he plays. He came but once a year to Sordan, if that, before you showed up to test my hospitality, and now I cannot shake him for a mere quarter moon. His interest in you leaves room for suspicion."

"What do you suspect him of?"

"Everything, until proven otherwise. The possibilities are endless. Essera is in fine disarray, if ever I saw one, and your usefulness in that part of the world is much to be pondered. You may be certain I am doing so. And so, I am sure, is our friend Endelarin."

"At least he's personable." Too late, Hans bit his tongue.

"And I am not." Dorilian caught the comparison meant in the remark. To Hans's surprise, he took no offense. "Count yourself fortunate. Most of those with whom I have been personable are dead. I have found there is little to be gained by it. And Endelarin's 'personableness' bears watching. It is but a mask for his quick mind. More than anything, I think he hides behind it."

Like you hide behind hostility?

Waves rolled in and washed their feet as they walked along the strand. Long moments passed in silence.

Movement upon the cliffs caught Hans's eye and he noticed men walking along a path among the trees. Guards? It made sense that Dorilian would have them. He was always guarded. But why hadn't they interceded when Dorilian and Hans had fought among the rocks? Because Dorilian had run too fast, too far? Outstripped his own guard? *He wanted to be alone with me, to see what I would do.*

"I just wanted to talk with you. We don't do a lot of that, and there are things—"

"Talk won't repair what lies between us."

"I think you mean Stefan."

Dorilian shot Hans a glance of steely reproval. "Your brother and I did not get along. You know that."

"Is that why you avoid talking about him to me?"

"Our conflict ended with us; I see no need for drawing you into it. He's dead. And I wish him to stay that way."

"But what if I want to know? What if it's important for me to know why my brother and the Hierarch of Sordan were mortal enemies?"

A skyrit called to its mate from the forested bluffs, a high, shrill cry of impatient waiting. Almost at once another call broke from the forest above, piercing the quiet of the beaches. Wave upon wave rolled in, little lapping things, a symphony of water running over sand.

"Mortal enemies? Is that what we were?" Dorilian scanned the running waves, his gaze upon some distance. "Stefan was a fool, then, to have tampered with *me*. He chose his enemies as badly as he chose his friends."

Looking at Dorilian's face, Hans saw sitting there in judgment an implacable god who would not be moved in a hundred years. Whatever wrong Stefan had dealt him, Dorilian had yet to pardon. Assassination attempts, surely, but Hans sensed something more. Clearly the subject remained closed, as wounds are closed, only to be opened with the probing tip of a knife.

"Marenthro said that I would have to find out—" Hans bit back his words too late.

Dorilian's eyes narrowed. "Find out what?"

"What happened. Find out for myself."

"Did he indeed? Yes, that would be your wizard's game, to leave the door ajar with not one lantern within to show what lies in wait. Usually when he does, one sees moldering corpses. Well, this is one corpse I choose to let lie undisturbed. I will not resurrect the dead. If your suspicions must be satisfied, there are Khelds enough willing to tell you their versions and leave no wrong unvoiced." A scant breath later, Dorilian spoke in a more conciliatory tone. "There is a man, a Kheld named Robdan Aelfricson, whose story I think can be trusted. He has, most recently, been Amallar's ambassador to the Archhalia. He was also present on at least one occasion of conflict between Stefan and me." Dorilian stopped walking and turned to Hans. "History will tell you the rest. Suffice it to say I will not hold Stefan's missteps against you."

"Other people do. Most people here avoid me like the plague. They're seeing him all over again." That was it, of course—everyone knowing that Hans was Stefan's brother. Stefan, whom Dorilian had detested so thoroughly that to this day his court dared draw no consensus as to what to do or think about Hans. Sordan's confusion was paralyzing.

To Hans's surprise, Dorilian looked like he understood. His mouth pulled into a crooked smile, one of the few Hans had seen. "Why do you think I hit you twice? I never got a chance to hit *him*." He shook his head and looked out across the lake. Long moments passed before he spoke again. "Do you know who *I* remind them of? My grandfather, Labran Sordaneon. He thought Essera rightly ours when old Endurin died—there were legal precedents to support him—and he never gave up saying that he, not your grandfather, was the real king."

"And what do you think?" Hans wanted to know. "Do you think he was?" It was perhaps the most vitally important question he had asked so far.

"Yes. Even Marenthro if hard pressed would admit it. After all, your grandfather was not even born in the land he came to rule; he was a Mentan by blood and birth. And Endurin Malyrdeon had decreed that the Sordaneons were to be his heirs long before his great-grandson was born. As I said, legal precedents, and historical ones as well. But Essera turned its back on us. They deserve what their betrayal has gained them. As far as I am concerned, your family is welcome to the forsaken lot."

"You mean that," Hans said, surprised. He had not thought to hear Dorilian say it so freely—not after everything Hans had heard others say.

"I have said so before."

"Your people are of a different mind." Hans could still hear the voices of the bargemen declaring that their Hierarch should claim his rights.

"They refuse to let Labran Sordaneon die. They have resurrected him in me, along with all their hopes. Sometimes, when I see him in their eyes, I want to go to the old man's tomb and kill him myself all over again." Dorilian rubbed his hand and the glinting Rill Stone ring he always wore. Hans had seen that ring at Permephedon, on the hand of Dorilian's father. Cleaved, as Dorilian's fingers had been. Thrust into Nammuor's sack. "We all have our ghosts, Handurin."

"Or shadows."

"Yes, that is more like it. Be careful how you place yourself, lest Stefan march before you like a shade."

"That won't be easy, if others insist on seeing him there." Hans paused, then pressed forward, whether wisely or not. "I hardly knew him, you know. That's part of what makes it so difficult—nobody wants to tell me anything about him."

They were on the sand again, a broad swath of unspoiled beauty. Most of those who visited Rhondda occupied themselves with the estate's other amusements. Hans could see that his comment had struck home.

"You speak of brotherhood," Dorilian said at last. He looked out over the blue water, or perhaps into his own thoughts. "Do you know what you invoke? The tie between siblings is the most sacred of all, even more than that between parent and child, for child and parent are strangers by nature, but siblings are formed of like stuff. To come between brothers is to stand in the face of that which makes each a reflection of the other. We have a saying: Say nothing to set a man afoul of his brother, for both will blame you for it."

Except Hans and Stefan had never been like that. Stefan had been too much older. And yet Hans remembered his brother as a defender, a teacher, even if Stefan had never let him win at swords. *You need to know that losing hurts, Hans.*

They paused beside a tidal pool swarming with sand urchins. The glistening, translucent creatures burrowed into the wet margins of the pool, burying their soft bodies from exposure to the heat and sun. At nightfall they would emerge to feed within the pool, their internal organs glowing through their silvery skins. Hans knelt down and touched a wriggler the size of his finger, feeling the smooth texture of its body.

"They are larvae," Dorilian informed him. "They mature into things with claws and teeth."

"I might as well get used to it," Hans reasoned with a slight smile. He hopped back onto his feet. "Who knows? Maybe I will mature into something with teeth too."

If I live. The thought nudged aside his momentary levity. And hope. His first challenge was to survive—in a pool where things already toothed and clawed fed upon the weak and immature.

Dorilian looked less bothered by such wayward notions. He stepped into the pool and let the water wash about his feet. "See if you can fashion advice into teeth. I will tell you this much: Stefan suffered most from blows he himself inflicted. He adopted policies that granted immediate satisfaction and never minded that those policies would in the long term bring him to ruin. He cut away foundations left him by your grandfather—and the worst of it was, he did not even know he was doing it. He was that ignorant. His overreliance on Kheld advisors alienated established administrators who would not have left him for any other reason. Essera's lords got a bad taste in their mouths. They may not be in a hurry to get their taste of you."

"But the Khelds supported Stefan," Hans maintained. "And they are wholeheartedly awaiting me," he added, recalling what Marenthro—and also Arne—had told him. "I should think they would be the least of my problems."

"They could prove the greater problem, depending on their expectations of you." Dorilian brushed sand from his arms. Both of them were still covered with it. "The balance will be delicate. Stefan gave them too much too fast. For that, they have amplified his virtues and made him the ideal to which they will hold you. They want another Stefan."

"And what do you want?" Hans dared to ask.

Dorilian grimaced at the question. "Anything but another Stefan." His very seriousness belied the predatory wolf-grin that claimed his mouth. "I might even settle for you."

As he and Dorilian continued their walk along the beach, Hans discerned a not unpleasant thaw across the yards dividing them. It was more than the morning sunlight. He wondered if Dorilian might not really mind being challenged in a small way. Of course, hitting him had been a mistake. Hans eyed the already purpling bruise marring the royal mouth and wished he had not done that. But then he touched his own sore lip and nose and was glad that he had.

Together they made their way along the silent, bluff-guarded strand. Much remained to be said, but Hans knew better than to press his luck. Instead he tossed lake-washed stones at flocks of gulls which defiantly stood their ground.

Before long they had come into sight of Rhondda's whitened walls, the red-sailed ship at anchor in the cove, her landing party on the beach and still out of earshot. Any argument entered now would be cut short, worse for having been concluded in haste. So they walked without words, each in his own thoughts, along the widening shore. Those standing at attention up ahead patiently watched them approach. Only Tiflan could be singled out of the growing crowd, standing tall above the others. And Endelarin, wearing marigold yellow.

Unfortunately, someone quickly noted Dorilian's damaged condition.

"What happened to *you*?" Endelarin grinned when Dorilian belatedly raised his hand to conceal his bloody lip. "And right where you most deserve it, I see!" Endelarin chuckled, quite taken with his own wit. Dorilian looked ready to kill.

Hans hoped against hope that he would become lost in the crowd, passed over somehow, but several sets of curious eyes marked him. By now everyone had noticed the two men's bloodied clothes.

"What happened, Thrice Royal?" Legon glared pointedly at Hans, just shy of accusing him. "Who did this base deed?"

"'Tis nothing." Dorilian's hand, held to his mouth, barely muffled his voice.

"That," Legon pointed to red-stained clothing, "looks like blood."

Dorilian pinned the Commander with a look. "Do you think we have been attacked?"

Legon stiffened at the question. "Clearly."

Dorilian nodded. "Then your course is clear. Take your men out along the shore and see if you can find the perpetrators."

But Legon's narrowed eyes never left Hans's face. "Perhaps we should begin looking closer to hand." Not everybody heard him, nor did they have to. Much the same thought was on everyone's mind.

Dorilian, however, had not lost control of the situation. "You have your orders, Legon. Go!"

"Yes, Thrice Royal." The man stalked off. It was obvious Legon knew full well he was being sent on a royal unicorn hunt.

Without saying anything more, Dorilian walked the path back to the villa, his entourage trailing behind him, strangely silent for a lovely, bright morning. Dorilian had declared off-limits the only matter about which anyone wished to talk. Hans walked at Dorilian's side, as effectively bound by that silence as by a spider's web—it could not really hold him or harm him, but he was acutely aware that he was being watched by the spiders.

Twilight had fallen and the sandstone bluff below the villa glowed purple. Hans followed Tiflan along a path of weathered planks and wondered why Dorilian would want to speak to him again so soon. Even though there really was no possibility of refusing a Thrice Royal summons, Arne had not wanted Hans to go. He'd been alarmed by having seen Hans's bruised face that morning.

"Don't do it! What if this time he wants to kill you?"

"Then he'll do it, I suppose. It's not like I can do anything about it."

But something had changed, of that Hans was sure. If not from that morning, then certainly since leaving Sordan. *Time*, he realized. He and Dorilian both faced challenges that would become worse through delays and indecision. Marenthro had warned that Hans's enemy was growing stronger, and if that was the case, Dorilian's enemy was getting stronger too.

Tiflan stopped at a point where the path bent to run along the bluff line and directed Hans to continue.

Hans followed the path until the planks ended at the overlook, a tree-framed pavilion that jutted from the bluff. Dorilian stood within the open structure, leaning against one of the sturdy timbers that supported the roof. It didn't surprise Hans to see hard-eyed

Commander Legon standing guard, making certain that Hans had to walk past to enter the pavilion. He was relieved when Legon didn't follow, but remained on the walkway, watchful but out of earshot.

"We need to finish our conversation," Dorilian said.

"Thank you." After the events of that morning, Hans was glad Dorilian would still talk with him. For this meeting, Dorilian wore garments of understated, unbloodied mauve silk. His lip, though no longer swollen, matched the bluff face for purple undertones. Hans's face, too, still bore traces of their earlier encounter.

"Put your brother behind us where he belongs. What do you know about my relations with Amallar?"

Caught by surprise, Hans bent his thoughts around what little he did know. "That you don't have any?" He watched Dorilian's gaze narrow. "I didn't think you'd ask about that. I thought we would talk about Nammuor."

For a long moment, Dorilian simply stared. "Nammuor." The name could not have sounded deader.

"I—" Again, just when he was possibly getting somewhere, Hans had wandered near quicksand. "I think he's our common enemy."

"Do you? What do you know of him?"

Hans clamped down on memories he had gained through a violation with which he was no longer comfortable. "I... was warned. By Marenthro. I told you that."

"Yes, though I'm certain he did not tell you all—or even enough." Dorilian paused before speaking again. Hans wondered what he looked upon. Was there something here Dorilian wanted him to know—or keep hidden? "Nammuor is a vicious enemy. I know this for having stood against him, not once but many times. More of my kindred's blood is on his hands than I can ever hold him to account for—and there is not enough blood in him for me to ever get it all back, not should I bleed him for a hundred years. You named Stefan and me mortal enemies; such was not the case. None have yet seen me take an enemy to mortal battle. But they will, because there is a battle in the offing between Nammuor and me."

"And for that you need my help."

Dorilian slid Hans a look of disgust. On the scale of things that Dorilian considered helpful, Hans did not even register except as a complication.

"You overestimate your usefulness. Yes, I dearly wish to fight Nammuor in the north, because I wish to drive him out from there—drive him out and defeat him. I have the armies to do this—and I have the Rill to move and supply those armies. I also have support in Essera I can bring to bear. But here is the matter: I cannot afford Amallar to oppose my entry there."

Which Amallar would be sure to do. Nammuor certainly knew this. By now, Hans had overheard enough to know Nammuor banked on Amallar to keep Dorilian in Sordan. With that surety, Nammuor could freely see to securing first Stauberg and then the rest of Essera. Amallar and the Khelds might not grow nervous until too late.

"Is that what you want? For me to guarantee Amallar for you?" Hans wasn't even sure he could do it, but he would be willing to try. Maybe. "What of your own claims to Essera's throne?"

Dorilian shrugged. "I will not resign that claim for naught. However, believe me when I tell you I do not want it. Essera is a bauble, a pretty toy. I could have had it were that my desire. Nammuor offered Essera to me not long after Stefan died—on a platter, held out with both hands."

"He offered it to you?" The revelation struck Hans as out of place, a twist of logic that, somehow, he could not make fit. "But at Permephedon he tried to *kill* you!"

The very air grew cold. Hans was reminded of that blood-curdling night on the terrace in Sordan. Dorilian stepped toward him. "*What* did you say?"

"Marenthro—"

"Of course."

Wanting to demonstrate that he, too, knew things and could be trusted, Hans added, "I know more than you might think about Nammuor and the Diadem and what it can do. About what he did at Permephedon."

"You tempt me to strike you again. You know *nothing* about that. Nobody does."

They might have been touching, so sharp was the withdrawal, the icy rejection that suddenly sheathed Hans in regret. Something hard and angry crashed down on the slender bridge of their contact, tearing it asunder. Instead of hitting him, Dorilian turned and walked, angry, to the other side of the outlook, where he stood framed against a bruised twilight sky and stared into some distance far out of Hans's reach.

Once more Hans knew he had done it wrong, all wrong. He'd tried to break new ground between them, tried to actually talk about that day, and he had uncovered an avenue of broken glass. Endelarin had warned him: to tread upon Permephedon tempted disaster. Marenthro's warning reasserted: *His thoughts were not your thoughts and may never be known to you—if the universe is kind.* More, even, than that Dorilian had experienced the mass deaths of his kinsmen, more than the torture and terror of that day, something was being guarded here. Something secret and deeply private.

"I'm sorry," Hans said. "I'm sorry if I—"

Dorilian faced him, still looking ready to throw a punch. "Do not speak half truths to me! I *see* them!"

Hans flushed, because Dorilian was right. He wasn't sorry for having made the attempt, only at the response.

"I'm not asking to revisit anything, or about what happened," he said. "But I'm also not going to pretend I don't know anything about Nammuor—or the Diadem."

Dorilian stared at him for a long moment, suspicious, weighing his response, before he relented. With a sigh, he tipped back his head.

"So Marenthro prepared you that much, at least. This Diadem you mention is monstrous," Dorilian acknowledged. "It's hard to know which to fear more: the tool or its master—or indeed which is which. The Aryati destroyed the world once, long ago. I do not believe they sought to do so."

"Marenthro told me a device like the Diadem corrupts the wearer." In this, at least, Marenthro's word would probably stand.

"Power twists even the strongest wills. Do you think I do not know it?" Over the lake, birds wheeled in the darkening sky. A chill slid into Dorilian's next words. "I am bound to an Entity; its power lies within my reach. Your regrettably deficient upbringing tells you this belief must be untrue, that gods do not reside in men, yet I know what I am. The temptation is ever present to seek out that power and use it."

Hans had no way to challenge such a... belief. Being descended from gods, or related to them, he understood; he'd studied these things. The Sapa Inka. Egypt's Pharaohs. But Dorilian was talking about something more, about having power of some kind. What kind? The power of his Hierarchate he tossed about easily enough. Something Stefan had said fell into place. *The Highborn blast aqueducts, Hans. They get inside peoples' heads. Tell me what's natural about that.* Plus Hans had seen what the Leur's Ring could do when Marc Frederick had wielded it. What if what Marenthro had sent Hans to find was not just a political ally, but a weapon? If Dorilian had powers like *that*....

"So Nammuor has this Diadem, and he does use it. Would this god you talk about, the one whose power you are tempted to seek, make you strong enough to oppose Nammuor?"

The question stood between them, naked. From the way Dorilian shook his head, Hans wondered if he had just sounded presumptuous... or stupid.

"I think we will save that for another time. You are possibly the most ignorant person I have ever met. Nammuor is poised to destroy us both and here we stand with no knowledge and less trust, unable to fight him."

"I'm a fast learner."

"This morning's adventure suggests otherwise."

Hans decided to try something else.

"We could form an alliance." It was a bold proposition, especially coming from him, and earned him another look of disdain.

"We could. But not as things stand presently. I need more, after all, than a brash young man with an accurate fist and the willingness to use it. I need Amallar." Dorilian's expression said he wished he did not have to admit it. "I need those damned Khelds off my back and against Nammuor. I need Essera too, but in its current state...." He shook his head. "Amallar. That is what I need from you. And then only if you can do it. It will be no easy task. Get your Khelds behind you, and then we will talk of alliances. Until then, you have much to learn. You are grievously unprepared for your future role, whatever that is to be. I shall assign tutors to you. Rhondda's library is among the best and books can be brought from Sordan if needed. Perhaps, in a few weeks, we can begin to plan what to do."

"Marenthro thought—"

"Marenthro," Dorilian emphasized, "sent you to *me*."

26

Life at Rhondda settled into a leisurely routine. Endelarin Nemenor sailed without further incident back to Ardaen, having accomplished whatever business he had pursued, and Dorilian was glad to see him gone. Tiflan, too, soon left, returning for a time to Teremar where he had his own duties to fulfill as Bas of that domain. Dorilian, for his part, tried to enjoy a less hectic schedule.

An hour into what should have been a peaceful morning, Dorilian focused unhappily on the woman in charge of the scholars he had summoned from Sordan. "Handurin… *what*?"

"The Prince refuses to undertake studies unless we also educate the Kheld."

Dorilian put the thumb and forefingers of one hand to either side of the bridge of his nose and pressed, forestalling a headache. The Kheld. Of course. A foreseeable complication. After a long moment, Dorilian resumed his audience with the Esteemed Archtutor Clothia Dalae. "Is Prince Handurin's request a problem?"

The scholar's mark centered on Clothia's brow had the bright glow of pure gold, designating her as a Disciple of the Order of Sages. By the way the Archtutor blinked, Dorilian knew his question had caught her by surprise. "Yes, Thrice Royal. For one thing, the contract—"

"Add the Kheld. We will pay the additional fees."

Clothia's consternation deepened. "We do not know how to educate Khelds. The language—"

"Teach him Stauba."

"Thrice Royal—"

"Do you think Khelds incapable of learning?"

Clothia saw where Dorilian was headed and lowered her gaze. "They can, of course. We have over the years instructed many of their kind. *This* Kheld, however... has had little exposure to refined education."

Which suggested a way to ensure this problem did not fall solely on Dorilian. He picked up a stylus and rolled it in his fingers. "Archtutor, let us be clear what we wish from you and your staff for the services of which we are paying an outrageous fee. Handurin is a prince but there are areas of study in which, we are certain, his education is deficient. There may be other areas in which he is not; it falls to you and your staff to determine these facts. As for the Kheld—" Dorilian made certain to capture Clothia's full attention and was satisfied by her obvious readiness to do whatever he asked. "That Handurin wishes to better his companion is laudable. A prince should have people around him who are educated enough to provide meaningful support and insight. This Kheld is loyal and Handurin trusts him; he will turn to him for advice. Make certain Master Anseldson at least has the tools to offer reasonable advice."

"Yes, Thrice Royal."

Using the stylus, Dorilian signaled to Mirrez, his chief secretary. Just prior to Clothia's audience, Mirrez had placed a stack of documents on the desk for Dorilian to address as soon as he ended this conversation with the Archtutor. "Prince Handurin will direct the Kheld's education. Consult with him about what subjects to teach. You may go."

Clothia performed a deep and deferential bow. She turned and departed with an elegant sweep of her fine linen robes.

"I can read and write, you know," Arne complained. It had been two days and already he resented his tutors.

"In Khelda. It's not going to hurt you to learn how to read and write Stauba. Or learn a little Staubaun history. It explains why they act as they do." Hans had also assigned Arne time with a mathematics tutor, though he heard fewer complaints about that. Arne was already quite good at numbers and eager to learn more.

Another discipline had been added to their schedule just that morning, though this one could prove to be fun. They followed one of the palace pages along a shaded walkway leading to the paddocks and playing fields that adjoined Rhondda's extensive stables. Even before reaching the stables they saw a handful of riders in the largest field engaged in an exercise or game. A man Hans recognized as the Hierarch's Chief Groom waited for them outside the main stable, along with two haltered geldings: one chestnut and one of pure ivory.

"Prince Handurin." The Chief Groom bowed. He did not acknowledge Arne. With a sweep of his hand, he indicated a nearby array of tack. "I am to assist Your Royal Highness, if needed."

They were to bridle and saddle their own horses. Another test, then, but fair enough. Hans grinned at Arne. "Dare I hope you grew up on a farm?"

Arne swallowed visibly. "I did, and I can put a bridle on a horse and ride it." They had ridden from Sordan to Rhondda the week before and he had done all right. "But I always rode bareback before. Never put a saddle on. Mostly I harnessed my ma's carthorse for trips to the market."

Hans glanced at the groom, who looked on without a hint of either interest or helpfulness. Although tempted to say something that might prompt the man to offer some assistance, Hans didn't feel secure enough yet in his position to begin ordering about Dorilian's staff. He had not even talked with Dorilian since their meeting at the outlook. Fine. He knew how to saddle a horse.

"Bridle him. I'll help you with the saddle."

Hans noticed how the groom's posture stiffened and his expression skewed to discomfort.

"If Your Royal Highness would—"

"I appreciate your service. You can saddle my horse if you want to help." That would allow the man to save face. And Hans would make sure Arne's horse was safe to ride. He laid a saddlepad and flung the saddle—an odd affair with double girth and a breastplate—atop the chestnut's back while the groom did the same to the ivory horse. Arne bridled his mount and stroked its smooth cheek, talking to it and saying he hoped they could get along.

"Here, I'll show you how to tighten the girths." Hans demonstrated the way the buckles worked and a trick to gauge the tightness. They had been given gentled and even-tempered horses. Next time, Arne could work at putting on the pad and saddle. "Riding is something we're both going to need to do a lot of, I think. Unless we travel to Essera by Rill... and probably even then."

Though working on the last girth strap, Arne twisted around, horrified. "*The Rill?* Hans, I can't ride the Rill. And there's a good shot you can't either! The damn thing kills Khelds if we even get near it."

"That can't be true. Stefan rode it. My grandfather did—and my mother too!"

"All right, maybe *you* can, because I heard how the Wall Lords did something special to your line," Arne conceded. He tugged on the leather strap. "But regular Khelds, folk like me, we can't ride it. The Rill hates Khelds because we killed some Highborn folk a time or two and it never forgets a death. Heard after I was captured that the same thing happened with the Wall. Man said Khelds killed the Wall Lords and now Khelds can't go to Stauberg."

"Not at all?"

"That's what I heard." Arne stepped back from his work on the girth. "How's that?"

"Good enough for now. Get up." A little loose, but Hans would tighten them once Arne was astride. He held the saddle in place while Arne used a block to get a leg up on the tall horse. After adjusting the stirrups, girth, and breastplate, Hans went to check on his own mount. The groom had done a good job and received a nod of approval.

The groom swung astride and rode ahead of them along a lane to the larger playing field where four riders—two wearing black tabards and two wearing green—appeared to be chasing each other from one end of the grassy expanse to the other. A large black post stood at the far end of the field and a similar green post at the near end, each with room to ride around it. Occasionally a rider did so. More often, two or more riders would run their horses at each other and mill around a bit, after which one of them would break from the melee to race up or down the field, the rider clutching what looked like a short-handled axe in hand. Upon reaching the painted post he would hit it with the axe, sending a loud crack through the air.

Pelekys!

Hans recognized the game. When he had still lived at Gustan, his uncle Jonthan had run a team and Stefan and Cullen had played on it. Revived memories burned bright: wild movement and the thunder of galloping horses, riders sporting tabards of blue and gold while scores of visitors to the Manor yelled from the grassy bank of the viewing rise. He'd sat with his mother for those games, watched the flow of excitement and dread on her face. Whenever Stefan got the *pelek* and raced for the other team's *herm*, Hans would jump up and down and scream for Stefan to win.

Unfortunately, Hans had never played. He had been too young and small, unable yet to ride a horse suited to the speed and violence of the game.

Arne, seated on horseback at Hans's side, watched the riders with visible admiration. The riders were clearly skilled, their command of their mounts forceful and elegant as the action flowed back and forth, the axe being passed or stolen. Following one more crack at the herm, the riders' movements changed and slowed. The players met at the center and Hans saw them exchange words and a brace of bows. The two green riders peeled off, cantering across the grassy swale towards the watchers, while the other two players headed to the stables.

As the riders drew near, Hans recognized Dorilian and Legon. Because neither was riding an ivory horse, he had not identified them sooner.

Even windblown and wearing sweat-damp clothes, seated astride a hard-run horse, Dorilian managed to look regal. Some people rode as naturally as they breathed, and he was one of them. With a sharp nod to his groom that signaled something Hans could not decipher, Dorilian patted his horse on its bowed and restive neck.

"Riding strikes me as more useful exercise than taking you on a daily run."

Though Arne tensed with affront, Hans took no offense. Dorilian had a knack for sardonic opinions. "Will we be playing *pelekys*?" The game required good riding skills, but Hans was willing to test himself.

At the Hierarch's side, Legon shifted in the saddle, prompting his blood-bay horse to dance back a few steps. Hans noted the way Legon's eyes narrowed on meeting his. He also noted the heavy, axe-headed *pelek* Legon held. Dorilian acknowledged where Hans's gaze had landed.

"Do you play?"

"No." Hans wished he could have claimed otherwise. It might have helped persuade Dorilian to take him more seriously. "Not yet, I mean. I watched at Gustan as a child, my uncle and brother, but… where I grew up, no one played it. I learned a different kind of riding. Trail riding. In the—" *Allegheny? Andes?* "—mountains."

Dorilian's gaze shifted to Arne. "You and your Kheld can learn together then. *Pelekys* is good for teaching how to keep a good seat. How to trust your horse and other riders." His head and Legon's both lifted as a voice hailed from the stables. Hans withheld a sigh. Getting more than a few words with this man was nearly impossible.

Dorilian gathered the reins of his horse. "I will see you tomorrow. At sword practice. Him too."

"Swords? I don't think—"

"I don't care what you think."

Hans watched, dismissed, as Dorilian rode away.

The groom gave them a wooden baton and set them to practice how to hand it off. Doing so from horseback was not nearly as simple as it had looked while practiced players had done it. Arne had trouble even turning his horse and had no understanding of using either stirrups or reins for communicating with the animal, whose frustration was nearly as pronounced as that of the groom. After a while Hans set Arne to riding wide figure eights on the playing field while he watched from the side.

"He will need a lot of practice, sir," the groom confided.

"I'm just glad he's learning now." At some point Hans was going to go either to Essera or Amallar, and more and more it felt only right to take Arne with him. Doing so would almost certainly involve riding horses.

"Are these horses to your satisfaction?"

Hans assured the groom they were and was informed that they would be reserved for his use for the duration of his stay.

Once Arne had practiced enough, they returned to the stables, where Hans directed the groom to see to his mount while he showed Arne how to unsaddle and care for his horse and tack. Hans fell back on teaching his own routine after trail rides: water the horse, feel down the animal's legs, check the hoofs, wash the bit, and look over the leather for wear.

"I always thought princes had people to do things for them," Arne said as he dried the bit after he had dipped it. "So how'd you get to know all this?"

"When I was a boy I had a horse—more of a pony, I think, that my grandfather gave me. Aster, I called him. Star, because he had one right here." He tapped his forehead near the hairline. "I loved riding Aster, and part of riding a horse is taking care of him. Your horse can't help you if it's not able; you can't ride a horse that's lame or sick because you didn't take proper care. Funny thing, but when I was sent away and forgot so much, I still liked to ride, so—" He smiled at recalling how Geraldine, short and round with a helmet of white hair, had doggedly led the charge into his every interest. Years of riding day camps had followed.

His moms. They had done so much for him, devoted their lives to him, and never known or even suspected that they were raising a wizard's pawn. Dorilian had called Hans that and it stung to know the label fit. Was that what he was—a playing piece on some gameboard for wizards and Hierarchs?

"What's wrong?"

A touch on Hans's arm brought him back to where he sat on a wooden bench in a stable's tack room. He looked up at Arne's concerned face. "Nothing. I—"

"You're sad. What about? It's got to be more than that I don't know shit about riding horses."

He might as well set that to rest. "No, not that. Not anything really. I just… I have questions I don't think anyone can answer. I guess I'm starting to realize I need to answer them for myself."

Arne hung the bridle where Hans showed him and together they walked out into the courtyard, a wide paved area surrounded on three sides by the grand barns where the Hierarch and nobles kept their horses. The Chief Groom was nowhere to be seen but Hans reasoned that their lessons were over for the day. Whatever assessment Dorilian had assigned, they had already performed. The stately arbor leading to the main palace lay before them, shaded and fragrant with white summer phlox.

"Tell me more about Stefan," Hans said. He caught Arne's look of surprise and added, "Dorilian won't tell me anything."

"And he's the one that could. Hans, even if he told you it would just be lies."

"The Highborn don't lie. That's what Ezhno said, remember? If they did, the lies would somehow become the truth. Maybe that's why he won't say anything, because the truth is ugly."

Arne rolled his eyes. The arbor, its stone paved floor dotted with thyme and sweetmoss, took a turn toward the long terrace at the back of the palace. "If the truth is ugly, Hans, it's because he made it that way. That bastard laid a curse on Stefan, did it to his face. Khelds were there to hear it! The whole of Essera heard it. And thousands died in Neuberland when the Hierarch broke a treaty your grandfather made. Just because he hasn't killed you yet, or me either, doesn't mean you need to learn more about Stefan—you need to learn more about *him*."

I'm trying.

"He's not making it easy." Hans had only to look at today's entirely too brief encounter.

"That's the way of it with villains."

Hans shook his head. "I think that's what I need to find out about Stefan, because I think he became one with Dorilian."

"Fuck that. You should be more worried about that Highborn bastard becoming one with you."

27

People think I've got the King's ear, and I do—
more than most. We swore our oaths in blood,
Stefan and me. Because of that, Stefan sits at my
shoulder even when he's not in the room. Trouble
is, I don't sit at his.
—Cullen Brodheson,
letter to Sinon Kouranos

Weeks passed and Dorilian was seldom seen. Affairs of state kept him busy with ambassadors and generals and the legion of administrators who ran his vast domains and government, many of whom he had summoned to visit his retreat. Dorilian was an exacting ruler who demanded that his subordinates work as hard as he did himself.

Hans spent those same days with history books and sword masters. Though he had proven he could ride a horse with some skill, in other areas he had been found sorely lacking. Dorilian had assigned even more tutors to correct any deficiencies. The trouble was that Hans had so many shortcomings—and thus so many tutors—that it was sometimes all he could do to squirrel away an hour for himself.

Most of all, he wished his native world had adopted a more advanced means of killing each other. Hours of practice in the weapons arena with the heavy wooden punts that substituted for actual blades often left him sore and bruised, too bone-tired to do more than eat his supper and go to bed—merely to face the wrath of his history tutor in the morning because he had neglected to trace the emergence of Wall Lords in various Malyrdeon lineages or study the Second Ardaenan War. He didn't even see the point of it. To him it seemed unlikely that Nammuor would be defeated in a sword fight. As for history, the Wall Lords had all died out and no one was even fighting Ardaen that Hans was aware of. But once a week Dorilian showed up at sword practice to test Hans's progress with real weapons, and each time Hans found himself backed against a wall or flat on the floor, Dorilian's sword at his throat. Only his determination to someday fight Dorilian to a draw kept him coming back for more punishment.

"Just once," he complained to Arne one night when his muscles ached particularly. "Just once, I would like to get him with *his* back to the wall."

"Seems like people have been trying to do that for years." Arne looked up from polishing his new sword. He took great pride in the weapon, which few Khelds bore. Only in Neuberland had they taken to doing so.

"I don't think I'll ever get the hang of it." With a sigh, Hans dropped onto the bed beside him.

"It's not fair, comparing yourself to him. Folk say he's one of the best there is, he's that quick. The sword master himself wouldn't take him on."

"No, I've noticed I'm the only one who has to. I suppose he just wants to make sure I don't get killed in my first battle."

"That's my job," said Arne. Dorilian had given him the sword and put him into lessons, saying that as long as he was so attached to Handurin, he might as well learn to protect his back. Arne grudgingly admired Dorilian for doing it. No one else in Sordan would have put a sword in Kheld hands.

A knock on their door brought Hans to his feet. He opened to Mirrez, the Hierarch's senior secretary. Mirrez bowed and said, "Your Royal Highness, your presence is requested."

"Now?" asked Hans. He was certain it was well toward midnight. "What time is it?"

"I know the hour is late, sir, but the Thrice Royal has requested you be brought to him. Shall I tell him you will be along presently?"

"No. I mean, yes—wait." Hans searched the nearest chair for his house chiton, which he had stripped off earlier, and his overmantle. "I will come along with you. I just need to make myself presentable."

"Certainly, sir."

From his perch on the bed, Arne simply looked mystified. He had told Hans earlier that evening how the use of royal address confused him. It turned on and off like cold water, he said, and depended on who was doing the talking. Despite having a teacher focused on protocol, Arne got it wrong more often than not.

Hans followed Mirrez along wide corridors softened by shadowed angles and corners, low light carpeting the floors and ceilings. Armed soldiers stood at attention beside a square archway but let them pass. After traversing more corridors within, they stopped at a door of carved gold-dark wood where Mirrez made a hand signal to two guards and then entered. Hans followed.

In all his weeks at Rhondda he had never been to the royal apartment. Dorilian had always seen fit to meet with Hans elsewhere, in the weapons room or the library where he studied. The rooms he now entered were spacious and regal, a style he had come to expect of his host. Mirrez walked over to a paneled door on the left and rapped quietly just twice before opening it and motioning for Hans to enter. Hans found himself in a private study with a floor of dark peacock green fashioned from slabs of some rare mineral and polished to the sheen of glass. Overlapping maps, many of them exquisitely drawn, papered the walls, and the heavy desk in the middle of the room was littered with papers, identifying this as a place of work. Emerald silk curtains hinted at covered windows, but a well-placed waterglobe on a broad, curved stand provided very good light.

Dorilian sat at the desk.

"Be seated." He indicated a brace of chairs. Mirrez softly closed the door as he departed. "What took you so long?"

"I had to get dressed."

Dorilian glanced at Hans's clothing, as if noticing only then that he wore any. "Yes. Well, I have been talking with your tutors. Two of them have been dismissed and will be replaced by others more suitable. The third has found herself inadequate and will not be replaced." Dorilian leaned back in his chair, gaze keen with questions. "Tell me, Handurin, were the Mentans who hosted you as advanced as your education seems to indicate?"

Stunned, Hans sank back between the wooden arms of his chair as what had started as dismay rearranged into relief. So that was what this was all about. He had done better than expected.

"Excuse me, but I'm not sure what you're asking." Hans tried not to sound too pleased with himself.

"I'm saying you demonstrate an advanced understanding of mathematics and sciences which many a Permephedon-educated student would be hard put to master. Your tutor said she had nothing more to teach you; that, indeed, you had taught her a thing or two." Dorilian steepled his fingers and considered Hans across them. "You have been back in this world for long enough to have reached some conclusions. This Creation within which we live is a paradox. On the one hand, we have the Wall and Rill and the Five Cities—really three Cities, because we count two that exist only in Myth—and on the other hand"—he indicated the imposing braziers standing near one wall, unused because it was summer and the room did not lack for warmth—"for the most part, our everyday technology is rudimentary."

Mindful of agreeing too readily, Hans asked instead, "Are you going to tell me the reason for that?"

"I might."

"Once you have figured out how much it is safe for me to know?"

For once, Dorilian looked amused. "Perhaps. You have just enough irreverence not to believe, as we all must, that the natural laws of our world differ in significant ways from those of the world before the Devastation—which is to say a world probably like the one your grandfather was born into or the one you so recently left. Whether you believe in them or not, those laws—Leur's laws—are in force. Just as, whether you believe it or not, there's godsblood in my veins."

"I'm not sure what to believe about that."

"At this point what you believe is not important. I am pointing out a fact." Dorilian placed something on the polished surface of the desk and slid it toward Hans. "What can you tell me about this?"

The Saint James medal, with its image of the mounted saint lifting a fiery sword, gleamed against the deep blue wood. Hans picked it up.

"It's a... symbol of protection. The Mentans, the people I grew up with, have a religion that venerates sacred people; they call them *saints*. This one is Saint James. He was a warrior, so he's on horseback and holds a sword of holy power."

"And the crown?"

"The halo?" Hans could see how someone might mistake it for a crown. "The light shining around his head is the sign he's a sacred person."

"It's not a diadem? A device?"

Like Nammuor's? Or the ones his tutor had told him about? "No."

"And you follow this… religion?"

"Roman? No. An old woman gave this to me after I asked her for help." Because Dorilian looked like he wanted him to say more, Hans continued. "It was the day after Marenthro came to get me. I was conflicted and she prayed for me and gave me this medal. To protect me, she said." Hans asked something just so he could be sure: "Are you giving it back?"

"Yes." Dorilian leaned back in his chair. "I find it fascinating that even an old Mentan woman recognized your need."

Hans ducked his head. "I realize I have come to this situation without much preparation."

"Without *any*. You barely have knowledge of who you are."

"I know myself well enough. Maybe the Sordaneons are living gods, but the Stauberg-Randolphs never made it that far."

"Just further than most ever thought they would—or could. It would be best if you could advance those gains, not throw them away. However, statecraft is an art, not a science, and there is not a text in three Worlds capable of teaching you all that you need to know. You are in for hard lessons, Handurin."

Was that an assessment—or a warning?

"There are, however, adjunct subjects you would do well to master. Like History."

Hans winced. He had been expecting this. So, he had surprised everyone when it came to math and science—all the more reason to find him deficient in something else. His grasp of history—*this* World's history—was a glaring weakness. All those years he had spent learning about another world's societies and past civilizations meant nothing here. Hans barely understood the Triempery's culture because he knew not a thing about where it had come from or what it thought it was going toward. Marenthro had taken no steps, made no arrangements at all, in that other world to mitigate his ignorance. Instead, Hans had studied the works of prophets and saviors and Inti the Protector, written a Master's thesis on

Dascanio's postcolonial econopolitics, taken a class on the poetry of the Kama Sutra, and translated *The Secret History of the Mongols* into a language invented by one of his professors.

All of it useless.

Nonetheless he attempted to defend himself. "I don't see why I need to know the names of all the Malyrdeons—or the Sordaneons, either, for that matter. I have already met the sole living Highborn princes. So I think that the knowledge of a few strategic dead ones should be enough, at least to start with. I can look the rest up in a book. And I know now that Stefan killed the last Malyrdeon princes and why that's a bad thing. He shouldn't have done it, but I just found out today he thought they were rebelling against him. I need to find out more about that. I understand. It's just—"

Why was this so hard for him to explain? Dorilian's gaze had not wavered, not even at that part about his murdered kinsmen. An empath—of course! No need to argue when he had only to sit and catalogue the manifold levels of Hans's response. Hans pulled his thoughts together.

"My tutor wants me to memorize dates and names. Dates are less important than the sequence of events—and the reasons and people behind them. Two-thousand-year-old patterns of settlement in Lacenedon or the Trans-Telarkan domains are hardly pertinent to what I need to do. I need to learn more about Khelds and *their* patterns of settlement."

"Who does what to whom—and how and where and why—is what history is all about. I can see you already know this." Dorilian flipped over several papers on the desk. "I agree at this point that you need only learn what is immediately useful." He rose and walked to an ornate stand in a corner alcove, a place of honor resembling a sort of altar, and took from its safekeeping an immense leather-bound tome, which he carried over to Hans and handed him. "Read this. If you learn—and understand the truth of—but half of it, all the world will mark you for a scholar."

"Cibulitus?" Hans read aloud the archaic lettering embossed in gold leaf upon the cover. He had his languages tutor to thank for his ability to do so. "*Annals of the Return?*" He glanced up in perplexity. He had heard of this author and knew he had written about an age long buried in the past.

"The only existing firsthand account of the Return and the first two centuries thereafter. Cibulitus, fortunately for all posterity, lived to be incredibly old and was a prolific writer to the end of his days. And he was personally acquainted with many of the persons and events whereof he speaks. Your tutor did not think you were ready for him."

"And you do?"

"We lack for time and must proceed directly to what is needed. And this"—Dorilian tapped the tome sharply—"this you need. Some call it Myth, some call it Truth—but it is, of all our history, the most useful to a person who would rule over others. Once I told you that I would have you understand me." Something of his intensity seemed to darken the shadowless waterglobe light that filled the room. "It is not for my own sake that I ask it."

"For whose, then? Mine?"

"When you know that, you know everything." Dorilian's expression, already thoughtful, turned pensive. "I wish we were not so very much strangers, you and I."

"We don't have to be." At the moment, Hans was not overly moved to pursue any closer relationship than what they now enjoyed, with which he was often, unaccountably, ill at ease.

"I wouldn't put you through the trouble." Dorilian walked back to his desk. "Still, the time has come for something more between us than guesses and innuendoes and the general courtesies a man owes to one he would have suffer his company. As things now stand between us, you owe me nothing but good behavior, and in exchange you receive an education. That is a good bargain for you because it costs you nothing, but a very poor bargain for me seeing as I gain nothing by it but your dubious company and a distinct nervousness in my domain and beyond. Given time, I have no doubt your cursed Khelds would attack Sordan in force to free you. I do not intend to wait for that to happen."

"Are you going to allow me to leave, then?" Hans could hardly believe it. It seemed too soon. He sensed something vital remained to be done, but here in Sordan he felt safe, at least. Just the prospect of being on his own alarmed him.

"In due time. As we stand now, you are doing me no real harm."

That much was true. Although ruled by hatreds and fierce resentments on all sides, Dorilian's subjects were not easily moved to conspire against him.

"Then what is it you want from me? What proofs do I have to give you that I can be trusted? That I am not another Stefan?"

"You've proven that already. He would have sought to kill me by now."

From what Hans had heard, that was certainly true. Stefan had never been one to sit still in the face of opportunity. "Would you have sought to kill him?"

"No."

Look after my family. Hans swallowed and sought for the right words. "Well, you don't have to worry about me trying to kill you. I can't even imagine doing that."

"For now. Situations change. So do people." Dorilian regarded Hans evenly. "It matters little if I trust you at this moment. You presently have no means by which to afflict me. But this moment will not last forever—it must give way to the next."

"What are you saying?"

"I require something from you: a proof I can deem fully binding on your honor that, should I turn you loose upon the world, you will not then turn against me."

Hans blinked at him in surprise. "Turn against you? Why would I do that? Besides, Sordan is too powerful—it would be suicide to do so." That, he was sure, was one of the lessons Stefan had learned too late.

"Small wisdom, though it serves you well. I would have taught you more."

"There are other things as well." Hans could not put into words his feelings about this man.

Dorilian's gray gaze latched onto his. "Are you willing, then, to seal a bond with me?"

The question was dangerous—because of who asked it. If studying myths had taught Hans anything, it was that promises made to a god were double-edged bargains. If ever there was a human he had to treat as a god, Dorilian was that man.

"A promise?"

"Of sorts."

"So long as you don't want my birthright, my life, or my firstborn child, or"—another possibility occurred to Hans—"or Arne as a hostage, then—yes," he decided cautiously.

"You may keep your Kheld, as well as any offspring you might choose to inflict upon the World." Dorilian looked amused by Hans's rampant imagination. "The bond I require does not depend on the lives of others." He paused, a possibility occurring to him also. "You have not already—"

"No," Hans assured him. "I haven't fathered any children. Anywhere." He had barely managed to have a few fumbling sexual encounters. Even so the subject made him uneasy. The manner in which Dorilian contemplated him reminded Hans acutely that he had no heir, and that Dorilian was the kind of man who might try to remedy that situation. Alliance by marriage was well practiced in every culture Hans had ever heard of. Thanks to his history tutor, he knew Marc Frederick had secured his throne by marrying the daughter of the Highborn Prince of Tahlwent. And Stefan had married a Kheld woman but fathered no children.

Which was how *Hans* had ended up in this spot.

"Just as well," Dorilian said. "Bastards bring down more dynasties than they profit."

That Dorilian did not mention marriage struck Hans as hopeful. With renewed interest, he watched his host rise and walk over to a tall cabinet.

"I wager all upon this outcome." Dorilian opened the heavy, inlaid doors, exotic birds with mother-of-pearl wings seeming to fly outward as the wooden panels flung wide. "Too much is at risk for me to be uncertain, and so I will settle the matter—I hope to our mutual satisfaction. You will not leave here if your bond does not prove binding."

Is this the alliance? Hans wondered. Was he standing on the verge of getting what he had come to Sordan to obtain for the Stauberg-Randolphs, for Amallar, for himself? Or was this yet another contrivance designed to keep him off balance? Hans shifted in his seat, not able to put his finger on what was causing his unease. It was the night, maybe, but everything about Dorilian tonight—his calm, his deliberateness, his too-obvious lack of guile, even Dorilian's choice of clothing—a plain chiton of sable silk that skimmed his body like black water and a single sash of scarlet red— made Hans uncomfortable in a nagging, pea-under-the-mattress sort of way. It was probably nothing more than that he was overeager, ready to read too much into too little.

Hans stroked the thick leather cover of the book in his hands.

It was old and beautifully preserved, with embossed gilded lettering, and he wondered if it was rare or valuable. In a society where few apart from the wealthy could read or write and common folk seldom saw, much less owned, books, Dorilian had lent Hans something more precious than wealth. As precious, perhaps, as the bond he offered.

This is important—as much to him as it is to me.

One thing was certain: if Marenthro had wanted Hans to learn about what it took to hold dominion over other men and command their loyalty, the work involved in securing a population's well-being, the wizard had chosen an impressive teacher. Hans was seeing firsthand and gaining a deep appreciation for the difficulty of the job. He was sure beyond anything that if he got the chance, he would want to work as hard and govern as well as Dorilian Sordaneon. About that, at least, Hans had some idea of how to go about things.

That was getting ahead of himself, however. The first part of what he had come here to do, plant his unprepared ass on the throne of Essera or give them some other, better, form of government, was going to be a damn sight harder to pull off. Maybe whatever Dorilian was proposing would help Hans accomplish that.

"Give me your arm."

Hans wrenched himself from his mental wanderings and back into the room, aiming a stare at the man who stood over him. "My what?" He looked down again, his mouth suddenly dry. In his hands Dorilian held a pair of scarlet cords.

"Your arm. You said you would be willing to seal a bond with me."

"Yes. And I am, but I had in mind swearing an oath, or something like that." Hans stared at the table where Dorilian had laid out a tray of instruments. Where Hans had thought to see pens and sealing wax, he saw instead cold metal and glass glinting on a tray of silver, reminding him of nothing so much as his own unreasoning fear of needles and all things surgical. He had watched a man die in an ambulance, threaded with tubing and wires.

"Does a blood bond frighten you?" Dorilian asked. Something probing lurked within the question.

Hans shook his head. It was not the bond, as such, that bothered him. "No," he said, tearing his eyes from the display on the table.

"Some Kheld taboo, perhaps?"

"No. Khelds count blood oaths more sacred than ties of birth." Those had come up during conversations with Arne, and Hans had his own childhood recollections of his brother's ritual with Cullen Brodheson. That one had involved knives. Something cold touched his spine as he remembered. *We'll be brothers, Hans, Cullen and me. He'll be your brother too.* Then, Hans had not wanted another brother. Nor was he sure he wanted one now.

"Then you understand something of the sacredness of covenants. Blood seals the oath, binds the Flesh to the Truth. And Truth is what I seek."

"Truth is good. I want truth too. It's just... does it have to be blood?"

Dorilian's expression turned quizzical.

Hans flushed. "I don't like needles."

Dorilian moved the tray out of sight.

This could be a good thing, Hans tried to convince himself. A blood bond was certainly not to be undertaken on a whim by a man in Dorilian Sordaneon's position. That Dorilian was Highborn could itself lend the rite all sorts of secret, even terrible meanings. Not to mention what Khelds would think of it, should they ever hear. Still, Hans could see that Dorilian was not proposing the blood bond lightly. He was as solemn as a priest.

Is he asking so much? If he needs this to believe in me...

Though he feared the far-reaching consequences of a sacred bond to so forceful a man, Hans decided he really could not afford to pass by this opportunity. Dorilian's offer of a personal alliance was a treasure such as even a king might kill for. At least Hans would be spared an ordeal of primitive butchery. Dorilian's instruments were clean and he was probably skillful.

"All right." Hans extended his arm. "As long as you don't remove my hand or a finger or anything."

He half-expected Dorilian to take up a scalpel and slash open his palm as Stefan had done with Cullen. Instead Hans found himself disregarded for the moment as Dorilian deftly knotted one of the silk cords above his own left elbow, then took up a primitive but elegantly made glass syringe. Hans winced and turned his head to one side rather than watch.

He looked only when he heard movement and suspected the

deed was done. White cloth covered a portion of the tray beneath a small bowl, beside which lay a syringe filled with vital, bright-red blood that was clear to the verge of translucence.

Dorilian then turned to Hans and took the arm that had remained extended to him throughout the entire procedure.

"You don't have to watch," Dorilian said helpfully.

Grateful for the consideration, Hans looked away and occupied himself with the ranks of books in various elegant bindings that lined the ordered shelves, the maps on the walls, the flow of green color through the tiles as they passed beneath the legs of the desk. The tourniquet looped around his arm and tightened. What was Dorilian going to do with their blood, once he had drawn it? Mix it in the bowl? Dip quill pens in it and use it as ink? From his studies, Hans knew some tribes drank blood as a part of sacred rituals. The thought turned his stomach.

Even though steeled for it, he hardly realized the needle invading his skin, finding and entering a vein. The tourniquet released and fell away, followed by a warm infusion at the puncture site...

Injection? He had received immunizations enough times to know what he was feeling—

Surprised, Hans jerked his arm away. The syringe flew across the room and shattered against the opposite wall. There was little blood to splash—the chamber was already empty. Only a few errant crimson spots stained the corner of one map. Dorilian moved before Hans could think, picking up the broken syringe and examining it minutely.

"Idiot! You could have killed yourself!" Dorilian hurled the useless instrument to the floor, sending yet another shower of slivered glass skittering in ruin across the gleaming mineral surface.

Dry-mouthed, Hans stared at him, more dismayed than before.

"The needle!" Dorilian's beratement bordered on shouting. "It could have broken off in your arm. Have you no sense at all?"

"Sense enough to know when I've been tricked!" Hans lashed out. All semblance of deference flew out the window. No one in his life had ever made him as angry as this one man. "*What* were you doing to me?"

"You agreed to a blood bond."

"You never told me you were going to give me a transfusion!"

"Don't be a fool. It was only this much." Dorilian illustrated the amount with his fingers. Truth to tell, it had not even been as much as that. His gray eyes narrowed as he studied Hans. "You do not seem much the worse for it," he observed.

"No thanks to *you*," Hans snapped. He had not yet cooled off, though Dorilian apparently had. "That's a hell of a bizarre way to make a covenant! I'm surprised I haven't broken out in spots!" He thought about it and added, "Or worse!" He examined his skin, checking for signs of reaction. His breathing seemed a little tight and his pulse was pounding, but that could be adrenaline more than anything else. Rage, most likely. He thought of another worry. "Did you even sterilize that thing?"

His concern made no impression on Dorilian, who handed him a square of white cotton. "I think you will survive in spite of yourself. And I require no more of you—other than your sworn word, which you can give me later, in front of witnesses."

"Seriously? Why not just perform this little trick in front of witnesses?" Hans pressed the cotton square to the pinpoint of blood dotting his arm.

"This bond is a personal covenant between you and me—*only*. I do not intend, at this time, to make a public statement. Indeed, I consider it fortunate that there was no one on hand to witness your reaction."

"You should have told me what you were going to do."

"Had you asked, I would have. And you should have watched. Always be aware, Handurin, of what others do to you." Dorilian turned away and began to put away his instruments.

Hans flushed so hot his skin was probably beet red. Embarrassment curbed his anger as nothing else could have. Dorilian might be the most insufferable man alive, but he was right.

"So that's all there is to it?"

"What more is needed? A signed document? Victory ribbons?"

"How about some gesture on *your* part?" Though Hans was mollified somewhat by Dorilian's belief that they had established a bond of some kind, the lack of reciprocity aggravated his sense of justice. "What you did was a little… one-sided."

"I assure you, the act is binding as it stands." Dorilian neatly slid each instrument into its corresponding sleeve. "Your feelings do not affect our bond one way or the other."

"Even if I feel it binds me to you—but not you to me?"

"Are you seeking to make us equals, Handurin?"

Hans wondered how much he dared to say. "I don't know. Maybe. I'd be a pretty sorry excuse for an ally if I wasn't at least close. It's not the worst idea in the world, for us to be on equal footing in something."

"True. And perhaps at some point you will be."

But I am not now. He never hesitates to remind me of that.

Hans swallowed. "You can do whatever you want. And you do," he said quietly. "But I don't have to like it. I'm not without some say in my own life. I was given the choice to return to this World or stay where I was. I chose to return. And I chose to come here. I am aware, you know, of when things are simply being done *to* me. I can't do anything to you. I don't even want that. But I do want something *from* you."

Dorilian went very still and thoughtful. Hans caught a fleeting expression he had not seen on Dorilian's face before. Something new and deeply aware. And then that impulse was gone, smoothed by a long habit of keeping secrets.

"We cannot repeat the covenant to your—or anyone's—satisfaction." Dorilian gestured to the glass-littered floor. "You managed to destroy the only proper instrument to be had on this part of the island. If you are willing to wait upon our return to Sordan, I will reciprocate the covenant with you then."

Hans sensed that the offer was genuine, that Dorilian would have done it immediately had there been another syringe. But to wait was too uncertain, an opportunity lost. This moment felt tenuous—and he knew how mercurial Dorilian could be.

"There must be something we can do now, here." Hans rose from his chair and surveyed the remaining instruments, considering alternatives. The instruments were few, but they were beautifully crafted for precision; most appeared designed for medical purposes. Was it possible Dorilian possessed a physician's skills in addition to his other talents? Hans no longer doubted it. "There is another way to form a blood bond." He hesitated, not certain how his idea would be received. "The way Khelds do it."

"And if I do not favor Kheldish bonds?"

Careful. Although he had seen Dorilian to be less hardened against Khelds than his reputation suggested, Hans faced a man who counted Khelds as enemies. Dorilian granted Khelds human standing, but he had said during a recent dinner conversation that he thought the incursion of Khelds into Staubaun Neuberland grossly violated every condition Erydon Malyrdeon had placed upon Khelds in granting them Amallar. Such a man would not regard Kheldish oaths as having much moral force.

"A simple blood bond, that's all." Hans noted the expected spark of opposition. "After all, what matters is that there be blood between us."

"There *is* blood between us," Dorilian reminded him.

"Yours. Not one drop of mine. That's what I meant about it being one-sided."

Hans watched Dorilian weigh what it would cost to call the bluff. It was easily done. A simple no and their meeting would be over. A call to the guard would make Hans a prisoner. The Rill might spirit him in the morning to Permephedon and his regent there—or to Leseos and from there to Amallar. And there was always the final option: to kill him. For a moment, Hans glimpsed the game board upon which they played and the way it possibly existed in Dorilian's mind, vast and intricate, populated by pieces and rules Hans did not yet know or even understand. Watching Dorilian, the shifting secret thoughts that moved him, Hans began to divine the nature of his adversary. He also noted the moment Dorilian decided that the game was yet worth playing.

"How do the Khelds do this?" he asked.

Willing his hand not to tremble, Hans lifted a thin-bladed knife from the sterile cloth and used it to show what must be done. "You make a cut across your left palm, the one closest to the heart." He recalled all he could of Stefan's act with Cullen. "It doesn't have to be deep, just enough to draw blood."

"The spilling of blood?" Dorilian's attempt to put the act in context recalled his priestly role during the Illumination.

"The *gift* of blood makes the act sacred," Hans hastened to explain. To a Staubaun way of thinking, the act was both. "You do it to consecrate swords; why not oaths?"

Dorilian took his time thinking about it. Hans had seen already that ritual use of Highborn blood was a sacrament deeply bound by myth. That a prince of the godborn house of Sordaneon would agree to spill blood in a Kheldish ceremony was beyond unlikely. Actually, it was unthinkable.

"Proceed then," Dorilian agreed. "If you must have your blood bond, I will do as you do."

A deeply drawn breath preceded Hans's initial attempt at the ceremony. Each participant in the Kheld ritual was required to draw his own blood as proof of sincerity and consent in taking the oath. Witnesses usually stood present, as he once had, but Hans saw no point in courting rebellion. He wrapped his fingers around the knife's cold metal handle. Steeling himself, he pressed the razor-sharp edge to his skin and drew it across his palm, feeling the quick hot fire of the cut. When he looked down, however, he saw that he had barely cut the skin at all and drawn only a few drops of blood. Fiercely embarrassed, if only because Dorilian watched him so closely, he managed a deeper incision on his second attempt.

When it became Dorilian's turn to perform, he slipped the ever-present dagger from his belt and drew its deadly point diagonally across his open left hand, which he then extended, exhibiting bloody beads welling from a clean, efficient cut the width of his palm. Hans had to admire the fortitude that enabled a man to disfigure his own flesh so neatly.

He took the offered hand and applied it palm to palm with his own, surprised by the warmth that suddenly tingled in his fingers as they arched against Dorilian's straight, strong ones. It was the hand that bore the Rill Stone, which even now blazed a brilliant green. It was also the hand from which Nammuor had sliced two fingers in Permephedon. *They feel real, both do,* Hans realized with fresh wonder. *Did that even happen?* But if it hadn't, how had Hans seen it? He forced his mind to focus on the task, welcoming the warmth that spread into his hand as though more than blood communicated when he pressed his and Dorilian's bleeding wounds to the fullest, mingling their different bloods in the Kheld way.

"By this act, I swear to do you justice." Hans interpreted the Kheld oath he had heard Stefan use as best he could remember. "Your hand bears now a part of me and mine a part of you. Should ever I offend the blood upon my hand, then may I lose that which I have dishonored."

The words reflected actual Kheld law: oathbreakers were traditionally deprived of their left hands as punishment. Marked by the enduring stigma of a disgrace so odious they became pariahs, the most wretched of people, no longer suffered to eat with or find refuge among folk of integrity, unfit to make contracts or handfast in marriage. To Khelds this was a terrible oath, written with the most inviolable of inks upon the most holy paper, binding mortals across boundaries of kinship and even death. Every oath breaker knew whose ghost would greet his in the otherworld. It was an oath Hans could be sure no Kheld would ever require him to break and one no Kheld would challenge. He alone bore the power to make it. He alone would bear responsibility for what it brought to pass.

And for Dorilian Sordaneon, Hierarch of Sordan, it must therefore be the same.

Dorilian clearly appreciated that the barbaric rite was in its way as solemn as his own. Gravely, as befitted his role, he repeated perfectly the oath he had just heard, adding, "As I have given my blood, so I give you my word. Let blood decree our way. We are bound to it for good or ill."

There was not a Kheld alive who could have said it better.

28

My father gave me the same training as he did his
son, and I was raised from girlhood to view the world
in political terms. My marriage to Erwan Cedrecson
was itself a statement of politics. What politics are
more enduring than that which commands the man
to whom a woman gives her body?
—Emyli Stauberg-Randolph, *Reflections*

Emyli wore her royal mantle of cerulean velvet embroidered
in gold thread with a repeat pattern of her family's crest;
white fox fur trimmed the hem and neckline. Gone were
her mourning weeds. The Archhalia was meeting and she wanted
her appearance to remind them of who she was—of who her father
had been. She wanted the mighty to look upon her as they debated
the fate of her son.

Permephedon's lofty corridors hummed with mingled alarm
and speculation, fueled by the news that had arrived a bare six
weeks before. Rumor of Handurin's return to their world had
spread rapidly throughout Essera's domains, followed by ripples of
disquiet.

Sordan's Highborn eagle had unexpectedly taken wing, prey in
its talons, and all lands watched with trepidation.

Within the Archhalia, a great beast of uneasy coalitions stirred
and rumbled. It had taken weeks for the members to convene, but
convene they did. From Essera's far-flung domains and provinces,
ruling lords and their representatives flocked to the High Citadel
to find out how much of what they had heard was true.

Since the day the Archhalia had stripped her of the Stauberg-Randolph regency, Emyli had clung to Marenthro's gift of sanctuary and never left the secure environs of Permephedon's Redoubt. That lofty retreat of scholars and exiles, outcasts and apprentices and those who craved solitary lives of study and service, had given her refuge. Now she again picked up the scepter of her family's power and made her way to the seat of government. That she had been born a Stauberg-Randolph had bestowed on her a life privileged beyond that of most women but had also laid on her a burden of obligation. Emyli could not put aside her duty to the land and people her family had been entrusted—indeed created—to rule. Even in the hour when he had felt most betrayed by them, Marc Frederick had not turned his back on the Malyrdeons and the trust they had placed in him. Now, because of that example, neither could his daughter.

What a Wall Lord and a wizard have conceived, it falls on me to midwife.

If only she were the sole force striving to give something birth.

Permephedon's supernatural walls allowed light and air into the citadel by means of open matrices. The expansive portals that presented such fine views also regulated the passage of air and light with extreme precision, screening out impurities, even grains of pollen. Emyli welcomed the breeze that teased her hair and delighted in the early summer scents cast up by the sun-warmed plain of Lacenedon. It made her wish, fleetingly, for her youth, when she had run with her long hair trailing in the wind, chased by Kheldish cousins through the meadows at Gustan. As always, she felt a pang for that girl and a childhood she had given over much too soon. Because of that regret, she found value in her younger son's extended stay among the Mentans. Handurin's removal from this world and the pressures Emyli had known it would heap upon him also had kept at arm's length those things that had caused Stefan's downfall.

Emyli's fear for Handurin now was that he was in the hands of a man whose complexity and ambition far exceeded his. Her son had not been brought up to desire the legacy he had inherited. Dorilian, from his very birth, had been shaped to desire nothing else.

But did he? Dorilian destroyed preconceptions. Emyli had expected him to pounce upon Stefan's death to press his claim to Essera's throne, but he had not. Neither had he thrown his considerable influence behind Handurin. Instead, he waited, even his caution bespeaking a power none cared to provoke. *Do we even know what he wants?*

Erenor's machinations were far easier to discern. Since Handurin's return had become known, Erenor's demand that Emyli deliver Prince Handurin to the Archhalia—and Erenor—had grown increasingly strident. Nor was Erenor's the only voice. Essera's domains wished to settle the matter of Handurin's fitness to rule and several of those lands, Emyli knew, openly supported a return to Stauberg-Randolph leadership. That Nammuor had taken up residence at Aral after bringing with him a large army and a fleet of Mormantaloran ships in support of Erenor struck many as a move designed for intimidation—and perhaps invasion. Following Stefan's death and Erenor's ascendancy as Regent, Essera's military fleet lay at anchor. Even sea trade had largely been subverted to Mormantaloran benefit. Every merchant in Essera heeded the fate of Zepheron's ship.

Only the Rill stood uncompromised. Even Nammuor respected the vast political and economic consequences certain to ensue if he tried to appropriate the Rill. It was not only that Rill operations were controlled via Sordan and, to a lesser degree, Permephedon. Nations carefully guarded the long-established balance of power—and flow of wealth—implicit in Rill commerce. Every domain had a stake in who controlled the Triempery's silver lifeline.

Emyli had chosen to wear the crown of sapphires Marc Frederick had given her in honor of the two sons she had borne—given on the day he had named them his heirs. "Always my Princess," he had said. In those days, such words had kept Emyli alive, such words and her sons. In her darkest time, she had found her life's purpose through what they represented to her and this land and to her family's legacy. The birthright of the Khelds. The continuation of the Highborn Triempery and legitimate rule. For as long as her sons lived, as even *one* of them lived....

She entered the Archhalia chambers after the last of the representatives had been seated. Though they might have anticipated Emyli's interest, none of the delegates had known ahead that she would attend. She dared to hope that none had prepared for her arrival or prepared a plan for how they would contain her. With nods to the lords and delegates who stood to acknowledge her, Emyli took her place at the Archhalia table. Though no longer head of that body and having purposefully not attended any

Archhalia session since the one that had removed her as regent for her son, she retained her seat as titular head of Essera's ruling family. *Dorilian and I have that in common. We are both legitimate heads of royal family.* And neither of them chose to dignify this assembly except on those occasions that suited their purposes. Emyli allowed a bitter smile at the thought of having anything at all in common with Dorilian Sordaneon.

"Princess." Erenor addressed Emyli smoothly, though his manner and expression looked tenser than his voice betrayed. He glared at her down his high-bridged nose. "We have waited upon you for several months. We trust that your appearance means you will now prove more obedient than in the past. As you recall, you were to have produced your son before this assembly. You are still bound by that order."

"Noble Representatives." Emyli rose from her seat to address them. Her gaze took in every person, to remind them of her royalty and sincerity. "As you are all by now aware, my son has indeed returned to the lands of the Triempery. I do not know by what means he arrived there, but I can tell you that Handurin is in the Hierarchate of Sordan."

There. That framed it nicely. There had been no announcement, only rumor thus far. For all that every person listening had heard those rumors, her words had the effect of stones shattering glass.

Erenor's jaw tightened with either disapproval of Emyli's manner or disbelief in her version of events. To Emyli, neither mattered.

"Then get him back from there!" Ionais, her bright hair piled atop her head like a crown, stood imperiously at Merrydn's table, surrounded by seated ministers and advisors. "Or are none of us now on speaking terms with Sordan or the Highborn tyrant who rules it?"

"Your cousin," Erenor stressed pointedly, giving Ionais a dark glower of censure, "has not responded to this council's inquiries."

The admission was revealing, Emyli thought. Erenor's friends on the Archhalia had tried to contact Dorilian—and been rebuffed.

In a fluid, much-practiced movement that immediately commanded every eye, the Sordani ambassador rose from beside the vacant Sordaneon seat. Diplomatic white silks, edged in velvet with bars of blue and the Hierarchate's emerald green, black, and silver colors, clothed his stately figure.

"Noble Representatives of the Archhalia." Emyli's dear old

friend, Sinon Kouranos, addressed the gathering in a voice so quietly distinctive that others always ceased their own talking to hear what he had to say. "As a sovereign Hierarchate, Sordan only answers questions of intent or policy from other states if these are submitted formally through proper diplomatic channels. In the case of this Archhalia, that would be me." He placed a hand on his beribboned breast to punctuate the reminder. "Every inquiry directed through this embassy has been duly forwarded and answered, as those who made them well know." Sinon paused to let what he had just said take root. Some inquiries, then, had been answered. Delegates looked to each other, the question rippling through the room as Sinon continued, in a darker tone. "I will now provide a formal statement of Sordan's position. My sovereign, Dorilian Sordaneon, the Thrice Royal Hierarch of Sordan, expresses grave concern over the young Prince's safety should he be delivered before this assembly. Prince Handurin will remain in Sordan. As my liege does not recognize the Tholeros regency, he does not feel compelled to respond to its complaints."

There was a general murmur of commentary—and alarm. Sinon had just confirmed that Sordan indeed had their Prince in hand. At least two Archhalia members rose to speak, but not before Ionais had again seized the floor.

"Nor, it seems, is Dorilian in a hurry to yield an heir whose uses he has yet to fully evaluate," observed the still-angry Ionais. "We will be here for months!"

"Is Prince Handurin being held prisoner or not?" demanded Kathanos Niarchos, the ambassador from Gweroyen. The old man, a close confidant of Emyli's since her childhood, must certainly wonder what she had not told him. His question evoked a chorus of agreement as others demanded the answer to that question.

Sordan's ambassador took his seat again. Emyli marked the confidence with which he did so. "My sovereign, Dorilian Sordaneon, the Thrice Royal Hierarch of Sordan," he told them, "has communicated to me that Prince Handurin Stauberg-Randolph is in no danger and is in fact his royal guest."

"Labran Sordaneon was a 'royal guest' of Marc Frederick's for thirty-five years." Kathanos spoke out of turn, prompting another round of murmurs and renewed affront. "I believe we can rightly demand clarification of that answer."

Reaching beneath the table, the Sordani ambassador pulled forth a plain cloth bag dimpled with bounty and set it on the table before him. To a man, the assembly groaned. With complete indifference, Sinon reached in to retrieve a small, pale nut, which he promptly cracked in his fingers. He pried forth the purple nutmeat. "My sovereign, Dorilian Sordaneon, the Thrice Royal Hierarch of Sordan, has communicated to me that Prince Handurin Stauberg-Randolph is in no danger and is in fact his royal guest," he repeated.

"Yes, we know that," another man, Phellan of Serrain, intoned. His perpetually strained expression did not look less so for all his attempt to sound coaxing. Serrain's relations with Sordan, while not warm, observed all the proprieties and were considered good. "Your Hierarch's assurances are appreciated, of course. But is Prince Handurin going to be returned to us any time soon?"

Sinon chose another nut from the sizable stash in the bag and cracked it open. The snap could be heard throughout the room. "My Sovereign, Dorilian Sordaneon, the Thrice Royal Hierarch—"

"Oh, be quiet, you blithering bore!" Ionais hissed. The famed blue Crescent of Caiseth at her throat blazed forth like a star as, regal in her rage, she turned to Emyli, leaving Sinon to his nuts—which he placidly continued to consume. "What do you say, sister? Have you been allowed to see your son? You don't know that he is even alive—or that Dorilian really has him at all!"

"You know I cannot travel to see my son." Emyli coolly provided the reason of which they were already aware. "Upon this body's orders, my Rill privileges were suspended along with my regency. I assume it was your intention to prevent me from travel, openly communicating with other domains, or using the Rill to foment discontent. As the Rill platform stands outside the boundaries of this Redoubt's veil of sanctuary, any attempt on my part to use it would put me at risk of losing my freedom. Much as I desire to see my son and provide him assistance, I will give this Archhalia neither cause nor opportunity to place me under arrest."

She did not tell them that she had received word, prior to any inquiry, from the Sordaneons themselves that Handurin was safe with them. However chilly her personal relations with Dorilian, Emyli's family possessed a unique relationship with Sordan's ruler. Marc Frederick's legacy now served Emyli well. Dorilian had sent word through Sinon that Handurin was alive, his well-being assured, his status to be determined. Furthermore, Emyli had received from Robdan Aelfricson, the Amallaran ambassador, news that his inquiry had been answered similarly. The message had reassured Emyli, and not only in that it had confirmed her own information. Asphalladra had verified that Hans was not imprisoned but had attended First Day festivities and been seated at the royal table. Asphalladra and Hans had even shared a dance. *He looks unafraid and is trying to figure out what he needs to do.*

Only three weeks ago, Emyli had heard—again from Asphalladra—that Handurin had accompanied Dorilian to Rhondda. Not a prisoner at all. A guest.

Dorilian promised. He wrote his death gift in blood.

Endurin's Paradigm was again in motion, but Emyli could not tell if the Wall's temporal construct was repeating its demented pattern or forging something new. *My family and his, forever at each others' throats. Or have we, somehow, altered that course?*

"You play a dangerous game, Princess," Erenor warned. He slid some papers he had just signed into an envelope and glared at her. "It is clear you mean to keep your son from us. I move that you intended all along to circumvent this body's orders to produce him. Sending him to Sordan is but your most recent insubordination."

Emyli turned on him with a fierce, brilliant anger. "Do you think I sent him there? For what purpose? You know my family's history with the Sordaneons! You know how wickedly and for how long that monster tormented Stefan. Dorilian made Stefan's reign impossible!" She faced the room again, chin held high. "After my father's death, I entrusted my youngest son to Marenthro Permephedeon. I told him to keep Handurin safe—and as far from the Sordaneon and his Highborn viciousness as he could take him. And he did. Can one be farther away than another World? But for Handurin to return, I had to trust to Marenthro again."

Emyli saw that she had succeeded in diverting them by the whispers that seized the room. *Marenthro.* All knew the wizard's ways were mysterious; that in conjunction with the Malyrdeons and the Wall he had brought Marc Frederick from an archived past to this world and then engineered his kingship; that he had helped make a captive of Labran Sordaneon and restored the Rill after Labran's bold attempt to stop it. Marenthro worked on a scale and by means unknown to the greater population. But the Archhalia also knew—Emyli counted on them knowing—that Dorilian had never been Marenthro's pupil or advocate. Indeed, Dorilian had banned Marenthro from Sordan. The Archhalia might think—Emyli hoped they would think—that Marenthro had gone against her wishes in returning Handurin to Sordan. Better yet if they thought that Marenthro had gambled on Dorilian's goodwill—and lost.

Erenor intruded. "Princess, the fact remains—"

"The fact remains that Handurin is in Sordan, and it matters not who put him there." Hebron of Lacenedon's saturnine face reflected the dark mood of his fellow ruling delegates. "What matters is that the rightful ruler of Essera is in Sordaneon hands. If that is not a violation of *something*, then this Archhalia should find more useful work."

Amallar seized the moment to make one of its rare successful motions, this one for a formal Archhalial censure and demand that Prince Handurin be remanded forthwith to the Archhalia. Others took issue with the exact wording of the demand.

From his chair at the Archhalia's head, Erenor seethed visibly as the council succumbed to the seductive pointlessness of arguing the right or wrong of Dorilian Sordaneon's action. Dorilian, who would ignore the edict and did not care what actions the Archhalia might take against him, was beyond Erenor's reach—and his power to punish. Emyli met Erenor's narrow stare across the expanse of table separating them and noticed the way his malicious smile hardened. There were other paths one might take to gain a throne.

Emyli shuddered, and it took every ounce of her strength to keep from giving Erenor the satisfaction of seeing her response. She must not show, not yet, not too soon, that she knew where the Prince-Regent's thoughts wandered.

If he succeeds in getting his hands on my son, he will kill him, just as he has killed so many others. He wants the throne—and with my sons dead, he has only to wed me to gain a path to Essera's kingship. With Erenor established as king through marriage, Mormantalorus would gain the one thing its puppet government yet needed: legitimacy.

And there was only one man Emyli could wed to prevent it.

She would not let things come to that.

Neither she nor Dorilian wanted to be in the same bed.

Erenor had just returned to the Emrysen Palace in Dazunor-Rannuli and dismissed his staff from his chamber when a glimmer of unnatural light caught the corner of his left eye. Usually such a display presaged a visit by Coram Barzanes. Erenor's jaw tightened and he inhaled sharply before he turned to confront the newly arrived visitor. He refused to call the Mormantalorans guests. Internally he called them *occupiers*. Or maybe *invaders*.

To their faces, he called them allies. Another word—*fiends*—came to mind when Erenor saw that Coram had not come alone. Beside him, white-haired and implacable, crowned with gold bearing a massive red gemstone and ringed with blood-filled spikes, stood the root and stem of all Erenor's successes and woes.

Nammuor.

Upon seeing Erenor's discomfort, Nammuor smiled ever so slightly. "I have been waiting. Or did you not promise to send a report?"

"I was about to. I thought I would include the current temper of Dazunor-Rannuli as regards the situation." A desire to amass all pertinent information in his account of the Archhalia session was only one reason Erenor had left Permephedon. The greater reason was that he had been descended upon by alarmed representatives from every domain and guild hall with whom he had forged alliances.

"And that temper is…?" Nammuor wandered to the chamber's south-facing window. Undraped, it afforded a magnificent view. The Rill, itself a crown of mighty rings and glorious arches, projected even more power at night than it did by day.

"I have not had time yet to survey the local powers that be." By that, Erenor meant all seven of the Seven Houses. Two of those houses had beset him following the Archhalia session. "They will be unhappy, of course. Everyone is unhappy." Was Nammuor? Erenor could not tell just by looking at him.

"Dorilian was not there." Nammuor had reached his own conclusion.

Erenor removed his jacket and tossed it upon a chair. He could tell his… allies would not be leaving soon, and the night was a warm one. He might as well be comfortable.

"No. Neither to take credit nor cast off anyone's fears about Handurin's possible fate. By all accounts, Dorilian is treating Handurin as a guest—albeit one on a tight leash."

"You must be worried. They could align." Finger pressed to the glass, Nammuor traced the shapes of the Rill's rings, then tapped once, sharply, between them.

"Hardly. At this point Handurin is just a pawn, a playing piece, and he is being treated like one. My source inside the Hierarch's staff tells me the boy is left to retainers to handle. Handurin traveled with Dorilian to Rhondda, but by accounts he spends his days with tutors, probably learning Stauba. The boy is unequipped for anything useful. Furthermore, he eats, sleeps, and shares his days with a Kheld who is either his servant or also a prisoner. He never speaks with the Hierarch."

Nammuor frowned at that. Perhaps he did not believe it. Erenor, however, knew his information to be good.

"You need not worry," Erenor assured Coram, who looked receptive to his explanations. "Handurin's presence in Sordan is actually a boon to us. His being there serves as a source of friction and dissent. The Khelds are livid about it. Their ambassador talks peace and compromise, but the rest of them talk about taking up arms. People in this city look across the river and thank their gods that Dorilian is blockaded in Sordan and not here in Essera stirring up trouble."

Nammuor turned his back on the window and rejoined Coram. Erenor noticed that tonight Nammuor's crown looked especially… bright. Except for one spike, which had darkened. Perhaps it shared the same fate as the darker gold of the two topazes in Coram's earpiece. Energy spent in translocation required crystals to be traded out.

"Yes. Blockaded," Nammuor mused. "Is that really the case? Or is our Sordaneon cowering in the protection of his Entity?"

Always, in every conversation, Erenor sensed something personal and deadly between Nammuor and Dorilian. "His Entity? Certainly. After all that has happened to his kindred?" So many Highborn had died in the last decade—indeed, the last few years—that Dorilian had to feel a bit… endangered. He and his Heir were the last two of their kind. "But his Entity is not only in Sordan." Erenor pointed to the window, though Nammuor did not bother to illustrate that point for him by looking at the Rillscape. "Dorilian traveled to Permephedon, lest we forget, and did his best to undermine my effort to be made Regent."

Dorilian had, in fact, put on quite the show by using the Rill Stone to illuminate—for the first time in decades—all *three* of the Thrones of Light. The damned Hierarch was not only Highborn but also Entity-bound and, quite possibly, powerful.

More than that, he held a claim to Essera's throne that rivaled Handurin's. Nammuor worried about Dorilian for the wrong reasons.

"The Seven Houses want Dorilian kept in Sordan," Erenor said, then made that case. "They don't want him to align with Handurin any more than I do, and they don't want him sitting on Essera's throne. They want him stripped of power, not given more. Marc Frederick had the Sordaneons exactly where they wanted them, and the Seven Houses are incensed by how Dorilian outmaneuvered their plans. They don't like where he is now. The Seven Houses don't give a damn about Handurin—nobody in Essera does except that as the Stauberg-Randolph heir he offers an alternative—but *everybody* prefers to see Dorilian confined to Sordan. That is where people want him, with Handurin and a nation of Khelds standing between him and Essera. Everyone except you, apparently."

Something acknowledging glinted in Nammuor's black gaze. His irises truly were nearly black and seemed to drink in any light that wandered near. "Oh, I do like to know where he is. At all times. You have no idea how dangerous he could become, but I do."

"Good thing he's afraid to leave his island," said Coram. He fingered one of the crystal wine glasses on a tray beside a filled decanter and stack of books. He turned to Erenor with a smile. "May I? Regent?"

An unsubtle reminder, stressing that word. "By all means."

Erenor would join them. He would drink the wine and watch in wonder and horror the lengths to which they would go. And he would use the full weight and power of his regency to aid their increasing grip on his country. Dazunor was next. He knew this in his bones.

By taking Dazunor-Rannuli and its Rill node, Nammuor would cut Essera in half.

29

Of the three sons Amynas begot with Leur, Derlon
shone brightest. Strong and moved most quickly to
action, he learned the arts of Hesphed. In preparation for war, he fashioned an armor that
amplified his body's natural gifts so that he ran like
the wind and could lift ships from the water. His
brothers thought him too occupied with kinetics.
—CIBULITUS, *ANNALS OF THE RETURN:
ORIGINS OF THE HIGHBORN*

Rhondda was Dorilian's haven of the heart, but Sordan was his royal seat, nerve center of his dominion, and eventually the business of government demanded his return. Hans and Arne rode with Dorilian into Sordan on the heels of a soft summer rain that left the city washed and fragrant with spice wood and jasmine blossoms. People turned out along the avenue leading from the Chasm Bridge into the Upper City, hurrying out from shops and courtyard dwellings to see their ruler's return along the Avenue of Heroes. Children ran in the wake of the royal entourage as far as the great Dekkora, where the riders passed under the soaring white arches of the Gate of Wings and into the Serat's shining heights. The morning mists drew back with the same light wind that unfurled the giant green and silver banner of the Sordaneons above the Serat, announcing Dorilian's presence within the City. It was as though the Hierarch himself had brought back the sun.

Hans was given different quarters than those he had occupied prior to leaving for Rhondda. This time he and Arne were allotted an entire suite of rooms in the oldest, and by that definition most sumptuously coveted, part of the Serat, adjoining the wing that housed Dorilian's own palatial residence. At first Hans took this as a sign of improved standing, and perhaps royal favor as well, but soon he noticed that the door to his rooms was still locked at night behind him and armed guards were stationed strategically in the corridor. Nor was he allowed to roam unattended as he had gotten used to at Rhondda. He needed to obtain permission to venture outside the manses and buildings of the Sordaneon Serat, and that permission was granted twice and then repeatedly refused. When confronted on one of the few occasions Hans could get alone with him, Dorilian made light of his alarm, citing reasons of security and pointing out that there were guards outside of his door too. But Hans detected hints of evasion and of plans underway about which he knew nothing.

Dorilian was not being entirely honest with him.

"Since when was he ever?" Though Arne had ceased jumping out of his skin at every encounter, he had never gotten past feeling that Dorilian couldn't be trusted.

"I don't know," Hans shook his head and sighed. "There are times..."

Overhead, the majestic Citadel soared in splendor while the Rill's mysterious portals moved in ways at once graceful and sinister. Below them, the city spread itself like a mantle about a clear blue harbor filled with ships. They were right back where they had started but with nothing to show for it.

"You ask me, it's not doing you no good, or anyone else, for you to stay here."

They walked along the open colonnade that led to the library that shelved books of lore. Dorilian had changed Hans's tutors again, and Hans was beginning to think his ordeal would end only when Clothia Dalae ran out of scholars.

A hum filled the air, more felt than heard, and Hans gazed up automatically to the shining body of the Rill. From the most distant portal, going north, a bolt of *something* shattered the day, glittering like the sun itself for a moment before shooting out of sight. Hans leaned upon the balustrade. "I can't help it," he said, frowning after it, "but I think that's the answer."

"What is?"

Hans gestured at the dome of a white building rising above the Serat and the shimmering structures spreading out from it like the limbs of a many-trunked, otherworldly tree. "That."

"The Rill?" Arne slumped beside him and eyed the wing-like arches and spans. "I don't know what you're thinking, Hans, but that ain't no answer to anything I ever heard of."

"It might be the answer to Dorilian."

"That? Well, of course it is. That thing is what makes Staubauns rich—and it's been making the Sordaneons rich forever. You heard what those men on the barge said. 'Wealth without end.' Look at this place!" Arne sighed. "I heard tell that even as king in Essera, Stefan was fearful of all the ways that bastard could use the Rill against him. Any sane man would be, and you should be too. That thing can't be stopped and it can't be captured. It's a deathless behemoth that shits armies and gold."

"It might be more than that."

"Like what?"

"Something I read in a book, a really old book, by Cibulitus." Hans had been delving into the incredibly difficult material, prying what meaning he could from a language expressing concepts that no longer existed and that he could not, without instruction, reconstruct. "Cibulitus says that the Rill, this Rill right here that we're looking at, was just ruins until Derlon, the very first Sordaneon—who was half-Leur, half-Aryati, and all immortal—became part of it. That's when it came to life and linked Sordan to Permephedon, which created the Triempery."

Arne frowned. "I always heard Staubauns say the thing is alive," he conceded. "Not that anyone can get close enough to check it out. The Staubauns won't let the likes of you or me get near it. And even if you could... Hans, that thing's deadly. Maybe it makes Staubauns richer than kings, but it kills folk every year along the run in Amallar."

"But you don't know what it *is*, do you?"

With a small shrug, Arne put out his hands. "Hells, Hans, nobody knows that. Even the Staubauns don't know that. All anybody knows is that the Rill gets from here to there, and that fast, carrying whatever people put on it. It flies like people don't matter to it. And it can't be stopped. I know, because Khelds have been trying to stop it for years! Anything gets in its way, it blasts right through. And the cold trees that are part of it, they can't be cut down—ain't nothing can cut into them or pull them down. The hardest blade in the world doesn't leave so much as a scratch! Maybe it *is* a god like the Staubauns say. Because if it ain't a god, it's sorcery—for sure there's nothing in the world natural about it."

Hans cut back a laugh. "Then I've seen sorcery that would pop the eyes out of your head. Ships that fly and wagons that speed along roads without horses."

"Well, that's Marenthro for you."

"It wasn't him, Arne."

"You don't know that," Arne asserted stubbornly. "You don't know that he didn't work it all up just for you. A whole world and all the things in it, just like the Staubauns say. You're the only one who's ever seen it, near as I can tell."

And to that Hans could conceive no ready answer. It seemed that most people he met truly believed that the world and everything in it was a construct of the Mind of Leur. Even Cibulitus had not fully explained the concept, but Hans gathered that Marenthro was more or less the Second Creation's guardian and that its continued existence depended in some way on the continuation of Highborn rule. Hans was inclined to view it as yet another instance of the divine underpinnings of monarchy. In primitive societies, it was pretty much expected that the ruler would be portrayed as having a special connection with the gods, and most claimed to be descended from them. It wasn't any wonder, then, that Dorilian was the Rill Lord, as the river folk had called him.

And yet the Rill was not a god, but an artifact. A machine. What other conclusion could be reached by a mind trained in logic? An artifact might well seem godlike to a society that had lost its science. But every memory from Hans's childhood was of people thinking— and saying—that the Rill was a god. It was also the god to which Dorilian thought himself connected.

Again, Dorilian had become ever more the question than the answer.

Once a month, Dorilian held three mornings of public audience. When Fahme came to Hans one morning, asking if he would like to attend one of those audiences, he leaped at the chance. It was about time he started appearing in public. He said as much to Fahme, who snickered.

"Why? You have more power if you don't."

The five months since his arrival in Sordan and inclusion in Dorilian's court had taught Hans much about the Hierarch's small circle of relations. Fahme had been the daughter of one of Dorilian's staff—his brother's governess, who had somehow died in that service in a way connected to what had happened at Permephedon. Dorilian had adopted the girl as an infant and raised her as his own, so Fahme and Levyathan lived in the Serat surrounded by the same extraordinary luxury, studied under the same tutors, and shared the same high expectations. As a result, Fahme was bright, opinionated, and as confident a child as Hans had ever met. She was also fiercely protective of her Sordaneon family. Her distrust of Hans had mellowed somewhat with Dorilian's apparent acceptance of him. Just the other morning, Fahme had shown Hans her tonal wand, a rod of smooth white material that took vocal intonations and changed them into colors and light shapes. Fahme had amazing command of her voice and could prompt the translator to create a nearly endless procession of patterns—rings, waves, lines and angles—in what she told Hans was a form of language.

"This is how Epoptes learn to work with Rill commands." As she waved her tonal wand, Fahme's ponytail of brown hair swung between her shoulders. They walked along one of the Serat's wide corridors. "I can do it. I have perfect pitch and nimble fingers, even if I don't have twelve of them."

"Twelve?"

"Like the Aryati. They engineered their mage techs that way. Your tutors really should teach you these things."

"I guess they skipped that part."

"It's a natural advantage for bespeaking Aryati machines." Fahme's frown deepened. "Even without twelve fingers, though, my scales surpass those of any other student. It's not fair they won't let me audition. They say girls' voices fail at lower registers."

"Who won't let you audition? For what?" Hans asked. That Fahme was confiding in him, he credited to her current state of pique.

Fahme slid a narrow glance his way, her young face sharp with scorn. "The Epoptes. You don't know anything, do you?"

"Not about that."

"A Kheld wouldn't. You can't even get close to the Rill or it will kill you."

They joined Dorilian in a light-filled hall that served as his private audience chamber. A raised dais drew eyes to the far end of the room, itself dominated by a single, eagle-winged throne. The wall behind that tableau boasted a mural of a younger Dorilian and his entire court, arrayed in magnificence, as they had been on the day of his coronation as Hierarch. That life-sized image melded seamlessly with the actual presence of the man seated on the throne, giving him the appearance of being backed by his court even when he was, as now, alone but for his close advisors. Kneeling before the royal chair were two widely separated figures, a man and a woman, both cloaked in upper-class robes and mantles, no doubt the best that they owned. Before the Hierarch and in this room, neither looked impressive.

Dorilian had just finished signing a document, which he handed to a secretary. Hans and Fahme took seats at the back of the room and watched as Mirrez entered through the main door, bringing with him an angry-looking youth in his teens. Like the people already kneeling before Dorilian, he was Staubaun and probably well born. When he was brought near the dais, he too dropped to his knees, head deeply bowed.

"Khoren Eliadures," Dorilian addressed the youth. "I believe this man is your father." He indicated the well-dressed man kneeling before him.

Khoren lifted his head only slightly. "Yes, Thrice Royal."

"You have no more to say about it… or him?"

"No, Thrice Royal. I do not think that I should."

Dorilian turned to the man in question, who waited silent and white-faced. "The Lady Phaidra will be a better guardian to her sister's son than you have been. Though Khoren is your son, I hereby remove his person and his finances from your legal control. The terms of the settlement for the inheritance you pilfered from him are as we stipulated. We expect the property to be turned over within the month. For all else you must answer to him. Allaon Eliadures, your son is soon to be a man. We suggest you remember that." Dorilian regarded Khoren less sternly. "Go with your father and discuss with him the terms of his restitution or, if you so choose, your reconciliation." But Dorilian's gaze moved to Hans and Fahme as Khoren and Allaon left the room, and the woman, bending deeply, spoke thanks and departed.

"You still think you want to rule?" Dorilian settled into his throne. He looked completely at home on one, Hans noticed. Everyone else in proximity, including the secretary and a brace of ministers, had retired to the far corners of the room.

"You appear to enjoy it."

"In this case, perhaps so. The boy deserves justice, and the man deserves his losses. He stole his son's inheritance so he could afford a new wife and start another family. To bring his case to me, Khoren worked his way upriver from Ilmar, begging meals and passage from men who thought nothing of selling him to others."

That Dorilian would speak this way in front of young Fahme surprised Hans. She looked unfazed and was watching with great interest.

"At least for him it turned out all right," Hans observed.

"Is that your preferred measure of a thing, that it turns out all right?"

Dorilian was getting at something, but what? "I happen to like happy endings." Hans hoped he didn't sound trite.

"And you believe justice makes people happy?"

He had wandered into a trap. Again. "I think injustice makes them unhappy."

"Not in every case. Justice is an imperfect measure. Many just outcomes make people miserable. What of your own case? Do you foresee things ending happily?"

Hans flinched. Despite himself, he looked to Fahme, thinking she might provide a clue on how to answer. The only thing he got from her was a sympathetic tilt of her head.

"I don't really know. My case is not about inheritance. I think we've settled that. We are caught in some middle ground, negotiating for bits and pieces of each other. I have too many questions to begin to guess how my case will end."

Nodding at an answer that, perhaps, satisfied him, Dorilian rose. The dark green silks of his state attire rippled with light. Behind him gleamed the glorious image of his ascension to his throne.

"Perhaps we can free ourselves of this middle. Ask me a question and I will answer it."

Hans did not know which Dorilian he faced: the philosopher, the Hierarch, or the god—or whether, at long last, he faced the man. Later he might kick himself for not asking something more profound, but for weeks one question had been driving him mad.

"Your left hand." Hans indicated the one on which Dorilian wore the Rill Stone, silver eagle aglow within the ring's glittering emerald matrix. "I know—I learned," he corrected as Dorilian looked at the ring, then to Hans, perplexed, "that you lost the first two fingers. They were cut off somehow. But it doesn't look like they were ever anything but whole."

Lifting his hand and flexing his fingers, Dorilian smiled ever so slightly. "So you heard about that." He spoke slowly, his words following thoughts that ran much faster. His smile took on a bitter edge. "Marenthro never quite killed the rumor. Enough people saw me after. But yes, I did lose them. At Permephedon. To a sword blow."

Fahme looked surprised. The injury, then, was not common knowledge, even in Dorilian's own household.

"But you have them now. How?" Hans persisted.

"I am Highborn, Handurin. What do you think that means? Only that I get to rule in Sordan for no other reason than that I am an accident of copulation by the man who sat here before me?" Dorilian held up his hand, showing the two fingers in question. "I *heal*, Handurin. All the Highborn heal. Our flesh differs from the solely human. Leur qualities reside in us as well and confer advantages. Our wounds do not fester; our tissues regenerate. Our bodies... resist corruption. I cannot get drunk and I do not get sick."

His fingers grew back. Bones and nerves and nails and skin. Not even a scar!

Understanding flared like dawn itself, the answer locking into place. An immortal and a human had joined to make Dorilian's race. Godborn. The Highborn had inherited only *some* of the human part. The rest was... the very thing Stefan had always said.

For the first time Hans glimpsed why people might think Dorilian was an abomination. Though Hans would have liked to ask more questions, Mirrez stepped forward with Dorilian's cloak to remind the Hierarch that he had scheduled to meet with the Epoptes that hour.

Hans considered for but a moment. He was learning so much, and only now the things he most needed to know. Like *this*. The Rill was something he had yet to see except from a distance.

"Dor— Thrice Royal." Calling him by name felt entirely too bold. Hans had not yet been given permission to address Dorilian familiarly. "Please grant me one more thing: I would like to see the Rill. I want to know more about it. What it is." Maybe if Hans knew more about the Rill, he would better understand what he was supposed to find—or learn.

Fahme snorted. Dorilian shot him a look of blistering scorn.

"I don't think you are yet prepared to know what it is. The Entity surpasses your current ability to grasp nearly everything about it."

"So does Sordan. So do you." Hans's best chance of success was to frame the request as a challenge.

"Well, this is not a sight-seeing trip to the Rill." Dorilian fastened a large brooch, an eagle bearing a great opal in its claws, to secure his cloak, itself a statement of state.

"I thought you were going to see the Epoptes."

Dorilian said nothing at first, then he gave a short laugh. "I will be meeting their Psilant in an anteroom. All you would see is a *building*." Something deep-seated and angry sheathed his words, the same anger that stole into his gaze and tightened the muscles of his jaw. "The Epoptes don't let me near the Rill. When I wish to travel, I am permitted upon the platform and, even then, they guard the thing with soldiers—which they will also be doing today."

"Why?"

"You boggle the mind. Perhaps I *should* bring you. It might be fun to watch as you annoy *them* with these questions."

"Can I go too?" Fahme piped in. "They don't allow me near either." She stepped in front of Hans the better to press her case.

Dorilian stared down her hopeful gaze. "We've talked about this."

Fahme scowled. "I will grow old and die before they realize their heresy."

"Then let us hope they find enlightenment, because I too might die before they ever bend." Dorilian accepted a circlet of flat green stones from Mirrez and placed it on his head.

"Heresy?" Hans tried to formulate a way for heresy to apply to an artifact of lost technology.

Fahme just rolled her eyes and shook her head when Hans looked her way, letting him know that he had just proven he'd been raised by cave dwellers.

It was called the Va Haira, that underground passage which ran beneath Sordan's crown of pre-Devastation structures. Horses awaited them in the cavernous vault below the Serat, ghostly shapes stamping in twilight-blue corridors where luminous arches, dimly green, showed the way. The cold was that of places that had never known sun. Hans shivered in his thin summer clothing, seeing now why Dorilian wore a cloak. The journey was not to be a long one. The reason for using the road proved to be more secrecy than speed.

Dorilian was accompanied by a full company of his bodyguard, commanded by Legon, all attired in full armament. Apparently the Epoptes were to be accorded every glimmer of power a Sordaneon could bring to bear.

"They will not like seeing you," Dorilian warned. He had forbidden Fahme from accompanying them. "As this is my City and it is my decision to bring you, let me handle it." He motioned to the Eagle Guard, who fell into place before and behind them.

A viridescent floor lit the subterranean antechamber, which was rimmed and vaulted with quicksilver in arboreal patterns reminiscent of the Rill's external structures. Hans could not tell if the chamber was part of the Rill or an adjunct structure, and there was no time for him to ask. No sooner had they walked up a flight of steps than scores of armed men wearing Epoptean yellow and black formed a vanguard that served both as escort and, as Dorilian had warned, security detail. If Hans had not fully believed it before, he now had proof that the Epoptes ruled more fully in the Rill environ than did Sordan's Hierarch.

That Dorilian brought his own troops was evidence enough he did not fully trust the Brotherhood.

It was only somewhat reassuring that each group appeared clear about their standing with the other.

An Epopte wearing a yellow robe trimmed with purple approached from a doorway framed with symbols traced in amber fire. The man bowed deeply, then lifted his head to display a broad face, a silver eagle emblem glowing in the middle of his forehead.

He addressed Dorilian. "We are honored by your holy person, Thrice Royal. I will escort you to the meeting room."

"I have a guest. He wishes to learn about the Rill, and I have given my approval."

The Epopte looked at Hans in surprise. "This is the Stauberg-Randolph?"

"His presence in Sordan is not a secret."

"However, his presence *here* is. You did not inform us of this turn."

"I am informing you now." Dorilian walked toward the doorway, every soldier in the room—his own and those of the Epoptean contingent—marching to each side. Hans simply kept pace.

"He has not been cleared!"

"And I can be accompanied by whomever I please. Don't force me."

For some reason, Hans had thought the Rill would inspire more serenity. Whatever emotion glided over the Epopte's guarded features contained enough opposition to alert Hans to something interesting. Much as he wanted to see the Entity artifacts of this world and learn more about them, he didn't want to alienate the powers that controlled them. Dorilian, it seemed, delighted in doing just that. Hans could see how Stefan—or anyone—might have engaged in lifelong conflict with this man.

As soon as they entered the passageway, Dorilian held Hans back by half a step. "Do as they say," Dorilian instructed in a low voice. "Gods are not nearly so jealous of men as men are of their gods. Do nothing the Epoptes can construe as an affront to their priesthood."

"But you—"

"We can talk about that later. I am another matter to them entirely."

Hans walked at Dorilian's side into the next room. His skin prickled as a delicate touch, as soft and brief as being brushed by a butterfly's wing, danced across his skin. A sensor, he decided. The sensation slipped from his thoughts the moment he stepped into a vast, sharply beautiful cavern of a room. Hans halted beside Dorilian upon an ornate overlook. A canyon of staggered platforms cascaded like honeycomb below, golden and gleaming. Ranks of immense Rill conveyances—*charysi*, Hans recalled from his lessons in economics—waited in gleaming silver to be laden. Cargoes of all kinds sat stacked upon the platforms, entire warehouses of crates and lumber and steel, silos and tankers waiting for transport. On one of the platforms a handful of human passengers stood in filtered sunlight, dwarfed by the soaring structures that surrounded them.

"Wait here while I notify the Psilant." The Epopte strode toward yet another doorway, this one grander still. Epoptean guards closed rank behind him and prevented any from following.

From every side came an oppression of voices, a sort of chanting, but those sounds were too distant to identify, not quite a hum and little more than a fleeting impression. Already the vista of platforms below overwhelmed Hans's attention.

"Is that it? Is that the Rill?" He walked forward, wanting to see more.

"*That* is the beating heart of the Triempery." Dorilian had followed. He stood at Hans's side and pointed to a group of people below. "Those people are traveling to the east, to Hestya and Teremar. On the other side"—he nodded at Hans's look of astonishment that the Rill terminal could be even larger than what he was seeing—"you would see even more people and cargo, traveling north. More nodes line that route." Dorilian managed an expression that was both derisive and proud. "Nearly the entire economies of both Sordan and Essera flow through the Rill. Nammuor would like nothing better than to get his hands on it. So long as the nerve centers at Permephedon and Sordan remain outside his control, he could man the length of the conduit from the Dazun to Permephedon with soldiers and not be able to do a thrice-cursed thing to stop it. We would continue to be able to communicate with our allies, transport goods, and travel. Those are vital advantages. I would storm the platforms myself before I would let Nammuor gain use of it."

Hans noted that the Epopte who had left them earlier had returned with three other men. All looked impressive. One, a tall, thickset man draped in ornate robes of priestly white, regarded Dorilian with a look of forbearance layered with disapproval.

"Who do you mock this time, Thrice Royal: this would-be prince of Essera, or the Order?"

"I am showing Essera's prospective king my dominion, Psilant."

"You are showing him the Rill."

"What little of it this vantage reveals, yes. I believe economics alone justify sharing this paltry sliver of a glimpse."

The Psilant flushed and his dark gaze flooded with condemnation. "And I am charged with the Rill's well-being, for which you show little regard. The Order's mission is set forth in the Covenant to which you are yourself bound. As such, it is my task as Psilant to be ever alert to threats."

"Threats." Dorilian clipped the word in a way that questioned its integrity. "Do you mean Handurin? Or me?"

The Psilant's lid-shrouded eyes narrowed. "You will always be a threat. As for him, I have been told that he may possess forbidden knowledge."

"Handurin? He can barely learn history."

That hadn't been necessary. Hans frowned at having been spoken of so dismissively. He flinched when the Psilant's voluminous robe brushed him. As the man walked by, a whiff of concealed malice accompanied him. Or maybe it was only that this space seemed shadowed by contrast with the honeycombed wonder gleaming in a golden blaze just beyond the terrace.

The robed man signaled his guards. He indicated Hans with a jut of his chin. "Remove him."

Dorilian signaled his own guards. "No. He stays here. The Rill falls into the realm of his education. The Entity will not oppose his seeing its operations."

"I oppose it."

"Your opposition bears no weight with me—or the Rill. Handurin stays, either to observe our conversation or to observe what little he can see of the Rill."

Hans saw what was happening. Dorilian was making matters too difficult, too time-consuming, for opposition. If only to get rid of them both more quickly, the Psilant would relent.

"Tharos." The Psilant singled out one of the two similarly but less-elaborately robed men standing just behind him. "Attend Prince Handurin. Inform his observations. The Hierarch and I are going to discuss... more important things."

With that, Dorilian and the Psilant walked to the far and enclosed end of the overlook, which was empty but for a table such as was used, obviously not often, for meetings. The third man and the Epopte who had met them first stayed near the door guarded by the soldiers.

Tall Tharos, whose paleness suggested he had never in his entire life set foot out of doors, gave Hans a guarded smile. "I take it you are unfamiliar with the Rill?"

Having fully expected to be patronized, Hans was surprised not to be. Tharos was fairly young, though probably older than Dorilian, and he had the gold-bright hair and amber eyes of the pure Staubaun caste, so he probably had noble blood as well.

"I think nearly everyone is."

Tharos softly laughed. "Probably. The Entity is mysterious even to we who serve it. And most people never look upon it except from afar. I will gladly attempt to answer your questions."

Hans glanced over at the other men in the room. "All right. What's with them?"

Tharos, too, looked to where the Hierarch and Psilant appeared to be talking heatedly in voices too low to be overheard. He gave Hans another thin, cautious smile. "Business, I would say."

It had to be more than that, of course. Much more. But Tharos was not going to open up about Order politics. Hans decided on a different path of questions.

"Why can't I get closer, see more?"

"Because you are the Sordaneon's guest—and he is not allowed in the sanctum."

"Why is that?"

Something quizzical looked back at Hans, suggesting he should know the answer. "The Sordaneons are a special case. The restriction originated with your grandfather."

Of course. For once, a history lesson came in handy. On the day of Marc Frederick's coronation, Dorilian's grandfather, Labran Sordaneon, had stopped the Rill and, for one terrifying day nothing in the Triempery had moved. Hans remembered enough conversations with Stefan, his tutors, and even Dorilian himself to imagine why that restriction remained in force.

With a look that said he had decided something about Hans, Tharos gestured for Hans to follow. They walked toward the opposite wall of the overlook, which Hans, drawn only to the view of the platforms, had not yet examined. Upon the wall's blue surface spread a map not unlike the one Marenthro had summoned on the table in Chuquiago, only many times larger, its blurred edges fading into the indigo substrate. Within the detailed central image ran lines of green, red, blue, and gold streaming from Sordan and its vivid blue lake. Similar lines, but fewer, snaked from Permephedon and another city far to the south.

"This is the Run of the Rill. Only the gold parts are active. For eighteen hundred years after Derlon awakened the Entity, the vital corpus extended to revived nodes between Permephedon and Sordan. *Only.* When Quirin took charge here, seven full decades before I arrived, those five nodes you see were the entirety of it. Five Nodes. Five cities, like the Five Cities of Leur. It was poetic."

Hans studied the map again: the scarlet, green, and blue lines, none of which glowed, and the blazing gold of the active Run that Tharos had traced for him.

"But the Rill's Run also extends to Teremar." Hans pointed to the golden spur that shot off to the island's southeastern end, across the lake. To a sixth node. Dorilian had said something about passengers going to a place called Hestya.

Tharos nodded. Then he added, in a much-lowered voice. "That bit of corpus only became active twelve years ago."

Hans felt his heart take a leap. "Out of nowhere?"

"Not quite, but almost. There were already intact Rill structures in place at that node. There are many such in the world. Unbroken. Undamaged, but inert. Some of these, Derlon raised before he assumed the mantle of the Entity, and others are survivors of the Entity's original incarnation. But no one was ever able to direct the Rill corpus to extend beyond Derlon's initial transformation."

"It looks like someone did."

"Yes. Someone did. The question is who. The Entity has been an inert intelligence for more than a millennium; it did not conceive the act. Which means something, or someone, expanded its awareness to *include* Hestya. Most of the Order believes that person to have been Sebbord Teremareon, the Hierarch's maternal grandfather. He was one of us and an Archmage of the Brotherhood's highest rank. He is known to have been there that day."

Tharos touched the glowing line of the new spur with a kind of wonder. "I was just an acolyte here when Quirin found the new Rill line on the map one morning, fully active. I witnessed the eastbound platform come alive. The first charys formed and shot out of here before our unbelieving eyes. It was inconceivable that the Rill would go the wrong way. I remember that. Nobody had thought it was even possible. It happened just after sunrise, and it was as if Derlon himself had spoken for the first time in a thousand years."

Hans could well imagine that day. Chaos. Panic. The exultation of something unexpected. What Tharos described had shaken the Triempery to its roots. Hans even vaguely recalled it—Marc Frederick and Stefan arguing, adults talking late into the night.

"No one could return the Rill to its previous configuration," Tharos continued. "There were many who wanted to, but how? Only the Entity itself could have made the alteration, and only the Entity could undo it. How does one reverse the action of a god? Quirin had to go before the King and explain how it happened that Teremar was now being Rill-serviced and there wasn't anything he could do about it. Marc Frederick was not happy." Tharos cocked his head inquisitively at Hans, making a comparison. "You have something of the look of him. Fairer, unlike Stefan who resembled him more. But like him. Marc Frederick nominated me to the Order. It was a sad day when he died."

That explained, then, Tharos's willingness to talk freely. Yet another debt to Marc Frederick. "You make it sound like my grandfather didn't want Teremar to have the Rill."

"No one did... in Essera." Tharos bestowed another telling smile. "I am a native of Tollech, myself."

Another southerner. Hans almost laughed. But his mind was already racing onto other things. Deeper things. Nearly every important event of the last years of Marc Frederick's reign carried echoes of that singular, rebellious act. That and other things convinced Hans—Dorilian had done it. And Marc Frederick had known.

It explained Marc Frederick's fascination. Or part of it. Brilliant, daring, game-playing Dorilian—how young had he been when he had launched the Rill into Teremar? The answer, once calculated, made Hans's jaw drop. *My age... no, he was younger!* But the Rill had not come without a cost. Hans again saw Nammuor's blood-streaked, hate-filled face, the murderous blade pressed to Dorilian's throat. The hesitation to kill him. *The Seven Houses would pay a lot to get their hands on you.* Behind it all had lurked an acquisitiveness and greed for which Hans now had a name.

More than ever, Hans was sure the Rill was the key not just to Dorilian but Marc Frederick as well. To everything.

"Is something wrong?" Tharos inquired.

"No." Hans broke out of his thoughts. "I was just thinking."

"I thought maybe you sensed the disruption."

"Disruption?"

"In the Overlay." Tharos indicated the map, then lifted his chin and opened his mouth. A low note, or rather a chord, soft but sure, came from his throat. The map disappeared to reveal another window wall—this one overlooking a cavern of shadows and glow. Dominating the room's center, encircled by shifting transient images seemingly printed on air and a lone ring of seated, gesturing men, hovered an orb—massive, dark, and traced with lines and glyphs of blue fire. "The Overlay is an array that communicates, to some small degree, with the Rill Mind, allowing us to organize the Entity's activity. It does not react to most people. It does not even notice them." Tharos looked across the room to where Dorilian and Quirin were meeting, and Hans looked too. Dorilian was gesturing, animated. "It is reacting to the Sordaneon."

Hans hadn't felt anything, disruption or otherwise. Neither could he see anything happening with the orb below. The map re-established itself, concealing that view.

As he gazed upon the map again, attending its details and strange writing, Hans saw something he had not taken note of before: A main portion of the active Run, the Sordan to Permephedon portion, passed straight through Amallar. From Sordan north, he traced the gold-ringed pulses of active nodes. The names and script on the map were different, Aryati, but his tutors had pounded the modern names into his head. Randpory Crossing. Leseos. Dazunor-Rannuli. Hans touched them one by one. But between those last two, clearly marked but unringed and unlit, was another node. He sounded out the Aryati name.

Trestethion.

"What are you doing?" Dorilian had come up behind him.

Hans's hand jerked back as though pulled by a puppeteer's string. Though anger surged into his veins, he fought it. He'd been asked a simple question… nothing more.

"I am looking at a *map*," he said with all the restraint he could muster.

Understanding slapped him in the face when he turned to look at Dorilian. Hans too was reacting to the Sordaneon. *Everyone* was. Dorilian's heated glare and tight face betrayed that he was as out of sorts as Hans had ever seen him—which could only mean that the meeting with Quirin, whatever its purpose, had not gone well.

Quirin, in fact, sported a jaw so clenched that Hans wondered he could speak at all. "Whatever your fate is to be, Prince Handurin, I am certain it does not include another visit to this Entity."

"Why?" Hans demanded. He looked from Quirin to silent, brooding Dorilian, then back to Quirin again. "Why shouldn't I learn more about the Rill and what it does? This map, you know, explains a great deal."

"Knowledge in the hands of ignorants can be dangerous."

"A map? Is there some reason I shouldn't know what everyone else knows?"

Quirin actually hissed instead of just saying no.

"This was a mistake," Dorilian said. He placed himself physically between Hans and the encroaching Psilant.

"But this map, it shows… the Rill *can* go other places." Hans wanted Dorilian to see that he understood, and shared, a vision of what the Rill could be—or rather become—a vision he was now certain Marc Frederick had conceived and hoped to implement. "Why shouldn't it go to Stauberg or… or Amallar? Look—" He pointed.

"This creature's heresy has no limit!" Florid with rage, Quirin addressed Dorilian. "We stand within a holy enterprise and you pollute it with this barbarian?"

"Oh, shut up, you insufferable toad!"

"What this creature suggests is laughable, a perversion even *you* should reject! How dare he speak so in the Entity's presence!"

"The Entity," Dorilian snarled at the raging Quirin, "does not hear the spoken word. It is as deaf as a block of stone! It does not yet know that Amallar *exists*. It does not *care*. It does not even know about the so-called Covenant your Order and a bunch of land-grabbing, wealth-sucking princes created to enslave it. It is immortal and the affairs and words of men are as nothing to it. *I am* the one who knows and cares. Your Entity has not spoken in a thousand years! Remember that, Epopte." Dorilian seized Hans by the arm and dragged him to one side, the tension in his grip both a warning and a threat.

Quirin shook with anger. "Do not dismiss the Order's holy purpose! The Rill is a sacred trust, to be held sacred, not paraded to impress loutish barbarians! The Entity may not hear, but it feels, and it rejects all but the most refined human contact. Who knows how the touch of low-blooded oafs might affect it? To even propose such a thing is heretical!" His stern gaze glowered beneath arched, almost delicate brows. "Not enough by far has been said about your actions, this day and for the months leading up to this day! I shall take your matter up at the Conclave."

"Yes, you do that!"

"One month, Sordaneon. Until then, do not come here. It would be unwise for you to court embarrassment."

Dorilian stopped to confront Quirin again. "Are you threatening me?"

"A warning, no more, Thrice Royal."

They had made it as far as the exit. Dorilian released Hans's arm to focus on Quirin. Both angry men stood face-to-face, neither ready to concede. Hans wondered what they had said to each other out of earshot that only now was coming to a head.

"This is not done, Psilant." Dorilian lifted his left hand to display the Rill Stone. Quirin took a step backward. "I will not have my own domains used against me. I do not bid men to plant Sordan's fields to feed my enemies, nor fire Sordan's furnaces to supply them war machinery. I did not raise high this City that the Order should sell it like a gold-draped whore. I must have a secure border, not a pipeline for spies. Too many shipments have passed under your nose and slipped between your fingers. Indeed, Psilant, you show signs of having open palms. So let *me* warn *you*. You would serve the Rill far better if you would honor my concerns."

"Thrice Royal." Quirin placed too heavy an emphasis on that designation, lending it the weight of insult. "Why do you insist on playing this dangerous game with my office? What suits you does not dictate the Order's purpose. The Order cares neither for your war nor for your politics. It is presumptuous of you to bring these to us. We serve an Entity, and that Entity is not Dorilian. The Rill takes no side in human conflicts, and the Order serves it for the good of all. *All!* According to the Covenant, it stops where it is most useful to stop, and it carries whatever it is given to carry under our enlightened auspices. These are things even the puissance of Hierarchs cannot dictate. Idle threats on your part will not influence my decision. Attempt more, and I will carry to the Conclave word of your interference and ask for an injunction that would limit your own use of the Rill—for any purpose."

In his months with Dorilian at the Serat and in the more relaxed privacy of Rhondda, not once had Hans heard any man, in any capacity, use that tone of voice with his host. Yet here the Psilant of the Brotherhood of Epoptes, undoubtedly a man of power and influence but not Highborn, nor in any way a Sordaneon's equal in rank, was lecturing Dorilian on what he could and could not do. The silence that gripped the room was that of a storm building within the very walls.

When Dorilian spoke quietly, all could hear him, so powerful was the mounting fury behind his words. "If you do not do as I ask of you," he said to the stone-faced man standing before him, "you know what I am capable of. What you will not do for me, I will do for myself—and if it cannot be done because of any tampering on your part, then I can and will see to it that you are unable to tamper with my plans ever again."

"You are good for words, Hierarch of Sordan." Quirin's mouth played with a smile, as though he held triumph itself between his lips. "You are Highborn, yes—but what does that mean anymore? Without the Rill, what would you be but yet another petty tyrant, tied to a trade-dependent island?"

The storm that had been mounting broke.

"By Arya's mighty Fall!" Dorilian thundered, full-blooded now in wrath. "Without the Rill, I would be no less than that which stands before you now! Hierarch of Sordan, Derlon's Heir, and heir by right to everything you cherish and serve. I do not need your thrice-cursed Order to make me what I am. For I, too, am an Entity, Epopte, such as you have never seen before. Let me remind you, then, that without the Rill, you—you and your entire Brotherhood—are nothing! Nothing! And *because* of it—I am everything."

Hans tried to keep his breathing silent. Gazes locked, neither man spoke. Quirin's staring face paled. The icy intransigence of Dorilian's glare was more frightening than his outburst. Having thrown down a gauntlet, he would let it lie there forever.

"I *am* your god, Epopte. And don't you ever forget that," Dorilian said as he turned his back on them all.

30

There are three sorts of entities one must never
trust—the amorphous, the amoral, and those that
vow upon the stars that you can trust them.
—Ergeiron, *Conversations with Leur*

Dorilian awakened to another morning and a calendar filled
with the pressing work of his empire. From the sitting area
of the Lesser Throne Hall, he gazed past the wall of
windows at sunlight dancing off the many-hued rooftops of Sordan's
Lower City. His City was just stirring, and the harbor had been
bustling with activity for hours. His day, on the other hand, was
starting badly.

Yesterday's altercation with Quirin had put nothing to rest,
neither his problems nor his temper. Things were not moving
forward as well or as quickly as he wanted.

"Princess Melenthas," Mirrez reminded. The secretary laid
that morning's collection of letters and memoranda on the table
beside Dorilian's hand. "First on your schedule."

An awkward situation, one Dorilian knew he deserved.
Melenthas's father, King Galanthias of Merced, had sent the princess
to Sordan for Dorilian to consider as a possible bride. Political
reasons existed for such a maneuver but Dorilian had known
within an hour of meeting her that he would rather mate with a sea
viper. He could have overlooked the imperative to copulate a few
times to produce heirs had Melenthas possessed any other of the
qualities he required in a wife. Intelligence. Wit. A deep sense of

duty. Tolerance and gentleness toward others. At least one of Sordan's ruling couple should be unterrifying.

Though he had tried his best not to compare her to Palimia, Melenthas had reduced Dorilian's every effort to dust. Whereas Palimia's laughter had been bright and joyful, that of Melenthas had the hard brilliance of diamonds, joyless and intended for display. Where daily conversations with Palimia had strolled into discussion of philosophy and poets, Melenthas traded in superficial commentary and wit that bored more often than not. The matter had come to a head with her display of rudeness on First Day. Handurin had remained closemouthed about their encounter—yet another admirable trait—but Endelarin, in exchange for an evening of wine and conversation in Dorilian's private garden at Rhondda, had been more than happy to spill the ugly details. At that point even Dorilian's political interest in Melenthas had ceased. No one insulted *his* guests at *his* table. For any reason. Only a desire to not offend her strategically advantageous father and people had held Dorilian from sending Melenthas directly back to Merced with a note of formal censure attached. With Nammuor's ships holding sway over northern seaways, King Galanthias and his island nation were important allies.

And so Dorilian had kept Melenthas at his court, though notably he had not asked her to accompany him to Rhondda. That would have been the polite thing to do, save he had needed to use that interlude to assess Handurin, not a woman about whom he was already decided. The time had come to put an end to the fiction that Melenthas could become his Hierarchessa.

"I will see her." He thought of something else. "Is Bas Morevyen in residence this morning?"

"He is, Thrice Royal. He returned just yesterday afternoon."

"Have Verlas find him and Bas Kolgya also. Have them report here."

"Thrice Royal." Mirrez bowed his head. He crossed the room to the Second Secretary's desk. The two men left the room together.

Bare moments later, accompanied by Mirrez, Melenthas entered, all pale beauty and allure. She was clothed in aquamarine silk from which billowed puffs of pearl-beaded organza. A tiara of crystals nestled in her elaborately braided and arranged hair, through which drifted trails of gold and pearl. Already she looked the part of a queen. With her was the Mercedan ambassador, a portly man draped in diplomatic blue. The Princess dropped a lovely curtsey and the ambassador knelt into a deep bow.

"Thrice Royal."

When Dorilian bid Melenthas to take the chair opposite his, she did so gracefully. The ambassador took his place just behind her right shoulder. "What did you wish to discuss?" Dorilian was acutely aware of his staff being at hand. Across the room, Mirrez had seated himself at his desk. Legon, as ever, stood in attendance nearby, though largely out of sight.

"Our understanding, Thrice Royal."

Dorilian smiled. "We have met and spent time together to evaluate our compatibility. That was the understanding."

He noticed that the ambassador's gaze lowered when Melenthas turned her head slightly to check his expression.

"We spent a few *hours*," she protested. "You accompanied me to a performance and a state dinner. And then you left me alone in your City when you removed to your estate. Are you telling me you have no more time to give, Thrice Royal?"

"Our schedule overflows into our every waking hour."

"Perhaps an hour before your day begins."

Presumptuous suggestions were a risk when dealing with royalty. "Few people can bear us before we fully awaken. We will sit together again at the next state dinner, however. In three days?" Dorilian glanced at Mirrez, who nodded.

"Thrice Royal—"

"In the meantime, our ministers and your ambassador will continue discussion about our... possibilities."

Understanding—and frustration—glimmered within Melenthas's dry, heated gaze. To continue to engage Dorilian would be pointless, yet she toyed with doing so. Her perfect lips parted to speak. That she did not was probably due to the Mercedan ambassador, who bent to whisper something in her ear. Merced counted Sordan as a principal trading partner. Melenthas stood and curtsied much less elegantly than before, an icy performance, then left with a straight back and strides as long and quick as her skirt would allow. Without deigning so much as a gesture of acknowledgement, she passed Tiflan and Tutto, who had just arrived and stood inside the door.

Both men formally nodded to the departing princess and the ambassador who trailed her.

"I can see that went well," said Tiflan. He and Tutto approached and took seats when Dorilian gestured.

"I would have killed her before the year was out, probably because she would have tried to kill me." Dorilian turned to Mirrez. "We will write to King Galanthias that his daughter is a paragon of beauty who conducted herself royally and with dignity, and that we gave her careful consideration. Compose something suitable and I will copy it in my hand."

Mirrez bowed deeply. He and Verlas left the room.

"You are well rid of that one," was Tutto's opinion. "Beautiful enough. Royal enough. Educated even. Too bad that when it comes to alliances, Merced supports all and opposes none."

"I believe you have just defined 'neutrality,'" Tiflan countered.

"Merced," Tutto clarified, "cannot be Sordan's true ally—and certainly not *his*. Galanthias is both in and not in Nammuor's pocket."

Tiflan lifted an eyebrow in agreement. Dorilian gave a nod to convey he concurred with the sentiment. The last thing he needed in his life was yet another of Nammuor's creatures. It was an even better reason than Melenthas's rudeness to have cut short this charade.

"I am weary of these attempts by my nobles and ministers to encumber me with a wife."

Although Dorilian considered Stefan's lack of success at reproduction a fortunate thing, seeing Emyli stripped of the Stauberg-Randolph regency had shown him the danger. A shortage of heirs had left Essera close to disaster. The thought of Erenor Tholeros—and Nammuor by proxy—ruling through a helpless child sickened him.

Handurin, at least, was now legally an adult. A young, raw, uncertain, and easily controlled adult. But possibly one who could stand up to his own regent.

Tiflan's deep voice intruded on his ruminations. "What are you thinking?"

"About Handurin."

Tutto grunted approval. "There is your answer. If you cannot find it in you to take a wife for yourself, perhaps you can get one for him. Tie him to us. Terveryen's daughter is of his age and—"

"If you think to marry my sister to—" Legon stepped toward them, teeth bared in a grotesque parody of a smile.

"*Enough!*" Dorilian fixed Tutto with a disapproving glower. "Cressia will remain unwed... as will Handurin. You know why. They're both *children*! As was I when my father forced *me*. I was sixteen!"

"Your grandfathers agreed to it," Tutto pointed out.

"My grandfathers—and my father—were cold-blooded dynasts."

Tiflan's gaze upon Dorilian warmed. "And you are not?"

"Not *that* cold-blooded."

Even so, Dorilian was pragmatic enough to know the risks involved in allowing Handurin to return to Essera without first securing the Stauberg-Randolph succession in some way. Had Handurin gone north instead of coming here, Erenor would have done so already, within these first months. Dorilian met that concern as it deserved.

"I cannot single-handedly decide Handurin's alliances without offending every domain in Essera; that would but turn them against the both of us. I will have Sinon Kouranos inquire—discreetly—of a few of Handurin's likely allies in Essera and see if we can come up with a mutually acceptable list of candidates for a possible betrothal."

"A wise move, Thrice Royal," said Legon, though his tone was icy and his gaze still fixed on Tutto.

Wise? Perhaps, but it was not an optimal move. Handurin was even less prepared for the yoke of a dynastic marriage than Dorilian had been.

"I will order that Melenthas be kept off the list. Handurin does not like her; he and I have that much in common."

Tiflan frowned. "Not to mention she made clear her dislike of him."

"Yet another burden he and I share. Women such as Handurin and I are obliged to wed would not want us at all save that our empires attract them. Could I but make a mannequin of the Hierarchate and bejewel it with Rill riches, they would marry *that*—and gladly!" Dorilian picked up the top document Mirrez had left for him.

Whatever woman eventually stumbled into becoming his wife, the result would be the same. She would be a broodmare of dynasty—and he would be a trophy, tolerated as the price of her position and wealth.

Damn, I miss Palimia.

"Stefan never appreciated this city. He never *valued* it."

As he stood on the balcony of his mountaintop stronghold, Nammuor's gaze swept the vista of Stauberg and its encircling Wall. The castle he occupied, a former fortified palace that had for several years housed the Wall Lord Austell Malyrdeon, provided the distance from the Wall needed for Nammuor to wear his Diadem while overseeing the Mormantaloran occupation of Stauberg. He did not *call* his operation an 'occupation,' of course; to do so would alarm too many people, including his erstwhile puppet, Erenor.

Who, fortunately, was playing king and dealing with matters in Dazunor-Rannuli.

"Stefan disliked the Wall." Coram Barzanes stood nearby, several steps away in fact, though he also studied the Entity. If one watched the Wall for long enough, they would see its almost translucent alabaster panels and towers rise and ebb and rearrange. "It made him deeply uncomfortable. Even before he murdered the Malyrdeon princes."

And after that, Stefan had not been able to approach Stauberg at all. The Wall had terrorized the city and driven out the Kheld king and his blood-spilling rabble before it had resumed its current equanimity. Had Stefan tried to enter the city again, scholars warned, the Entity would have either killed him or driven him mad. Stefan had stayed well away from Stauberg in the last year of his reign.

Nammuor turned his back on the vision of Entity-encircled palaces and reentered the tower. In this high room constructed to provide a panoramic view of the Wall and its city, he removed his Diadem and placed it on the secure deathstone plinth he had ordered installed days before. Only today had he worn the increasingly powerful device for an hour and felt none of the brain-piercing, jolting pain he had experienced when he had pursued Zepheron's ship dand come into proximity with Stauberg's Wall-guarded harbor. Both the Wall and the Rill blanked the Diadem's energies and punished *him* for wearing it.

At least from this remote vantage, Nammuor could use other devices to translocate into the city if needed. It was important that he make his presence known to his underlings and personally review his armed forces in the city. Stauberg was one of the prizes of his soft war.

He pressed the lock that lowered the Diadem into its deathstone vault and sealed it within.

"What are the chances of luring Dorilian out of Sordan again?" Of all the things Nammuor craved, one thing remained foremost: getting his hands on that Highborn prince.

"Slim. The Hierarch knows of your plans for him."

How could he not? Dorilian had seen with his own eyes the fate Nammuor intended. Daily—indeed hourly—the Diadem clamored for more godborn blood. It was for good reason Dorilian never left his Entity-protected island.

"So you believe he will send this Stauberg-Randolph prince, this Handurin, north, return the boy to Essera, but not venture forth himself?"

"Himself? No. Handurin's fate, however, remains to be seen. Though Erenor sent a demand to have the prince returned to the bosom of his kingdom and regent, Dorilian has done what he usually does with such demands: ignored it. He does not recognize the Tholeros regency. Perhaps if the Archhalia as a body—"

"Or Handurin's bitch of a mother."

Deep intelligence played at the edge of Coram's smile. "Perhaps. The Hierarch is known to have a soft spot for mothers—and also for Marc Frederick's descendants. Despite a popular belief that he had the late king murdered, there is no evidence other than accusations that he ever actually sought to end Stefan's life."

Set against a great deal of evidence that Stefan had sought to end Dorilian's—and Levyathan's also. Nammuor had killed Stefan to put a stop to those attempts.

"I want you to travel to Dazunor-Rannuli. I trust you placed the new crystals?"

"Two sets, yes, for translocation. While you were talking with Erenor."

"Good. I have a job for you to do."

Nammuor walked down into the sunken center of the room. Bookcases ringed the lower level and overflowed with tomes of classic editions of history and lore. Though Nammuor intended to replace them with volumes of *Ir* genesis and crystallokinesis, he had yet to disturb the Malyrdeon library. A hastily installed workbench hunkered at the chamber's center. Nammuor unlocked a drawer and lifted a hen's-egg-sized crystal of burning orange that held within its core an inner fire as dark as obsidian, from which shadows uncoiled in all directions. Placing it within a depression in the igneous tabletop, he next chose from the rack a broad curved black blade, which he raised and then brought down with precise force. The sharp contact released two events: a dark lingering note like doom itself and a vast flicker of shadows that lasted but an instant. Cleaved, the crystal lay in two parts. Nammuor picked up these pieces and placed them separately into pouches of black velvet. He handed one pouch to Coram and tucked the other into his robe.

"I will weld the half I carry into the Stauberg array this afternoon—I plan to make good use of this city's array as our plans move forward. Take *your* half to my artificer downstairs for a setting suitable to your mission."

"Which is?" Coram placed the black pouch into the bag at his belt.

"Keep company with Erenor. Once you are in Dazunor-Rannuli, find reasons to be with him. Wear your new device. It will allow me to observe him directly. We must maintain our Prince Regent in a strong position. Find out who are the supporters of this Stauberg-Randolph prince and monitor what moves they make. Now that Handurin has returned and his situation is known, those factions will reveal themselves. I know Dorilian, and he may well hold onto his pawn prince. It would amuse him to do so. But he might also find some clever way to use him."

Nammuor walked away from the tools of his arcane power and again ascended the steps. Magery did not exist only for its own sake; such power needed focus, an end. Finally, after so many years, Nammuor stood upon the brink of pulling his true foes out into the open. He crossed the chamber's mosaic floor with its sun-splashed images of mountains and seas until he emerged again onto the tower's broad balcony. Once more his gaze followed the slow, even ponderous, movement of Stauberg's towering Wall. He had more things to say about goals yet to be met.

"While you are in Dazunor-Rannuli, I think we should punish

Dorilian for holding the prince. Take every opportunity to paint Handurin the victim. Call attention to the youth's plight, imprisoned by Sordan's cruelty and Essera's incompetence. Ignorant and childlike and kept that way by greater forces."

Coram grinned. "I shall be certain the Khelds in particular find that news poured into their ears."

Nammuor nodded and watched his best weapon against Essera depart. It was proving surprisingly easy to play Essera's many factions against each other, to churn the fog of confusion. Essera would get nothing done, possibly not even the return of its prince. Erenor would remain in power. The Khelds would continue to serve as a bulwark between Dorilian's stronghold in Gignastha and greater Essera.

If Dorilian would not leave Sordan, Nammuor could at least clip the Sordaneon's wings. He would turn up the heat and watch the Khelds keep Dorilian penned in Sordan, his range diminished and talons dulled. Until it was too late.

Nammuor eyed the Wall and wondered if Essera's mighty Entity had foreseen this turn. Foreseen *him*.

He fought a smile.

31

Do not think Ergeiron is a gentle god. His Wall
form makes cruel demands of its keepers, who must
balance foreknowledge with ignorance, compassion
with calculation. Today will see the success of
grand designs. Tomorrow will rain blood.
—Austell Malyrdeon,
letter to the Lahgaelan Initiate Umhed

Sordan lazed out her summer days like a vast, white-horned lizard sunning itself on rocks, the lake a glittering carpet at her feet. Eyes hurt just to look upon that water, now become a windless glassy plain that saw fewer ships and laid the harbor into torpid waiting. Heat melted the hours together and welded them into interminable days, then weeks, always the same but for frequent brief rains that cooled the streets and kept fragrant tree-lined avenues in bloom. People conducted business behind latticed windows and within the shaded privacy of secluded courtyards, or beneath tented awnings in the marketplace. For several weeks each year, Sordan sweltered, Sansordan and Suddekar breathing hot across the water, leaving the city praying for the cool winds out of Teremar to return.

Hans, though, was no longer content with waiting. He suspected he had waited too long already: waited for himself to feel comfortable in this new skin called Handurin, while the Hans of his fabricated childhood drifted further and further away into that corner of himself which would be forever a gawky Dominioner and history student. Instead of moving forward, he perceived himself sliding backward, his situation becoming less and less certain as a rumor from the City below reached his ear: that the Hierarch was keeping the Stauberg-Randolph pretender hostage and had installed him—much as King Marc Frederick had done to Labran Sordaneon so many years ago in Essera—in luxurious confinement in the Sordaneon Serat. Reasons for such an imprisonment abounded and speculation passed from lip to lip along city streets and into diplomatic chambers, and finally into the Serat itself, no ear untickled by the slightest innuendo. Hans noticed the way conversations died when he drew near, how glances withdrew upon meeting his. That people were obviously avoiding him bothered Hans because he had so few other ways to gauge Dorilian's intentions.

Mostly he tried to do it through books. Levyathan had pointed him to volumes by Xenocles, *Lives of the Sordaneon Hierarchs*, and Dorilian's favorite poets. Hans knew from his studies that the poets and writers a ruler favored could tell a lot about them. In that way, at least, Hans remained a Dominioner, thinking he might find answers at the intersection of History and Art. This morning he pursued answers as he squeezed in a short spell of reading while he waited for Arne to finish lessons with the Stauba tutor. Feet up on the marble bench, Hans lounged in an alcove tucked against a lecture room from which emerged the sounds of Arne repeating pronoun declensions.

The alcove was one Hans favored because it faced a pretty courtyard frequented by songbirds. The book in his hand today was a volume of poems by the Esseran poet Myron.

> *Without passion, he lays upon your gilded bed*
> *Without promises, he returns your heated kiss*
> *And you dream you have conquered the city*
> *And you dream you are happy with this.*

Just how such a verse might either appeal to Dorilian or explain him was something Hans had yet to figure out. Probably something to do with unhappiness rather than conquest. He closed the book and instead watched a small gold and blue bird hop along a marble balustrade. Loud, jostling voices approached around the nearby corner.

"What needs the Hierarch with this Kheldish courtenjay he coddles?" the first man said. "Dorilian's own claim is irrefutable—he put it forth again, just last week, before the Archhalia."

"Did he so?"

Hans recognized neither voice. Wishing not to alert them or in any way prevent them from saying more, he moved not a muscle.

"Indeed, though not in person. He did it but to hear those pigeons squawk and show their feathers, demanding that he return their prince to them. Yet there is not a thing they can do. He holds their card and plays it as his own."

"There's the fox."

"Or the serpent."

"Speak not too loudly!" Though they dropped their voices, the speakers had stopped walking and stood but feet away, the corner keeping them from view. "And what for it now, if he gets his way?"

"Your guess or mine. The Stauberg-Randolph will not outlive his usefulness. This Sordaneon has been known to look aside at the fates of princes."

Upon coming into the colonnade, they went the other way and never saw Hans wedged into the alcove. Who they might be did not matter. Hans made no move at all until they had disappeared into the next corridor.

Dry-mouthed, Hans struggled to put what he had heard into place. *Look after my family*. Marc Frederick's plea resounded in his mind along with Dorilian's promise. But was that what was happening here? Dorilian had not protected Stefan. He had *punished* him. Turned his back on Stefan and Essera and everything Marc Frederick had built or stood for. What if he was doing it again? And if so, why?

"Do you want me to tell you what to do about it? How about nothing." Herberth, the Trongorian Elector, had been in Sordan for months, hammering out the details of a trade agreement. Sordan was his nation's greatest trading partner, with Rill commerce providing vital traffic and revenues as well as access to markets in Essera's interior. "Stefan had his chance and threw it away. Don't do the same with yours."

Hans stood with Herberth in the Serat's Atrium of Ceremony following a reception honoring a scholar whose daughters both had married well in Essera and so could be counted on for news. Herberth had lingered an additional week in Sordan to deal with problems stemming from Dorilian's worsening feud with the Epoptes. Dorilian was threatening to implement an embargo by posting soldiers around every Rill station within his domains. In response, the Epoptes were threatening to cut service, which would seriously hamper the upcoming harvests. Aside from prospects of grain spoiling in the bins and widespread hunger as a result, the effect on overall trade would be devastating if the two factions did not soon end their dispute. Even Herberth, whose nation did not have direct Rill access and prospered primarily through minerals and other goods shipped by water, foresaw grave consequences. Many of the best buyers of Trongorian metals were in the Dazun Basin, receiving their ores by way of Rill through Randpory Crossing. Trongorians did not wish them to seek other sources.

For his own part, Hans was happy to find someone who would talk to him. For all Dorilian's smooth assurances to the contrary, Hans felt enough grating suspicion to want to put their relationship to the test. Deep within him an urge to action stirred and would not be quieted.

"Do you believe it? That Dorilian has decided to keep me prisoner?"

"I believe it—if that is what he says. I have not heard him say it."

"But he is *using* me!"

Herberth shrugged. "So, let him use you. Come out of it with that man at your back, and you will have done more to assure your ascension in Essera than even a host of Malyrdeon princes could provide. Dorilian is not given to announcing his intentions. Do not give up on him too soon."

"I may have to. I cannot be expected to stay here forever, sitting on my hands like a schoolboy and doing nothing. If Dorilian won't help me, maybe there are others who will." Hans paused, uncomfortable at being bold. "You have a ship." Out in the harbor a tall Trongorian ship and two escorts sat at anchor, provisioned, crews aboard and ready to leave in the morning.

"Yes, but do I look like a fool? If it were any other man but him—" Herberth clapped Hans on the arm but would not look him in the eye. "This is his City. I will not cross him in it. If and when you leave Sordan, should you find yourself in Trongor, approach me then. It may be that I could aid you. But I will not do it here."

Hans swallowed and nodded. Herberth turned at the approach

of others, and Hans, taking his proper leave, could but watch as Herberth walked away. The Elector's offer might be nothing more than an empty promise, but it was the closest Hans had come, in all his months in Sordan, to obtaining a pledge of support. Few other men of influence would even condescend to speak to him, as though his undefined status was contagious. Stefan's name swirled around corners when people didn't know Hans was listening. Marc Frederick passed in whispers. Emyli. Marenthro. A ghostly army, at once feared and insubstantial, impotent and mighty.

Later that day Hans met with Asphalladra again, almost certainly with Dorilian's knowledge. She related that Emyli was working on Hans's behalf, defying his regent and hampering actions proposed to the Archhalia. But Essera, too, was becoming contentious. Those domains that wanted their prince returned battled resistance from those who favored other candidates.

"I can put that matter to rest," Hans reasoned. "Just send me north. Why is he holding me here?"

Asphalladra sat on the wide marble rim of a pool at the top of the Long Court located in the heart of the Serat's formal gardens, her ankle-length skirt skimming the tile paving. Guards stood nearby, though out of sight and earshot. Her children, a boy and girl, studied alongside other students—the children of nobles and high officials—with a tutor in a quiet corner not far away.

"Ask him."

"I do. He never answers!"

Asphalladra laughed. "Dorilian is so very good at that."

"You're his friend, aren't you?" Asphalladra was beautiful and easy to be with. Hans wished he could trust her more than he did.

The smile on her lips turned thoughtful. "Not really. He helped me, which I suppose makes him a friend, but it was more for Cullen's sake. They knew each other."

"The only thing I ever heard was that Dorilian broke Cullen's leg." Stefan had returned to Rhodhur that one winter solstice and ranted about having to leave Cullen behind.

"Oh dear! No. I heard your late brother say as much, but...." Asphalladra sighed and softly shook her head. "I was there when it happened. Cullen broke his leg playing *pelekys*. Another horse collided with his. His Thrice Royal Grace was not even in the game at the time."

Hans was learning a lot about Stefan; mostly, how much of anything Stefan had said—or that was said about Stefan—could be believed. "So not your friend... but *his*?"

"Not precisely, although the Hierarch had a good opinion of Cullen and never believed him a traitor, not even with the way things happened."

"The way what happened?"

"How Stefan was murdered. You have heard about the hunt?"

Hans nodded. His tutor for political studies and recent events had included a noticeably truncated chapter on Stefan's reign. Wanting to know the full story of how Stefan had died, Hans had asked for and been shown primary sources, among which had been several original documents by Esseran and Hierarchal informants. Each report had touched on elements Hans had dreamed. A few had given him new nightmares.

Asphalladra tore her gaze from his and looked down at the pool. "Then you know it was Cullen who killed him."

Dismay trembled in Asphalladra's voice and lent a quiver to her lips. She was afraid Hans might hold the facts of Stefan's death against her.

"I hope you understand that I will never blame you—or Cullen either—for what happened to my brother," Hans said.

Asphalladra looked across the courtyard to the children, to something hopeful and affirming, before she spoke again. "It was a hunt and Cullen thought—they *all* thought—Stefan was a stag. Cullen and the others never received a trial, so there's little testimony. The aspect of a stag was an illusion, it had to be, because it fell from the King only after... Anyway, the official report doesn't say that. Erenor and others claim Cullen lied about the illusion or that Dorilian created it using Highborn magic. Except the Highborn don't create illusions. I'm not sure they can. It is clearer by the day that people are forgetting what the Highborn are and can do. In Essera people are forgetting so much. They are more and more willing to believe things that are false."

"About Dorilian?"

"About themselves. About Sordan. About Khelds." She blinked tears from her eyes. Water rippled around Asphalladra's fingertips as she trailed her left hand through the pool. Tiny fish followed the resulting wake. "About you too. About anyone and anything that can oppose Erenor and Nammuor. You appear to understand that Nammuor is your real enemy—and that Erenor is too. Continue to believe that."

"Is that what my mother wants me to believe?"

Asphalladra lifted her gaze to meet his. "She wants you to follow your own mind."

That was what Hans wanted too. And Marenthro had said something similar. His own mind. Yet for Hans, Sordan had become a bottomless well with him at the bottom, his voice nowhere to be heard.

Hans had only to appear in Staubaun company and all at once the Serat became a prison, Dorilian an avenger, and Essera a battleground where phantoms vied for power. The factions that opposed or supported Hans did not see him at all. To them he was fleshless, invisible, a name consigned to a living grave. Even the heat of the south, the sun and the hot desert winds, could not take the chill out of his heart. Sordan threatened to become a sepulcher for all he wanted to be or might become.

He must leave.

But Dorilian held court upon a seat of adamant, wrapped up in the concerns of his myriad battles, and try as he might Hans could not find a way to reach him.

Even once, just once, Hans wanted Dorilian to acknowledge that he mattered.

Hans should not have been surprised when that afternoon, answering a royal summons, he found himself brought before the Hierarchalia Dodecai, Sordan's Council of Twelve. The Twelve were the highest nobles in the Sordan Hierarchate, rulers of the eleven hereditary domains under Sordan's dominion, with Dorilian at their head as Prince proper of Sansordan in addition to his being Hierarch of Sordan. Hot summer sunlight poured through the windows to fill a marble-lined chamber, wherein it touched each Bas or Basarchessa with a golden finger as if in benediction. Hans determined that he faced for the first time the formal power of the Triempery's aristocratic bloodlines. Most of the men and women before him looked upon Khelds as barbarians, and each's opinion of him on that basis would be implacable. Worse, not a few of their families had been persecuted during Essera's occupation of Sordan and they held deep hatred for his family in particular.

Only Tiflan and, to a lesser extent, Deleus of Suddekar, showed Hans friendly faces. The other man he halfway knew, the Bas of Kolgya, Tutto, was not of Staubaun birth, though no more friendly for that. However, the heads of every other ruling house—lording over domains with names like Anit-Rebir and Tollech, Ilmar, Ildurria, Sandalya and Kyknossa—were hereditary aristocrats who exuded privilege so ingrained that it had the stiffness of ancient leather. Hans saw in their faces, filled with defiant knowledge of his reliance on their Hierarch's goodwill, that they little sympathized with his plight. Instead, they saw the last gasp of the hated Stauberg-Randolphs and the Esseran power against which they had vied for three generations in succession battles that had shattered the Triempery.

With a sinking stomach, Hans realized that these nobles were the foundation of Dorilian's rule. Powerful people who when summoned would convene to do things. And they would do things the way Dorilian wanted them done. Hans had nothing like this for himself.

Dorilian, regally attired in deepest green silk and wearing the silver crown with its seven blazing stones of emerald green, met Hans in the antechamber. The question that leaped to Hans's tongue, about the possible meaning of this meeting, died unasked. Dorilian instead issued a warning.

"This is a day for humility. Whatever I say, bite your tongue, and whatever I do, stay your hand."

"Why?" Hans had asked.

"Because we are going to give them a chance to humble you."

With the practiced ungraciousness of which he was master, Dorilian wasted no time but gave Hans a shove that caught him by surprise and sent him stumbling toward the door, through which they walked together to stand before the risen Council of Twelve.

"My Lords and Ladies of the Dodecai, this day we bring before you a Prince of Essera, Handurin Stauberg-Randolph, who holds himself Prince of Dazunor. I have no doubt that most of you are already familiar with his presence here."

Dorilian indicated that Hans was to be seated. Hans hid his

nervousness and quietly took the seat that was offered, at the head of the table, beside his still-standing host. The Dodecai also took their seats.

"Honored Basarchs," Dorilian said, "as you know, Handurin has been our guest these past months. As such, he has enjoyed our hospitality and gained us little save intense speculation as to our interest in him. We have much pondered his situation and our own. This Hierarchate is not in the habit of keeping insignificant prisoners. Therefore, we propose some steps be taken to increase this one's value." A pause. The gathered nobles leaned to hear more and Dorilian continued. "Lest you misunderstand me, I propose that this Council of Twelve in Sordan vote to invest Handurin Stauberg-Randolph with his late brother's names and titles."

The entire chamber drew in its breath as one. Hans sat back, stunned, a sick feeling beginning in the pit of his stomach, as Sordan's Dodecai released its pent-up breath in a burst of laughter. They thought it was some kind of joke—and only the strange, self-satisfied gleam in Dorilian's eye kept Hans from thinking it was all a misunderstanding, a mistake. But this was not a mistake, none of it. It was deliberate—a mockery, a farce.

Damn you, he thought, *damn you, damn you*—

But even saying it would not have taken the edge off his humiliation.

"Dodecai, all," Dorilian's voice acquired an edge of reprimand. "I told you I was serious. Believe me when I say that I am." Why, then, could even Hans see that he was not?

"Thrice Royal, we must ask your pardon if our reaction is unseemly." Hans recognized the Bas of Tollech, a younger lord with whom he had never spent even a moment. "But your request is... unusual, to say the least."

"Why unusual?" Dorilian fixed each man with a look that challenged their reasons. "Stefan is dead. And Handurin is his Heir. Heirs should be invested with their inheritance."

"What difference would it make?" Old Bas Terveryan seemed especially put out, perhaps because more sunlight flooded his table than the others. "Stefan never held any lands in Sordan, thanks to you, nor did he ever hold a title in our eyes, not even those which he claimed in Essera."

"Even to call these half-breed Khelds by the name Stauberg-Randolph is to stretch our tolerance," said another Bas, whose chair displayed a crest of snow-capped mountains. "Emyli's sons were both bastards, by strict definition. And this one," he smirked, "is one by any definition."

A general murmur of agreement circulated about the chamber.

Hans started to rise. He was done sitting as a target for aged vipers to spit upon. His family name was still worth something. Not much, maybe, as he had yet to make anything of it, but it was a name worth defending and Staubauns didn't have a monopoly on pride. A sudden hard pressure clamped onto his shoulder and forced him back down in his seat.

"Sit still, you fool!" Dorilian hissed sharply into Hans's ear, not releasing his iron-hard grip. Those fingers tightened until Hans, humiliated and furious, reluctantly submitted and did not try to rise again. But the episode had not gone unnoticed. The gathered Sordani nobles exchanged knowing glances.

"Basarchs," Dorilian resumed, and his tone bore a new edge. "Let us get back to the point. Handurin's name is not up for discussion, nor his legitimacy. Those are already established. His grandfather settled that matter when he formally adopted him. He did so by laws we hold in common with Essera. But what is a name if it bestows no value on the bearer? Even with that name, what good does Handurin do me, or any of us, as he now sits before us? A dead king's younger brother is no great prize. To put my point more precisely," he said with blunt persuasion, eyes narrow and cold, "why hold a pawn, a prince only by name, when just by the saying one can hold a Prince of Dazunor and Heir in fact?"

An old man spoke up from the table's end in a sharp, strident voice: "Thrice Royal, even if we did wish it so, we cannot make this Kheldish by-blow a Prince of Dazunor. That is the Archhalia's work."

"This is true, Thrice Royal," said an older woman whose chair bore the crest of Ildurria. "The Archhalia has done this work for us. You yourself did vote on it."

"Then this council admits Handurin to be Stefan's Heir, and Heir to the kingdom of Essera?" Dorilian queried pointedly.

Several of the Council exchanged glances. "Forgive our confusion, Thrice Royal," one of them said at last. "The Archhalia's ruling has no legal force with this Council of Twelve. We have deliberately withheld ratification of our votes so as not to place an obstacle to your own superior claim. The Archhalia's declaration is meaningless in Sordan. As this council never acknowledged the validity of Stefan's investiture in the first instance, how can we then say we would confer this status on Handurin?"

Bas Terveryan cleared his throat. "Are you suggesting, Thrice Royal, that we grant Handurin a meaningless investiture?"

Dorilian took his seat at that point and regarded them from his chair of green marble, raised as a throne above them all. "Not at all, Basarchs. The investiture of Dazunor and the Stauberg-Randolph titles would be valid. Your twelve votes, plus mine—which I, too, would reconsider—added to the votes already registered in the Archhalia, would accomplish this. Handurin's investiture of titles has been held up by the fragmentation of the Esseran domains, many of which have been won over to the cause of Erenor Tholeros." The royal smile hardened and vanished from Dorilian's eyes. "Investing Handurin would win me two ends, good Basarchs. As you know, I do not favor the ascension of Erenor and would deny him Dazunor. I do not wish that man to have lordship over any domain in which there is an operative Rill mount. So I will do what Erenor cannot. But just as importantly, I would as soon hold Marc Frederick's fully invested Heir rather than Stefan's useless brother. Essera held as prisoner the Hierarch of Sordan and saw my father hold a worthless title all his life. I merely seek to redress that insult."

A murmur of understanding and agreement drifted outward from the Council table. For once, the Council of Twelve held the power to grant their formidable ruler a great favor. As any power Dorilian wielded ultimately enhanced their own, the Dodecai had little to lose.

What Dorilian wanted, they were willing to give him. The rest of the afternoon was spent on the hows and wherefores, deciding at last to vote first to acknowledge Stefan's legitimacy and then his legal claim to Dazunor. Having done so, they were able to vote to invest Hans with the titles to which the Archhalia had already declared him heir. Tiflan and Deleus—neither man willing to look Hans in the eyes—said nothing, did nothing, but voted as their Hierarch required.

Through all the proceedings Hans sat stiff and numb. Though he willed himself to let the insults roll off like so much water, he could not get past the knowledge that this Council of Twelve, and Dorilian too, were making a mockery of Stefan and Hans both. Of his family. Of everything he had come here to do. But the one time he caught Dorilian's eye, unable to hide his own disbelief and pain—the betrayal he had been warned to expect and had never expected—he was struck by a look so thoroughly cold that every thread of heated anger in his mind turned to frost and rendered him immobile.

Stunned by the knowledge that he had been duped, Hans sat still and unmoving, like the victim Dorilian had made of him. He simply watched Dorilian maneuver, subtleties Hans could not even begin to grasp sliding between every word and its meaning, every action and what it provoked. When the Council of Twelve was done, Hans was Prince of Dazunor and Stefan's fully legal Heir, for all that the words were worth. Monarchist gibberish. Nothing and less than nothing, a bestowal intended for but one purpose: to increase his value to the man who held him prisoner. The political distance between him and Dorilian, always suspect, had become a gulf, and there was not a man in Sordan who would not know it.

Hans went quietly with the soldiers who came to take him to his rooms.

"You are formally under house arrest, Prince Handurin," Dorilian told him calmly. "Behave yourself."

32

I will bring you water from the mountains,
Sweet and bright,
Cold from snow,
Heated by volcanoes.
—Issahan, *Seven Springs in Agalor*

Hans did not speak all that afternoon. Only when the steward brought their evening meal, and Arne begged him to eat, did it begin to dawn what had happened.

Taking his seat at a table large enough to seat an ambassador's household, Hans forced himself to pick up a spoon. The server had not given him a knife. The princely suite had become a prison, and its luxuries now seemed cobwebbed and gray. Even the caged bird in the corner, usually full of song, had fallen into sullen silence.

"I'm not going to take it anymore." Hans pushed at the food on his plate, unable to eat it.

"You ask me, you shouldn't've taken it this long. He's a cold bastard. All plots and plans. You knew that before you came here." Arne stood with his back to the windows that overlooked the lake and the city below.

"I bought into it, his stupid game. I actually thought he was treating us well." One look at the amount of food on the table supported that thought. "And at Rhondda, for a while there, I believed—" Hans shook his head, not knowing what to think. "He's changed since we came back to Sordan. It's the Rill, the Epoptes—Nammuor—I don't know. Something is going on, but he won't tell me what it is." Hans sighed, then brought the wine cup to his lips and drank. The wine was warm and heavy, sweet.

"He's probably up to his old tricks again," Arne snorted. "Wolves can look like dogs, you know. Didn't I tell you he's not to be trusted?"

"You did. I just—I don't know." An emotion Hans could not name gripped at his throat. Maybe he finally sensed the wolf.

He laid down his eating utensils and stared out the window at the lights slowly appearing throughout the city, bejeweling a growing dusk. That web of lights, enticing and beautiful, had enchanted his evenings—but tonight it seemed cloying and deadly, strands of a sticky net into which he had fallen unawares. He shook his head, defeated.

"Dorilian is impossible. It's like he's two different people... or three, or even more. He presents a different face whenever it suits him, and I never know when he's being for real."

"Maybe he's never for real."

Hans glanced over and saw that Arne was being serious. "Maybe not." He frowned into his cup. "Maybe I have never seen anything real."

Arne looked about to protest, then he too shook his head. "Sleep on it," he suggested. "That bastard won't be on your mind so much in the morning."

"I'm under house arrest, Arne. That means he's decided what to do with me—and I don't think I'm going to like it."

"Me neither, then. What goes bad for you goes worse for me."

Hans sighed. "I don't know what went wrong. It was supposed to be easier than this."

"Wizards don't tell you everything." Arne's eyes looked very blue in the clear waterglobe light. "If they did, nobody'd ever do what they wanted."

"And who would blame them?" Hans lifted his cup and drank again. Even the wine tasted flat and unpalatable. His mood was tainting all it touched. Absently, he swirled the contents. It was only then that the residue caught his eye. The wine, normally rosy and clear... wasn't. Sediment curled in a dark shadow at the very bottom of the cup. And he had swallowed it. All at once the heaviness in his stomach was dangerously real.

It hit him quickly.

He bent over as a sudden cramp wrenched at his vitals. He grabbed a bowl and, by thrusting his fingers down his throat, managed to vomit. Bile splashed against the glimmering glass. But he knew that it was already too late, that some of the poison had already been absorbed into his system. He hadn't eaten all day, had nothing in his stomach to slow it.

"Hans, what's wrong? Are you sick?" Arne leaned over him, his face a study in concern.

"Poison." He managed to gasp out the word before another gut-wrenching cramp bent him in renewed agony. "Don't drink it."

"What?" Arne looked confused, then he understood, and his horrified gaze sought the wine flask on the table and the fouled bowl. "Sweet givers! Did you toss it all up in time?"

"I don't know. Probably not." Hans forced himself back to a sitting position. From the table, the goblet continued to glimmer at him, shimmering with dangerous beads of moisture.

"Is there any way to find out for sure?" Arne looked helpless, his voice trembling.

"No. I'll have to wait it out."

"I should fetch the leech. She was just here an hour ago." Thuraya had poked Arne's ribs and pronounced them sound.

"No, don't. Wait—I only drank a little. Maybe—" A surge of nausea interrupted Hans and he strained weakly, bringing up another stream of blood-tinged bile.

"Oh, Mothers. But it was the same man who brought it as always does, the Hierarch's own steward," Arne told him. "That same man who makes sure we get a little extra. It surely couldn't be him."

"It could be anybody."

With Arne's help Hans managed to make it to a couch, where he lay curled on his side, too sick to move, while every light in the room danced in slow circles behind his eyes. Blood roared in his ears, breaking through and filling his skull with lines of vivid red. Before his mind danced images of the wine cups in Permephedon.

Teremar wine, red and sweet; Marc Frederick smiling, lifting the cup. His hand—Dorilian's hand—lifting a cup in answer.

Hans had a face to put to that man now.

Another pain wrenched at his gut and he collapsed into knots of visceral jelly, too twisted to care. The misery was the worst he had ever known. From this hell there was no escape into unconsciousness, no merciful relief. His body itself held him captive to its throes.

Hans didn't know how long it lasted, only that it seemed to go on forever. His world went white. His breathing turned rough, then smooth. He heard sounds of other breathing, thick, nearby.

After what seemed an eternity, he opened his eyes to see Arne staring down at him, white-faced and worried.

"Thank the gods, whoever they are." The Kheld dropped to his knees beside the couch. "I thought you were dead."

Hans lifted his hand to touch Arne's tear-stained cheek. "Not quite. Almost, maybe." He still felt sick and had not done with empty retching, but the throbbing in his head had dulled to a manageable ache and his limbs responded as if filled with lead.

"I didn't know what to do. There were a couple times I almost ran out to get the Hierarch or his men. But I couldn't, I couldn't." Arne's voice broke when Hans wrapped his hand around Arne's head and held it as he collapsed against him. "What if *he* did it? Poison is how he killed them at Permephedon, folk say. Oh, gods, Hans—what if it was him?"

"We don't know. It doesn't matter. I'm all right." Hans did his best to control a fear that, already, threatened to hurl him headlong into panic. He couldn't afford that right now. "I'm only glad you didn't drink as well."

Arne smiled tremulously. "Good thing I prefer beer. I'd not have lasted." He pushed himself to his feet as if embarrassed by their sudden closeness. "You're not well yet."

"I could use a drink of water. It should be safe from the spout. And Arne," Hans said as the Kheld hurried to accommodate him. "Don't use the goblets—nothing you would drink with normally." Just saying it aloud, exercising that precaution, brought into focus the extent of their peril.

Someone had just tried to kill him. If not Dorilian himself, there were countless others living at this court, separated from Hans by mere doors and walls, whose hatreds now spoke too loudly to be ignored. And not this court alone. Someone, somewhere, was expecting him and maybe Arne to be very dead by morning. Worse was the possibility that those people were still at hand and might take steps to be sure of it.

Arne rushed over with a deep glass bowl in his hands. Hans felt its slick, smooth weight, wet and heavy, as Arne placed it in his hands. Before drinking, Hans said, "We can't stay here. I don't know what is going on, but it's too dangerous for us. I can't trust Dorilian to protect us anymore."

"I never did. You ask me, he's the one that did it!"

"I don't even want to think about that." Hans lifted the bowl, which smelled and tasted of green leaves, and remembered the flower bowl that had graced the table. He had not realized his thirst until he began to swallow. The cold water flowed like a healing balm, cooling and soothing his abused system, replenishing bodily fluids depleted by vomiting and deprivation and the dubious mechanisms of the unknown poison.

"You know what I think." Arne stood with arms folded. "You could wager your crown and Essera itself on him doing it and not be worried about losing a flake of gold or a blade of grass when it all comes out. He'd not do it himself—he's too smart for that—but he's got a hand in every pudding and that damn well seasons it. His palace, his food, his steward—that cold-blooded snake's got poison written all over him, has had it from the first, only you didn't want to see it."

Hans sat on the edge of the cushions and held his arm across his stomach. Only now did he see it had all been a game, a deadly game played for keeps. Dorilian keeping him and Arne as his guests for months, training them to use swords, tutor Hans in politics, economics... everything. Deception covering deception, treachery hiding within the folds of elaborately constructed lies. Dorilian had known all along he was educating a corpse.

Other thoughts gripped Hans just as powerfully, adding their own kind of pain. It stung to know he had actually begun to like Dorilian a little. Trusted him, believed him. *We made an oath! Made it on our blood!*

What an idiot.

He'd been so green, so ready to buy whatever Dorilian wanted him to believe. He hadn't seen through it.

The Highborn don't lie, he recalled. *Isn't that what Ezhno said? Because if they did, so could the World, and reality itself would be a lie.*

Or maybe, this whole time, that reality had been nothing more than how desperately Hans had *wanted* Dorilian to be someone he could trust.

"It doesn't matter who did it," Hans said at last. "We're not going to stay around here long enough to find out."

Ignoring his body's demand to rest, he rose from the couch. A meal would have relieved much of his weakness, he suspected, but he remembered the blood he had vomited and reasoned that it would be wiser to wait before eating. Also, who knew what poisons might lurk in the food? Instead he drank another bowl of water. The best thing he could do for himself now was to flush his system—and think of a way to get out of this prison.

So, Handurin. What do you think of our prison?

One way or another, Dorilian had meant it all along.

"What are you doing?" Arne protested when he saw Hans standing. "You're too sick! And where are you going to go anyway? We're locked in!"

Hans went to his clothes chest for a fresh everyday chiton. He slipped this on over his undergarment. "I'm not going to wait for someone to come and finish us off—or for Dorilian to send us for our own 'protection' to some cell in the Citadel either. They come for the dishes in the morning. We have until then. I've got an idea," he said, "but I don't know how much hope to put in it."

"Maybe not any. But I'm with you, you know."

"Then pack our gear. Just what we need and make it light. And be quiet about it," Hans warned. "If we start making noise, it's possible someone might come in to put a stop to it."

Arne nodded grim obedience.

Making his way to the bedchamber, Hans went to the wide, lake-facing window. No one had bothered to secure it. Escape, while difficult, might not be impossible: the Serat had been built for seclusion and aesthetics, with the intent to limit access to its residents rather than prevent guests—almost none of whom were prisoners—from leaving. By balancing on the window's broad ledge he could angle out for a better view of what lay below. With sunset, darkness had fallen over the Serat and softened the terraces below with shadow. Low lighting at points along the parapet showed him the long, unguarded terrace that was common to the Serat's residential lower level.

Now that he looked more closely, Hans saw that the ledge outside this bedchamber window, if properly negotiated, might allow him to drop onto that terrace. He was stronger again, no longer woozy.

Taking care, he crawled out on the smooth, ghostly ledge as moonlight cascaded down the Serat's courtly walls, pooling in silver on the terraces. Securing a good grip on the stone with his hands, he spread his fingers along the edge, looking again for roughness and measuring its hold. All he needed was a good launch and enough momentum to land him squarely on the smooth surface below. A straight drop might cause him to land badly or plunge past the terrace wall to a certain death. He wouldn't think about that.

"I think we can make it," he said upon coming back into the room and seeing Arne standing there, mystified and holding in his hands the packs he had thrown together.

"Make what?"

"A rope."

Hans moved about the room, in quick succession stripping the bed of its covers, the windows of draping.

Arne paled as he realized what their plan was to be. "Lud's Balls, Hans, you can't be serious! That wall's a thousand feet high straight down!"

"Then it'll have to be a very long rope, won't it? We'll need to strip your bed too. Everything." Hans took the packs from Arne's hands. Into one of them he stashed what little wealth was his—the golden circlet Tiflan had given him to wear, an enameled armband, the belt with turquoise overlay, and two plain rings—as well as his dagger and the *deiknya* and the Saint James medallion. He added the silver eating utensils from the table. The silver amounted to petty thievery, but he wasn't about to let that stop him.

"Hans, what are you doing?"

"We'll need the money." Hans got down on the floor and began tearing at the fabrics, knowing that dawn came early on these short summer nights. He turned to Arne, who was staring at him, dumbfounded. "You do know how to make knots, don't you? The kind that don't slip?"

"Can't we just sneak out or something?" Arne entreated. "There must be some way easier to get out of this place."

"Not for us." Hans ripped at the sheets, tearing them into sturdy strips. Dorilian owned good sheets, cotton thread and densely woven.

"But, Tiflan—he wouldn't be in on it. He'd help us."

"Arne, listen to me. At this moment there is not a soul in this Serat I would trust to help us, and only a handful I would swear don't want us dead. Even if Tiflan wanted to, he couldn't help us. He wouldn't go against Dorilian. Don't you see? Dorilian is the only one who matters. If he's turned against us, if he's decided to look the other way—or if he cannot stop it, whatever it is—we're dead, and I don't give us the first chance in any god's hell of getting out of here alive come morning." Hans grabbed for another length of sheeting, pulled, and was rewarded by a loud rip as the fabric tore down the middle. "And even if it isn't him and he isn't behind it, it doesn't matter anyway. Being kept under house arrest is not exactly what I had in mind."

Arne looked about the room in dismay, at the draperies, the sheeting, littering the floor. "But how can it work, I ask you, how can it? All this stuff—it's too heavy, it'll never hold together."

"Oh, yes it will," Hans told him fiercely. "We are going to make damn sure that it does."

Arne, probably because he saw they had no choice, got down on his hands and knees alongside Hans, took up an end of sheet, and began knotting. Three hours later, as the moon was setting, they had the longest rope that was in their power to make. The apartment had yielded no more sturdy fabrics. They would have to make do with what they had.

Hans went out the window first. Nodding to Arne, who grinned at him weakly, he secured a good grip on the stone with his hands, spreading his fingers along the edge, then swung himself over. The terrace was just one floor below, with only a small portion directly beneath him. But the odds were good that he might reach it. Using his arms, he pulled his body high upon the ledge, let his weight pull him down, into an arc, his grip slipping a little as he pushed with his hands, the arc carrying him back. He landed in a crouch, fell off balance for a moment, then rolled to his feet. He had been quieter than he had expected. With a last signal to Arne, he dodged into the shadows. Voices approached, then faded without ever coming near.

When he was certain that no one watched, Hans left the shadows and stood in the moonlight under the windows. He waved to Arne, who tossed one end of the rope down to him. It took two tries before Hans could grab it and pull the long, heavy thing knot by knot into thick coils at his feet. That done, Arne secured the other end about his waist. Then, with the painful slowness of uncertainty, Arne lowered himself out the window. Both packs, which he had tied to his back, swung side to side like pendulums. He tried to make the jump, but he started badly. He would have tumbled past the terrace had not Hans pulled him up by the rope, then grabbed his clothing and hauled him to safety. Now that they were down, there was no going back, no way they could get back up to the window.

Together, they leaned out over the terrace wall and peered down into the dark, a gray distance so deep it became forever. They had both seen this same wall from lake level, and from the Dekkora level of the City, yet looking down somehow made it seem that much taller.

"I don't think the rope's going to make it," muttered Arne as he squinted through the murk, trying to make out the ground they knew had to be there.

"This way," Hans urged quietly. With Arne on his heels, he darted along the terrace to the other end. The ground rose toward this side of the Serat. It would still be a long way down, however.

Hans secured his end of the makeshift rope to a stone bench that was set against the terrace wall, double tying the knot to make sure of it. He then dragged the remainder of the rope to the rampart and dropped it over, watching as it snaked its way down the glimmering white wall, the dark segment he had fastened to the very end swinging in wide sweeps, disappearing far below. He exhaled sharply. "We are going to have a drop at the bottom." He could not even guess how much of a fall there would be. He picked up the pack Arne had made for him and secured it across his shoulders. "I'll go first," he said, preparing to go over the edge.

Arne grabbed him by the arm. "No. I'll go first." He sounded serious.

"Look, Arne," Hans reasoned, "if it's going to break—"

"That's just it," Arne said, looking over the edge at the lumpy line of their homemade rope dangling down the sheer face of the wall. "If it breaks under me, then maybe I'll be dead or something. And you'll know better than to go, and maybe you'll get north somehow later. Make it to Amallar! But if it breaks under you, and you going first, then you're dead, but I'm left up here—and I don't want to think what that bastard would do to me with you gone!"

He had a point. Hans had to admit that he stood a better chance of looking out for himself in such an event than did Arne. Stranded among Staubauns, and in Sordan yet, the Kheld wouldn't stand a chance.

"All right," Hans agreed. "You go first."

Shaking only a little and clearly trying to be brave, Arne took the rope in his hands, then leaned on the top of the rampart and slowly edged his legs over. Hand over hand, he began lowering himself down the white face of the wall. Hans watched his friend's agonizingly slow progress from above, worried that a guard would come and cut the rope, or that Arne would make it and Hans would not. Then the rope suddenly went slack and swung free and Arne was gone, swallowed by the shadows at the base of the wall. Either he had fallen, or—and here Hans's heart started beating again—he had merely reached the end. He could be safe on the ground.

Hans took the rope and checked it again for strength, the knot for security. It had held Arne's weight on the way down, and Hans was pretty sure he didn't weigh that much more. With a last look at the majestic, many-terraced Serat, he sighed and lowered himself over the edge. He hung against the wall in a gray world, a middle ground between the white cliff of the wall and night's waning darkness, with only the knotted rope in his hands to give him any tether on reality. That rope became everything. He lowered his body slowly, carefully at first, mindful of the knots that he had tied, dreading the strain he put on them for fear they would give way. But they didn't, and halfway down he allowed himself to rely upon those junctions, hanging there while he rested muscles unused to climbing and surveyed the terrible beauty of his vantage point. What man had ever looked upon Sordan from this place? Above him reared a wall of milky glass, reflecting the last silver glimmer of moonlight, a mirror brightness, while overhead, higher still, the Serat lived out an angular dream of terraces and shadow. Higher still, the Citadel raised tall shining towers, unreachable in darkness, a City of Light.

Beautiful Sordan.

And he was leaving.

Not only was he leaving Sordan, he was leaving Dorilian too. The man he had traveled so far to find. That emptiness was crushing and felt like a punch to his gut. Even with the bitter aftertaste of poisoned wine still in his mouth, Hans didn't believe in his core that Dorilian wanted him dead. Maybe something else had happened... someone else. Nammuor spies, or even one of their guards. His own regent wanted him out of the way. Even if Dorilian was not to blame, all his precautions and protections had not been enough.

Hans looked down again and saw that the gloom had parted. And there was Arne, barely more than a shadow, standing on the ground below and anxiously, eagerly, waving him on. Hans groped down the last several lengths of sheet and drapery cord. Reaching the end, he let go. He fell for a second only, perhaps twice his height, and crashed feet first into the shrubs that grew at the base of the wall. They broke his fall, though the branches cut his arms and clawed at his legs as he waded out of the thicket. The bruised leaves gave off a scent sweeter than any perfume he had ever known.

"We did it! We did it!" Arne exclaimed softly, though it was unlikely that anyone in the Serat, even if there were guards on the walls, would hear him. He jumped up and down with excitement, embracing Hans.

"We still have to get off the island," Hans reminded him. There would be time for amazement later. For now, it was enough that they had done it without injury. They weren't off the island yet. "We need a boat. Let's go."

"Where to?"

"Ezhno. The bargemaster." Hans had been racking his brain for a way to obtain either transport or a boat. The wharves might yield something. Sordan was certainly not without smugglers, or an underclass of men willing to provide any sort of service for the right price. But such men might also rob them or hand them over should a reward be dangled before them. Hans had another idea.

"You think he can get us a boat?" Arne asked, picking up on that thought.

"If he's here. If anyone can, in a hurry, at this hour, with no questions asked." Hans still had the *deiknya* that had commanded the old riverman's reverence.

The Serat overlooked the bluffs at the edge of the Old City, although the New City had begun to extend that way and eventually would surround it, as in the myth of old. Sordan through the ages created even her legends anew. Hans and Arne made their way along the beach for a while and then through city streets past closed up shops and houses. It was still dark when they came to the wharf district and the first of the fisherfolk directed them to the house of Ezhno Ezhnar—just back a week, they said, from Suddekar. A large green capstan stood before the low shack, ropes holding back a tidy garden of smoke leaf and yellow pulpfruit.

Ezhno answered their persistent rapping at his battered door. "Cease now," he grumbled, surly with sleep. "Who be you at this hour to disturb a man's slumber?" He opened the door barely a crack and squinted at them around it.

"It's me, bargemaster. Hans? You brought me in time for the Coming this past spring."

"Did I? Give me a look at your face." Ezhno struck a candle with his hand flint and held it to them through the crack in the door. Hans flashed the *deiknya* in the thin thread of light. "So be it, I remember you," Ezhno said. "I brought you from Ben Aranath, and in time for the Coming, you and this blue-eye here." He continued to hold the candle before him, then opened the door and bade them come in. "On the run now, eh?"

"What?" Hans stared at him. Arne pulled back into the shadows.

"You. Handurin, that's Prince of Dazunor and who knows what else in the north." Ezhno sat down and the chair creaked beneath him. "He first turned up in Sordan after you did. Looking for the Hierarch, you said, and I said to myself, 'That's the lad. That is Permephedon working through him.'"

"I had to come. It was the only way."

Ezhno nodded and lit another candle. Yellow light played across the oilcloth he dropped over the windows. "You came under your own will. I'll grant you that, though I may be the lone soul who knows it. You came, and word rained down that the Hierarch took you in—and now you want to leave?"

"I have to. My life may depend on it. There are men who want to kill me here."

"The Hierarch?"

Hans ducked his head. "No. At least, I don't think so. But someone does. Someone tried. I don't feel safe here anymore."

"It weren't like no one warned you."

"I know that." Hans waited a moment before trying to convince Ezhno to help him. "I need to leave Sordan. You said that you would help me if ever I needed it. Will you?"

Bright eyes set in a weathered face studied them both. Hans knew what matters Ezhno weighed. Sordan commanded his first loyalty. The City was his home, his heart. He held fast to the godhood of its ruler.

"You saved my vessel and the lives of its crew, so it's holy writ

I owe you a good deed in turn. I've my own ideas what that means. It was for a reason you were put into his path. Dorilian is mighty, that he is, but I brought you to him—so maybe it stands for me to get you away. Has this to do in any way with harm to him?"

Hans understood what was being asked. He shook his head. "None... but he might be unhappy."

Ezhno sighed, then asked. "What do you need?"

Barely controlling his nervousness, Hans said, "A boat, a small boat, but seaworthy. And I need it tonight."

After Ezhno had scratched his chin and looked toward the ceiling, he made a sound between tongue and cheek. "Maybe. How big is it you're looking at?"

"Small enough for two men to handle, and big enough to make it to Trongor."

"You'll need hard barter."

"Can you get us the boat?"

"I can. A seaworthy little ketch the man might sell for the right price. Small, but solid. It was good wood that made her twenty years ago."

"I've got gold and some silver," Hans told him. "But I need to have the boat tonight."

"I'll be back inside the hour." Ezhno disappeared into the next room, re-emerging in short order fully dressed. He gestured for Hans and Arne to sit as he went out the door into the paling predawn night, leaving them to wait in the quiet, cramped dark until he returned. Hans weighed his sack and hoped it would be enough. It was all they had in any case. He also weighed the possibility that Ezhno would turn them in, seek out the City Guard. But there'd been not even a hint of ill intention in the man. Hans had gone with his gut this far and would continue to do so until it failed him. After a while the door rasped open.

"The man will sell," Ezhno told them. "Come with me."

They followed him out into the darkened street and from there down to the wharf. The boat was a shabby vessel, weathered and needing paint. But Ezhno assured them she was tight, and the sails when raised were in good condition. With the ancient owner standing by, Hans emptied his pack on the dock to make the purchase. He held back only his coins. The exchange was quickly done, no names asked and no names given. The man selling the ketch picked up the circlets, rings, armbands, and silver and left as soon as he had wrapped it up again. Ezhno stayed a little longer, acquainting Hans and Arne with the vessel and reassuring himself that they could sail it.

"I've sailed before." Hans could hardly explain that he had spent several summers sailing the powerful tides off the coast of Maine. "Just not in these parts."

"Take on fresh water in port once you pass Renet. The Sansordan coast is poison to those who don't know it well enough. Almost no good water until you get to the Randpory or cross to Ardaen."

"I will." Hans looked at Arne, who nodded that he too would remember.

"She's seaworthy, lads, and maybe you are too. But you got to remember she ain't one of those." Ezhno pointed to the dark Trongorian frigates riding at anchor across the harbor. "She can't take what a big ship can and won't have near the sail. She's tidy but small. Will you name her? Rid yourself of old luck by it, bless her with new."

Hans pondered. "*Destiny*," he decided after only a little thought. "It's a Mentan word."

"A fortunate one, I hope."

"Yes. Very fortunate." If destiny existed for Hans, he was definitely in those hands now. He had a boat and his freedom, and if he and Arne lacked the money for provisions, they were free to sail on empty stomachs.

Ezhno pressed into Hans's hand a weathered chart and a warning. "Sorand'ruil will be kind—there are settlements enough and the downstream currents will favor you. But the Kolpos is unruly and hard to travel. Look to the chart—it will tell you where there's shoal."

"Thank you again, bargemaster. We'll manage. I hope."

"I but honor Permephedon and Leur, and hold that Truth resides within us, if we can find it to follow. It is an old way, but straight, and not likely to lead to ruin. I was put in your path also. The Light of Leur guide you, lad. Now… go quickly."

Morning had not yet risen when they set out onto the lake, tiny *Destiny* dancing beneath her sail as the wild wind from Teremar rose for the first time in many weeks, carrying them ever more swiftly toward another horizon and the waiting Sorand'ruil, the long road to the sea.

33

Dorilian Sordaneon never hesitated to use his
advantages. He always had the pulse of his
opponent and understood the consequences of
bringing Rill godhood to the table. Politics was
his natural voice.
—Princess Palaistea, *Before the Storm*

That morning, taking breakfast on his private terrace, Dorilian sensed that something was wrong. He had not slept well the night before, a restless sleep much disturbed by an incessant, clamoring wakefulness that even now plagued him. During the night some fleeting impulse had moved him to leave his bed and walk onto the terrace, to look over the edge. But nothing lurked in wait; only the dark, shadowy folds of night and Sordan's ghostly splendor, with silence the only thing to speak to him. He had stood there, ruler of all he surveyed and yet none of it was his to grasp. Though Levyathan slept nearby and within reach, Dorilian had felt inexplicably alone. Even now that feeling darkened his morning. Seeing him up so early that day, the servants had reason to suspect a rough edge to his mood and their attention, always superb, was quickly upgraded to being above reproach.

Someone unwisely disturbed his solitude and he glanced up to see Legon, looking even grimmer than usual, walking toward him. At Legon's side strode the tall, broad figure of Tiflan. The combination annoyed Dorilian. He hated when his friends felt the need for reinforcements.

"What now? I thought I was the only fool up at this god-forgotten hour."

Legon took a deep breath before speaking. "Grave news, Thrice Royal."

Dorilian looked at him sharply. Legon only called him Thrice Royal when servants or nonfriends were near.

"Handurin Stauberg-Randolph has fled the Serat."

Dorilian froze, his hand poised over his bowl. "What did you say?" he asked, though he had heard every word.

"The Prince's quarters were locked, but empty, Thrice Royal, and"—Legon swallowed, casting a glance to Tiflan's steadying presence—"we found a rope of knotted curtain cords and bed linens and such hung over the west terrace this morning at first light. Naturally, I have ordered the area searched, but so far—"

"And the Kheld?"

"Gone as well."

"What are you standing here for, then?" Dorilian launched to his feet, all thought of enjoying breakfast gone. "What job did I give you but to keep him safe under lock and key? This is an *island*, be it filled with imbeciles, not easy to get off from—tear it apart if you have to but find him!" He paced to the wall of the terrace and looked out over the harbor, still in the first stirrings of a new day. A black-hulled Trongorian trader with two escort ships was just making it past the fortifications of the harbor gate, out into the open lake.

"Wait!" He called after Legon, who had not yet gone out of earshot. Legon turned on one heel. "Tell no one else. Not one word. Down to the harbor. Ready my ship!"

"Thrice Royal—"

"Do it!"

Legon ran to do his bidding with all the haste of someone fleeing demons. Dorilian heard him call for horses to carry them into the City.

"Damn it!" Dorilian swore to Tiflan as they left together. "This changes everything!"

"Sir!" The captain of the Trongorian ship *Wothe-kopp* handed her spyglass to the Elector standing on the deck beside her and pointed to a rapidly growing point on the horizon set against Sordan's fading towers. "It is the *Vata!*"

"*Vata!*" Herberth repeated the name and an oppression came upon him. The *Vata* was Dorilian's ship. "Heave to," he directed the captain. "We wait."

The other ship came alongside as swiftly as the wind blew, her great emblazoned sails fluttering then tightening as she hove alongside. *Vata* was a warship, smaller and lighter than her martial brethren riding at anchor yet in Sordan but measuring quite favorably with the two Trongorian escort ships hanging astern of the *Wothe-kopp*. Those ships had received signals from the Elector that they were not to interfere.

Dorilian, dressed in royal colors but not armed for battle, hailed from the deck. "Your leave to board!"

Herberth saluted his consent, there being no point in doing otherwise. "Himself in person," he muttered aside to the captain. "I think I have an ear on what this is about." His crew assisted in tying the *Vata* to the side and Dorilian, wasting no time, sent over a complement of his bodyguard before he himself crossed over while accompanied by two other men, both of whom Herberth knew: Tiflan, Bas of Teremar, Trongor's other single greatest trading partner, and the dangerous Legon Rebiran, Commander of the Eagle Guard. Legon, especially, looked exceedingly alert.

Dorilian made only the most minimal of courtesies, demanded by the fact that he had boarded a sovereign vessel. He followed Herberth and the captain to the fore of the bow, where they could speak without being overheard. "Handurin Stauberg-Randolph disappeared from Sordan last night, and his Kheld with him," Dorilian informed them. Herberth winced, though he had half expected it. "I would like permission to search your vessel."

A demand cloaked in a request. Herberth knew he was being given the courtesy of consenting. The other option, and one Dorilian could well enforce, was to subject Herberth's ship and crew to an ignominious forced escort back to Sordan. Out of the corner of his eye and not unnoticed by the rest of the crew were several Sordani ships of the line crowding sail just this side of the harbor entrance.

"They are on maneuvers," Dorilian told him. "'Tis monthly." But the effect was one calculated for intimidation.

Because he was certain Dorilian did not desire to force a confrontation, Herberth made a try at dissuading him. "I assure you, Thrice Royal, that Handurin is not aboard this vessel, nor any other vessel that sails under the flag of Trongor. You have my word, I would deny him passage." He did not see fit to mention that Handurin had approached him two days before. To do so might only feed suspicions.

"That may be," Dorilian conceded. He knew Herberth well enough to rest upon his honor. "But he may have come on board by pretending to be one of the crew."

The captain spoke out. "Thrice Royal, your pardon, but I inspected this crew before the Elector boarded. And he was the last man to do so. I know each member of my crew by sight, name, and reputation. I would not have overlooked a pretender."

"Good Captain," Dorilian said firmly, "I respect your judgment. But I cannot trust to it. This matter outweighs any opinion but my own."

"Then I must protest," argued Herberth, a shade less politely.

"And I must search this ship." Command rang in those Sordaneon words like steel, cutting through all that would stand in his way. "Shall we be discreet about it?"

For a moment, Herberth Estol Tammett toyed with righteous indignation. His will rebelled and the blood in him rose to an ancient call to battle. His pirate ancestors would not have stood for it. But he also understood his situation to be different. He had never confronted Dorilian in any conflict worthy of the name, though he had seen others take up that sword and now, coldly, knew that he was not the man to do it. Only one of those many others had ever emerged the victor—and Herberth did not have the conceit to imagine himself Marc Frederick Stauberg-Randolph's equal.

With that thought cooling his response, Herberth indicated that he would himself direct the tour of his ship. It was prudent, after all, to permit the search. On the one hand, he could trust that Dorilian Sordaneon, in all ways a true Highborn prince, would be able to perceive his professed innocence as truth. If, on the other hand, Herberth did not permit the search and Handurin was somehow discovered aboard the ship... no amount of truth would then offset the appearance of collusion.

More than ever, Herberth wished he had never spoken with Handurin Stauberg-Randolph. Better yet would be if he had never heard of him.

The search took all morning. Nerves on both sides approached their limits as cargo holds were opened and officers' quarters were unlocked and given over to inspection. Dorilian and his men were cool and thorough, but Herberth's officers and crew were less contained: offended by the violation, they cooperated only because their Elector pointed out the need for diplomatic restraint. At length Dorilian was satisfied.

"He is not here," Herberth heard him say to Tiflan when he and Legon came back onto the hot deck beneath a sun fully risen and beating down on the lake's gleaming anvil. "Search the escorts," Dorilian commanded. And he leaned upon the *Wothe-kopp's* rail, unmindful of the Trongorians' heated glares, his rain-cloud-colored eyes searching the golden-hued lands to the north, as if by force of will alone he could ferret out and follow the ones who had eluded him.

"He got away from me," Dorilian said as he and Herberth stood on deck before the Hierarch returned to his own ship. "I never thought he had it in him."

Morning was long gone into deep afternoon before the Trongorian flotilla proceeded on its way, striped sails catching the lake winds which would carry them to the Sorand'ruil corridor and the sea. Before their leaving, to soften injury, Dorilian had made his apology and had patched together with the disgruntled Herberth a purely diplomatic glossing over of the incident. In addition, he had agreed to a less than favorable trade pact to settle the matter. Little permanent damage would come of it, but the fact he had strained a needed alliance because of Handurin galled Dorilian to no end. He stopped short, however, of ordering a general search and alarm. Outside of himself and his close circle of advisors, none of whom would betray any knowledge he told them to keep, and the Trongorians Herberth and his captain, whom Dorilian had bound to secrecy, none knew that Handurin and the Kheld were no longer in Sordan.

At least Dorilian now knew with some certainty why they had

left. Tutto had conducted an efficient investigation. Blood-laced bile and unnatural sediment pointed to an attempted poisoning. The political game had taken a dangerous turn. Someone, somewhere, had good reason to believe Handurin might be dead. Dorilian knew better—but whoever had tried to kill Handurin could be left to believe they had succeeded… and that Sordan's Hierarch would seek to conceal the death.

"I have decided." Dorilian spoke with Tiflan over a late supper shared that night under the pale light of half a moon. Tiflan had provided the meal. Heavy sweet wine glimmered deep in their silver chalices, the nectar of the gods such as their ancestors had been in ages past. "I will follow him."

"He has escaped into the river or made the north shore by now."

"Yes, but I know where he is headed." Dorilian took a deep drink from his cup before he put it down again. "I will not leave this business unfinished! Someone tried to kill Handurin, and if he has even a shred of intelligence, he suspects it may have been me. He did not think enough of me to ask my help. Am I to now watch from afar while my well-laid plans fall to ruin and my hard work comes to naught?"

"Where you saw hard work, it might be he saw hard lessons," Tiflan mused. "You humiliated him before the Dodecai. Do you think he heeded the rumors you planted?"

"Apparently so, though I told him not to. More than likely he could no longer stand my handling of him. So what does he do about it? Over the wall! And to Gsch with what alliances he might have had." Dorilian slammed his hand hard upon the glass top of their table, setting the dishes to ringing. "I had the bit in my teeth, the race before me—and the damned rider jumps off!"

Tiflan burst out in rich, throaty laughter which the night drank up like wine. "More horse than he cared to ride, eh?"

Dorilian glared across the table, irked by Tiflan's amusement. "Nammuor would thank him for it. And may yet do it once he knows him gone. Handurin is in more danger than he knows. I can conceal his absence some three weeks, maybe more—but not to the end of Time." Dorilian frowned into his cup, then drained the dregs. Too many thoughts cluttered his mind this night. "Have a prisoner taken by secret and upon my orders to the highest cell in the Citadel. Have him always guarded, never seen. Those who care to speculate can guess, if they wish, that one of them, either Handurin or his Kheldish slave, is dead. That should buy us time."

"While you send someone in pursuit?"

"Whom could I send that I might trust? Tutto would terrify him into fleeing again. And Legon might kill him given even the smallest provocation. There is no one else." Dorilian frowned at Tiflan. "I would send you, except you are recognized on sight throughout the Triempery and would only draw attention. You are the opposite of blending in."

That being true, Tiflan tipped his cup in salute and lifted it to take another drink.

"That leaves only me."

Tiflan choked in his cup. "*Yourself?* Have you lost your royal wits?"

"I told you I will not leave this business unfinished."

"Concealing *your* absence would be by far more difficult."

Dorilian upended the chalice in his hand, spilling the last drop onto the table, and set it down again, his fingers twining absently about the stem, weaving unseen designs.

"Jharbala," he intoned. "Say I have sought out the Initiates for a retreat. I have done so before. That redoubt of Zamenes' sits in a desert in the middle of nowhere. Lev will stay here, of course. I will talk with him before I go. And Fahme too."

Tiflan's brow furrowed, his disapproval clear. "If Nammuor should guess something is amiss, both you *and* Handurin will be in danger."

"When have we ever not been? It is a trap to think that safety resides in inaction." Dorilian's resolve hardened with a fit so well adapted, so firm, that it bore the mark of fate upon its cloth. Why wait for another opportunity, when opportunity had come to him already? "My enemies would like nothing better than for me to cower here in Sordan, trapped, wearing the chains they forged upon me—*and* the ones I forged upon myself. I will not stand by while yet another fool runs headlong to ruin! He's still a boy, and he did not grow up among us. What if he has not learned enough? Nammuor would love nothing better than to hold me here, for the mere sport of it, while he plays Handurin just as he played his brother."

"Which takes care of Nammuor, for I should have guessed you would not listen to reason. You risk all our lives. But what of Handurin? He fled your hand. What makes you sure you can lure him back and still turn him to your advantage?"

"He came to me first. I care not if Marenthro put him up to it—our confederation is necessary. Moreover, he knows this: dangle a proper alliance before him and he will not turn away a second time. He was fair certain of me before he left." Dorilian paused and looked out across the harbor lights. "Does he believe nothing good of me? What sort of fool's game is he playing?"

"Hide and seek? Catch as catch can?" Tiflan suggested. He laughed when Dorilian stopped, bemused, then comprehended. "Have you remembered then, how another man played this game before, and better, in Neuberland those many years ago?"

"It was a different game with different players. And different stakes." But lambent remembrances bubbled from the depths, breaking the surface. "I never thought Marc would come after me the way he did." That Dorilian could say the familiar name aloud was new. It caught him off guard.

"Sometimes a thing is that much worth having." Tiflan waited a full several moments, then asked, "You say you know where Handurin has gone?" By his tone alone, he was warming to the plan.

Dorilian roused himself from the dark pull of his memories. "Where else would he go but to Amallar? And by way of Trongor. Rill travel is too restricted; overland too difficult. That leaves him the sea, and Trongor the most likely destination. As for Essera… even he knows the kingdom is too fraught with danger for him to simply appear on its shores without allies." He dipped a fingertip into the condensation rings on the table and traced a crude map. "He had words with Herberth—of that I am sure, or I do not know the man. Nothing either one would admit to, and Herberth denied him passage on his ship. Which is just as well, for had I found him there we would then be ten steps back of where we had started. So Handurin found some other way. A boat or a merchant who would sell him passage. He has coin, after all. Either he or the Kheld stole the silver." Dorilian grimaced at Tiflan's laugh. "Handurin knows his best path to Amallar lies through Trongor. He will be nearly there as soon as he gets to Ogarth."

"Ogarth? If you are to travel there you will need companions."

"You? Legon? Tutto? Any of you would draw attention, if only by your absence from the City. No, I need you here in Sordan to maintain appearances."

Tiflan frowned as he pondered. "Tutto and I you can trust to act on your wishes. You have often left us to see to matters here when you make your retreats. Legon will be more difficult."

"I will speak with him."

"I see great risk in that you should travel unattended."

"I have been on my own before this." Taking up a misty ewer of wine, Dorilian refilled their cups. No servants intruded on their privacy this night. Indeed, his entire staff was being investigated. Even the wine had come from Tiflan's personal stock.

"Not since your father died. Not since you became Hierarch of Sordan. Thrice the danger now that you braved then—and thrice the consequences."

"And what are the consequences if I remain in Sordan and nothing gets done, and Nammuor is left sitting proud-feathered in Aral, poised to swoop on Dazunor? New intelligence places him in control of Stauberg also. Our time grows short. If we are to salvage Essera at all, Handurin is the weapon I must have. It will take both of us to defeat Nammuor and our other enemies there. Think about it. If Handurin can secure Amallar—and I think he might—and I swing what influence I have left in Essera to his side...." Dorilian traced a new map in the water rings left by the base of the ewer, illustrating the geography of that decision, and studied Tiflan across it. "Tell me the coalition does not have possibilities."

"To spare," agreed Tiflan.

"Then why is it your expression sours my enthusiasm?"

"Care for you," Tiflan answered honestly. Few people loved Dorilian, but he was one of them. "And I am thinking, too, of Sordan. These are troubled times. A strong hand is needed here as well."

"The Hierarchate is stable, Tiflan. Well defended. None will know that I am gone, and between you and Lev, Sordan would have better government than Essera now has."

"Granted. And Levyathan barely needs a regent. So the City is safe and your dominion secure. But there are others who will seek to take advantage of your absence. Nammuor will find ways to do so. And with the Epoptes permitting Rill access even to our enemies—"

"Say no more." Dorilian took the Rill Stone from his left hand and displayed it in the moonlight only for the two of them. Even off his finger, the device's emerald matrix glowed with supernatural light. While Tiflan watched, inquiry in his gaze, Dorilian grimly smiled. "For too many years I have played at being powerless, and for what if not to make my enemies complacent? The Epoptes stand in the glory of the Rill. It so blinds them that they cannot see anything else. And they are not alone. The World has forgotten what it means to be Sordaneon." He met Tiflan's gaze across a covenant of bitter purpose and slipped the ring back onto his finger, where it flared again to full brilliance.

"I am going to remind them."

Fahme wore a yellow dress, her favorite, as she danced along the dawn-brushed river path, barefooted before an audience of giant, moon-faced malva blossoms. Her left hand cradled her tonal wand while her throat extended to produce pure, sublime chords—for perfection of which she practiced night and day. High and full, those notes carried above the Viridian River and anointed the stone wings of the Eagle Barge with song.

Dorilian wondered if it was even possible for man or boy to sing such notes.

Levyathan, seated on cushions near Dorilian, was less taken with Fahme's prowess. Neither had he shown interest in the light repast Dorilian had ordered for the morning meal. Instead, Levyathan leaned forward, chin propped in his hands as his gaze fixed beyond the Serat walls on the towering, ever-in-motion structures of the Rill.

"You would leave behind your safety."

Where Fahme had accepted Dorilian's impending absence as an adventure, Levyathan saw only danger.

"Perhaps I will find greater safety where none know me." Dorilian had thought this through. "I will look like any man."

Levyathan's unhappiness did not relent. "You are not just any man, and never will be."

True, but Dorilian might be able to pull off the *appearance* of one. "I am not without weapons."

"No Coronal. No armor." Levyathan pointed to the light-filled rings painted against the morning sky. "No Rill."

Dorilian showed his left hand and the ring that blazed green upon it. "I always have the Rill."

"Not in Ogarth. Not in Trongor. You will not have it there should Nammuor find you."

Dorilian had told the children only what they needed to know. For Fahme, that would always suffice. Not for Levyathan, whose mind touched Dorilian's in ways Fahme's never would and whose memories fostered vastly different perceptions. And intimacies. Dorilian understood that he, in many ways, surpassed the Rill in Levyathan's eyes.

"He will not even know I am gone. And I am only going away for a little while. A few weeks, a month. I have done as much when I go to Rhondda. My gear includes a message cylinder; I will send to you if I need help. You will stay in Sordan, protected." For Dorilian, that mattered most.

"I do not need message cylinders to know when you are in danger."

"Only to send help if I want you to do anything about it. Losing *you* is the real danger to this World."

The boy climbed over cushions, moving nearer, until Dorilian put his arm around Levyathan and pulled him close. Head nestled on Dorilian's shoulder, Levyathan relaxed. Warm. Safe. When together like this, Dorilian always felt at peace. Little else in the world made him so.

"Are you going to bring Handurin back?"

"Perhaps. If I can."

Levyathan gave another unhappy look. "And if you cannot?"

Indeed. "In that event, I will do whatever I must. You know what awaits us on the road ahead. We cannot simply let Handurin go out into the world armed only with his ignorance of it." Dorilian maneuvered himself free of Lev's weight and stood. It was time to leave the young ones to their own day. He had preparations to make. "We knew this day would come. I cannot continue to let the minions and creatures of this world dictate what I do." *Or am.*

"You will test their chains?" Levyathan asked.

"Yes." Dorilian looked up at the Rill. "And if possible I will break them."

"No." Legon shook his head, though his disbelieving gaze never left Dorilian's. Only in private would he have dared use that word. "You cannot go out into the madness beyond these walls and not take me with you. I promised you—"

"To always be at my side, shield to my sword." They had been ten and in Teremar when Legon had made that vow, ardent and kneeling before Dorilian in a self-made ceremony conducted on the Stairs of Tulamanta.

"A vow I will keep to my last breath." Legon stood with Dorilian upon the Eagle Barge, Sordan's Citadel at their backs and the lake before them gilded with morning. He spoke through clenched teeth. "Put me in a cell if you would keep me back, but I will find my way free and I will follow."

"No, you will not," Dorilian countered. "Because if you do that, Nammuor will follow *you*. He has spies in this City and they will be watching. I want them to watch you go to Jharbala with Deleus, to pretend along with him that he is me. You will convince them, more even than his resemblance to me ever could. Be my shield for the world to see. All know you never leave my side."

Fuck. Legon did not need to speak the word aloud; it took shape in the way his lips moved, lower lip tapping upper teeth. Legon was taking this about as well as Dorilian had expected. "So I am to draw the eyes of the world while you wander unprotected."

"No, unnoticed. My protection will be that I am not where they think me to be. You, and Lev also, and Tutto and Deleus will all be here. And Tiflan, too. All of you in roles so well understood none will question where I am. As for self-defense, I will be armed, and I am better equipped than most men for detecting danger."

"You are not immune to injury."

"No. My goal will be to avoid any."

Legon's upper lip bared teeth and his eyes narrowed. "I will kill him, this Esseran prince. Stefan's brother. If any harm comes to you because of Handurin's stupidity, because he could not trust you..."

"I forbid you to murder him, even if that should happen. If you still obey me, heed me at least in that."

Early sunlight glinted along Legon's lashes. His sigh burdened the bright hour. "Though I obey you to the end of days, I am loathe to release Handurin from blame should any harm befall you—or any of us! Any harm that lands on you lands on us all."

And on the Rill. And on the World.

Dorilian placed his hand on Legon's shoulder, earning himself a look filled with surprise and a flare of deep feeling just as quickly pushed aside. Twenty years of memories filled the space between them.

"Protect us all, then. Help me sheathe myself in obscurity a little longer. Be my shield, Legon, as you have promised. Because the time has come for *me* to be a sword."

34

Ardaenans are a proud folk. Royal blood passes
through the female, so that the king is always
brother to the Queen, to whom he is not wed and
whose son will succeed him. The king may wed as
many women as he can maintain. It is not
uncommon for an Ardaenan male of high rank to
have a dozen or more wives, or for their kings to
wife-bond to commoners.
—Patroculos, *Journeys to Many Lands*

After making way around Ilmar and into the sea, *Destiny* crawled along the coastline of Sansordan for many days, following the Kolpos north along a sparse, rock-bounded land. Cursed with few rivers and lacking fresh water, this stretch of coast supported only a meager population, unlike fragrant Ilmar, left behind to the south where the mighty Sorand'ruil emptied at last into the sea. Here the land was drier and less friendly, often spectacularly colored but never green, its only patches of life showing among the rocks where surging ocean tides left pools to evaporate in the sun. On the other side of the Kolpos, that great body of water dividing the Staubaun lands from those of Ardaen, lay the peninsula of Callorn, notated on the map as being pine-forested and misty. Hans and Arne knew Callorn was there but also that they would never see it. They kept close to the eastern shore, fearful of losing their bearings if too far from land, and mindful that Trongor would be found along this coast. Often they spied full-rigged Trongorian merchant schooners in the distance, moving swiftly to the north.

On their journey down the Sorand'ruil, they had become sun-browned, their garments weathered and stained by sweat. Hans had taught Arne enough of the basics of sailing to trust him with the helm during the day. So long as the weather held they made good time, though the wind was not always favorable and there were days they languished offshore, sometimes fishing, bobbing on the water like the gulls that waited for them to throw scraps overboard. Those days they studied maps and charts and spoke Kheldish, Hans brushing up on the language he would need to use when they reached Amallar. He no longer doubted that they would. Had Dorilian really wanted to catch them, the week spent making their way down the river, porting in small towns and sailing at night, convinced Hans that he could have. Hans never thought for a moment that Dorilian would not guess where he was going. "It's perfectly obvious, after all," he told Arne.

One late afternoon, after days of good sailing, a strong wind rose with pelting rains and Hans knew that he would be risking their lives to attempt to ride out a storm in such a small boat. Much safer, he thought, to beach for the night, not merely drop anchor in some cove as they had done before. Wind and lashing waves already threatened to dash the tiny *Destiny* against hidden shoals. As the skies darkened, and with Arne's growing competence with the sails, Hans managed to guide them into a sheltered inlet where they were able to haul the boat up behind some rocks. That done, Hans tapped Arne on the shoulder.

"Stay here!" he shouted above the wind, "We are almost around the headland." He pointed up the cliff. "I am going up there. I want to see what's on the other side."

Arne huddled against the ropes. "Can't you do that later? You might get blowed off, it's that nasty."

"No. It's almost night. I don't want to waste time in the morning. Don't leave the boat!"

Hans picked a path up an incline of brittle rock in some places so fragmented that it was easily crushed to fine powder beneath his feet. With his fingers, he pried loose flakes of stone and crumbled them to dust in his hand. The tableland above the cliff was a sea of brittle dust, like ashes but harder, crunching underfoot even though dampened by the brief rains that had wetted them and passed on to the east. Shielding his eyes, Hans looked north. The headland he had noted earlier was no narrow tongue but a great thrust of land much bigger than he had thought it from the map. It would be another day at least until they got around it. And days more until they reached the mouth of the Randpory.

Dark clouds hastened upon the horizon, pushing nearer, promising more rain. A tall thrust of rock caught his eye, its symmetry prompting him to walk toward it. The ruin stood above the sea of ash, a semicircle of stone columns worn to featureless smoothness but too perfect in spacing and size to be nature's work. He reached out and touched the crackled surface of the nearest column. It crumbled away beneath his fingers and, moved by an uncertain awe of what he had found, he brushed that powder away and dug deeper, the pillar falling away under his hand like sand. He went on to the next column and stopped.

There before him, the only dark thing in a landscape of gray, garments floating tendrils in the wild wind, stood Thaa.

Huge dark eyes, set in that mask-smooth face, regarded him. Thaa spoke in that hollow voice Hans remembered in the pits of his bones. "Go. The sea is safer for you."

"What do you—?"

Before Hans could finish the question, darkness came full upon them, night and fast-running clouds blotting out the sun's feeble rays. An eerie luminescence rose as darkness fell.

Thaa turned and pointed to the north. "Behold Mulsor."

A tall city rose before Hans's eyes where none had risen before, mighty, crowding the heavens, Sordan's rival in grandeur. A vision that struck into his very heart because neither map nor chart had shown it.

Ghostly dark, Thaa spoke in a voice more like the dying whisper of the wind. "Mulsor lingers. Great Mulsor! The Aryati turned her to dust. The sea flooded in and carried her away. Time moves us to forget, but Leur does not forget its children. Here on the edges, the land remembers and so great Mulsor lingers. See… and remember!"

Towers shaped like crystals of perfect light glimmered at Hans across the ages, achingly beautiful, that Leur city imprinted forever on the fabric of the World. Looking through those wavering, distant towers, Hans saw the dark shape and outline of the land beyond, lightning streaking the haunted shore.

"Devastation?" Hans asked.

Thaa pointed to the flickering vision of the dead city, forever trapped in the ghost of the World's remembering. "You have seen Mulsor—tell them that."

From a lesson learned in Sordan, Hans knew he was seeing, in however bizarre form, the destruction of the First Creation. One of the Five Cities... being torn apart.

Thaa knelt and gathered a handful of pitiful flaked earth into one hand, let it dribble from cupped fingers into a little pile. Thaa did this again and again, lovingly, as one strokes the hair of the dead, with remembering. "Mortals do not come here except to die. The land turns their bones to water, it peels the skin from their fingers and burns out their eyes. The land is cruel, yes—as cruel as those who did this to it."

It struck terrible fear through Hans "Who are you?"

"Go. You and the one you travel with are in danger. Witness. See how the rains tell the tale."

Thaa showed to Hans the shallow pools of his footsteps, filled now with water that sparkled and danced, webbed with light. Hans followed his wraithlike guide across that landscape pocked with glowworm lights until at last they came to the crown of cliffs overlooking the sea and the inlet. He was left there to climb down on his own.

At the foot of the rocks, still with the boat, he found Arne soaked and anxious, more than ready to abandon their haven for the open sea. "Look at the water," Arne said. The very waves spewed ghostly light at their feet and the coastline wore a deathly shimmer.

"You're right, let's go." Hans helped Arne drag *Destiny* back into the choppy water that surged above their waists before they could climb in. As quickly as they could manage, the sail was set and a fierce swirling wind had pulled them out of the inlet.

The Kolpos rose and fell in gigantic swells. Every muscle, every movement—every trick Hans had ever learned or even overheard coupled with a few earned by sheer prayer—served to keep the tiny boat from capsizing or, worse, from being dragged back onto the rocks that edged the forsaken shore like teeth. Arne doggedly did what he was told, trusting completely, too terrified of the crashing waves and wild wind to do anything less than throw himself headlong into the struggle. When the waves started dying, Hans did not think it could last... but then one star shone through the thinning clouds and then two more and he knew for a fact that the storm had passed. Drenched and worn, Arne lay down on the deck of the boat and slept the sleep of the dead.

Just as exhausted, Hans fell asleep with his hand on the helm and his body propped against it, holding it steady, having judged by the stars just before falling into slumber which way lay north. But his dreams were consumed by visions of Mulsor. Mulsor, beckoning from the shore, the beautiful city with its crystal towers, to which Hans waved his hand in greeting. Mulsor, glittering madly, blinding bolts of energy breaking from deep within those clustered pinnacles to strike out at the heavens. The explosion that had ripped out the doomed City's heart, unleashing a mushrooming blast and heat that had shattered everything, even hope. The beginning of the end. From afar he watched the wounded earth convulse and open before sliding into the seething sea, Mulsor dissolving into nightmare beyond legend.

Hans woke up sweating, his gaze seeking the fateful east shore where in the night nothing had been visible and then the dark waters over which he sailed, half fearing to see Mulsor glimmering still beneath the waves.

But the waters were dark and lightless, the night quiet, so he slept again, this time until dawn broke across a dark blue sea.

"We're stranded."

Destiny dipped with each wave that heaved toward the first gray-brown clumps of land far to the east. The broken lands of the Randpory estuary to the north of them dumped so much silt-laden water into the sea that even from this far away they could see the golden-brown shadow of it. For the last hour, while morning spread pale light across the bay, they had tried to repair the damage from last night's storm. They had finished bailing out the water without trouble, but the sail was far beyond their skills to mend and, to make a bad situation worse, the mast had cracked so badly Hans feared it would break if they raised sail. So they were left at the mercy of the sea.

"Maybe we could make shore." Arne searched the almost sea-hidden land mass to the east.

"We will, eventually." Hans sighed, for the currents pulled them in that direction. "That is, if the weather doesn't change." It had changed fast enough the day before. Ezhno had warned that the Kolpos was changeable, a tempestuous water trough of a sea. "I wonder if we could fashion some oars or something." He began looking for anything that looked even remotely destined for that function, but hadn't gotten far in his search before Arne nudged him in the back.

"Hey, Hans! Look at that!" A flash of scarlet to the west had caught Arne's eye and it was fast coming nearer.

An Ardaenan ship.

The great black-hulled vessel, crowned by magnificent red sails emblazoned with ensigns of white, cut toward them like some great bird of the sea touched down to water, slowing as she neared.

"Alloo!" a woman called down from the lofty deck. "Need help?" Without pausing for their answer, she signaled two other women to begin tossing down lines. Then she continued in a kind of multilingual patois. "That boat, it not go far!"

"Thank you!" Hans grabbed one of the lines and tied it to the battered *Destiny*. Arne grappled to do so with another.

"For you!" the woman shouted down. "Come aboard!"

A rope ladder rolled down the vessel's side. Hans grabbed it on the third try and first he, then Arne, climbed up the side of the black-hulled ship. By the time Hans reached the top, he was out of breath but glad for the solid deck. Arne flopped over the rail and lay on the planks, gasping.

"Are you the captain?" Hans asked the woman who joined them.

Gray eyes squinted at him from beneath black brows set in a brown and toughened face. Arms akimbo, the woman answered with a broad grin. "No. This ship be Nemenori. I take you."

She led them aft along the deck, then through a heavy wooden door with fine brass fittings and down a broad flight of stairs into what looked like an antechamber. The door at the center of the opposite wall could have graced a palace, with pots of flowering, miniature trees on each side and a frame made entirely of gilded seashells. A gentle knock elicited a bid to enter.

"*Kolpos hraegaethar*," their rescuer announced, and indicated they should enter also.

Hans gaped. Captain's cabin or something else, the room was one big bed, covered with mounds of exotic skins and curtained by enough brilliantly colored silks to swaddle an elephant. In the bed's center lounged a man with a familiar face: big-nosed, toothy, and grinning from ear to ear.

"Handurin!" Endelarin popped up and gave a shake to untwist his robe. "Strange flotsam for such a sea! Did your ship sink or what?"

The woman interceded. "Small boat, bad way. We tied 'er up."

"It's a long story, Your Majesty," Hans said. After the events of the last few weeks, seeing Endelarin now came as only a minor surprise.

"A favor, Gija? Run tell the cook we have company!" The sea king waved off his sailor. No sooner had she left than Endelarin rolled to his feet and began rifling through a nearby sea chest. "Join me for breakfast on deck and tell me about it. Where are you headed?"

"I'm headed to Ogarth," said Hans.

"Why, so am I!" Having quickly retrieved some brocade breeches and a doublet quilted with velvet and pearls from the chest, Endelarin tugged them on, then threw one arm across Hans's shoulders and together they mounted the steps back onto the main deck. Once there Endelarin pulled Hans along to the prow of the ship. Hans gestured to Arne to keep up. "We must travel together, really—I could use the company. I owe Herberth a visit and I thought I would get it over with. It wouldn't hurt you to cultivate an acquaintance, you know. He is an important man in his own slow way. Dull, but important. And we kings, especially, have to keep up appearances. Also, the women of Trongor are lovely, truly lovely. Clever too! I hope to come back with another wife."

Hans shot a glance at Arne, who hurried at his side, wide-eyed with amazement at this talk of wives. Endelarin was rumored to have over a hundred.

"I am coming off an interlude in Callorn," Endelarin continued. He sidestepped a bucket. "All work and no play—well, my wives would never stand for it! I have a summer palace on the cliffs, a truly delightful little pleasure dome by the sea, home to all my loveliest and most accomplished wives and, of course, the most charming company I could drum up on short notice. I never quite know when I am going to be there. What a shame we did not know you would be in the vicinity!"

Hans was thinking much the same thing, although he was not thinking in terms of Callorn or, as was obvious by Arne's expression, Endelarin's lonely wives. This ship could have had them in Ogarth a week ago. As it was, he was not about to complain.

"Set the sail! Man the mizzen!" Endelarin commanded his crew, who for all Hans could see were deaf to his orders. And just as well.

Hans smiled as he leaned upon the prow struts and looked out across the waves. How different the ocean looked from up here among the ropes and beneath huge sails! The turbulent Kolpos, so deep and unruly, actually appeared tame. A shifting vista of grays and shadows with white-capped waves that would have swamped the tiny *Destiny* barely made themselves felt against the thick hull of the larger Ardaenan ship. Red sails unfurled and billowed at his back as Endelarin briskly shouted, "More sail, sea slugs! More sail! Young Handurin here wants to see what she can do!"

A man trotted up and pointed urgently to port. "*Veser Varuna, Nemenori—*"

Endelarin perked up instantly. "*Varuna!*" he cried, leaping to attention. "What luck! Is she going our way?" He hung out over the rail, peering sharply into the distance, as his ship's captain, who used a looking glass, answered affirmatively. "Why then, she will rise to our challenge. On our toes!" he shouted aloft. "Let's show her our foam!" To Hans he said, "Sorry, lad. We are cutting loose your derelict. Too much dead weight!"

"What is it?" Hans didn't understand why every sailor on deck scurried into action. He scanned the sea where Endelarin and the others had been looking and drew in his breath.

Riding the waves to the west and coming into focus as they drew nearer was a great tall ship with silver-tipped spars and masts, emerald blazons rippling on her white canvas sails. No merchant's trader, this proud vessel, but a warship fully armed.

"Sordan," Hans said. An icy chill crept into his heart. Beside him, Arne turned pale and looked sick. To have come within hailing distance of Trongor only to have failed!

"What's that?" said Endelarin, who in his excitement had not caught what Hans had said.

"That ship, it's from Sordan. It would have found us if you hadn't first."

"*Varuna*? Well of course she would have! She patrols these waters. I should think she is good for something." Endelarin, at least, seemed unconcerned.

"But won't she intercept us—now, I mean?"

"Intercept us? Whatever for? Sordan and Ardaen are not at war. Surely you do not suspect her of hostile intentions." Endelarin paused to shoot Hans through with a shrewd look. "You didn't do anything foolish, did you? You didn't kill anybody? Give Dorilian indigestion?"

"No." Hans didn't see the point in telling anything but the truth. "But I did leave Sordan rather… suddenly. Without leave."

"Oh-ho!" Laughter returned to Endelarin's bright gaze. "If that is all, then you have nothing to worry about. Even if she knows you are on board, she cannot take you off unless I agree to it. This is an Ardaenan ship!" He laughed wholeheartedly. "So you've fled Dorilian's fold, have you? We will have to talk about this!"

Talk would have to wait. They were fast closing on the *Varuna*. The black-hulled Ardaenan ship gathered wind in her sails and cut forward, parting waves into curls of white and leaving them in disarray behind her. Nor was the *Varuna* merely biding her time. Men swarmed across the decks of the Sordani ship and climbed aloft in the masts, lashing sail into place. Both ships turned to catch the wind and ran parallel, sleek swift vessels with a mind to speed. Hans grabbed at the ropes and held on as, far to the east, Sansordan faded to a haze.

Hans chided himself for his fears. He was just relieved and also astonished by having eluded pursuit. Had the *Varuna* arrived sooner, or Endelarin later, Hans and Arne might well have found themselves back in Sordaneon custody. He wondered if the *Varuna* even knew to look for him. If so, it was strange that the Ardaenan ship had not been challenged. Unless Dorilian had no intention of pursuit.

Hans watched the unfolding contest, a race eagerly anticipated by both vessels, a natural outgrowth of their traditional rivalry. Control of the Kolpos was claimed by both Sordan and Ardaen. So it was with fierce competitiveness that the two ships worked feverishly to capture every bit of breeze, every current that these sailors knew to flow beneath these waters. Endelarin Nemenor was reduced to shouting, "More wind! More wind!" as he waved his ship on.

Sails bellied before a swift west wind, carried up from the mountains of Callorn and rushing eagerly into the open gulf between land masses. The *Varuna* was built for power and speed, but the Ardaenan ship was lighter, not so much a warship as the personal transport of a king. Soon the two ships were so close that cracks of sail spoke loudly overhead while crew hurled taunts and ribald insults at each other across the spray. Gray-eyed Ardaenans and bronzed Sordani Estols exchanged boasts and slurs, breaking the loneliness of the sea and lending excitement to their salt-filled days. Some time later, when the excitement had become work, the Ardaenan ship surged to the front of the match and pulled ahead. The Sordani ship, conceding graciously, dropped sail to salute the victor.

Endelarin stood forth on the deck in his brilliant red coat and waved back at them magnanimously. Like a dancer, *Varuna* turned and retreated, sails rippling lightly in the wind.

After the race, the voyage settled down and spirits remained high. "The slugs like a good run," Endelarin explained.

They sat to a hearty breakfast of honey-smothered bran cakes and fruit porridge and pots of steaming amber *wort*, the favorite drink of bleary-eyed sailors. Even at sea, the king of Ardaen dined royally, beneath a canopy erected on the deck to shield them from a strengthening sun. Both Hans and Arne had been given fresh garments—certainly not the king's equal in scarlet finery, but serviceable and clean. They felt like new men and even joined with the men and women of the crew in song, the rousing choruses of the sea. Not far to the west lay the sailors' homeland of Ardaen, and to the east and north lay Trongor. It was in that direction they sailed.

Is this what it feels like to be an Ardaenan? Hans wondered afterwards. *This pride of victory? Just mastering the sea will give it to a person. It's in their blood. Irmgard and Geraldine would have liked them, maybe even fit right in.* He smiled to imagine his moms laughing and singing it up with a crew of Ardaenan sailors.

To the west a smudge upon the horizon became a wall of cliffs and the first green shadows of land.

"That is Skalmrimvor," said Endelarin. He stood beside Hans at the rail. They were alone, Arne having gone back to ask the cook for a second breakfast. "The Skal, we call it. It means 'borderland.' For centuries it has served as a land bridge for invading armies, including the ones with which Ardaen attacked the Highborn Triempery."

Though Hans wondered why Endelarin was telling him this, he did not think it was just to make conversation.

"Oh, yes, it's true," Endelarin said, misinterpreting his look. "You can see Ardaen almost from here, but not quite. And Trongor"—he moved so that Hans could look out across the other side of the ship—"lies over there. And if you follow the land just a bit to the north you need only cross a river to be within a days' striking distance of Ogarth. A strategy we Ardaenans have been known to practice."

"But Skalmrimvor—"

"Is not Ardaenan. Not any longer—although our people live there. Still, by treaty, the land belongs to Sordan and their lot have taken over, building guard posts everywhere to make sure we don't take it back. They call it Caerdon, which is to say they call it tribute. It seldom pays to lose a war."

"Was that the Second War?" Hans had found the whole study of that war to be a convolution of superstition and politics. Dorilian included Prince of Caerdon among his many titles.

"Oh, yes. Fairly recent, really. Haven't you learned about it?" Endelarin huffed to think his kingdom's place in history had been overlooked.

"I ran out of time." Hans padded the truth a bit liberally.

"To think that Dorilian, of all people, would let that slip by your education. Why, he wouldn't be here if that war had never been fought. We did him a favor. And you too! But that is another story. And it all happened because we lost the war. As part of the treaty, the Triempery's Highborn rulers demanded that we cede Skalm- rimvor. Well, of course we refused. But we wanted to end the war, so a compromise was reached. Essera got Skalmrimvor, and the royal house of Nemenor got Endurin Malyrdeon's spare son to marry our Queen's youngest daughter."

"How did you get stuck with the Sordaneons, then?"

"Politics, my boy. Not by choice, certainly. We wanted a shot at some Wall magic, to be truthful. The Rill does us no good at all. But Endurin's younger son died tragically while on his way to the wedding, you see, and Essera was not about to honor the bargain with Endurin's Heir. That might have meant turning over throne and Wall alike to a plague of mongrel, non-Staubaun offspring. That's when he noticed that his cousin Tarlon, the Hierarch of Sordan, had three strapping sons—Highborn, all—and between Endurin and the rest of the Malyrdeons they convinced him in the end to accept Skalmrimvor in exchange for the youngest and scrawniest one marrying the girl. A small sacrifice, they said, seeing as the lad was reported to sire only daughters, so no one expected anything to come of it."

"But something did."

"More than they bargained for, as is usually the case. It seldom pays to lose a war, but it never pays to cheat a bargain."

Hans looked again at the forbidding land that had played such a powerful role in the history of two nations. It formed out of the haze like a giant stone fortress falling into ruin, crumbling but still mighty. Those rock walls cloaked in gray swirling mists belied the bright morning and from time to time he saw ghostly sentinels of stone loom out of the fog, looking out, it seemed, at Trongor across the water. Almost, he could imagine that a city lay hidden in the mists.

"I saw Mulsor last night," he said to Endelarin, who stood daydreaming beside him. "All that mist and the rocks rising through it remind me."

"We all face a healthy fear of the gods now and then." Endelarin waxed philosophical, then his rosy face froze. He turned to Hans. "I just had the most frightening thought that you meant that."

"Meant what?"

"That you saw Mulsor. Tell me that you meant it the way most people do."

Puzzled, Hans explained, "But I did see it. We beached the boat on the headland and I went up onto the cliffs. When I looked north I saw this city—Thaa told me it was Mulsor." Looking at the pale and increasingly alarmed face of the Ardaenan, he added, "Thaa told me to tell people that."

"You met the Dark Watcher?" Endelarin glanced about to see if any of his sailors could overhear them; then, satisfied that they could not, continued in a much lower voice. "They spoke to you?

Truly? Then you are either mad or greatly blessed. Or perhaps you are a sorcerer. Strange, you don't quite strike me as the type."

"What are you talking about?" Much as Endelarin's odd conjectures amused him, Hans felt a prickle of alarm.

Endelarin leaned nearer. "You saw Mulsor? That puts you in another class of people altogether. Most people never see Mulsor—and fewer ever want to, but there are the strangest tales about those who do. Everyone knows that to see Mulsor is the greatest of fortunes and the worst of fates. And I will tell you why." Something in the sea king's wary gaze came alive, perhaps with remembrances of tales he had heard. "Mulsor is only visible to those who stand on the brink of their own doom. Most die themselves, poor souls, but those who don't have sealed the fates of nations. 'Tis a dangerous enchantment to fool around with. There was a Nemenor king who saw Mulsor once: Thorondar, the Scourge of Essera. And later in a dream of Mulsor, he was foretold that he would achieve his highest ambition. So he overran Trongor and Amallar and invaded Essera. The Malyrdeons were helpless against him. But he hated the Highborn King Erremon and so he slew him in battle—and that's where the wrath of the gods comes in. Unknown even to Thorondar, killing Erremon, not conquering the Staubaun north, turns out to have been his highest ambition."

Hans thought he understood. "You mean—"

Endelarin sighed. "Yes. That done, Thorondar was no longer enchanted to achieve. He tried, but the Highborn have an enchantment of their own—a very powerful one—and theirs says that any land where Highborn blood is spilled is Highborn land thereafter. So, of course, after Erremon was slain on the spot… well, I suppose we should be grateful that Thorondar did not bring his enemy back to Amroset and kill him there."

"I suppose so."

"Of course, seeing Mulsor does not always mean that you will fall victim to a deadly curse. Not all men are doomed to terrible fates. Some few are doomed to greatness. You are not yet dead, which so far speaks well for you."

Was this why Thaa had wanted Hans to talk about Mulsor? Might it have been a way of warning him? "Maybe it means something else." Hans hoped to reassure himself more than anyone else. "Maybe because I'm going north… you know, to meet my destiny."

"Well, don't get carried away with telling people about it. This fate of nations stuff makes most powerful men—other than me, of course—most skeptical. They might throw you out on your ear. Or maybe simply kill you off, just in case it's true."

"But you wouldn't stoop to that, of course." Hans managed a thin, careful smile.

"If you would stay in your own country, it would help."

The Bay of Murre was a wide deep gorge carved into the heart of Trongor, dividing the wet, fertile Rua Plain from the drier Plain of Trongor. Ogarth lay at the mouth of the river Rarr. As the Ardaenan ship glided into the land-cradled passage, other ships began to converge from the sea, funneling into Trongor's major port. Barges and traders' boats hailed them with clanging and a few with shouts of greeting. Ardaenans, when they were not enemies, were welcome trading partners. Before they made port, Hans told Endelarin how and why he had fled Sordan. Much to Hans's surprise, Endelarin supported him completely.

"Well, of course no one expected you to sit there like a dunce for the next decade." Endelarin sounded philosophical about it all. "Essera couldn't be in a worse state. Nammuor's tearing up the place and no one has much use for Erenor. He was an incompetent Bas and he is an even bigger idiot as Prince Regent. I would hate to see what kind of king he would make. And if Nammuor is promoting him, all the more reason to steer clear! I wouldn't put it past either of them to have opted for poison in your drink, and you cannot rule out the Seven Houses. In all fairness to Dorilian, he would do something a bit more personal."

Hans was inclined to agree. Dorilian was already suspected of the poisoning at Permephedon and would more likely do something that didn't point directly to him. If only Hans could actually be sure about that.

"Do you know Nammuor?" Not very many people in Sordan had wanted to talk about the sorcerer who threatened their very existence. So much so that Hans had concluded Nammuor was another of the subjects Dorilian forbade people to talk about.

"Nammuor the Nasty?" Endelarin wrinkled his nose. "He's not exactly the kind of acquaintance I choose to cultivate. Still, I know him as well as I care to. The man rules Mormantalorus, after all, and as King of Ardaen, I sometimes find it necessary to give in to diplomatic considerations."

"I was just wondering. I don't know nearly enough about the kind of person he is."

"Why, no kind of person at all—as you'll find out, my boy, should you ever be so foolhardy as to set foot in Essera. Still, I suppose that is where you must go."

Hans grimaced and nodded, his gaze seeking the mountainous country beyond the city in the bay ahead of them. "Nammuor killed Marc Frederick and Stefan, and before too long he will want to kill me. Anyone who stands in his way. That's why I have to move now, get Amallar behind me. I have to start somewhere."

"Spoken like a true prince." Endelarin patted Hans on the shoulder. "But you probably should have started in Sordan."

35

The Sons of Amynas strove to restore all they
could of the ruined World. Many Leur creations
had survived but few that were Aryati. The Rill
presented a challenge in that most of its structures
had been Aryati and been destroyed, in particular
its core interfaces and propulsion arrays. Yet
enough of the system survived that Derlon burned
to revive it. He conferred with Hesphad, who
knew how it might be done, and together they
went into the heart of the machine.
—Cibulitus, *Annals of the Return:
Origins of the Highborn*

"Hierarch's left the City. *Vata* sailed yesterday for the western shore. Jharbala, they say." The Epopte charged to oversee boarding of the northbound *charys* exchanged papers and pleasantries with a well-fed Rannuli merchant he apparently knew well.

"Taking advantage of the Psilant being out of town, is he?"

"May the Initiates enlighten the Thrice Royal," the Epopte said. "We're just glad that he is out of the City."

When the Epopte signaled to him next, Dorilian stepped forward. The voucher in his hand was marked for Randpory. He had darkened his hair that morning with a tincture of branroot, wore the somber-hued clothing of a Trongorian tradesman, had turned his horse over for boarding earlier, and his personal belongings waited at his feet. The Epopte checking passes barely glanced at him, then his papers, then waved him through.

Dorilian had known from the start that he could carry it off. Early encounters in Teremar and Essera had taught him that when he downplayed his station, people readily assumed him to be of lower birth. Downplay it more and they thought him common born or, on one occasion, a servant. Now at last he found a useful application for his mixed-blood looks. The other part of his deception, acting as though traveling by Rill were routine, also came to him easily. Rill travelers were a privileged lot, and if Dorilian had experience at anything, it was being privileged.

Inside the *charys*, he detected its imminent departure when the air enfolding his torso acquired more density, buoying his body. Thus cradled, he prepared for travel.

Other travelers might celebrate feeling enclosed in a tangible vessel or perceive safety in the swaddling of invisible restraints. Dorilian felt exposed. Ever since that day at Hestya—no, ever since bloody *Permephedon*—the Rill had laid claim to his flesh. How did a man stay undetected by something that would know him from a single droplet hung in the air?

For now, the *charys* was a self-sustaining environment. That would change when the Rill's energy field fully enveloped and infused the vessel. Already delicate currents, precursors of the Entity's nervestream, trickled over Dorilian's skull and into his nose. Prickles of energy penetrated his skin.

It was that near.

Even the Epoptes did not suspect how close the Entity had come to claiming Dorilian ten years ago—so close the thrice-cursed thing considered him a sliver of its own immortal being. Every. Time. For that reason, Dorilian could not allow the Rill's actual corpus to touch him. If it did, even for a moment, the Rill would seek to make itself whole. To incorporate him, it would dissolve the *charys* and expose his fellow travelers' fragile bodies to be torn apart by unnatural forces. His body would be destroyed also—at least momentarily—and although his life might continue in some form, it might no longer resemble anything human.

He did not want to test that outcome.

At any other time, Dorilian could command the Epoptes to summon the shielded Sordaneon charys for travel. Today, his need for secrecy barred that safety. For him, the greatest danger was not in leaving Sordan but in the manner he had chosen to leave.

Eyes closed, hands behind his neck, fingers laced, Dorilian bent his head and focused on sheathing the pathways of his nerves and blood vessels, then his skin and hair—his entire body—with an ego shield that would reject any outside incursion, rendering him invisible to the Entity. The people around him, if they noticed anything at all, would think him merely coping with Rill sickness.

When the Rill energy flared, permeating the *charys* while the corpus created a portal through which to fling the vessel, Dorilian was ready. Senses dulled, disconnected, but ready. Epoptes and travelers and city dwellers looking on from far below would hear the whine and see the gleaming *charys* hurl into the open air above Sordan's white sprawl, speeding toward distant Randpory and beyond. Dorilian heard nothing, saw nothing.

The journey barely registered. Even had he tried to watch the scenery, the *charys* traveled too fast for the brain to differentiate what the eye saw, and the view blurred into a colorless stream only remotely resembling its parts. Sometimes Sansordan emerged as a faintly golden ribbon, Amallar as a smear of green during the proper season. How many times had he witnessed the Triempery reduced to a spectrum? Like so much sand funneled through a timepiece—when he emerged on the other side, it would be gone.

The *charys* hit the first deceleration arm and slowed perceptibly, breaking speed with each succeeding arm until it entered a last slow glide across the river coming into Randpory Crossing. Bare moments later it stopped and the Rill's corporeal strands retracted. Dorilian unlocked his fingers and released his shields. He drew a breath and waited a full several heartbeats to expel it.

When he stepped onto the platform, he saw that Randpory was every bit as ugly as he remembered. Booming and overgrown, the Crossing crowded between a sluggish river and a few naked bluffs of the Telarkan mountain range. A jumble of wood and stone buildings lined cluttered streets loosely looped around a towering mount and adjacent palace at the heart of the city. Upon that mount loomed the Rill, easily the most important structure that side of the mountains. In Sordan, where neighboring architecture echoed its soaring arches and enlaced portals, the Rill was a vision. Rising above the squalor of Randpory Crossing, it was a glaring and disquieting anachronism.

Dorilian retrieved his horse, a brown, lanky gelding Tiflan had chosen for him and for which Dorilian had yet to feel a liking. He led the horse from the platform down a ramp into an adjacent courtyard, where he tethered the animal among others at a post which served the local station. There, he paid an attendant to ensure his gear would still be strapped on it when he returned.

The departing Rill whine receded into the distance. After a suitable wait, Dorilian approached the station guard and presented another document, this one a letter authorizing him to dispatch communication by way of Rill. Waved through, he paused in the entrance of the low building. Although many times smaller, the structure retained some of the elegance of Sordan's sanctum. The detection devices cleared him—he had left his weapons and any other thing the station sensors might find objectionable with his horse. After Dorilian had waited long enough to start becoming annoyed, a tired-looking man, his fair hair gone gray beneath an Epopte's headband of rank, arrived to learn his business.

"I have a message to send." Dorilian extended the document he had shown the guards.

The Epopte accepted the paper and perused it with a frown. "You could have sent it by *charys*."

"I did not make the schedule. I was supposed to appear with this in person. Now I will be unable." He gestured after the departed *charys*, long since vanished. He knew as well as the Epopte that there would be no other to or from Randpory that day. He had chosen this hour for that very reason. "It is very important that this message reach"—he leaned forward and pointed to the name written prominently in several places on the page—"the Esteemed Lord Philemon Leander." Leander, a man of considerable influence in Dazunor-Rannuli, had a secret and lucrative partnership with the Sordaneons and knew only as much about this letter as what Tiflan had directed him to write. He had also been instructed to be available for the call.

The Epopte handed the letter back. "Send it tomorrow."

Dorilian refused to take it. "Lord Leander needs this document immediately. This is a field report on two ore properties he is thinking to purchase, and the offer expires tonight. I examined the sites. One property is crap ore and most of that unmineable. If he purchases it and takes a loss—" He trailed off, leaving the Epopte to draw his own conclusions.

The Epopte's sour expression conveyed understanding. Leander already had extensive mining operations in the region. Given Psilant Quirin's policy of accommodating influential patrons in matters that might enhance Rill revenues, the request assumed more importance. "Where are you sending?"

"Dazunor-Rannuli." Dorilian relaxed. There had been a chance, a small one, that he might encounter an Epopte who recognized him. This man clearly did not. Dorilian added an important point. "Lord Leander may wish to speak with me personally." It was a reasonable assumption.

The Epopte glanced at the name at the bottom of the page, an Estol name which meant nothing to him, and nodded. "Very well," he said. "Come with me."

Only one Epopte was needed at Randpory Crossing, although three Epoptes of rank and several acolytes were assigned to the port to oversee loading, handle slot passes and fees, and manage a fairly heavy communications load. The Rill itself followed timetables dictated by chantors at Permephedon or Sordan. The real business of Randpory station was communications, and sometimes during peak seasons the boards maintained waiting lists as long as those in Sordan. Due to war raging in Neuberland, disrupting mining in Lower Neuberland's strata, business had suffered and the current communications load was light. With his superiors attending the Conclave and the remaining shift acolytes assigned to warehouse duties, this low-ranked Epopte was operating alone.

Though the interior of the station lacked the honeycombed wonder and fulgent grandeur of its counterpart in Sordan, the curved chamber was larger than the exterior presented and perfectly functional. The console dedicated to Rill operations, seldom manned, looked vaguely abandoned. The communications console showed more signs of use, with papers littering that area. An ornately carved and gilded table at the rear of the room held the station's hospitality supplies: a firepot and brazier, a polished wooden box with tiny drawers holding an assortment of leaves and spices, bottles of fine spirits, and an elegant set of utensils and drinking vessels. Comfortable chairs were arranged in a nearby alcove.

The Epopte walked to the communications section. "I will transmit your message to Rannuli node," he said. "You may partake of refreshment in the alcove."

The man seated himself facing the screen, his back to Dorilian, and painstakingly confirmed that Lord Leander was, indeed, awaiting a message. Then he fit a silver disc against his temple. Before he began the exacting process of obtaining payment and sending, he pulled a ceiling-hung curtain to better obscure the mysteries of his vocation.

Dorilian walked around the wall to the alcove, where he chose a bottle of spiced wine and glass to set upon the table. After listening for and hearing the Epopte fully sunk into a tonal trance, he stepped into an adjacent corridor.

What he sought waited behind the shimmering wall just around the corner. Symbols flowed across the wall in a script incomprehensible to anyone unlearned in Archaic Aryata. Only a scholar might know what the inscription said, and only an Epoptean Archmage—the highest members of their order, bearers of a Ring of Order—could perform the necessary unlocking. An Archmage… or a Sordaneon Hierarch. With a precision born of practice, Dorilian opened the case of the compass he carried and removed the ring within. It blazed to life in his hand. Locating the mechanism within the pattern, he touched the Rill Stone to the nexal point. Scrolling blazed blue, then white. With just a hint of ionic sigh that no Epopte laboring under a chantor's disc would hear, the wall vanished.

Awash in faint light, the room Dorilian entered curved around a deep chamber bathed in the heavily shielded pulse of an active core array. A pillar of light. A single console. A single chair. Dorilian slid into the chair and passed his left hand, now wearing the Rill Stone, over the console until his fingers rested lightly on the operational rings. They glowed seductively beneath his fingertips, transmitting the web of subliminal contexts that ordered the system. He tensed as the Overlay tested his nerve endings with psi-neuronic constructs.

It was ironic that the Brotherhood had endeavored for so long to keep him unschooled in the mechanisms by which twelve-fingered Aryati mages had conversed with Leur's intelligent creations. The Epoptes, fearing a repeat of Labran's aptitude, had refused to train any subsequent Sordaneon heir in Rill mechanics.

They had failed to consider that a Sordaneon might not *need* training. Sebbord's books had taught Dorilian many things, including that through the Rill Stone he could obtain instruction directly from the Rill.

With only barriers of technology, metal, and Leur matrix standing between him and the pulsating corpus two deep floors beneath him, Dorilian was perilously close to actual contact. After so many centuries of godhood, the Rill retained few vestiges of its former humanity—save for memory of being Sordaneon. Dorilian opened himself to peripheral contact, skin to sensors, and detected Derlon's flare of recognition. He stabilized the incursion as Sebbord had trained him to do—as he had done before, so many years ago, with Levyathan. If Dorilian held the separation, he could maintain contact. He could order the thing.

The Derlon Entity caressed the terminal receptors in Dorilian's fingers, sang into his synapses. Impulses flared, entwined. Patterns flashed across his eyes, responded to his attempt to order them. Immersed in contact, Dorilian matched resonances, his own to those of the rings, adjusting for the six-fingered Aryati mutation for which the core panels had been configured. Smoothly, his fingers moved across the board in patterns seen in books, in ways to which his nerves were already attuned, linked to the god. His eyes skimmed shifting patterns of Rill glyphs and through the Entity itself he gained entry to a neural path no Epopte had ever reached. His flesh carried the string of cell-based code his grandfather Labran Sordaneon had imparted to Dorilian from captivity in Stauberg—bestowed beneath the very eyes of Labran's captors—the gift held by the Sordaneons for generations that allowed them to bespeak not the Aryati entity-machine, but what remained of Derlon, their forefather.

Father, see me. I need… this.

Derlon presented the requested interface without hesitation, flawlessly and silently performing what to the Rill was as natural as thought. What *did* constitute thought to such a being.

Dorilian's focus remained on his fingers, in them, as he queried the elegant mind of the god, evoking answers without hesitation. *How?* He glanced only briefly at the complex schematic that presented itself for inspection on the ionized air beside his hand, a pattern webbed with Rill lines out of memory to places that no longer existed. He bade the image narrow to the main artery of the Sordan-Permephedon corridor, enlarged it, focused on Randpory, enlarged that.

While the Epopte, oblivious to the silent goings-on in the room behind his back, still slaved over transmitting the highly technical data and samples in the field report, Dorilian pressed ringkeys, the Rill itself telling him how to proceed. Energy, blue and delicate, laced his fingertips… his hand. Were he to remove his jacket and bare his left arm, he was sure he would see the entire limb patterned blue from the Entity's incursion.

Every contact made the connection stronger.

The day might come when he could not break it.

Today, however, he merely touched, made a request a machine would find inconsequential—*I want to do this*—and it was done. That and install a restore key. When he had finished, Dorilian broke contact. He sighed and pushed himself back from the core console. Though he had severed all connection and the blue lacing overlaying his skin had faded, his fingers shook with fine tremors.

Anxiously, he looked at the timepiece he carried. Bare units had passed. The lighted rings had dimmed once more to muteness, the console as ghostly and remote as half-remembered dreams of Aryati greatness. In Randpory, at least, there was as yet no sign of what he had done. Settling his nerves, Dorilian bade the secure door close again and returned the Rill Stone to its hiding place. He then retraced his steps back to the table where his glass of spiced wine stood untasted.

Dare he? What reason would the Epopte—or anyone—have to poison a random mine inspector?

Now was not the time to tempt fate. Dorilian left the glass where it was and waited for the Epopte to conclude his communication. Outside the station windows, the town of Randpory Crossing crowded the river and its wooden bridges.

"You can be going." The Epopte had finished and moved back his curtain.

"You got through?" Dorilian had picked up the glass to imply he had been tasting it. Now he set it back upon the gilded table.

"Yes. You are in luck." The Epopte walked over and handed him an elegantly penned slip, tangible proof stating the communication had been completed. "Lord Leander is grateful and has agreed to pay for the transmission, with an added gratuity for the inconvenience. You can proceed with the written report by Rill in the morning. He did not seem to think it necessary to speak with you."

Dorilian nodded, unsurprised. Leander had followed instructions in not asking to speak with him. Taking the bulky report, Dorilian folded it and slid it into the document sleeve of his jacket. At this point it made no difference what happened to the document, but it was a masterpiece of sorts and might later prove useful to his masquerade.

Taking a polite leave from the Epopte, he stepped out into the cooler air of the open platform, where he walked past the bored-looking guards. Two men hurried toward the station, almost certainly in need of communication service. Depending on where it was directed, their message might make it.

The last sun of the afternoon threw hot glaring slashes across the curved architecture of the Rill and painted the platform in bold strokes of gold. As he looked north across the clutter of the town into the hazy mountainous distance that was Lower Neuberland, Dorilian felt immense satisfaction. Somewhere beyond the towering peaks of these great Telarkan mountains, the lights were already winking out, the system dying like a vine to its roots while scores of frantic Epoptes tried unsuccessfully to bring it back to life.

He had done what he had threatened. He had brought the Rill to a grinding halt.

What Dorilian liked best about his maneuver was that he had stranded their damned Conclave, including Quirin, at Permephedon. Moreover, he had not shut down the Rill completely, only that part of the system that serviced his enemies.

Sordan, Randpory, and Hestya still had the Rill. Dorilian stood on top of the civilized world—and he had locked Sordan into a shining circle behind him. Somewhere in the Vault of Incorruption, his grandfathers were laughing.

He left the area and retrieved his horse. Quirin would talk to Marenthro, of course. The wizard was the sole complication Dorilian needed to consider, the only person whose access to the Rill possibly exceeded his. It had been Marenthro who had cleared the stoppage effected by Labran during that Hierarch's brief and doomed rebellion against Marc Frederick.

This time, Dorilian was sure, Marenthro would do nothing.

36

The first true blow of the War of Ascension was
not struck against Nammuor or the Khelds. It was
aimed directly at the heart of Essera itself.
—Emyli Stauberg-Randolph,
Reflections on Kingship

The *charys* to Sordan, fully loaded and prepared for its first
leg to Dazunor-Rannuli, sat stranded on Permephedon's
platform.

"With so many of us attending the Conclave, less experienced
brothers are carrying out responsibilities throughout the system."
Quirin spoke reassuringly to the alarmed merchant at his side who
was bleating of deadlines and penalties. Gold-hemmed white robes
floated about him on his own man-made breezes as he strode to the
control center, directing technicians as he went. "We probably
have signal confusion, a simple lockup."

Quirin gazed past the Overlay to a broad portal overlooking the
steady blue gleam of the core. The Rill's vitality burned as brightly
as it had for eighteen centuries. That it did so pointed to other,
human causes for the current situation. As to *where* the disruption
had started....

Three chantors manning the console responsible for transport
stood helpless in front of their instruments. The brother at another
console turned to Quirin. "Direct oration is unresponsive also. We
cannot raise Sordan!"

*I will disband them! They'll all be stitching ceremonial stoles before
the week is out!* Quirin had little doubt as to what had happened. The

only thing left to wonder was which of his Epoptes at Sordan had seized this opportunity to capitulate to the Sordaneons. A few of the younger brethren came to mind. *I should have staffed Sordan only with Esseran Brothers.*

Pitar Kisthoda, Archmage at Dazunor-Rannuli but today attending the Conclave, approached from the huddle at the console. His saffron robe flared to his hurried stride. His pale face only heightened his pinched air of worry.

"Dazunor-Rannuli is also unreachable. The entire system is unresponsive. It will not accept our inquiries."

"Not accept? You mean the Entity does not acknowledge? Or does not understand?" Quirin's brow lowered. The Rill was a powerful deity but not at all a willful one. "Let me."

Moving authoritatively, Quirin took the oration position at the Overlay. Epoptes fanned out behind him to watch. He had been an Epopte and Archmage for a hundred years, nearly fifty of those spent as Psilant in Sordan. His gifts were such that he was able to query the Overlay intuitively, without using ritual chants to relay loci-specific requests. Placing his six-fingered hands on the rings, eyes lidding as he voicelessly brought the circles to a glow, Quirin sorted through appropriate neuro-linguistic queries for when he made contact. Before he could deliver the query, the glowing rings faded. He released and his eyelids snapped open. He had managed only to summon a small amount of residual energy. Beyond that, he felt what he had never felt in the Overlay before—

Nothing.

Quirin rose from the console and faced the core. Though the immense central spindle still glowed strongly within the cavernous housing, its halo of subsidiary arrays had gone dark. He stared at the unresponsive console.

"The Rill cannot just stop!" And yet the Rill had done just that.

"Eminence," the merchant intruded fretfully, "this delivery is vital. It cannot be delayed!"

"The delivery be damned!" Quirin bellowed. "You will just have to find some other way to move your goods to Dazunor. We have bigger problems!"

He turned and the wall of Epoptes surrounding him parted so he could march to the view overlooking the vast complex of platforms, many never used because their corresponding nodes had never been awakened.

"The Sordaneons and their games! I have charged an entire staff to do nothing but follow and report on the Hierarch, just so I can keep a finger on his meddling. For years, he has done nothing save show up on occasion to plague me. And now this!" Quirin noticed how his fingernails cut into his palms, so tightly had he balled his fists. "If I find out Dorilian had anything to do with this, I will kill him myself!" He looked around at a roomful of helpless Rill mages and the sight inflamed him even further. His entire Order was being subjected to confusion and ridicule. "Damn him! Dorilian has been trying to wrest control from us for years. This is the fruit of Hestya. We are paying today for not having dealt with him then."

"You speak rashly, Eminence." Kisthoda drew Quirin aside. A knot of ranking Epoptes formed about them. "Should the Sordaneon come to misfortune, I would not have it said we wished it. To do so would be sacrilege! Infuriating as he is, we do not know what would happen to the Rill if the Sordaneon line were to fail."

"He has enemies enough seeking his demise," another Epopte ventured. "What if that is exactly what has happened here?"

Quirin had not thought of that. "Just another Highborn myth," he dismissed. "Stauberg's Wall was supposed to fail if ever the Malyrdeons left the city or perished, but the last of them died two years ago and the Wall is still standing in all its might."

To that, the gathered men could only concur. The Order had been prominent in King Stefan's effort to reassure the Stauberg populace—and all of Essera—that their fabled Wall had survived the deaths of Rheger and Elhanan Dannutheon. Quirin himself had sounded the Wall and pronounced that Entity's continued vitality. The tragedy had proved to be not the Wall's demise, but that the deaths had forever destroyed the means to use it to look into the past and future.

A sudden silence fell over the room. Quirin turned to see what had stopped every human movement and voice. He exhaled with relief to see the bright-haired figure of Marenthro walk onto the sanctum floor. Marenthro peered up at the no-longer-active arrays attending the core, his expression curious but not alarmed.

"Now maybe we will get somewhere!" Quirin declared to Kisthoda and his gathered administrators.

He walked to where Marenthro stood in solitary study of the arcane structures surrounding them. With greatest deference, Quirin spoke for his order. "Tell us, Highest, that the Rill is not dead."

"Oh, no." Marenthro smiled reassuringly. "Derlon is very much alive."

Exhalations and whispers of relief accompanied his pronouncement. The structure of society itself depended on the Entity. So long as the Rill lived, the Triempery's economic and military might continued and the Order had purpose.

"Then why this?" Quirin pressed. "Dare we hope the Sordaneon is dead?"

Marenthro's expression darkened. "If I were you, I would not wish for that." He walked to the console, Epoptes trailing in his wake, and touched the circles there. They awakened to his fingertips but died again as soon as he lifted his hand.

"How long will it take you to restore service?" Quirin asked. There was still a chance to salvage the schedule—and avoid undue commentary outside the closed ranks of the Epoptes.

"That is not the question you should be asking." The gathered Epoptes stepped back to make way as Marenthro walked out of the command room.

Quirin followed. "But you can restore it, Highest?"

"The Rill does not need restoring. Derlon's integrity is intact. He is still quite active—south of Randpory Crossing. Look for yourselves."

The system map generated by the Overlay indeed showed a golden, glowing line from Randpory to Sordan to Hestya.

Quirin blinked. What had started as relief finished as realization. If the Rill was still running south of Randpory—

"But it is not running *here*. Something is wrong!"

"Not wrong, Psilant. Changed. The Rill is not malfunctioning. Derlon just no longer performs tasks north of Randpory Crossing. It is as simple as that. I think you can guess what happened."

A deep silence settled upon the vast viewing terrace on which they all stood, overlooking ranks of silent platforms. To each side, Quirin saw his Epoptes look from one to the other, communicating a growing certainty where before there had been only the first flickering of suspicion.

At last someone spoke: "Sordaneon." Pitar Kisthoda's voice held the first hint of something reverent.

"That's impossible," Quirin asserted, though his chest felt tight. For the last hundred years of his life, he had monitored that trait in the Sordaneon lineage. "Dorilian was *tested*. I was there as a witness. He was never trained by this Order."

Marenthro acknowledged as much. "True, though he was never retested after he completed puberty. Highborn talents often do not manifest until then—or even later if latent. And Dorilian might not need the Order to teach him mage skills. Or have you forgotten everything you ever knew about Highborn connections to their Entities?"

"You cannot let him do this!"

The wizard's gaze hardened. "This"—he indicated the silent platforms behind him—"is not the result of a machine obeying a command, as it was when Labran configured the Overlay to keep the *charysi* locked in their slips. What you see before you today is Derlon's doing. The Rill itself decided to implement a new configuration of its active nodes. I cannot reverse the Rill's actions. Even if I wanted to, I cannot impose *my* will on the Entity. Derlon has *chosen* this shape."

"You can ask the Entity to reconsider."

"That, I will not do."

"The Rill Covenant—"

"Is a legality. Men create and are bound by legalities. Gods are not."

And the Rill, however the Epoptes defined such, was a god. Self-created, powerful—answerable only to itself. About Marenthro's godhood, Quirin was less sure, but he could see the wizard would prove as unswayable.

"Then bring Dorilian here." Quirin had never felt so helpless, so thwarted. "I, as Psilant of the Brotherhood of Epoptes and Arch-Eminence of the Order of Rill Mages, Keeper of the Rill Covenant, petition you. I will convene the Conclave in full and have it issue a formal request. I will convene the Archhalia! You have the power to bring Dorilian before us. Highborn he may be, but he *is* a man and answerable to law. We can make him restore the Rill again north of Randpory."

With a sigh, Marenthro frowned and shook his head. "I doubt you could. But even so, I cannot do what you ask."

Quirin felt the door of finality close. He had seen Marenthro bring ten men into a room upon a time, just by willing it so. "Why can't you?" he demanded. "Because he is Highborn?"

"No. Because I cannot see him. I cannot *find* him." Marenthro's golden gaze stared into a distance Quirin could not decipher. "For the last ten years, Dorilian Sordaneon has been invisible to me."

37

Trongor was settled by miners and outlaws. They
live by trade now, but they started out as thieves.
The first person they elected to lead them was a
pirate named Helda the Harpy.
—Peredun Nemenor,
Lessons from the Second War

Though Hans procured a meeting with Herberth within hours of his arrival in Ogarth, it took two days more before he could attempt to gather support of any kind. Trongor's government was vastly different from Sordan's. Each region of the confederation was administered by an elected governor, most drawn from families grown rich on trade or mining. Herberth's kin group owned ships and he'd guided the family enterprise before Trongor's governors had elected him to be their nation's representative for purposes of state. The Elector's main responsibilities were the handling of relations with other countries and the negotiation of treaties. Unlike Dorilian, Herberth could not simply order Trongor to support Hans. Neither could he provide troops or funds. The best he could do was call together whichever governors were available on short notice and give Hans a chance to persuade them.

Late summer, both in terms of trade and the region's agriculture, was a busy season. Only three governors were in the capital. Hans met with them at a stone table on a terrace of a great house overlooking Ogarth's ship-filled harbor.

"My mother has assured me of support in Essera," Hans repeated what Asphalladra had told him, "and Amallar will follow me. I am going there to secure that support and raise an army. I think I'm going to need one. I don't see Erenor stepping aside just because I show up."

Ogarth's governor, Kaetel Estol Remaus, was older than Herberth. Braids of soft white hair wove into a halo that framed her pleasant face. Her skirt was of fine soft linen, supple and smooth, its bright pink color striped with purple. Only the gardens' urns, overflowing with fuchsias, were brighter. "And how does Trongor fit into your plans?"

"As a friend. I'm asking only for help for myself and my companion to get to Amallar."

The governor to Kaetel's right, a rotund man named Garick whose polity lay near Caerdon, spoke up. "I think I need to bring up this point: we heard you were a *prisoner* in Sordan."

"That has been the rumor," Herberth interceded from his perch upon a nearby wall. He was party to the meeting yet retained a degree of separation that acknowledged the primacy of the governors. "I have damn good reason to believe, however, that Dorilian merely wished that to be what people thought."

Hans wondered what Herberth knew that he didn't.

"People will find out Prince Handurin is here in Ogarth. You realize that?" Garick pressed.

"I'm trying to leave," Hans pointed out. "To go to Amallar. All I need are supplies."

"But what if Sordan wants him back?"

Kaetel turned a testy frown on Garick. "We are a sovereign nation not obligated to do Sordan's bidding. Handurin has come to our soil in friendship. He is a rightful prince of Essera, however few of that lot might want him. We certainly are not going to turn him over to anybody!"

That, at least, was favorable news. Hans had liked Kaetel on first meeting and now liked her far more. Garick hung his head and murmured agreement.

"Just to be clear," Kaetel proceeded, gesturing to Hans with a purposeful finger. "Do you have an agreement with Sordan?"

"No," he admitted. "But I think I can get one."

All three governors exchanged glances. Herberth rose and stepped forward from his perch beside the potted flowers. "We would be investing in a potential here."

"We would also be opening ourselves to being drawn into a

war." Kaetel resumed her critical study of Hans. "We suffered a fair bit of hardship when we aided Stefan."

Herberth shook his head. "Maritime inconvenience. A few impounded cargos and ships that Dorilian later released after he had made his point. Nothing we did not overcome with a bit of privateering."

Kaetel fixed Herberth with a hard gaze. "Sordan keeps Ardaen from annexing us. Ardaen keeps Sordan from throwing around too much sail in the Kolpos. And it takes both of them to keep us safe from Mormantalorus. We don't need Dorilian withdrawing his ships to fight elsewhere. We cannot pick up the military slack."

"I discussed this concern when I was in Sordan. Both Dorilian and Endelarin said they will uphold the terms of the Augull-Periskleron Treaty."

Hans knew when he was out of his depth. Best to let Herberth handle this part of the conversation. Hans's part would consist of what he had to offer Trongor. Arguments that had seemed good when he had passed them by Arne during their days at sea now appeared flimsy. The governors of Trongor were right: Hans's support in Essera was questionable and he had no agreement of any kind with either Amallar or Sordan. That blood pact with Dorilian was not even worth talking about and worse, if Dorilian was angry about his leaving, any support shown to Hans might present more problems than opportunities.

Hans spoke up when the governors stopped talking, the better to ponder what Herberth had said. "I can get that agreement with Sordan. If I secure Amallar's support, and I think I can do that, Dorilian *will* talk with me. He told me flat out what he wants from me, and what he wants is for me to win over Amallar."

"He wanted Amallar less when Stefan was king." The third governor, Sammel, a white-haired man from Damna, had sailed into Ogarth just two days before on business. He wrinkled his nose. "Doesn't Sordan have armies there, still fighting that rabble? That is the last I heard."

"In Neuberland—fighting Khelds, yes," Hans affirmed. *Because of my brother.* Among the most useful history he had learned was how that war had started. "Things have changed, though. Dorilian's real enemy, the one he *must* fight, is Mormantalorus. They are in Essera and getting stronger there. That's where the fight must go. And he can help me regain that throne. He said he would help me, but only if I can keep Amallar from opposing him in Essera."

Kaetel nodded sharply to herself and turned her gaze upon Ogarth's busy harbor. On the other side of the deep blue bay the land rose in a great hill, the summit of which was crowned by a hulking brown fortress. In the harbor below, sails billowed on full-bellied ships leaving for other ports.

"Yes, things have changed—so many things—the greatest of which is that Stefan is gone. That means less reason to continue the conflict. That also means Dorilian's promise is ended." To Hans's questioning look, Kaetel offered a cutting smile. "Dorilian swore he would not set foot in Essera while Stefan lived. Highborn oaths hold them stronger than iron. With Stefan's death, Dorilian is now quite free to go there."

"And has," said Herberth. "He attended the Archhalia meeting which acknowledged Handurin as Stefan's Heir."

The governors exchanged glances. Sammel poured himself another crock of sour spirits.

It fell to Garick to voice their concern. "The Hierarch was not exactly... supportive, as I recall. You were there, Herberth. He vetoed Erenor's bid for kingship, yes, but he did *not* vote to make Handurin king."

"This is true."

Sammel added another worry. "Dorilian has a claim of his own for that throne."

Kaetal snorted. "Which Essera rejected. Again."

"And which he might pursue at this young man's expense."

Herberth nodded, though he remained difficult to read. "I have thought long on this. What I saw while in Sordan puts new wind to that sail. Why would anyone, but especially someone with their own claim to put forth, support a youth they had never met? Someone about whom they know next to nothing and who furthermore is brother of a king against whom he had waged a bitter war? Lineage would not be enough; Dorilian's bloodline is far higher. I think something else changed the shape of that map."

"So what are we dealing with?" Kaetel demanded sharply.

Herberth pointed to Hans and walked up to the table, drawing all gazes. "They met. Handurin going to Sordan may well have convinced Dorilian of something. Maybe something he hoped to find or needed to learn. Maybe just that he has an opportunity. We may never know." Herberth crossed his arms across his chest, upon which the Elector medallion, gold ship dominating a red sky and azure sea, stood forth boldly. "But I do think Dorilian will want to make use of Handurin, if only to thwart Nammuor in Essera. Dorilian is Highborn, remember that. Essera is home to Rill ports—and the Wall."

"Yes," said Sammel. "And we do not want Nammuor there any more than he does. Nammuor's ships and those of his arse-licking allies clog Aral and Stauberg's harbors. Mormantalorus underbids our contracts at every turn. We have lost substantial business." Sammel eyed Hans with fresh interest. "A change of rule in Essera would almost certainly work to our advantage."

"If it is to be done, Handurin will have to move quickly," Herberth warned. "Once Essera is overrun, Sordan will no longer be enough to protect us—any of us. On the voyage back I ported briefly in Ben Aranath and spoke with Joaar of Lahgael. He is… concerned. Mormantalorus has been making inroads with some younger members of the royal family."

"Is Lahgael aiding Mormantalorus in Suddekar or threatening to disrupt the Sorand'ruil?"

"Not yet. Or at least not openly. Lahgael remains Sordan's strong ally."

The governors looked troubled. How not, when Trongor's prosperity and well-being depended on traffic from two great rivers, the Randpory and the Sorand'ruil, both downstream from Rill ports. Lahgael shared a portion of the Sorand'ruil with Sordan and was a valued trading partner. A nation without Rill access, Trongor could not afford a disruption of river or sea trade.

The time had come again for Hans to speak up.

"If I could go to Amallar with Trongor's backing and can show this backing to potential allies, I will be in a better position to claim not just the Esseran kingship but Kheld support also. I'm not asking for military or naval help. I'm not asking you to finance me aside from horses and provisions enough to get to Amallar."

Kaetel sighed and once more her aged gaze drifted to the harbor. She peered in that direction for several long moments before she turned again to Herberth. "What is the latest word on his standing in Essera?"

"The Stauberg-Randolph claim to the throne continues to command great loyalty." Herberth spoke from his experience in meeting with the Archhalia. "Handurin has strong support from the rulers of Merrydn, Dannuth, and Gweroyen, all of whom continue their intense loyalty to the Wall Lords who named the Stauberg-Randolphs as Essera's heirs. The domains of Lacenedon, Serrain, and the Eleutheron fiercely oppose Erenor and would accept Handurin, I think, though their participation is less certain. Dazunor and Rannul should support Handurin, but the Seven Houses hold great sway and they—"

"Will not move against Dorilian—and neither would Lacenedon, whichever way *that* goes," sniped Garick, the man from Caerdon.

Herberth's pained smile conceded the point.

Was Dorilian, even in this endeavor, going to stand in Hans's way? More and more, Hans felt Marenthro's warning loom large.

"Governors, I may be a gamble," Hans pleaded, "but I am a *good* gamble. Essera will not become a better trading partner under Erenor, and Nammuor would only be worse. As for Dorilian, he can't ask for me back if I'm not here." He had to try. If he did not succeed, he and Arne would find work in Ogarth until they could earn enough for gear. If he had to, he would walk to Amallar. "Please think about it. That's all I ask."

The Telarkan Mountains, a wall of saw-toothed peaks capped by late summer snow, reared abruptly above the ore-rich Trongor Plain. Those shadowing mountains looked over Dorilian's shoulder as he made good progress for three days along the busy and well-guarded trade highway to the town of Hortha. On the northern side of the range, forests wrapped the mountains in plush robes of soft-needled pine. On the south face toward Trongor, however, the mountains stood unclothed and fiercely barren, daring any man to challenge their determined stance against the sky.

The point where plateau gave way to plain was famed as a rich ore site, the remains of an ancient city, which the terrible fires of the Devastation had literally melted, depositing vast pools of metals into pockets and layers beneath the surface. The resource-greedy Aryati culture had poured metals from their own world and many others into their mighty cities. Now miners sought those legendary places.

The city of Hortha squatted on a bend of the Randpory where

the sometimes fast-flowing river became easy and deep enough for big merchant ships to come up from the sea to take on the precious ore or stone ported from quarries upriver. These cargoes they carried to Ogarth or Aleni or Sordan, or even to Stauberg in the far north. For all her dusty, haphazard sprawl of shacks and cluttered riverside docks, Hortha was prosperous and some of the men living in those shacks were as rich as princes.

Rain began to fall by the time Dorilian reached the city's outskirts. Using Trongorian coin, he purchased dried fruits and grain cakes, a supply of sugar, and two additional skins in which to carry water for the journey overland. Dorilian was not especially worried that he would not find water on his way—Sansordan, after all, was drier—but he did not trust the ground water in Trongor, which he knew seeped up from under the dead Aryati cities. Poisons lurked within those crystal pools.

Another coin bought him a private room and pallet at a small, shabby inn. The weather dictated that he sleep beneath a roof, but it was best not to court discovery by seeking better quarters. Traveling incognito remained his greatest protection. After three days of sleeping off-road and bathing in ice-cold mountain waters, the steaming tub of hot water Dorilian coaxed from the reluctant innkeeper with an extra krugzat of copper quickly proved itself the greatest luxury in the world. He soaked for an hour before ordering up a meal and a bottle of wine, and settled down to study his maps in a tiny closet of a room so spare that it lacked even the bare comfort of a good lantern. In the morning, he was glad to be gone.

The fast-moving storm cleared the skies, and for two days the weather was good. The road, a major thoroughfare to the capital, was both well constructed and in good repair. Dorilian made good speed through treeless ore fields, pocked by digs and shallow pools used by miners for ore washings, that revealed the harshness wherein great wealth was produced by a few. Miners frequently became rich but seldom lived long. For that reason and others, Trongor was not densely populated away from the banks of its rivers. Sea trade was as lucrative in its way as mining and somewhat less deadly.

On his ninth day, as Dorilian rode toward Ogarth, he met with two miners returning to their claims after a week in the city. From horseback they asked him about the status of a watering hole he had used, which they knew sometimes ran dry. In return for his assurances, they shared news that the late Esseran king's brother, Handurin of Dazunor, had shown up in Trongor, having escaped from months of imprisonment in Sordan. One man's sister in service to Ogarth's governor had spilled that nugget. The only other news she had been able to state with any certainty was that Handurin had already left the Trongorian capital.

"Rode out the morning we did, right? Same day we watched that fancy Ardaenan ship set sail, the one she said he came in on?" the one man inquired of his partner, whose face showed crusted patches of black skin and who nodded without any real interest.

"Where to?" No piece of information was more vital.

"Said Amallar, and that the Elector went with him. Watch my back and I watch yours, looks like." The miner broke into a sudden smile that showed metallic staining on his teeth. "Them Khelds need refined metals, I hear. Maybe he'll bring back a new trade pact or something. Elector came back from Sordan with a dandy one this last time out." That agreement had involved ore, so the miner knew about it.

Dorilian found it a physical strain not to scowl. When the miners continued on their way, he no longer held back. He had followed Handurin halfway across the Triempery—and missed him! How in the world had Handurin reached Ogarth so quickly?

The answer burst through his thoughts like a maddening bubble. The Ardaenan ship. Though there had been none at Sordan the morning Handurin had escaped, he could have boarded one at another port along the way. A fast ship could have halved the boy's traveling time. There was no knowing what agreements young Handurin might have come to with Trongor in that time—or even with Ardaen for that matter. The thought of the Stauberg-Randolph princeling weaving a web alongside his own made Dorilian distinctly nervous. He contemplated his next move, and his horse pranced under the sudden tension of his hands upon the reins.

He had hoped to settle their business in Ogarth, under the respected auspices of Trongor's traditional and well-recognized mercantile diplomacy, as satisfactory a negotiating ground as he had dared hope to find. And a reasonably safe one as well. Dorilian's personal safety mattered; Sordan had an embassy in Ogarth as well as a contingent of troops. And Trongor was a country intent on remaining politically neutral. But now....

To pursue Handurin with any chance of success, Dorilian would need to bypass Ogarth—bypass diplomacy and safety and troops. He would have to ride straight after Handurin in the hope that he might catch up before crossing the Trongor Pass.

The alternative was to enter Ogarth, announce himself and collect his troops. Put aside his secrecy for safety. Nammuor's recent display of magic had made sea travel too dangerous for any Highborn prince, which meant a straight hard ride back to Randpory Crossing and the Rill so Dorilian might return safely to Sordan. Send spies to locate Handurin. Dispatch an emissary. Exchange communications. Arrange a meeting. The process could well take months. Months of contentious politics and certain interference. Months of unsustainable Rill disruption.

Months Dorilian knew Essera did not have.

Nammuor's reach was growing rapidly. Dazunor under Erenor's sway hosted Mormantaloran troops. Dannuth had been openly invaded. Soon Lacenedon and Serrain would be besieged. It would be madness to let another year pass without confrontation. And Handurin, among the backward Khelds, was in a far more vulnerable position than he might know. Erenor and the Seven Houses yet stood by, almost certainly waiting for their chance to rid the kingdom of its inconvenient prince. Dorilian had reason to think they'd tried to do so already.

He eyed the distant line of high mountains to the north. A day… two days. A lone rider on a fast horse *might* be able to overtake them. He had provisions enough for the ride and coin enough to purchase more. Should he meet with trouble, his gear included two swords, one long and one short, both of excellent steel, and he knew how to use them. Most importantly, his secret remained intact.

Even had it been in his nature, to give up his pursuit felt premature. Not once in all these months, not since the morning he had rescued Handurin from death at the hands of Sordan's Halia, had Dorilian found Stefan's brother to be other than genuine, his every feeling open to the world. True.

They had pressed a bond—sealed a blood oath.

For now, though, only Dorilian glimpsed what the world did not yet see—that both their futures were being written in that blood.

38

Hans includes me in just about everything, which
is good, because I watch his back, you know. He's
always looking ahead of him. I never knew him
but he had something in front of him he wanted to
get to. I just follow along and make sure nothing
worse than me is coming up behind him.
—ARNE ANSELDSON, PER ROBDAN AELFRICSON,
JOURNALS

"Well, there it is. The Gate."

Hans looked where Herberth pointed. The way to Amallar lay through a massive break in the mountains, guarded on either side by sheer, snowcapped cliffs draped in clouds and legend. A wintry chill blew upon the wind. They were far now from the seacoast and its more temperate clime.

Trongor's available governors had given Herberth provisional approval for the expedition. Herberth was to accompany Hans to Amallar, and assess how he was received there and how much benefit Trongor might gain by backing him. The first obstacle, however, would be the mountains. Even with a train of forty men and a string of pack animals in tow, Hans knew they were barely more than a smudge on the landscape.

"How much trade moves along this road?"

"Not as much as could, but all it can bear." Herberth nudged his horse to continue their journey. Hans rode beside him, with Arne and the captain of the soldiers riding not far behind. "Those who travel this road pray for neither rain nor dry weather."

"Why is that?"

"Heavy rains have been known to wash away the road. And dry weather leaves the shale looser than sand, so that too may cave. The whole damn mountain is crusted through."

That he could die on this road, or any road, no longer surprised Hans. Since leaving Sordan, he'd hardly felt safe for more than two straight days. Ogarth at least had been unthreatening and his and Arne's time there had been productive. Long hours spent in the Elector's company had lifted Herberth higher in Hans's estimation. Geographically, Trongor could have been swallowed by either Sordan or Ardaen, but it suited both countries—and Essera also—to have the Estol nation as a buffer. As such, Herberth possessed a sharp sense of politics in service to Trongor's array of tight alliances.

"Why isn't Amallar more important?" Hans wanted to know. "It's literally in the heart of the Triempery."

Herberth shrugged. "No Rill, no sea, no reliable roads. And it's a tangle besides. All bogs and deep forest and, all pardons to your friend, but the people are intractable and difficult. No two of them agree on any one thing, it seems. Little can be had from Amallar that can't be had from somewhere else for half the haggling and half the price. I can't blame the Malyrdeons for letting the lot of it sit on the shelf like a jar of murky wine they hoped would settle."

"If it had the Rill, would that help?"

"The Rill always helps. But the Rill runs *through* Amallar, not to it."

A day later they reached the steeply cut gorge of the Gate. Hans saw for himself how the tale of the passage's origin might be true. Herberth claimed that it was a fissure in the spine of the Telarkan mountains caused by the Devastation, when the First Creation had literally broken into pieces. Though the Second Creation had restored much of the World, not all its wounds had healed. The splintered sides of this fracture were laid with loose slabs of brittle rock that sometimes broke free from fragile moorings to slide with great rending noises down into the debris-laden abyss below. When this happened, the sound of the valley's torment was heard at great distances and had earned it the name of Roaring Vale.

They halted briefly to water their beasts at a walled and bridged stream which gathered runoff waters that then plummeted in silver ribbons down the sheer-cut face of the mountain. Hans and Arne dismounted along with the others.

"Drink up," said one of the rangers, the captain named Farrl. "We'll find no more good water 'til we reach the top of the Pass."

"Where does this stream go?" Hans walked to the cliff edge and peered over but could see no river below. It vanished once it reached the canyon floor. "What's down there? Does it go underground?"

"The Ardaenans drink it, legend says."

"Ardaenans?"

"The ones buried there. They drink it all and there's none left. Thorondar the Nemenor King and his army—they were fleeing this way back to Ardaen when a rockslide caught them and carried them to the bottom of the Vale. Buried them. No Ardaenan has tried to invade since, but then we like to say that the Vale is hankering for more of them. There's a pool of water at the bottom that we call Thorondar's Tears."

Poor Thorondar. In the littered gorge below, Hans glimpsed the terrible fulfillment of Mulsor's curse. Thorondar had gambled on his vision and lost. So what did Mulsor mean for Hans?

They spent the night on the floor of a broad ledge carved into the Gate's sheer cliffs, a space protected somewhat from the wind and spread bare beneath the stars. As darkness fell, campfires built using wood carried on the pack animals cooked the travelers' suppers and warmed the mountain cold from their bones. Hans huddled near Arne before one of the fires. Wrapped in blankets of coarse warm Ruan wool, they dipped bread crusts into pots of aromatic goat stew and talked of what they would find on the other side of the mountains.

"It's pretty bad when your own language starts sounding strange to you," said Arne. They were speaking Khelda and doing a bad job of it. "All my life I spoke like a proper Kheld, then I start speaking Esta and Stauba and all those fancy languages they talk in Sordan and listen to me now! I can't speak anything right!"

"Your Khelda's perfect and you know it." Hans balanced another chunk of dripping goat meat on his bread crust and shoved it into his mouth.

"Not to me, it ain't. But yours is."

"I learned it as a boy," Hans said once he'd finished chewing. "Stefan and my mother spoke Khelda a lot. It's probably the first language I ever spoke. You don't think I picked it up out of thin air, do you?"

"Maybe you did. You seem to learn awfully fast."

To that, Hans had no ready answer. Being quick on the uptake had never kept him from making mistakes. He set his bowl aside and stared into the flickering light of the fire. "I don't know, Arne," he said, "Sometimes I wonder if I haven't jumped from the frying pan right into the fire."

"What's that?" asked Arne. He looked puzzled.

"Going to Amallar this way. It's all on me now. I didn't get anything done in Sordan—no money, no promises, no support of any kind. I'm bringing nothing with me but my name."

"As names go, it's a pretty damn good one." Arne hunkered down and pulled his blanket about his knees. "You've got family there, you know. Close kin."

"Second, third cousins, once or twice removed."

"Same thing. Once a Kheld, always a Kheld, we like to say. And the Staubauns think so too—just ask them once, they'll tell you what they think you are, deep down. Even Herberth and his bunch."

Arne was right, of course. No matter that Hans had the height and skin tone to carry off being mostly an Esseran Staubaun—his brown-tinged hair and blue eyes made a lie of it. Just as Dorilian's eye color, skin tone, and not-quite-blond hair marked him apart. Had people ever put him—a Highborn prince—down as less? Hans had overheard enough on the river voyage to guess that at least a few people had. Stefan, for one. More than once Hans had heard Stefan say Dorilian had eyes like a mackerel. Only he didn't. All at once Hans felt an aching kinship, something he should have seen but recognized too late.

In that at least, Dorilian and I are alike. He's not Staubaun either, not entirely, even if some people want to think he is.

Because it seemed like as good a time as any to start making plans, Hans launched into that. "With whom should I deal in Amallar, if I want to get somewhere?"

Arne scratched his head and thought for a moment. "Well, I suppose if you had to go to the top, you would call a Council of Elders. They decide the laws and things. But a Witan of the Clan Chiefs might carry more clout. They levy the men for battles and that, and the Elders always take to mind what the Clan Chiefs have to say."

"I need clout," said Hans.

"While you're at it, it never hurts to make good with the Old Mothers. No man gets far if the Mothers hang a bad reading on him."

Women, then. They could be as terrifying as Dorilian.

Hans looked across the yellow glare of the fire to where Herberth and his men crowded around their own cook fire, trading good food and laughter. If one wanted clout, one did not look to Trongorians—they were angling for clout themselves.

"What about Robdan Aelfricson? Back in Sordan, you said he's your uncle."

Arne shrugged. "He's everybody's uncle. You ask me, that's his problem. He's a fine fellow and I think everybody likes him. He's learned too—can read and write real good, in Kheldish and in Stauba, and with a fine hand, I hear, which is saying a lot for a Kheld. That's why he represents us to the Archhalia these days. He knows how things are and what's going on. But he's not much of a leader. Given his kin ties, he could have been Thegnard if he'd wanted, but he never went after it. Probably he just sat down to read a book one day and forgot all about it. Not too many people listen to him anymore, and a few say he's too much about avoiding fights."

"Maybe he just doesn't like war. Or seeing people get killed."

Arne merely grunted in answer. Khelds, then, preferred war, which was just as well. There would be no victory in Essera without it. Nammuor wasn't going to be defeated by negotiation.

Hans sighed. What he really needed was what Marenthro had sent him after in the first place: an alliance of Sordan and Amallar. If he could get the Khelds to listen, to follow him, then at least he'd have an army. *And something tells me that if I come to Dorilian with an army of Khelds on my side, he would not refuse that alliance.*

Hans was pretty sure he and Dorilian had reached the same conclusion: that the way to victory over Nammuor was buried deep in Amallar.

The next morning dawned overcast and gray. Hans and his party started out again in rain. The mountain road turned slick, awash with runoff from the slopes above, while gusting winds flung sheets of rain at them around every bend and turn. In some places, water cut chasms in the stone and churned beneath bridges of heavy planks laid down by travelers before them. By the time the rain stopped, sunset painted the top of the Pass.

A simple guard station stood upon the open, wind-swept summit at the point generally accepted as the border between Amallar and Trongor. The modest compound included a rough inn of sorts that also sold provisions, a chicken house, and a fenced pasture of thin, dry grass that provided forage for the animals. A small lake glinted nearby. A wool trader making the crossing from Amallar told them they would find nothing so good on the Amallar side—only a well, a run-down cookhouse, and a half-built inn—so they spent the night beneath Trongorian stars.

"It's a disgrace, that's what this is." Arne threw down his pack and began to unsaddle his horse. Hans did the same with his pack and bedroll. Because Hans wished to continue traveling in secret, they had passed on the inn for Herberth and his captain to share with the wool trader. "Not even sentries on our side, just an old cook in the cookhouse, man said, and a few rangers wandering the woods. What the hell good is it to stand guard at the front door and windows when you leave the back door wide open! If I could see that Sordaneon bastard right now, I'd tell him to stop fighting in Neuberland. Just come on in this way and make himself at home!"

Hans would have laughed had Arne not been so clearly furious. Unlike his friend, Hans was not particularly bothered by the absence of a welcoming committee. "Herberth is flying a diplomatic banner. Whoever is on the Amallar side will probably decide to let us continue. They'll just keep an eye on us. We're not exactly an army, you know, and Trongor is not at war with Amallar."

"Yeah, I know that. But you'd think we could come up with some kind of decent welcome for these people. Or an escort or something. Folk are never going to think much of us if we don't start putting on a few respectable airs like they do in other countries."

"That'll come. Khelds have a reputation for hospitality."

"That's true enough. The best inn in the world—and the biggest—is at Rhodhur." Arne perked up at having that to boast about. He flipped a stirrup over the saddle to get at the billets. "We're a good week away from there, I reckon, and that only if the weather stays good." He grimaced at the stone walls of the squat, single-floor building that housed the Pass's guards and a few guests. "I got my doubts about old Herberth in there. I heard him talking, him and his captain; he won't stick with you all the way, you know. He'll get out at the first sign of things getting tough."

"Maybe. He's not a mercenary, Arne. He's with me for other things." Hans thought Herberth's reasons for helping him were clear enough. Under Erenor, formerly Trongorian markets in Aral and Stauberg—primarily for rare ores and spices—were being converted over to Mormantaloran sources. Hans had spent an entire day with Herberth and the governors, going over the advantages of equipping him and what might be expected in return. Amallar might not be a rich trading partner, but it was at least still available.

"My trouble is that things are *going* to be tough." Hans finished undoing the cinch and hauled the heavy Trongorian saddle from his horse's back, setting it down on the stony ground alongside his packs. One of the Trongorians, a sturdy youth in charge of the horses, unbridled and haltered both Hans and Arne's mounts and led them away.

"Not as tough as all that. You're Stefan's brother, aren't you?"

"I don't think that's going to help a whole lot."

"What do you mean? Stefan was our king! King of all Essera, even Dazunor-Rannuli—even the Royal North. And you're his brother. Even in Sordan that meant something."

"It meant that I had to endure a lot of Staubaun crap." Hans turned to Arne and tried to explain. "I wish that when people look at me, or talk to me or about me, they would see Hans, Handurin, whatever—not just Stefan's brother."

"But I see you as Hans."

"Are you sure?" Hans asked. "If that's true, then why do you insist on bringing him up every time?"

"I don't do that. You know me better. It's just that, well, you *are* his brother, and... being a Kheld, I can't forget that."

"It seems nobody can."

"Hans, Stefan did us a lot of good. He made us bigger than we'd ever had the chance to be before. He made our chieftains into nobles, gave them palaces and stuff. We were part of his councils! That's not something we're going to give up overnight. And I don't see why we should."

"Because if you can't give up on what Stefan *tried* to give you, you won't be able to grab onto what I *can*." Hans shook his head and confronted Arne's stricken surprise, pleading with him to understand. "I can't give Khelds all the things you thought Stefan gave you, because he never succeeded! Those men to whom he gave titles and estates—they all were killed when he died. They got stripped of power as fast as they got it handed to them. To make the powerless powerful and the powerful powerless only serves to replace one set of aggrieved people with another. Whenever one group is placed in power over unwilling others, there is trouble."

"Well, if there's anyone knows about that, it's Khelds," said Arne with a muted, withdrawn, angry pain. "Ask me about it sometime."

"Do you think I ever forgot a word you told me? I can't." Hans ached at knowing that he could never set right the wrongs that had brought Arne to the fetid, sordid waterfronts of Ben Aranath. "But the only way I can put anything right is to prevent it from happening again. I want Amallar to have a place in the Triempery—the whole Triempery—but I want it to be a *just* position, a place of honor and respect. Not the swagger of a bully nor the cower of a slave, but a free stance among equals. Isn't that what you want too?"

"Yeah. Maybe. I guess so." Arne shuffled his feet but kept his face averted, looking down. "But don't you think other people have tried?"

"They never had the chance I have."

A bright glimmer awakened in Arne's blue gaze, caught by the low flickering light coming from the nearby campfire of Herberth's rank-and-file guards, who droned in a muffled conversation of their own. A heady aroma of spiced beans and corn wafted their way.

"The Staubauns need us this time, don't they?"

"Yes." Hans matched that brittle smile with one of his own.

"They've needed us before, but we never got nothing for it 'cept an extra kick in the teeth for having listened to them in the first place." Arne shouldered his bedroll and they prepared to join their Trongorian companions around the cookfire. "What makes you think that this time will be any different?"

As they crossed a stark mountaintop beneath the watch of a night-goddess moon, Hans did not speak the only answer he could find.

I am the difference.

39

I bring you water from wells
Black and deep,
Untouched by light—
Tasting of the bones of ancestors
And children unborn
And the dead hopes of nations.
—Issahan, *Seven Springs in Agalor*

At dawn, Dorilian sought an outcropping with a good vantage and gazed down at the road that led away from the summit, descending in curves and bends following the mountain's shoulders toward the misty promise of a river valley. The land beneath those cloud drifts was probably green. Breaks displayed grass dotting the mountain's flanks, interspersed with stands of pine. Above the clouds, sharp peaks stood etched against the horizons to every side.

He breathed thin dry air and suffered icy cold to bite the surfaces of his eyes.

It had been late afternoon the day before when he had reached the guard station at the crown of the Trongor Pass. His single question to the guard on duty had answered all he needed to know.

The Elector had been there two nights before and departed with his party the next morning. Depending on travel conditions and the fitness of his escort, Handurin was at least a day, maybe two, ahead. Worse, Dorilian's quarry had entered Amallar. This changed matters entirely.

There would be small chance of getting Handurin back to any negotiating table once the Khelds got hold of him. Once that happened, perhaps nothing would get done. Dorilian had dealt with Khelds before, and agreement with them was almost impossible. Worse, Khelds hated Sordan for a hundred reasons, some of them founded. As for Dorilian's safety—toward him they wished only murder. He knew that had not changed.

But Handurin was different. With Handurin, young though he was—inexperienced as he was—there remained a chance they might work something out between the two of them. An understanding, even, that could in some way be binding on the whole. In order to do that, however, Dorilian would have to follow Handurin into Amallar—and *that* had not been part of his plan.

Dorilian gazed upon the one place he had always thought he could not and must not go… and tested that perception. The Wall lurked somewhere within this moment, just as it had so many others. Interesting that he should feel the mighty Entity here, guardian of a past for which he had no chart and a future against which so many had raised monumental obstacles.

Among them was a Wall Lord's ancient promise.

Erydon Malyrdeon had ended Essera's bloody conflict with the newly arrived and violent Kheld invaders and he had done so by granting Amallar to the hairy horde as their new home. He had also given them a Promise. His most solemn vow, locked into the Mind for all generations and all Time. Erydon had sworn that Amallar and the Khelds who lived there would not be attacked or harmed by any Highborn-ruled land or person. That oath still included Sordan. It included *Dorilian*.

To not *attack*. Did that mean he could not enter? Or did it mean that he could?

Interpretation of Erydon's intent was pointless—the promise was such that Dorilian, if he did enter Amallar, would not be able to do bodily harm to Khelds, even if they meant to kill him. Perhaps if they attacked him first… But did he really want to put that part of Erydon's Promise to the test?

If Dorilian went into Amallar and Khelds learned who he was, they would almost certainly kill him. He had nothing with him but the Rill Stone, two swords, a message cylinder, and his wits. The cylinder, at least, he had been able to put to good use. He now owned new papers more suited to his mission—should he choose to continue—and he had refreshed his purse with more coin.

Forget it, some part within him counseled. *It is up to Handurin now, not you. He has chosen this path. Now you must choose yours. You have Sordan and power enough to keep it. You have the Rill and one of the Five Cities. You have your life. Why risk that on this?*

Because he too had made a promise?

Even Marc would not have asked *this* of him.

To every side, the purple shadowed Telarkans thrust daunting shoulders high above the fleeting concerns of one man standing atop a cliff in Trongor and contemplating destiny. In the swirling nexus of this moment, Dorilian stood alone.

But not *quite* alone.

Nammuor, too, haunted this desolate mountainside—along with a chance to defeat him that might never come again. Dorilian could defeat no one if his enemies succeeded in keeping him isolated in Sordan, his power constrained and his options restricted. In stopping the Rill he had already revealed too much. Forewarned, his adversaries would not stand aside to see what might happen next; they would move to contain, if not imprison, him. In doing so, they would imprison Levyathan also, along with a Wall design yet to unfold. To go backward from this point would but make victory harder to attain.

Handurin was the only path forward.

A train of traders' wagons had arrived at the guard post the day before. Teams of oxen lowed as the merchants prepared for their own morning departure. They would be slow to travel but... they could serve Dorilian's purpose at least for a short while. He carried Trongorian papers and bore a warrior's weapons. The head of the train had agreed he could ride with them. To any Kheld who might be watching, he would be taken as their armed escort.

Dorilian strode toward his already saddled and ready horse. So be it.

Ten years ago he had chained himself to inaction rather than engage Stefan in a war that would destroy them both and tear to shreds all that he had promised Marc Frederick. Had made an unbreakable oath to uphold an unbreakable oath. He had given Stefan three gifts: his freedom; his life; and a chance. By doing so, Dorilian had bought time for the two of them—and for Sordan and

Essera. It was no fault of his that Stefan had failed to use his chance well.

Dorilian's oath had run its course. But his oath to Marc Frederick had not.

Look after my family.

He had sworn it. Dorilian mounted and turned his horse north toward thrice-cursed Amallar.

— END —

To be continued in Book IV

THE GOD SPEAR

Turn the page

for a peek at what comes next!

THE GOD SPEAR

The best Hans could say for Amallar so far was that it didn't feel dangerous. Their few encounters with fellow travelers along the road had been with the occasional small trader or people, generally women, intent on reaching the next town to treat the sick. As for hospitality—the most pressing inconvenience was that the handful of inns along the road were inadequate establishments capable of sleeping or feeding only a few, not the number of men Hans and Herberth had with them. Save for Herbeth and his captain Farrl, both of whom Hans insisted be housed under a roof each night, the Trongorians ended up camping nearby. At least, as Hans had predicted, people they met along the road were more curious than suspicious and never seriously challenged them.

A brisk, chill wind had kicked up overnight, reminding them that they were in the northlands now. The further north they rode, the more the trees wore autumn colors, so that the hills looked to be afire. They made good progress along the dry track and stopped at midday to water and rest their horses.

"You'd think someone would wonder who the hell we might be or what we might be up to." Arne commented on the lack of scrutiny as they prepared to move on. His riding skills had improved and he easily swung atop his sturdy horse.

Hans patted the shoulder of his own dapple-gray mount and checked the cinches one more time.

"We're being watched," Farrl assured the party. "Essera's kings have long ordered Kheld rangers to not interfere with mercantile or diplomatic missions, which our banners declare us to be. They act only if they suspect trouble. Consider too that it was not so long ago your land was protected by powerful interests. Highborn promises on the one hand and Essera's might on the other are powerful deterrents."

"Seems to me both of that lot are dead and gone." Arne was having none of such explanations. "Guess it's a good thing Trongor never got a craving for land over the mountains."

"Our folk prefer the sea and the riches mining brings. We are interested in your country and people only for what trade we might share." Herberth lifted his hat to wipe at his brow. "Can you tell me how far we are from Rhodhur?"

"Day or so." Arne scratched at his head as he considered. "We should reach the Rhodhur Road tomorrow once we get to Uggwil's Pitchfork. The road branches there. One road will head up Rhodhur way, one will cross the Brennan to the Toregh Trail, and the other will run over to Eastmeary." Just speaking the name made Arne brighten. "That's where I grew up. Eastmeary Brenna. Good land, all farms and towns." He slapped a hand to his forehead. "Damn it all, but I should have thought of this before! We don't have to stick to this road or wait to get to the Fork to turn north. We're going northeast now. All we have to do is set out cross-country from here, point ourselves north, and intercept the Rhodhur Road about halfway. We could cut a day off our time, easy."

Herberth eyed the surrounding hills. "The forest is thick. We could get lost in it."

"Nah," said Arne, "I have cousins in these parts. Had an uncle too near Uggwil. My brothers and me visited every year until a bear got him. Point being I got a map in my head. The hills are taller not far from here, and I know *those* hills with their insides out and backwards. I can find Rhodhur blindfolded."

"I sure hope so," Hans said. "I don't remember it being quite this tucked away." He was willing to count on Arne as a guide. None of the Trongorians had deep knowledge of Amallar whereas Arne, at least, was a native.

"And I am for staying on the Trongor Road," Herberth insisted. "We know where *it* goes, and there are certain to be inns along the way, as there have been thus far." He generously did not question the quality of that housing.

Arne refused to be swayed. "We'll make Rhodhur by tomorrow

night if we get a good start today. You can't do better for inns than Rhodhur's and you can't do better for food. We should travel fast while we can. This time of year the weather can change like a mad goat's temper and when it does it'll rain like the heavens come falling in, or I'm not a Kheld!"

Herberth turned to his captain. "Farrl?"

"I think it safe to cut overland, sir. At this point any course that takes us north will bring us to the Rhodhur Road."

The Trongorian leader then nodded his assent and returned to join his men. Hans mounted his horse and gave Arne a weary, hopeful smile.

"I'm not making trouble," Arne said in his defense. "This is better. It's a shortcut. There's a trail and all. You'll see."

"There should be a road."

"There should be a lot of things, if people did a better job of getting them done."

They set out riding north into forested hills that would not end. Soon they began to ride downhill to the river bottom where some lesser tributary of the Frendel rushed swift and cold. The sun was still above the trees when one of Farrl's men, riding ahead, returned to say he had spotted people on horseback on the other side of the narrow valley between the hills.

Herberth turned to Arne. "Should we be worried?"

"Nah. We're too far from the road to start running into ruffians."

"What if they followed us and are now circling to cut us off?" Herberth's words prompted the Trongorian rangers to exchange glances and nods. "Is there any way to turn back and go around?"

"We'd lose a day or more," said Arne, his expression cross. "Aside from the bridge at Eastmeary Brenna, the only place to cross the Frendel is at the Fords."

"Perhaps you should have thought of that when you proposed this adventure," Herberth snapped.

Arne's ears burned bright red. "Look, I might have groused a lot, but we never seriously thought we'd ride all this way without nobody seeing us. It might be someone who's followed us, and it might be someone who don't even know we're here. The Fords aren't secret, and there's those who use them."

"I have no wish to be set upon by bandits."

"And I tell you bandits wouldn't want to be set upon by *us!*

Whatever that lot is, they're not Staubaun robber lords." Arne looked affronted by the thought. "There aren't enough rich travelers in these parts to make a business of robbing folk. It's young hooligans, mostly, and nothing your swords here wouldn't set to running."

"I say we go ahead," Hans decided. "He's right about us being well-armed." He suspected forty veteran Trongorians could hold their own against even Staubaun robber barons. Meanwhile, standing here was getting them nowhere. He had adjusted his own sword and tested his grip. Even though he, like Arne, had never used a blade in actual combat, it wouldn't hurt to look menacing.

They set out again, more cautiously than before. The rangers riding in front and behind the party, respecting the possibility of ambush, rode with their weapons ready at their sides. Herberth, at least, was mollified. In weather dry and cool enough to not overtax the horses, they covered ground quickly. The trail they were on broadened to become a path as the stream it followed spilled into the lowland. Ahead, not that far, flowed the glittering trace of a river.

The Frendel below Rhodhur was not yet mighty; in fact, the river above the Fords was barely navigable and then only in seasons with abundant rain. Above Rhodhur itself, the Frendel was wild, untamed, a young torrent of water imprisoned for much of its length by narrow valleys. It presented churning stretches of whitewater only a fool would attempt to cross. Arne assured them their journey was nearly at an end and they would join the Rhodhur Road at the Fords below the town. There would be good water there and, once they crossed, there would even be inns, for the Frendel Road between Rhodhur's port of Swintha and the city of Eastmeary was well traveled and dotted with prosperous holdings.

They had barely rounded a bend in the path when a spray of dirt and stone erupted on the trail ahead of them. A second shower, this time of splintered rock, shattered from the stony hillside close above their heads. The party rapidly dismounted and sought shelter along with their horses among the scrawny pines just off the path.

"Madrock's hells!" Arne swore. "They've got us pinned and proper, all right!" Below them, precariously near, was the stream. Above, the path was wide open to attack, with only two outlets, both narrow and easily bottled.

"Maybe if I get up and talk to them…" Hans moved to push to his feet. The attack had been sudden but not entirely unexpected. Their attackers had merely bided their time, knowing there was no way out of the gully but to go forward or back, and able to control both from the surrounding bluffs.

COMING IN 2024 FROM FOREST PATH BOOKS

Author
Acknowledgements

Books have many parents. Aside from my sister, to whom this book is dedicated, the people who contributed most to the creation of the story that became the Triempery series were my three sons: Michael, Anthony, and Kenneth. They were children when I first started writing this book—which was called *Sordan* at the time (I tend to name works in progress by location)—and they were teens when two of them read it in hard copy. I have recently had the most amazing discussions with their adult selves about what they remember. What I remember: Mike's discourses about the parts or characters he found interesting and Ken's comments about which images he would like to draw or paint. I put their views to good use. Tony did not escape his author-mother entirely: from him I lifted Dorilian's ability to stare down *anyone*.

My husband Steve, while not part of the series' creation, played a key role in the evolution of *The Second Stone*. With his helpful editorial insights, I revised, rewrote and slapped a few characters into shape. He is gamely tackling the next book, which he hasn't read in several years.

A certain chapter in this book owes much to the wordsmithing of Jeanine Hennig and Carole the Copy Editor. Their hard work helps the story shine through. So too does that of advance reader and drawer of maps Christina Wooden, whose wonderful input has enriched every book.

Many thanks to the people who are helping me bring this series to readers. Cover artist Larry Rostant, for his gorgeous covers. Illustrator Margarita Bourkova's beautiful illustrations of artifacts and other items from the series bring magical parts of the story to life. Much gratitude to Sarah Stanitis for her creative assistance with social media.

And to all the reviewers and readers who have taken a chance on reading this series... thank you for embracing this world and its characters! I promise you this series is fully written. I only have edits to make.

Triempery Appendix

CHARACTERS

MALYRDEONS—Past

Ergeiron One of The Three, son of Leur and Amynas. After his brother Derlon gave life to the Rill, Ergeiron founded the Wall, sealing dangerous Time Rifts opened during the Gweroyen War, protecting the Malyrdeon stronghold at Stauberg, and serving as a means by which his descendants could discern past and future events.

Cienorr Son of Ergeiron, founder of the Mormantalorus Nuarchate.

Telarion Son of Ergeiron and founder of the Stauberg Principate, first Esseran king and ancestor of current Malyrdeons.

Emrysen Wall Lord and great-grandson of Ergeiron, who bestowed a conditional pardon on the Hen Kyon.

Erremon King of Essera, great grandson of Emrysen. Slain by Ardaenan King Thorondar in the First War with Ardaen

Erydon Great-great grandson of Emrysen, who granted the Khelds the wilderness of Amallar for their homeland.

Endurin Last true Wall Lord and last Malyrdeon King of Essera. Endurin's Heir died unexpectedly, leaving only a natural daughter, who fled to sea and was caught in the Rift. Endurin later brought her son Marc Frederick back to the World.

Ariande Granddaughter of Endurin. Mother of Marc Frederick.

MALYRDEONS—Present (and associated characters)

Apollonia Queen of Essera (family name Halasseon); daughter of Elegiros, Prince of Tahlwent. Wife of Marc Frederick and mother of Jonthan.

Austell Wall Lord, third cousin of Endurin and distaff cousin to Marc Frederick. Brother of Enreddon II. Died in the Demise.

Elegiros Prince of Tahlwent (family name, Halasseon); third cousin to Endurin. Father of Apollonia. Died in the Demise.

Elhanan Son of Rheger Dannutheon; Wall-gifted; one-time tutor of Stefan and Dorilian at Permephedon. Deceased.

Enreddon II Prince of Stauberg; cousin to Endurin and distaff cousin to Marc Frederick. Scholarly, but not Wall-gifted, Enreddon supported Endurin when the aged king named Marc Frederick to be his Heir. Both of Enreddon's wives died in childbirth, failing to produce living sons. Later wed Palaistea. Died in the Demise.

IONAIS Princess of Merrydn; daughter of Regelon and betrothed of Jonthan Stauberg-Randolph.

OSTEMUN Prince of Dannuth (family name, Dannutheon); distant cousin to the Stauberg Malyrdeons. Sired three daughters. Grandfather to Kerr. Died in the Demise.

PALAISTEA Princess of Lacenedon; daughter of Lakron. Married Enreddon II. Mother to Eldon II and Enreddon III, Heirs to Stauberg and Lacenedon. Deceased.

REGELON Prince of Merrydn (family name, Merrydeon); matrilineal cousin to Sebbord Teremareon. Father of Ionais, betrothed of Marc Frederick's son Jonthan. Died in the Demise.

RHEGER Prince of Hespera (family name Dannutheon); brother to Ostemun. Father of Elhanan. Possesses strong spatial ability and is one of few Malyrdeons who can use an enhancer for translocation. Deceased.

MARGARID A princess of Gweroyen who weds Elhanan. Daughter of Kathanos. Sister to Estevan IV Niarchos.

SORDANEONS — Past

DERLON One of The Three; known as the Rill-Giver because he integrated his immortal body and life with Rill's remnants, facilitating its rebirth. Epoptes believe Derlon's integration still directs the Rill's actions, though he has lost the ability to interact with other beings.

DEBEN I/II/III grandson and great-grandsons of Derlon (collectively known as the Three Debens), ushered in a Golden Age of Rill expansion and Triemperal growth that secured the Sordaneon dynasty. Builder/creators of Leseos, Bynum, Gignastha, and the Vermillion Aqueduct.

PELEOR Son of Derlon; slain by the Aryati, who poisoned his blood and spilled it on the mount at Simelon to be absorbed by the Rill. His blood still stains the platform and Rill structures.

TARLON Hierarch of Sordan during the Second War with Ardaen. The youngest of his three sons wed an Ardaenan princess to secure the truce. Tarlon was the last manifested Rill Lord, able to communicate with and influence the Entity. Opened the Rill node at Randpory Crossing.

SORDANEONS — Present (and associated characters)

DAIMONAERIS Princess of Mormantalorus. Daughter of Camas, the Mormantaloran Nuarch; half-sister of Nammuor. Married Dorilian. Mother of Levyathan II. Deceased.

DEBEN IV Sordan's Heir and regent. Son of the captive Hierarch, Labran, and Ermenthalia, daughter of Mezentius, Prince of Suddekar. Deeply paranoid, Deben had not set foot outside of Sordan's Serat in thirty-five years. Married Valyane, daughter of Sebbord Teremareon. Father of Dorilian and Levyathan I. Died in the Demise.

DELEUS Son of the Heir to Suddekar; great-grandson of Mezentius and grandson of Sebbord. Although a first cousin to Dorilian, Deleus is not Highborn.

DELOS Deben IV's twin brother. Son of Labran. Used the Lacenedon Crown to break the Vermillion Aqueduct and end the siege at Gignastha. Died after that deed from plasm shock.

DORILIAN Son of Deben IV and Valyane. Brother of Levyathan I. At the age of seven, witnessed his mother's murder. His precocious physical and empathic gifts allowed him to save his neonate brother. Determined to right wrongs done to his family.

ERMENTHALIA Daughter of Mezentius and a Mormantaloran princess. Wife of Labran, mother of Deben IV. Bears title of Gracious Hierarchessa. Inclined to favor alliance with Mormantalorus, from which her mother hailed.

LABRAN Grandson of Tarlon; his mother was a princess of Ardaen. He wed Ermenthalia, daughter of Mezentius, Bas of Suddekar, and is father of Deben IV and grandfather of Dorilian. He objected to Endurin Malyrdeon naming Marc Frederick as Heir to Essera and at Marc Frederick's coronation refused to acknowledge him as King. Labran fought his way into the Rill node at Permephedon and was able to command the Rill to stop running, creating wide-spread panic. Taken captive by Marc Frederick and considered too dangerous to release, Labran was imprisoned at Stauberg, far from any active Rill nodes.

LEVYATHAN I Son of Deben IV and Valyane. Grandson to Labran and Sebbord. Brother to Dorilian. When enemies poisoned his mother, Levyathan was born months too soon to survive. Although saved by Dorilian, Levyathan's development was affected, and he suffered neurological deficits. Deceased.

LEVYATHAN II Son of Daimonaeris and Deben, raised by Dorilian as his own son. Heir to Sordan.

MEZENTIUS (family name Suddekeon); Bas of Suddekar. He wed a princess of Mormantalorus. His eldest daughter Ermenthalia wed Labran and gave birth to Deben IV. Died in the Demise.

SEBBORD (family name Teremareon), Prince of Teremar. Possibly Rill-gifted, Sebbord trained as an Epopte and rose to the level of Archmage in service to the Rill. He wed twice and sired three daughters. Grandfather of Dorilian, Levyathan, Deleus and Tiflan.

TIFLAN (family name Morevyen). Bas of Teremar. Grandson of Sebbord but not Highborn. Seven feet tall, he is Dorilian's first cousin and a loyal ally.

VALYANE Princess of Teremar. Sebbord's daughter, wife to Deben IV. Mother of Dorilian and Levyathan I.

LEGON (family name Rebiran) Son of Terveryen, Bas of Anit-Rebir. Youngest of six sons. Sent to Sebbord as a boy to enter Sordaneon service. Dorilian's friend. Commander of the Eagle Guard.

TERVERYEN (family name Rebiran) Bas of Anit-Rebir. Father of Legon and Cressida.

CRESSIDA (family name Rebiran) Daughter and youngest child of Terveryen; Legon's sister.

TUTTO (family name Rhunnard) An Estol who served as Sebbord's sword master and now serves Dorilian. Later Bas of Kolgya.

SINON KOURANOS Marc Frederick's administrator in Sordan during that city's occupation; later governor of Neuberland. Stefan's Archhalial Ambassador. Shifted allegiance to become Dorilian's Archhalial Ambassador.

BERSYAS (family name Garheleon) One of Dorilian's generals.

PANDAROS (family name Vidyamemnon) One of Dorilian's generals.

NOEMI Wet nurse to the infant Levyathan I, later his governess. Mother of Fahme. Deceased.

RAXA Levyathan II wet-nurse, trained by Noemi.

THURAYA (family name Lares) Sage Physician; Dorilian's house physician.

CLOTHIA (family name Dalae) Archtutor; Sage Scholar. Arranges Hans' education in Sordan.

HERAN (family name Albos) Mormantaloran agent who wed Noemi. Father of Fahme.

FAHME Princess of Sordan. Noemi's daughter by Heran. Adopted by Dorilian.

HAESKOS (family name Periskleron) Dorilian's Admiral.

TIDUS Sailor on Dorilian's ship *Raudra.*

QUIRIN (family name Chrysolemnos) Psilant, or leader, of the Brotherhood of Epoptes.

PITAR (family name Kithsoda) Arch Epopte/Arch Mage; chief at Dazunor-Rannuli.

THAROS (family name Odakkon) Epopte at Sordan.

PALLAS (family name Trophoneos) Speaker of the Sordan Halia.

MIRREZ Dorilian's chief secretary.

VERLAS Dorilian's second secretary.

STAUBERG-RANDOLPH (and associated characters)

MARC FREDERICK King of Essera; great-grandson of Endurin Malyrdeon through his son Estevan II and Brenna Almarresda. Son of Ariande Malyrdeon and William Randolph. Considered a Malyrdeon in recognition of his relation to and support from them, but he is not Highborn. Marc Frederick first married Thora, a Kheld woman. After Thora died of a miscarriage, he wed the Highborn princess Apollonia as a condition to becoming Endurin's Heir. He has two children: Emyli, his daughter by Thora, and Jonthan, his son by Apollonia. Died in the Demise and interred in the Vault of Incorruption.

EMYLI Daughter of Marc Frederick and Thora; was betrothed to Deben IV Sordaneon but ran away at age fourteen with charismatic Kheld rebel Erwan Cedrecson. The pair wed and Emyli gave birth to Erwan's son, Stefan. To free Erwan from prison, Emyli helped Kheld rebels gain access to the stronghold of Gignastha, resulting in three Highborn deaths and the bloody siege of that city. She later gave birth to her second son, Handurin.

JONTHAN Son of Marc Frederick and Apollonia. Prince of Dazunor. Married Ionais, princess of Merrydn. Their union was childless.

STEFAN Son of Emyli and Erwan; grandson of Marc Frederick and adopted by him after Jonthan's death. Succeeds Marc Frederick as King of Essera. Marries Nilla Lowenda. Deceased.

HANS (full name Handurin) Son of Emyli, reputed son of Erwan. Grandson of Marc Frederick. Brother to Stefan.

GARETH (family name Morgen) Marc Frederick's steward, in charge of his household.

TREVOR (family name Allen) Captain of King's Guard.

MARENTHRO Wizard of Permephedon; ageless and possibly immortal. No one knows much about him save that he is apparently benign and possesses both Wall and Rill affinity. Responsible for finding Marc Frederick for Endurin and bringing him back to this World.

MORMANTALORUS (and associated characters)

NAMMUOR (family name Varehos) Ruler of Mormantalorus, half-brother to Daimonaeris. Reputed to have Aryati blood. Has recovered the lost Diadem of the Devaryati. Responsible for the Demise. Is intent on collecting the blood and lifeforces of the remaining Highborn princes.

OARZAS Nammuor's Chief Crystallier.

CORAM (family name Barzanes) Was with Nammuor at the Demise. Nammuor's emissary to Stefan. An adept in mage arts.

Balathu Archmage.

Salkren Zel Mormantaloran general. With Nammuor at the Demise.

SEVEN HOUSES (and associated characters)

Chyralane (family name Rannuleon) Denizen of Phaer, most prominent of the Seven Houses. Daughter of a Highborn prince of Rannul. Opposed to any action that would lessen the cartel's control over the Rill. Very tall.

Rhynos (family name Tybenos) Denizen of Koillos.

Iphithus (family name Kheprion) Nephew and heir to Chyralane.

Philemon Leander Wealthy Staubaun merchant, not noble but aspiring to the nobility. His daughter married the Denizen of House Haralambdos.

ESSERAN STAUBAUNS (and associated characters)

Asphalladra (family name Velos) Youngest daughter of the Enlad of Chennor; weds Cullen Brodheson. Sister to Zoranna.

Jaron Velos Enlad of Chennor. Father of Asphalladra and Zoranna. Ambitious nobleman intent on arranging high-ranking mates for his three daughters.

Eldonus (family name Kastryon) Enlad of Velsitha; late husband to Palimia. Very old friend of Marc Frederick.

Palimia (family name Attora) Daughter of a high-ranking Sordani noble killed to facilitate confiscation of his estates. Later married Eldonus Kastryon. Mistress to Marc Frederick, and later Dorilian. Deceased.

Erenor Tholeros Cousin to the Halasseon rulers of Tahlwent; grandson of a natural daughter of Elegiros. Friend of Stefan. Commander of the King's Guards.

Kondros (family name Bragord) Ally of Erenor.

Estevan IV (family name Niarchos) Bas of Gweroyen. Son of Kathanos. Maternal grandson of Estevan III, last Highborn Prince of Gweroyen.

Kathanos (family name Niarchos) Archon of Peleddor. Father of Estevan. Friend of Emyli. Son of Smaragda.

Smaragda Venerable mother of Kathanos. A princess of Stauberg.

Evlann Wife of Kathanos. Daughter of Estevan III, Prince of Gweroyen. Mother of Estevan IV and Margarid.

Hebron (family name Ursenos). Cousin to Lakron, Prince of Lacenedon, and Palaistea. Bas Regent and later Bas of Lacenedon.

MACHON EPIROSI Archon of Penrhu. Breeder of blood horses.

ALBAN ESKEROS Gignasthan lord whose lodge Dorilian used during his rebellion.

PHELLAN ILLARION Bas of Serrain, married to Linne, one of Ostemun Dannutheon's daughters. Father of Lucien and Raphelon.

LUCIEN ILLARION Heir to Serrain. Supporter of Stefan.

RAPHELON ILLARION Younger brother to Lucien.

GRENANT AIGELLEROS Minor lord loyal to Ostemun. Wed Raeva, eldest of Ostemun's daughters. Father of Kerr.

KERR (family name Aigelleros) Son of Grenant and Raeva. Grandson of Ostemun. Nephew of Rheger and cousin of Elhanan and Raphelon.

BURELAN (family name Phaeros) Bas of Rannul. Grandson of the last Prince of Rannul.

EUELLA (family name Phaeros) Burelan's sister.

THEMACRYSA (family name Rannuleon) Daughter of the last Prince of Rannul. Mother of Burelan and Eulla.

ARTON (family name Metagoras) Third son of the Archon of Eddethel (Merrydn). Assistant to Cullen Brodheson. Later weds Euella Phaeros.

KYROS (family name Eulodes) Son of the Enlad of Rhiarren.

ALKRON (family name Eulodes) Enlad of Rhiarren. Kyros' father.

KHELDS (and associated characters)

ARNE ANSELDSON Friend and companion to Hans; a slave whose freedom Hans purchased in Ben Aranath on his journey to Sordan.

CULLEN BRODHESON Cousin and best friend to Stefan. Keeper of the King's Trade. Enlad (later Archon) of Heddros and Wyre. Weds Asphalladra.

ERWAN CEDRECSON Son of Cedrec Aelfricson; ran off with young Emyli Stauberg-Randolph. She later bore his sons, Stefan and Hans. Died at Gignastha.

TOBOLD FORBASSON Thegnard (leader) of the Thegnkeld, the foremost clan of Amallar. Died at the Demise.

LOWEN TOBOLDSON Son of Tobold and father of Nilla.

CEDREC AELFRICSON Late Kheld representative to the Triemperal Archhalia. Father to Erwan. Grandfather to Stefan and Hans. Died at the Demise.

ROBDAN AELFRICSON Cedrec's brother; a scribe. Uncle to Stefan and Hans.

GOFF HORVADSON First Minister during Stefan's reign; Enlad of Kelmene.

NILLA LOWENDA Daughter of Lowen Toboldson and niece of Goff Horvadson. Marries Stefan. Deceased.

OTHER CHARACTERS

THAA non-human. Rift Guardian; the Dark Watcher. Aligned with Marenthro.

ENDELARIN (family name Nemenor) King of Ardaen, brother to the throne queen. Romantic and rumored to have one hundred wives. Cousin to the Sordaneons and fond of reminding them of it.

HERBERTH (family name Tammet) Elector of Trongor.

FARRL (family name Hennek) Captain of Trongor.

KAETAL (family name Remaus) Governor of Ogarth.

GARICK Trongorian governor.

SAMMEL Trongorian governor.

MELENTHAS (family name Helaosun) Princess of Merced, daughter of King Galanthius. Prospective bride for Dorilian Sordaneon.

GALANTHIAS (family name Helaosun) King of Merced, father of Melenthas. The island nation of Merced, while economically allied with Sordan, embraces ties with Nammuor.

EZHNO (family name Ezhnar) Bargemaster on the Sorand'ruil.

DERN Deckhand on Ezhno's barge.

TERK Deckhand on Ezhno's barge.

CEF Herdsman in Sansordan who helps Hans.

YANPO Riverman who helps Hans.

MALLOGH troublemaker in Sordan.

ACHREIOS GAR assassin in Sordan.

JOOAR ZETHARNNA A prince of Lahgael, not in the line of succession. Governor of Ben Aranath.

BARAN REDHARG Hen Kyon leader, Lord of Gloanneach. Looks nearly fully human.

ENTITY-BOUND DEVICES

THE LEUR'S RING Fashioned from the body of The Leur as last living act. Rejects non-Leur flesh and can only be worn by the Highborn. Used at coronations to identify the true king of Essera (Heir of Ergeiron). Manipulates real world/Leur's Creation. Removes barriers. Opens doors. Reveals truth and restores Leur's reality.

THE RILL STONE Device created by Derlon, who encapsulated his immortal blood in Rill matrix. The Rill Stone will identify a Sordaneon who wears it by glowing green. The Rill recognizes Sordaneon wearers and will not arm itself or lock locations against them. Can be used to burn a permanent Eagle mark onto any other substance, including human skin.

THE WALL STONE Shard of the Wall containing Ergeiron's immortal essence. It connects directly to the Wall, regardless of proximity, and must be used carefully by individuals open to its gifts. Allows wielder to peer into discreet temporal flows. The Wall Stone unlocks the Aidion and provides access to the Archive, which it assists in revealing.

OTHER ENTITIES

THE DIADEM The Undying Crown; the Diadem of the Devaryati. Pre-Devastation device created in secret by the Aryati from the immortal core that remained of Vllyr after that god was destroyed by Amynas and the Leur. Generates and commands arcane forces. Vastly powerful when fully tapped into an immortal being. Retains vestige of Vllyr's godhood. Malevolently self-aware and fixated on destroying that which destroyed Vllyr. Succeeded in corrupting the Aryati, destroying Mulsor and the First Creation.

GREATER ENHANCERS

SORDAN CORONAL Also called Derlon's Crown. Most powerful of the Greater Diadems. Now in possession of the Sordaneons.

STAUBERG CORONAL Also called the Star Crown; Ergeiron's Crown. Now in possession of the Malyrdeons.

MORMANTALORUS CORONAL Also called the Crown of Fire; Ciennor's Crown. Now in possession of Mormantalorus and its ruler.

LACENEDON CROWN Also called Ulnossi's Bane. Used by Delos Sordaneon to break the Vermillion Aqueduct.

OTHER DEVICES

DERLON'S ARMOR The fabled Eagle Breastplate, helm, and gauntlets. When activated sheaths the wearer's torso and limbs. Kinetic negation. Any blow to the armor is absorbed. Invincible to nearly all weapons.

SWORD OF AMYNAS Also known as Derlon's Sword or the Gweroyen Sword. Greatest of the *tullun* blades made from Vllyr's skeleton. Most effective when paired with more powerful enhancers.

RINGS OF ORDER Three rings created by Derlon Sordaneon before the Inception. Used in accessing Rill stations and communicating with the Overlay. The Head Epopte (Psilant) keeps one of the rings.

BACKGROUND — Highborn Origins

ARYATI Human strain engineered to replicate the powers and immortality of Leur. Creators of greater and lesser devices that generate quasi-magical powers. The Aryati rose to extraordinary heights through

genetic manipulation and technology but were arrogant and acquis-
itive; they ultimately destroyed their world. A remnant of the Aryati
survived into the new Creation but most were slain following their
defeat by the Highborn during the Gweroyen Wars. The survivors
scattered. No pureblood Aryati survive but the strain persists in noble
Staubaun lineages.

Leur Immortal beings that created the World. Elusive, mostly hidden
from humans until technological advances revealed them. Leur magic
built the Five Cities, each in a day, and, combined with Aryati
technology, engineered the living matrix of the Rill. During the
Devastation brought by the Aryati, the Leur sacrificed itself to create
the temporal disjunction that preserved the Creation. The lone Leur
survivor mated their immortal bloodline with that of the Aryati clone-
prince Amynas, conceiving three immortal sons known as The Three.

Malyrdeon Descendants of Ergeiron, one of the three sons of the gods
Amynas and Leur; Ergeiron settled in what is now Stauberg, where
he created the Wall as a barricade against the Rift. The Wall exists
throughout all Time. Some descendants of Ergeiron are able to "walk
the Wall" and by that means divine future events or reveal the truth
or import of past events.

Sordaneon Descendants of Derlon, second of the three sons of the gods
Amynas and Leur. Derlon settled Sordan, home to one of the surviving
Five Cities of Leur, from which he gave life to the Rill by melding his
immortal body with that of the vast machine. The descendants of
Derlon carry the potential to connect with and communicate with the
Rill, which would allow them to alter the god-machine's operation
and physical structure.

HUMAN RACES

Highborn Males descended from the immortal sons of Leur and the
human Amynas. Leur traits pass only to male offspring, who must mate
with human females to reproduce. For this reason, the adage is that the
Highborn take the race of their mothers. Almost exclusively, the Highborn
have chosen to reproduce using Staubaun lineages.

Staubaun A people originally created by (and related to) the Aryati
and still manifesting some traits of the parent race. Some can wield lesser
devices. Tall, fair-skinned, brown or gold-eyed blondes, beardless (with
little body hair), Staubauns are intelligent and long-lived. They also, after
generations of success and prosperity, tend to be rich and privileged.

Estol Amalgamation of races, the general population. Disdained as
mongrels by Staubauns, Estols nonetheless rise to positions of influence
and become minor nobility. Most are servants, laborers, soldiers and

craftsmen. Because they are of mixed blood, Estols can have any human color of eyes, hair, or skin.

KHELD Barbaric people that entered Essera through the Rift during a period of instability following the First War with Ardaen. Khelds generally have blue or green eyes. They also have dark hair, sturdy builds and are shorter. Adult males are usually bearded. Their language is completely separate, as are their ways of life. Kheld naming differs from the Staubaun, as does their system of inheritance.

NEMENOR Seafaring people that forms the ruling families of Ardaen, Callorn, Lahgael, and the Isles of Maskos. Traditional enemies of the Triempery in the past, a marriage by treaty to a younger son of the Hierarch of Sordan instilled Ardaenan Nemenor blood into the lineage of the Highborn Sordaneons.

NONHUMAN RACES

LEUR Magical race, as explained above, creators of the original World and the tripartite Creation they fashioned to salvage it from destruction. Originally the Leur people inhabited the area now known as the Bogs, a marshy delta where the Dazun River flows into the sea. The last Leur was slain by the Devaryati and the race is now only legend.

HEN KYON The Dog Men, created by the Aryati as hunters and servants, specifically to track down and kill the magic-gifted offspring of Amynas and Leur. Intelligent and reclusive, the Hen Kyon are bipedal, often with fur covering parts or all of their bodies. The most true-to-breed have long, wolfish faces with well-developed olfactory organs. They have incredible stamina and strength. They can interbreed with humans, from which race they were originally fashioned. The Hen Kyon nearly eradicated the young Highborn race. Though they later repented their deeds, the Dog Men were abhorred and hunted nearly into extinction until the Malyrdeon King Emrysen cloaked them in obscurity and gave them the haunted wilds of the Kragh in which to live unmolested. They have since become feared and avoided.

PLACES (background)

(MENA)TROHJANA The Second Creation. The present World that moves forward in Time.

(MENA)TANTAUREUS Archived world/Past world, living remnant of the First Creation. Birthplace of Marc Frederick.

GSCH The World of Fire. The moment of Devastation, forever happening, never completed. A single moment in Time that has both already occurred and will never occur.

FIVE CITIES Eternal cities built in the First Creation by Leur and continuing in the Second Creation. Îs (vanished), Permephedon, Sordan, Mormantalorus, and Mulsor (destroyed).

Mulsor Destroyed in the Devastation. As a Leur creation part of it remains eternal. A ghost city whose appearance portends doom.

Daln Barrier Created by Leur to separate the World in Time. Past World/Gsch/Current World.

The Rift Transient instabilities in the Daln Barrier that permit passage between the Past World and the Current World. The appearance of Mulsor is one such occurrence.

Triempery A confederation comprised of three aligned Highborn empires: Essera, Sordan, and Mormantalorus.

ESSERA

Stauberg Capital city of Essera. Home of the Malyrdeons. Major seaport. Location of the Wall. Site of a dormant Rill mount.

Asae Eranos The Malyrdeon Serat or Malyrdeon Tower. Royal palace in Stauberg.

Aidion Heart of the Wall. Located under the shrine at the Gate of Transformation. Where gifted Malyrdeons walk the Wall.

Gate of Transformation Original city gate of Stauberg. Transformed by Ergeiron and now site of a shrine.

Eleutheron Domain also ruled by the Prince of Stauberg. Rich and deep in history.

Bynum Foremost city of the Eleutheron.

Danae Palace Princess Palaistea's seat. Near Bynum.

Gweroyen Domain in Essera, north of Stauberg. Former stronghold of the Aryati.

Ennsa Capital city of Gweroyen.

Iddolea Destroyed city in Gweroyen. Former capital of the Aryati.

Permephedon City-State presided over by Marenthro. One of the three remaining Five Cities. Neutral seat of the Triempery and home of the Triemperal Archhalia. Northernmost Rill city and a major Rill hub.

High Citadel Central redoubt of Permephedon's city core. Also called Marenthro's Tower. The Leur Arcana and Harmonic Hall are here, as are the Archhalia Chambers.

Jewel Tower Malyrdeon tower. Floats above the Mirror in Permephedon's city core.

Sordaneon Tower Sordaneon hold in Permephedon's city core. Congruent with the Rill, which it is near.

Lacenedon Domain in Essera, north and east of Permephedon.

Kenelm Capital city of Lacenedon. Site of a dormant Rill mount.

Serrain Domain in Essera, just west of Permephedon

SIMELON Capital city of Serrain. Site of a dormant Rill mount.

RANNUL Domain in Essera.

TERNA Capital city of Rannul.

DAZUNOR Principality in Essera, holding of Essera's Heir.

DAZUNOR-RANNULI Pre-eminent city in Essera due to its position on the Dazun River and presence of a major Rill node. Home of the Seven Houses.

DAZUN RIVER Largest river north of the Telarkan Mountains. Major economic resource and highway. Has no navigable egress to the sea.

THE FAN Egress of Dazun; fens, marshes and channels that go nowhere. Also called the Bogs. No one knows how or where the Dazun empties into the sea (or even if it does).

RILLHOME Sordaneon palace in Dazunor-Rannuli

CUSTOMHOUSE Seven Houses seat in Dazunor-Rannuli.

ILLYSTRI PALACE Malyrdeon palace in Dazunor-Rannuli, located on island in the Lago.

LAGO Lake in heart of Dazunor-Rannuli near the Rill mount.

EMRYSEN PALACE Esseran monarch's residence in Dazunor-Rannuli, on the Upper Canal

UPPER CANAL Large canal north of the Rill mount and Lago, where the wealthy live.

LOWER CANAL Main canal of Dazunor-Rannuli. Largely commercial properties along it.

BEARD FEN Kheld neighborhood in Dazunor-Rannuli

MERRYDN Principality in eastern Essera. On the Dazun River. Home to the Merrydeon Princes. Site of a dormant Rill mount.

MERATH Capital city of Merrydn. Famous for its palace and walls of blue stone.

DANNUTH Principality in Essera, holding of the Dannutheon Princes.

KYRBASILLON Capital city of Dannuth. Famous for its beauty and public places. Four gateways of Virtue: Arch of Mercy, Arch of Truth, Arch of Courage, Arch of Justice.

TAHLWENT Principality in Essera. South of Stauberg and on the sea. Home to the Halasseon Princes.

ARAL Capital of Tahlwent. Major sea port.

HALASSEON SERAT Palace of the Halasseon Princes.

GUSTAN Town on the Dazun River near the Fan.

GUSTAN MANOR Marc Frederick's personal residence, which he designed and built using materials from his home world.

TRULO Major city on Dazun River. Seat of the Princes of Dazunor.

GOLDEN PALACE Highborn palace in Trulo.

KRAGH Badlands of high hills and dangerous gorges. Home of the Hen Kyon. Near Trulo. Site of the destroyed Aryati city of Gyges.

THE MAW Huge hill in the Kragh

AMALLAR Semi-autonomous domain of the Khelds. Considered part of Essera.

THE BOGS Kheld term for The Fan; endless marshes of terminal Dazun River.

RHODHUR Capital of Amallar. Site of Rhodhur Hall.

EASTMEARY BRENNA City in Amallar.

AURDOLLEN Sanctuary near Rhodhur and site of a school for girls.

BELLAN TOREGH Town on eastern edge of Amallar. Site of a dormant Rill mount.

FLOHE River that flows through Bellan Toregh. Tributary of Dazun River.

ORQHO Mines in southern Amallar near Leseos.

NEUBERLAND Esseran domain/protectorate. Kheld and Staubaun populations often in dispute over land.

SAEMOREGH Kheld town in Neuberland.

AMUNDHAL Kings grant holding of Aubrey Amundda. Near Saemoregh.

GOBBA Frontier holding east of Neuberland, loosely affiliated with Essera.

ANNECH Frontier holding allied with Gobba, increasingly at odds with Essera.

LESEOS Former Principality of Essera, now a semi-autonomous Basarchate. Rill city. Located south of Amallar and west of Gignastha.

GIGNASTHA Former Principality in Essera. Made a Crown Protectorate after its Highborn Princes were murdered by Kheld rebels.

SAR'PRYANNIS Poisoned lake in Gignastha. Gignastha is built on cliffs overlooking this lake.

VERMILLION AQUEDUCT Raised by Deben II Sordaneon to provide water to Gignastha and also power the locks securing the impregnable gate of the Watergilt Palace. Broken by Delos Sordaneon during the Gignastha War.

LOWER NEUBERLAND Part of the Principality of Gignastha, south of Gignastha and bordering Randpory, the northernmost territory of Sordan.

HORCROD Fortress in Lower Neuberland.

SORDAN

SORDAN One of the three remaining Five Cities. Called the City of Light, City of Amynas. Site of the Inception, originating point of the Rill, and a major Rill node. Island city surrounded by a large and very deep lake.

SORDANEON SERAT Palace of the Sordaneon Hierarchs, in Sordan, and congruous with the Rill. Portions of the palace are part of the immortal Citadel forming the core of the city.

VIRIDIAN RIVER Man-made river contained within the Serat. Site of numerous features, including a waterfall over the Serat walls.

WELL OF BIRDS Located in a courtyard of the Sordaneon Serat.

THE PRISM Rainbow-laced waterfall and deep gorge on grounds of the Serat.

VA HAIRA First Creation underground passage connecting the Rill, Citadel, Serat and other pre-Return structures in Sordan's city core.

THE INCEPTION Sordan's Rill mount. Largest Rill complex, where Derlon's presence has fully completed its transformation. Multiple levels, platforms, and crown of portals.

KING'S HOUSE Palace near the Serat, connected to the Va Haira. Former residence of the Malyrdeons.

SARKUAN Lake surrounding Sordan.

SORAND'RUIL River that flows from Sarkuan to the sea.

SANSORDAN Domain attached to Hierarchate. Largely desert/wasteland. Western coast poisoned by destruction of Mulsor.

IRIDONOS Fabled treasure city of the Aryati, rumored to lie in poisoned Sansordan.

ILMAR Domain of Sordan. Located at mouth of Sorand'ruil.

IVERNESSE Capital city of Ilmar.

NEREID PALACE Sordaneon palace in Ivernesse.

KOLPOS Gulf between Sansordan and Ardaen. Also known as the Gulf of Mulsor.

LAHGAEL Kingdom of the Gaels, a Nemenor-Estol people allied with Sordan.

BEN ARANATH River port of Lahgael on the Sorandruil.

SUDDEKAR Principality located on the southern shore of Sarkuan. Borders Mormantaloran domain of Othgol. Home of the Suddekeon Princes.

BATRAZ Capital city of Suddekar; location of the Palace of Dawn.

ILDURRIA Domain located on northern shore of Sarkuan.

TOLLECH Principality located north of Ildurria.

RANDPORY CROSSING City-State. By agreement a free trade city because of its Rill mount.

RANDPORY RIVER Navigable river that forms the border between the Sordan Hierarchate and Trongor.

ANIT-REBIR Domain located north of Teremar. Mountainous.

TEREMAR Principality located on eastern shore of Sarkuan. Rich and powerful, home of the Teremareon Princes.

ASKORRAS Capital of Teremar.

TULAMANTA Palace at Askorras.

HESTYA River port in Teremar. Site of an active Rill mount.

TIRIS Estate on Sordan island given by Dorilian to Daimonaeris.

RHONDDA Sordaneon estate on Sordan island. Personal estate of Dorilian.

TRONGOR Independent nation of sea folk located on Kolpos north of Sansordan, west of Randpory, and south of Amallar. Separated from latter by the Telarkan Mountains.

OGARTH Capital city of Trongor. Site of a dormant Rill mount.

ARDAEN Monarchy located on large peninsula west of Trongor. Seafarers known as the Sea Kings.

SKALMRIMVOR (see Caerdon)

AMROSET Capital city of Ardaen.

CALLORN Region of Ardaen.

CAERDON Principality. Former region of Ardaen, ceded to the Sordaneon Hierarchate as part of a treaty and now included among the Hierarch's title domains.

MERCED An independent island kingdom near Ardaen, loosely allied with Ardaen.

MORMANTALORUS

MORMANTALORUS One of the three remaining Five Cities. Sits on an active volcano and is livable only because the City itself creates an environment conducive to human habitation. The environment immediately outside the city's bubble is toxic.

DZALARAD The volcano.

ILGAON Main tower of the Citadel of Mormantalorus, where Nammuor creates his arcane crystals and devices using the energy of the volcano.

NUARCH'S TOWER Residential tower of the Citadel of Mormantalorus.

MAGISTRY Part of Ilgaon tower where mage work is done.

ORM Domain. Borders Suddekar.

OTHGOL Domain. Borders Teremar.

TELEG Southernmost domain of Mormantalorus.

NALAPAR Eastern domain of Mormantalous.

XEBBETH Large island domain west of Mormantalorus.

ULAN-JANA Mountainous domain south of Teremar and northeast of Mormantalorus. Gifted by Nammuor to Dorilian and Daimonaeris on their wedding.

WORDS and TERMS found in the Books

CHARYS Rill conveyance. Created by the Rill at need and uncreated when no longer needed.

DEIKNYA An oval medallion created by Marenthro that displays the royal or noble house to which that person is bound. Given exclusively to Highborn, royal, or high nobility.

FRA'DON Means 'royal brother.' Used by the Highborn for another of their kindred.

GYNEKOS used for a Highborn lineage that has reverted to purely human. This happens when a Highborn sires daughters instead of sons.

ORBUS/orbi Balls of light Highborn princes generate in their hands. A minor power.

THRICE ROYAL Proper form of address for a Highborn prince regardless of age or rank. Highborn are considered royal three times over: Father. Mother. Entity. Generally, a Highborn prince is born to a royal father and mother, though the latter is not always the case... but it usually is.

TULLUN Material created from the god Vllyr's skeleton. Can be sharpened to an edge that can cut anything but itself. Shaped by the Aryati into blades from daggers to swords. The Sword of Amynas is a *tullun* blade mated with device matrices.

L. L. STEPHENS

has been writing science fiction and fantasy full-time for several years. Published works include a debut science fiction novel in the deep dark past and a medical journal, as well as lots of short stories, and local brochures, newsletters, and pamphlets for everything from local politicians to an international airport.

The Triempery series, which begins with *Sordaneon*, is a six-part series and life's work. For excerpts from existing or upcoming books, lore, maps, and other related content, visit the L.L. Stephens website at:

https://triempery.com

Twitter: @triempery
Facebook: L.L. Stephens Author

INDEPENDENT PUBLISHERS ROCK!

We appreciate your purchase of a Forest Path Book. We do our best to cultivate distinctive and compelling stories for our readers.

If you enjoy our authors' efforts, kindly consider that a reader review at your favorite online outlet can help spread the word.

To keep track of our latest releases, sales, & happenings, please join

INTO THE FOREST

https://forestpathbooks.com/into-the-forest/

(the Forest Path Books reading group and newsletter)
When you sign up for the newsletter, as our "thank you!" you'll receive a code for 25% off your first purchase at our store!

FOREST PATH BOOKS

https://forestpathbooks.com